WATCHMEN OF ROME

Alex Gough

To all my loved ones, family, friends and pets.

Chapter I

Rome, AD 27, September

Elissa sat alone in a dark room. Shadows cast by a single candle flickered on the walls. Her eyes were closed and she intoned a prayer quietly.

"O Lord Ba'al Hammon, O Lady Tanit, Face of Ba'al. Hear the prayers of your Priestess. Guide me now. Show me what I must do, so I can further your glory, and cast down your enemies."

She threw some knuckle bones and examined how they fell. Then she drew a small chicken from a box. It tried to flap its wings, but Elissa drew a knife quickly over its neck, taking its head off. Even as it convulsed, she was expertly opening its belly to examine its entrails. Blood spurted out of the neck, over the warm organs, over Elissa herself. She closed her eyes again, emptied her mind. A vision came to her, half-formed, not even an image. A colour. The colour of danger, of blood, of anger, of fire. Red. It had to be red.

Rufa sang a gentle lullaby to her daughter, Fabilla, who lay with her eyes closed on the straw mattress in the corner of the tiny room they shared with another family of slaves. The two children of the other family, a boy and a girl of about four and five years respectively, played with a carved wooden toy, while their parents rutted noisily. Rufa stroked Fabilla's lush red hair, so like her own that no one would doubt whose daughter she was. Fabilla's breathing grew deeper and slower, and Rufa marvelled at how easily the seven year old could ignore the noise that came from outside the walls of the house and from within. She wished she could sleep as well, but she hadn't been born to this life the way Fabilla had. Which was worse, she wondered, to have never known freedom, or to have known it and had it taken away?

As Rufa brushed the hair out of Fabilla's eyes, she noticed a red mark on her forehead. It was smudged, but in this light, Rufa thought it had the vague shape of a woman with outstretched arms. She rubbed it away with a moist thumb, deciding that Fabilla must have knocked herself at some point during the day, playing while Rufa was working.

The man on the other side of the room emptied himself noisily into his partner, who clutched him in the throes of her own pleasure. The man rolled off and within moments was starting to snore. The children too were starting to tire of their game, and lay down, cuddled together. The woman, a slave called Natta, sighed and rose, rearranging her tunic.

"Rufa, we should attend our duties."

Rufa gave Fabilla a light kiss, nodded and stood. She stripped from her dirty, ragged clothes and and pulled on a clean plain white robe that she was obliged to wear when serving. Natta and Rufa opened the door and walked through to their mistress's *triclinium*. The dining room was being readied for a feast. Shafat, the steward, caught sight of them.

"You are both late," he said, his voice heavily tinged with an Eastern accent.

They weren't, but both women mumbled apologies. They fetched jugs of wine from the kitchen, and stood behind the top couch, which remained empty. Time passed, the lamps sputtered and smoked. Rufa shifted from foot to foot, legs starting ache, bored and tired from the forced inactivity. The other slaves had finished their work, and all had now either retreated to the kitchens or their quarters, or stood as Rufa and Natta did, waiting to attend.

At last their mistress arrived. Rufa surreptitiously watched the woman who legally owned her. She was tall, slim, with long, dark hair braided behind her head. Following her were two men and a woman. Her mistress reclined at the top couch, and the others arranged themselves on the other two couches at either side.

Her mistress held up a decorated glass, and Rufa stepped forward swiftly, filling it deftly from the wine jug she carried. She moved on to the two men to her mistress's right, while Natta took care of the woman on her left. The man on the mistress's immediate right was enormous, with tanned skin, and a livid diagonal scar sweeping from his forehead over his eye and down to the corner of his mouth. Rufa was scared of him. He lived in the house, and sometimes acted as the mistress's bodyguard, though he was a free man. She wondered if he was the mistress's lover, but she had never seen any evidence of that. Often, he would look at Rufa, an expression on his face that she was sure was full of violence and lust. As she filled his glass, he grabbed her arm, firmly and painfully, and held her gaze with one good eye and one clouded.

"Glaukos," said the mistress in a low voice. Glaukos held her for a moment longer, then looked at Elissa, bowed his head and released her.

The guests waited for the mistress to raise her glass to her lips, then they all drank. All eyes were on the woman on the top couch, none speaking. Rufa's mistress swallowed, then placed her glass on the table before her.

"Friends," she said. "Thank you for coming tonight. I hope my simple offerings refresh your palates and satisfy your appetites."

She flicked her fingers, and Shafat directed the slaves to bring forward the food from the kitchens. It was simple food by the standard of Roman banquets, as the mistress had said, but the cheeses, ham, eggs and market vegetables looked mouthwateringly good to Rufa. She swallowed as her mouth filled with saliva, and tried to ignore the tempting smell.

Again it was the mistress who started eating first, and the others followed suit. After a few mouthfuls, she spoke again.

"So tell me, what news from the Urban Prefect's office, Scrofa?" asked the hostess.

"Mother Elissa," said Scrofa, a plump man with broken purple veins over his cheeks. He touched his forehead in a gesture of obeisance. "Work continues on the restoration of some leaking aqueducts and pipework. The citizens persist in bashing holes in them though, to get their own private water supply. The Temple of the Vestals is having some paintwork restored…"

"I was referring to the games," interrupted Elissa.

"Yes, Mother, I…I'm sorry," stuttered Scrofa. Elissa inclined her head and waited.

"Well, the Prefect has procured a shipment of cameleopards from Ethiopia. The jails are full of bandits and escaped slaves to be given to the beasts. There will be some gladiatorial combat, of course, though the details still need to be worked out regarding the appearance some of the biggest names. Fees to the *lanista*, you understand."

Elissa's face was cold. "I trust you will give the Prefect every assistance to make these games as spectacular as possible. You know what depends on it."

Scrofa glanced around him nervously. Rufa noticed with surprise that the female guest was regarding Scrofa with open hostility.

"Of course, Mother," he said.

"Glaukos!" Elissa snapped at the large scarred man.

Glaukos had been leering at Rufa, but turned his attention to Elissa as soon as his name was spoken.

"Do you have anything to contribute?" asked Elissa.

"Yes, Mother. We have recruited a number of new followers in, um, useful positions in the city. We have an initiation ceremony for them planned tomorrow in the temple, and we would be honoured if you could attend. "

"Of course. Make sure there is an appropriate sacrifice, to mark the occasion."

Finally, she turned to the only female guest, who was sitting to her right. She held out a hand, and it was taken and gently gripped. Rufa thought this woman very beautiful, long, light brown hair flowing the full length of her back, tied with a simple ribbon. She appeared around thirty years of age, but had made no attempt to cover the first sign of lines around her eyes and the corners of her mouth. Her lips held a faint smile, but to Rufa, her eyes seemed sad.

"Metella, treasured friend," said Elissa. "How are you?"

"I am well, Mother. As well as can be expected."

"Thank you so much for joining us tonight. It was a delight to see you last week at our little gathering."

"The gratitude is mine. The peaceful ceremony was such a comfort at this difficult time, and your followers were so kind to me."

"You are no nearer to finding your husband's murderers?"

Metella shook her head angrily. "A month now, since we interred his body in the family tomb."

"And still no witnesses have come forward? The urban cohorts have nothing?"

Metella looked at Scrofa accusingly. "The Urban Prefect refused even to see me. He told his lackeys that if I brought a suspect before him with evidence, he would be happy to judge the case, but until then would expend no resources on the matter."

Scrofa nodded sadly. "It is the way of things. True justice is only for the powerful. For the rest of us, justice is whatever we can mete out ourselves."

Elissa looked sympathetic. "The elite care nothing for the rest of the people of Rome. We have to look to each other for succour and comfort. It must have been so traumatic for you, finding him in that alley."

Metella's mouth tightened, lower lip trembling. "There was so much blood..."

Elissa squeezed Metella's hand tighter, but Rufa saw a brightness in her mistress's eyes that unsettled her.

"As you know, our followers have made enquiries, but we found nothing. I fear that the more time that passes, the weaker memories grow. I am very sorry, Metella."

Metella looked at Elissa through tear-brimmed eyes. "Thank you, Mother Elissa. For your kind words, and the support of you and your people."

"Our people," corrected Elissa, laying her other hand over Metella's. "You belong with us now. And of course, we should thank you, for the generous donation to our group."

"Money," said Metella, waving her hand dismissively. "My Decimus was rich beyond most men's dreams. We had a town house on the Palatine, a villa in Baiae, fifty slaves, and dozens of clients paying their respects at our *atrium* every morning. What did it gain him? His blood emptied out in a dirty back alley." This time she did sob, and Elissa patted her hand gently.

"You are with friends, Metella," she said. "Tonight you will join us for the first time in our mysteries."

Metella smiled through her tears. "I can't wait to know more about the Lord and Lady, Mother Elissa."

"Tonight, Metella, you will learn much."

The meal continued with subdued small talk. The guests seemed to Rufa to be a little on edge, although she often felt the same around her mistress. It wasn't that Elissa had ever mistreated her as such. There was just an intensity to her gaze, a tone to her soft voice that sent shivers down Rufa's spine, the same way the squeak of a rusty cart wheel could if it was just the right pitch. Her attention started to drift, as it usually did on these occasions where her tasks mainly consisted of standing around doing nothing. Her mind wandered to her past life of relative freedom and relative luxury, as much as was afforded any female child. Only eleven years old when she was sold into slavery, over half her life had been spent in bondage, including all her adult days. But even now she missed the still vividly remembered time with her father before he died, and with the others who looked after her as their own, before she was sent to the slave market. She sighed, which drew a disapproving glance from Shafat. She stiffened her back, set her face to a neutral expression once more, and let her mind go blank.

She was called on to serve a few more times as the meal progressed, welcoming the movement so she could stretch her legs, but despite her inactivity she felt quite tired by the time the guests rose.

"Dismiss the slaves," said Elissa, and Shafat sent them on their way with a gesture. Rufa bowed deeply, and headed back to her room with Natta, rubbing her sleepy eyes and looking forward with anticipation to the bed in which she hoped Fabilla was fast asleep.

When she opened the door to the room, Natta's family were all asleep, but Fabilla was sitting up, crying quietly. Rufa ran quickly to embrace her.

"What is it, precious one?" she asked, drying the girl's eyes on her tunic.

"It's Arethusa," sobbed Fabilla. "I can't find her anywhere. I think she is lost, mummy. She must be so lonely and scared."

Rufa hugged her daughter tight, stomach sinking. There were many fears that plagued Rufa, but Fabilla losing Arethusa, her doll, was one of the acutest. Her daughter's only real possession, Rufa had made the little doll out of rags, coloured wool and glass beads she had saved and begged for while she was pregnant. Arethusa had been Fabilla's constant companion since the day she was born.

"Where did you see her last?" asked Rufa with concern.

"I think it was this afternoon, after I had finished my cleaning chores. Natta said I could play in the *peristylium*. I sat her on one of the benches while I played ball with Cossa. Then Shafat came along and sent Cossa away, and he asked how I was, and he said some words in a foreign language, and then he rubbed something on my head, and I got a bit scared, so I ran away, and I forgot all about Arethusa until a little while ago, and then I woke up and she wasn't there and you weren't there and..."

She started to sob louder, and Natta's family all started to stir. Natta shot Rufa an angry look. Rufa held Fabilla close, gently easing her sobs, worried that she would be in trouble with Natta's man, Cossus, if he woke. Cossus wasn't afraid to dole out a physical punishment when he was angry, to his own family and to anyone else not protected by someone more powerful than him, although he was careful not to damage his mistress's property.

"I'll find her," whispered Rufa. "I'm sure she will still be where you left her. And even if she isn't, someone else will have seen her."

"Please bring her back for me, mummy," said Fabilla. "I love her."

"I will," promised Rufa, saying a silent prayer to Juno Quiritis, the goddess of motherhood, to help her fulfil her vow.

She settled Fabilla back to bed, where the little girl lay, calmer, but still awake, trust in her mother showing now in wide eyes. Rufa quietly slipped out of the room, and made her way from their quarters at the back of the house to the *peristylium*. She heard voices as she rounded the corner, and found Elissa, Shafat and the dinner guests seated in a circle on the floor of the *peristylium*, illuminated by the light of a few small oil lamps. Metella sat in the middle of the circle, holding a small piglet who wriggled occasionally. She seemed over-aware, eyes wide, body twitching a little.

Rufa ducked back into a shadow behind a column, frustrated. She didn't want to go back to Fabilla empty handed, but clearly she was not invited to this meeting, and she didn't think it would go down well if she started rummaging through the bushes and under the benches looking for Arethusa. She decided to just wait for them to finish whatever they were doing.

Elissa had her eyes closed, and was chanting in a low voice in a language Rufa didn't understand. The others were still, keeping their eyes fixed on her. Elissa raised her hands upwards, and they copied her movements. She then opened her eyes, and fixed each one with a stare in turn.

"Children, we are here today to bring this child, Metella, into our sacred circle. Since the days when our Lord and Lady's city, our spiritual home, was founded, thirty eight years before the first Olympiad, my ancestors have worshipped the Lord Ba'al Hammon and the Lady Tanit, Face of Ba'al. The office of the Priestess of Tanit has been passed down from mother to daughter through the generations, and though our city has been destroyed by the Romans, our people scattered into the desert and across the seas, our Lord and Lady live on, and will rise again. We, their obedient followers, will carry out their commands, until the day when finally they exact their retribution upon the city of Rome, and revenge all the people of Carthage, and all those across the world who suffer under the Roman yoke!"

The men gave a firm, low, "Aye." Metella fidgeted in her seat, but kept her gaze fixed on Elissa.

"Metella, we bring you into the worship of our Lord and Lady. Do you swear to worship, honour and fear them, and to worship, honour and fear me, their representative here in Rome?"

"Yes, Mother," said Metella, speaking quickly. "I swear it on the bones of my ancestors, and with the blood of my children to come."

"It is unfortunate, Metella, that your marriage did not produce issue. But there is an ancient Punic tradition, that in place of a sacrifice of your own blood, the blood of another can be substituted. Hand me the piglet."

Metella did so, nearly dropping it as it wriggled. Elissa calmed it with some soothing words and a gentle stroke down the back of its neck. Then she drew a sharp, curved knife from the folds of her robe and slit its throat. She held the thrashing animal up so that the bright red blood spurted over Metella's face, hair and white robe. The thrashings ceased, and Elissa handed the limp body to Metella.

"Commit your moloch, your sacrifice, to the fire," she said.

Rufa noticed that the odd bronze statue that had always sat in the middle of the peristylium, arms stretched upwards with palms facing the sky, now had a fiercely burning fire in an open urn in its centre. With some gentle direction from Elissa, Metella placed the body at the top of the statue's arms, and let it go. It rolled down the steep incline, and landed in the middle of the fire, where it immediately started to hiss and sizzle. The smell of roasting pork drifted over to where Rufa still crouched, motionless.

"Accept our gift, Lord Ba'al Hammon and Lady Tanit, Face of Ba'al," said Elissa in a sing song chant. "And with it, accept your new follower, Metella, into your family."

Elissa leant forward, and used her thumb to make a sign on Metella's forehead in the blood. The sign was hard to make out in the flickering light, but it looked similar to the strange mark on Fabilla's head. What had Fabilla said earlier? That Shafat had put it there? Rufa's stomach clenched involuntarily, and a wave of nausea rolled over her.

"Metella," continued Elissa. "You are now part of the family of Ba'al Hammon and Tanit. You are bound to us by blood, and will keep our secrets till death. Do you understand?"

Metella nodded. "I understand, Mother."

Elissa smiled. "Congratulations, Metella. You belong now. One of the foremost among the followers of the Lord and Lady. A special one."

The others gave their congratulations with a word or a touch, and Metella smiled at them, appearing somewhat calmer now. Rufa wondered if it was anxiety and anticipation that had made her seem so jumpy, or some type of herb or potion.

"And now," said Elissa. "To the next matter. The day of retribution. First, though I should explain some things to Metella. Child, do you know the story of the wars between Carthage and Rome?"

"Of course, Mother. We Romans have been brought up on tales of the terrible Hannibal, his defeat by Scipio, the eventual destruction of the city."

"Brave Hannibal," corrected Elissa. "His name means beloved of Ba'al, and truly he was. How else could he do the impossible, lead an army over the Alps, stay for ten years in Italy, terrorising the Romans, never defeated, except with the favour of Ba'al and the Lady?

"In the end though, it was the cowardice of men, not the grace of the Gods that brought him down."

Rufa wondered what Elissa meant. Hannibal was a name every Roman knew, a name that even to that day was used to scare children into better behaviour. She listened, interested despite her growing anxiety.

"The elders of Carthage betrayed him and their city. Then fifty five years later, they did it again, and this time, Carthage was burned to the ground."

The listeners nodded solemnly as Elissa described the scenes of Carthage's destruction. Rufa listened in wonder and horror at the stories of the children and the elderly burned to death, or crushed under the hooves of the Roman cavalry and tossed, living or dead into vast burial pits. She heard Elissa tell tales of looting, raping and murdering, and heard her curse people she had never heard of, like Scipio Aemilianus and the cowardly Carthaginian leader Hasdrubal who surrendered the city. In spite of herself, she was held rapt by Elissa's hypnotic voice. Metella and the others listened, rapt, the monologue punctuated only by crackles and sizzles from the fire.

"Everyone that survived the siege was sold into slavery," Elissa said, voice hushed now. "Every building was levelled or burned. Scipio cursed the city and salted it. He performed the *evocatio*, claiming by doing so that he had driven the Carthaginian gods from the city."

Elissa paused, took a deep breath and looked around her. When her gaze drifted past Rufa's hiding place, a fist clutched Rufa's heart, but Elissa's attention did not linger, and she continued to speak, voice firmer now.

"But there were others, in the countryside and towns around Carthage, where the spirit of the city, the tradition, and the gods, lived on. When Julius Caesar re-established his colony at Carthage, the descendants of the city found their way back, mingling with the Numidians and the Romans. Many lost their way, turned their backs on the old religions, and embraced the Roman pantheon, and called themselves Romans. Some of us though, we never forgot."

There was a silence, which eventually Metella broke. Her eyes were filled with tears.

"Mother. I am so sorry for the anguish my ancestors caused your ancestors. The horror, the injustice they inflicted on them."

Elissa reached out to hold her hand. "Rome has turned its back on you too, Metella. With your husband dead, you have no protector, no one to stand up for your rights. The city does not care to investigate your loss, and soon the vultures will be circling, trying to wed you to get their hands on your husband's fortune, committing you to a life of servitude and lovelessness."

Metella trembled.

"Don't worry, child," said Elissa. "You are with us now. You have a new family, who will care for you and protect you."

Metella smiled and blinked the tears away.

"And Rome's punishment is overdue. Soon, Rome will face her own *evocatio.*" Elissa turned to Shafat. "The sacrifice that was chosen is safe and well?"

Shafat inclined his head. "She is, Mother. And today, I marked her with the sign of Tanit."

"Good. And we have a symbol of the sacrifice now, to ask for the Lord and Lady's blessings on our preparations?"

"Yes, Mother."

Shafat produced something from beneath his robes, and for a moment in the dim, flickering light, Rufa could not make out what he held. Then terror grabbed her chest as she realised the identity of the little object. It was Arethusa, Rufa's doll! As she watched, Shafat bowed his head to the statue, and placed it at the top of the outstretched bronze arms. He let go, and the little bundle of dry rags slid down and disappeared into the fire.

Chapter II

Dusk was rapidly giving way to darkness when Carbo arrived in the Subura. The path of his ride, a rickety cart of animal fodder that he had hitched a ride on from Veii, had diverged from his own before he reached the Tiber, and he had walked through a chill, gloomy Rome for at least an hour to reach his destination. The Argiletum, the road connecting the Forum Romanum to the Subura was a great artery of a road, choking at night time with the wheeled vehicles that were banned during the day. Carbo picked his way cautiously through the traffic, aware that death could come to him beneath the axles of a laden ox cart as easily as it could at the hands of a barbarian warrior in battle, with maybe a little less glory.

Eventually, he recognised the turn into the street leading to the part of the Subura in which he had grown up. Though once the area had been as familiar to him as the hilt of his *gladius* now was, much had changed. Delapidated apartment blocks collapsed with regularity, especially in the poorer districts, where unscrupulous landlords skimped on quality building materials and quality builders, and then erected dangerously unstable dwellings to replace them.

Multiple wrong turns and dead ends lengthened his journey. The character of the Subura changed dramatically as night fell. The throngs of people and hordes of merchants were replaced by those brave or stupid enough to venture out into the unlit streets. Every dark alley, every recess was a potential hiding place for a cutpurse, or cutthroat. Carbo kept his hand tightly gripped on his *gladius*, striding calmly and purposefully forward, but with ears straining and eyes darting from side to side. Several times he thought from the corner of his eye that someone was watching him, gaze burying into him, but when he turned, no one was paying him any attention.

A flurry of wings startled him, made him duck. A black crow, disturbed from its nesting place by a prowling cat, flew close over his head, and landed on a wall. It cocked its head and regarded him steadily. Carbo shivered, picturing the memory of scores of the birds picking through the human remains of a battlefield. He walked on and the crow cawed, the sound resonating in his head like a discordant, broken bell.

At last, he recognised a small fountain, a familiarly twisted tree, and a stone statue of Augustus. He traced his fingers around the statue base, and found the writing he remembered, engraved there twenty five years before. *Carbo sat here, then left for the legions.* It was all he felt anyone needed to know, at the time.

Twenty feet on, facing into a small courtyard, was the *insula* in which he was born, where he had been raised. He paused for a moment, looking up. It had evidently survived longer than many of its neighbours, although large cracks in the fascia made him question how much longer it could hold out.

He looked around. The buildings seemed smaller than he remembered, though he knew that was just his adult perspective comparing the view to his child's memories. But Rome seemed different too, something unsettling him that he couldn't define. His stomach felt like it contained a lump of cold iron. He swallowed. He knew how his past could affect him, take hold of him, and cursed himself inwardly. He set his shoulders and started for the *insula* in front of him.

The staircase was external on this building, and he started to climb the narrow uneven steps to the higher apartments.His old family apartment was on the third floor. Reasonably sized compared to many in the district, it had three rooms, a bedroom for him, one for his mother and father, and a communal eating and cooking area. He sighed as he remembered his father. The letter he received had been dictated by his mother to a scribe, informing Carbo of his passing. That had been at least ten years ago, he realised. Carbo reached his old front door, and knocked gently.

There was no response, so he hammered more forcefully. This time, he heard low muttering and curses from within. He frowned. A male voice? His mother's last letter hadn't mentioned a new man in her life, though it was several months since he had her heard from her.

The door was pulled abruptly open, and Carbo found himself staring into the bleary-eyed, suspicious face of a man in his twenties.

"What do you want?" he growled.

"A fine welcome home," said Carbo.

"Home? Have the gods taken your senses? What are you talking about, man?"

"Get out of my way, I want to see my mother."

Carbo pushed the man firmly in the chest, making him stagger backwards, and brushed past him into the apartment. The old place was how he remembered it in shape and layout, but completely different in appearance. The walls were painted in brighter colours than his mother would ever have tolerated. The furniture appeared reasonably new and in good condition. On the table, illuminated by a dimly burning oil lamp, was a cheap vase, and a child's rattle. A rattle?

"Lucius?" came a voice from behind the curtain separating the living room from the bedroom. "Who is it? Is everything all right?"

Carbo strode to the curtain and ripped it aside. The young woman in the bed screamed, and snatched up a baby from the cot beside the bed, clutching it to her. The baby woke and joined in the screaming. A roar from behind Carbo alerted him, and he spun to find himself caught full in the chest by the charging Lucius. They landed together on the bed, the young woman jumping deftly out of the way.

Disorientated by the confusing turn of events, Carbo allowed Lucius to get the first blow in, a punch to the mouth, softened by proximity, but enough to split his lip. He rolled the man off him and onto the floor. Lucius rose quickly, and snatched a dagger from beneath the bed. Carbo stood, putting some distance between them.

Lucius feinted, thrust, and Carbo dragged the curtain down over his head. Lucius swung wildly, but the curtain temporarily blinded him. Carbo stepped forward, an elbow to the temple causing Lucius' legs to buckle beneath him, allowing Carbo to disarm him easily. He stepped back, and let Lucius regain his feet.

Lucius eyed Carbo, able now to take in Carbo's large frame, and the easy, seasoned way he held the knife he had just taken. Carbo saw the change in his posture that meant he had thought better of taking him on.

"We don't have anything worth taking. See for yourself. But I will kill you if you touch my wife or child, if I have to come back across the Styx to do it."

"Where's my mother?" asked Carbo.

Lucius looked nonplussed. "How should I know where your damned mother is?"

"Because this is her damned house!" shouted Carbo.

For a moment, Lucius stared at Carbo, and then he looked at his wife, and an understanding seemed to pass between them.

"Are you Atella's son?" asked the woman, her voice a little shaky, but soft.

"Yes, I'm Carbo. Where is she?"

"Carbo, I'm sorry. Atella passed on three months ago."

Carbo stared, understanding, but not believing. He let the dagger fall to the floor. Lucius spoke, voice also softer now.

"Gnaea and I were living with Gnaea's father, in the next *insula*. We knew Atella, knew she was ill. Gnaea helped look after her, as best she could, brought her bread and water, tended her when her illness became too much for her to get out of bed. When she died, the landlord offered us the flat. We could afford it, just, so we moved in."

"She didn't have many possessions," said Gnaea, "and she owed some rent, so the landlord sold most of what she owned. We put some things aside, though, for safe keeping."

Gnaea took a small, carved, wooden box from under the bed and offered it to Carbo. Numbly he took it, opened the lid and looked inside. It contained all the letters he had written to her over the years he had been serving in the legions, pitifully few, he now realised. He picked one at random and read it. It must be twenty years old, written when he was not much more than a boy, still serving in the XIXth, before that legion was destroyed. The words were brief, informing her of his good health, and wishing her the same, hoping the enclosed money was of help, and telling her he loved her. Beneath the letters, his fingers touched something hard, and he pulled it out. A lead legionary soldier, his prized toy. How he had wanted to be a soldier, all those childhood years. If only he could have known what it would be like.

Carbo looked up. Gnaea and Lucius were regarding him, still cautiously, but also with sympathy.

"I owe you both an apology. I've travelled a long way, and I... I thought I was home."

Lucius put a consoling hand on his shoulder. "If you don't have anywhere to stay tonight, you can sleep on the floor here. But you need to be gone in the morning. There isn't enough room for you here, you understand."

Carbo smiled sadly. "You are a good man. But I will not disturb you further. Please accept my apologies again, and thank you for your kindness to my mother. Your kindness to me, too, for saving me these memories."

He turned to the door, then paused. "For the damage, and the trouble," he said, handing them a coin that was unnecessarily large to compensate them for both. Lucius' eyes widened at the value, and he thanked Carbo. Then Carbo walked out of the door of his childhood home, and made his way back down the stairs.

Carbo woke to a spatter of foul liquid landing on his head. He realised from the smell and the solid chunks that one of the occupants of a flat above had emptied their chamber pot on him. He was lying in the doorway of a shop that smelled as if it mainly sold *garum*, the ever popular sauce made from rotted fish guts. He wiped his face, cursed, and stretched, joints that had had twenty five years of hard wear and tear courtesy of the army protesting. His backside was numb, and although he figured he had got an hour or two of sleep, his mind and body felt drained. He stood, and limped his way down the street, stroking the poorly healed war wound in his leg.

Rome was waking. Shutters on shops were opening, and the keener citizens were hurrying out to meet their patrons to be first in the line for a dole out of cash. Some of the more enterprising ones would be visiting several different patrons that day, and making a decent living from what amounted to professional begging.

He came across the fountain that had served as his landmark the previous night, and dunked his head in, rinsing off the worst of the excrement and grime. An old woman cursed him for polluting the water, and filled her jar from the trickle of clean liquid flowing from the pipe that served the fountain. He ignored her and looked around, taking stock.

He was back home, but what was here for him? No family remained, and he was sure there would be few friends who remembered the unnaturally large teenager who had left to join up. He felt the weight of the purse suspended around his waist, concealed by his tunic. The years of campaigning had left him a comparatively rich man, at least by the standards of the citizens of this district. Of course, he would never hope to see in his life time even a fraction of the wealth that the poorest of Rome's elite, the senators and equestrians, owned.

Nearby, a tavern opened its doors. A sign of a cockerel was painted on the wall. A man dressed in tunic and apron came out and looked up and down the street. He was tall, but starting to stoop, and the remaining hair that rimmed his bald pate was white as goose down. He seemed ill at ease, but after a few moments, he sighed, and put out his sign, which declared him open for business. Carbo decided he had no other place to be, and walked in.

The tavern was like a thousand others he had been in throughout the empire. The floor was tiled with a plain pattern, the walls decorated with poorly painted depictions of bacchanalian scenes. Tables and chairs were scattered around. A low bar ran along the back wall. Large depressions in the bar held pots of various stews and sauces. Jars of wine and other drinks sat on shelves behind it. Behind it, a small door led to what Carbo presumed would be the kitchen and living quarters of the tavernkeeper. A small room, little more than an alcove, was separated from the main part of the inn by a tatty curtain. This could be drawn across to give the alcove a semblance of privacy, but was currently pulled back to reveal a low, stained couch within. Carbo knew what sort of services were performed in that room, had paid for them himself often enough.

He took a seat by the table that served as the bar, and the tavernkeeper approached him with a nervous smile.

"What would you like, friend?"

Carbo nodded, not feeling in the mood to return the smile. "A loaf, and some watered wine."

"Of course, sir, *poscum,* I presume will suit?"

Carbo grimaced, realising that his dirty clothes and unkempt appearance must have him marked as a street beggar, come into a couple of *asses* to fund a drink. He reached into his purse and took out a *denarius.* "I came here for wine, not vinegar and water. Make it a Falernian."

The tavernkeeper looked a little shocked, both at the value of the coin, which was sixteen times the value of the copper *as* that would usually be enough to buy wine, and also at the request for the fine vintage.

"I'm sorry, sir, this is just a humble Suburan tavern. We don't keep such fine wines here. Maybe I could suggest a Mamertinian."

Carbo considered, then nodded. The tavernkeeper poured a small amount of wine concentrate into a cup, then topped it up with water. Carbo took a sip, not bothering to comment on how dilute the drink was. He wasn't intending to get drunk anyway, at least not yet. The tavernkeeper retreated through a back door. A short-legged bitch with a shaggy brown and white coat came and sniffed his hand, and Carbo stroked her rough-coated head. The tavernkeeper returned with a loaf that was still warm. Carbo devoured it, only now realising how hungry he was, but saved a small crust for the dog who had stayed at his feet throughout, gaze fixed on him. She gobbled the offered morsel in one swallow.

"I apologise for Myia," said the tavernkeeper. Carbo raised his eyes questioningly. The tavernkeeper indicated the dog. Carbo waved the apology away.

"Think nothing of it. She is good company."

"I haven't seen you in here before, sir. I'm Publius Sergius by the way."

"Carbo," said Carbo through a mouthful of bread. "And I've been away."

"Oh," said Publius, realisation dawning. "The legions?" Carbo nodded.

"I would have loved to have fought in the legions. The glory, the riches. But I am just a lowly freedman. Just able to buy this place after a lifetime of servitude, due to a small bequest on the death of my master."

Glory and riches. Maybe the latter, compared to the people living in this district at least. The former, precious little.

Before Carbo could retort, the door to the back room swung open, and two arguing slaves strode in.

"You are a lazy boy, Philon," said the first, a tall, well built, dark haired girl in her twenties, with a strong Germanic accent. "Master should punish you. But he won't. He is too weak. Just be thankful you aren't my slave, or you would feel the rod on your backside every day till you mended your ways."

"You are just spiteful, Marsia," Philon shot back angrily. "I do my chores. And the master would never hurt me. I am his favourite after all."

Carbo looked at Philon, an effeminate looking teenage boy, and then looked at Publius. The tavernkeeper appeared to be doing his best to ignore the altercation, and when he caught Carbo's eye, he gave him a small shake of the head and a weary shrug of the shoulders.

"Publius!" said Marsia. "Why don't you correct this slave, like a true master of his household should? He was supposed to have cleaned the bedroom, and when I checked this morning, I found six spiders, two cockroaches and a dead rat. I had to slap his face just to get him to wake up."

Philon rubbed a red mark on his face, and gestured at Marsia. "Master, shouldn't you correct this slave, who takes it on herself to discipline your property without your say so?"

"Enough. We have a customer. Sort your petty squabbles out between yourselves."

The two slaves seemed to notice Carbo for the first time, wrapped up as they had been in themselves. Philon's demeanour changed instantly, a coquettish smile appearing on his face. Marsia put her hands on her hips and regarded Carbo steadily.

"And now we have become a home for all the beggars and destitutes of the streets. I knew business was bad, Publius, but how desperate are we?"

Publius hissed at her. "Marsia. Enough. He paid in silver."

Marsia raised an eyebrow. "I see. And who did you rob?"

Carbo held her stare. "Several thousand Germans," he said, evenly.

Marsia paused, then nodded her head. "So, you are a war hero. Good. We are honoured. And stolen German money is as good as any."

"As are stolen German slaves. Publius, get me another loaf, I'm still starving."

Carbo spent the morning sitting in a corner of the tavern, sipping slowly from his drink, and gradually restoring some energy with the simple food he bought. Philon and Marsia busied themselves, Marsia efficiently, Philon only with constant encouragement and bullying from Marsia. Publius tried to engage Carbo in conversation, but soon became dispirited by the one way flow, and got on with his own tasks. Other customers drifted in, and Publius soon forgot about Carbo, as he chatted to his regulars.

One early visitor caught Carbo's eye, a thin, balding man, with a long grey beard and a deeply lined face. He moved purposefully to an empty table next to Carbo's and spent some time settling himself, groaning as his elderly joints accommodated the change in posture. He gestured to

Marsia, who came over with a cup of wine and some bread and *garum*.

"There you go, Vatius."

The man nodded his thanks, and slid a coin across the table with an arthritis-twisted hand. He then looked around the room, and his gaze rested on Carbo for a moment. He gave him a calculating look, then smiled and winked. Carbo couldn't help but smile back at the friendly face.

"Haven't seen you here before," he said, in a gravelly voice.

"I haven't been here before," said Carbo.

The elderly man seemed to digest this for a moment, and then gave a nod that seemed to suggest this was a satisfactory explanation.

"Gaius Annaeus Vatius," said the man, and stuck his hand out. Carbo leaned over and grasped it.

"Gaius Valerius Carbo."

"Enjoying the games, lad?"

Carbo smiled to himself. A lifetime in the legions with all the accumulated wear and tear on his body, coupled with a night spent sleeping rough, had left him feeling like anything but a lad.

"I'm new in Rome. There are games on?"

"Aye, lad. The *Ludi Romani*. The greatest of the Roman games. Chariot racing in the Circus Maximus, gladiators in the arenas, plays in the theatres, if you like that sort of thing."

Vatius' grimace suggested he didn't like that sort of thing, and Carbo couldn't help but agree with him - what little theatre he had seen seemed to be either convoluted tragedy or low farce, neither of which appealed much.

"New to Rome, then? Where have you been?"

"Away, in the legions."

"Ah, one of our heroes. Then it is even better to meet you."

"You never served?"

Vatius shook his head ruefully. "Not I. I'm a mere son of a freedman."

"What was your trade then?"

"Oh, this and that. Actor in my wilder, younger days. Tutor. Itinerant philosopher."

"Is there much call for an itinerant philosopher?"

Vatius eyes seemed to twinkle. "You would be surprised. It made me enough money that I can sit here and eat and drink and watch the world go by, rather than live under the arches of the aqueducts and try to support myself and my wife with the corn dole."

"You are married? You prefer to be in here than with your wife?"

"Socrates said that everyone should marry," Vatius said with a grin. "If they get a good wife they will be happy, if they get a bad one they will become a philosopher."

"Oh," said Carbo. "I'm sorry."

Vatius fixed him with a stare. "Don't be. Happiness depends upon ourselves." Carbo returned the look questioningly.

"Aristotle," said Vatius by way of explanation. "I am content with my life."

Soon, the room filled enough that there was a constant background of noise, clanking cups, laughter, the odd raised angry voice, chatter. Once, a rather drunk customer rolled in and declared in a loud voice that he had won on the blues at the chariot races. He bought everyone a drink, then gave Publius a coin and grabbed Philon by the hand, guiding him to the small alcove. Philon sighed, and pulled the curtain closed behind them. A surprisingly short while later, the curtain was drawn back. The man, clothing awry, winked at Carbo and staggered back out of the inn. Philon emerged, his clothing undisturbed, wiping his hands on a grimy cloth.

Carbo took everything in, but his mind was wandering aimlessly. He felt paralysed with indecision. Since he had left the legion a few weeks ago, he had had only one aim, to go home. Now he found out he didn't have a home. He didn't have a family. The only people he called friends were still serving in the legion. He owned some land he had never visited, a purse full of money, a pension, his clothes, a stiff leg, and nothing else.

The sun rose high in the sky. The tavern was full, which surprised Carbo after Marsia's earlier comments about business being bad. He started to wonder whether to stay here for lunch, or to make an effort to overcome his lethargy and inertia and make his way out into the streets of Rome. He didn't know where to go, or what to do, but he had to do something, didn't he?

Or did he? The life Vatius described suddenly sounded appealing to him. Just sit back, watch and take no further part in the world. Myia, who had been sniffing around his feet, stood up on her hind legs to put her paws in his lap, and he stroked her head absent-mindedly.

The door to the tavern flew open so forcefully that the noise as it banged against the wall silenced the clientele. A small crack appeared in the masonry, making Carbo look up nervously at the ceiling for a moment, wondering what it would take to bring the building down.

A well-muscled man with a pock-marked face swaggered in, and gave an exaggerated grimace. Myia stood facing him, taking a step back into the shadows of the table, teeth bared and a grumbling growl coming from the back of her throat.

"What a dump," he said. "It doesn't get any better, does it?"

He looked around to the clients in the tavern, who studied their drinks intently, avoiding his gaze.

"Maybe it's the atmosphere," he said. He walked to the bar, elbowing aside anyone too slow to move out of the way. Carbo regarded him with curiosity.

"Cilo," said Publius, droplets of sweat appearing on his forehead, a tremor in his voice. "What would you like to drink?"

"*Mulsum*," said Cilo, and waited impatiently while Publius poured a cup of the honeyed drink with shaking hands. Marsia had moved close behind Publius, saying nothing. Philon was at the opposite end of the room, trying to remain unobtrusive. A few customers slipped discreetly out. Cilo downed his drink, and Carbo noticed that he didn't offer to pay, and nor did Publius ask.

"Cheap muck, as usual," said Cilo, wiping his mouth with the back of his hand. "I've come to expect no better. Now, give me what you owe, and I will leave you and your customers in peace."

Publius hurried into the back room. As he came out, he avoided looking at Marsia, who was regarding him with narrowed eyes. He thrust a small bag of coins into Cilo's hand. Cilo hefted the bag speculatively, then laughed.

"There was supposed to be a week's payment here. This barely covers a single day."

"There are ten *denarii* in there," said Publius indignantly. "That is the price your father agreed."

"I've put the price up. One hundred *denarii* a week."

Publius gasped. "I can't afford that. My entire takings wouldn't cover it."

"Maybe you should think about a price rise. I'm sure your customers here would be glad to pay extra for the wonderful service they get here."

"I can't, Cilo, please, you will ruin me."

Cilo touched a knife at his belt, and looked hard into Publius' eyes. "There are worse ways to ruin someone than financially. Give me what you owe."

Hastily, Publius emptied a pot from beneath the bar. "That's all my takings from last night and this morning. That's all I have."

Cilo weighed the money. "It will have to do as a down payment. I will come for the rest tomorrow."

"I don't have any more," said Publius, pleading. "I don't even have enough to buy new stock. How am I supposed to pay you if I don't have the means to make money?"

"Your problem. Maybe you should make those pretty slaves of yours work a bit harder at what they are good at. Talking of which, I think I fancy a turn with the handsome German." He turned his gaze on Marsia, who held it defiantly.

"Cilo, sir, Marsia doesn't provide that service. Take Philon. "

"No, I have taken a shine to Marsia. Even more so, now you tell me she isn't for public use." He strode over to Marsia and grasped her by the wrist. Marsia glared at Publius, who turned away, eyes downcast. Cilo started to pull the struggling Marsia towards the cubicle, and as she resisted, he cuffed her hard around the head, dazing her a little.

"If you struggle, I'll leave you so you are no use to any man again."

"Please," whispered Marsia. "No."

Cilo drew his knife and stroked it around her throat, causing her to freeze. A livid line encircled her neck where the tip had touched, one bead of blood oozing out where it had bitten deeper. He led her, unresisting now, towards the cubicle.

Carbo's voice was low, but it carried across the room. "She said no."

Cilo turned in surprise to see where the voice had come from. He took in Carbo's appearance with a glance, and laughed.

"Fuck off you idiot, or I'll hurt you as well."

Carbo stood, and Cilo's eyes widened momentarily, then he pushed Marsia aside and face Carbo.

"You don't understand the size of your mistake." He waved his knife in small circles in the air. "But it doesn't matter, as it will be your last one."

Carbo regarded him steadily, hands by his sides, unmoving. Cilo struck with the speed of a snake, knife flashing to plunge into Carbo's stomach, and up under his ribs. But Carbo was no longer there. The knife stabbed at the space out of which Carbo had side stepped, and Cilo staggered forward, his momentum unbalancing him. Carbo grabbed the knife hand, twisted, and stepped back. Cilo found himself suddenly disarmed. Carbo tossed the knife aside and took a menacing step forward. Cilo retreated before the large, furious looking man confronting him.

"You're a dead man," he hissed at Carbo. "You too, Publius. My father will destroy you all, and this tavern with it."

"Get out," said Carbo. "One chance to walk away."

Cilo hesitated, pride warring with prudence in his face. With a last obscene gesture, he stormed out, slamming the tavern door behind him.

Carbo let out a breath. His heart was racing, the anticipation of an imminent fight that did not materialise leaving him tense. He looked around, to see Publius sitting with his head in his hands.

"They'll kill me, they'll kill me," he was muttering, over and over.

Carbo sat back down in his seat and sipped his wine, letting the drink soothe his jangled nerves. The tavern was silent.

Marsia walked up to him unsteadily, fingers dabbing intermittently at her neck, which was still damp with blood. "Thank you sir, that was a kind thing you did."

"Thank him?" cried Publius, leaping to his feet. "Are you mad, Marsia? You know what Cilo and his family are like. This fool has destroyed us. We will need to leave Rome. Who will buy this place from me at such short notice? And with those men ready to terrorise anyone here. We will have to leave, and we will have nothing. I will have to sell you and Philon, but the money I get for you worthless pair won't be enough to start a new business. Dead or ruined. Those are the choices I face."

Carbo looked around him. The customers looked conflicted, maybe pleased at the humiliation of the thug, but worried about the consequences. Philon and Publius both looked terrified, but Marsia was standing straight, a half-smile on her place. What would it be like, he wondered, to have somewhere to belong? Somewhere to have pride in. He suddenly realised how terribly lonely he was, since he had left the insulated life of the legions.

"I'll buy the tavern," said Carbo.

All eyes turned towards him, Publius, the slaves, the customers. Publius gaped at him. "You? But you…surely you couldn't…I mean… could you?"

Carbo pulled out his purse. "I'll give you thirty *aurei*. And throw in the slaves. And the dog."

Publius' expression turned calculating. "Thirty? The slaves alone are worth that. And the building, the customers, this is a nice steady earning business…"

Carbo knew he was driving a hard bargain, though the tavern owner was clearly overvaluing the slaves. The small farm Carbo owned was worth around a thousand *aurei*, but though he had never visited it, he knew it was a nice estate, bringing in an income, whereas this was a dive in the worst part of town.

"You were ruined before I stepped in, Publius. You couldn't afford to pay the money to those men any more. Thirty is a fair price, given the circumstances. Take it or leave it."

Publius took in Carbo's set features, and nodded. He disappeared out into the back of the tavern, and returned shortly afterwards with a surprisingly small sack of belongings. He held out his hand to Carbo. "Give me the money, and the place is yours."

"Wait," said Marsia. Both men looked at her, annoyed by the interruption. "This isn't legal. By law of *mancipatio*, you need five citizens as witnesses, some scales and an ingot of copper."

Carbo raised an eyebrow. There was obviously more to this Germanic barbarian slave than met the eye. Looking around the tavern, he counted only four men remaining, the ones brave enough to have wanted to witness how the scene played out, or too drunk to leave. Vatius was one, grinning broadly, but neither he nor any of the other customers looked interested in the idea of participating, and although there was a rusty pair of scales behind the bar, finding a copper ingot seemed unlikely.

"I don't think you are going to come back to Rome to dispute my possession are you, Publius?" said Carbo.

Publius shook his head anxiously. Carbo counted the coins out of his purse. Publius snatched them, and with one last glance around, was gone. Marsia stared at the door he had just departed through, disbelief on her face.

"Gone, just like that. I have served him for three years, and he didn't even say goodbye." She faced Carbo.

"Well, Master. You are now the proud owner of your own tavern, and two slaves. What now?"

Carbo thought for a second. "Pour me a drink, I guess. And then carry on as you were. I presume you two know how to run this place?"

"Of course," said Marsia, as she poured Carbo a cup of wine. "You don't think Publius did any work, do you?" Carbo smiled, then walked round behind the bar, and sampled the unfamiliar viewpoint. He didn't think of himself as an impulsive person, but he realised his current frame of mind had pushed him into a decision he wouldn't normally have made. Maybe that was a good thing, though. He suddenly felt like he had some vague sense of purpose. Or at least, something to do.

First, though, he had another task, now the morning's torpor had been lifted.

"Good," he said. "I'm going out."

"May I ask where to, Master?" asked Marsia.

Carbo looked at her, surprised at the presumption for a moment, then walked out into the street.

Elissa stood before the worshippers, who knelt in hushed silence like obedient schoolchildren. The initiation ceremony was finished. The new follower, a Numidian freedwoman called Dahia, knelt at the front, beaming in pride.

Arms raised, Elissa chanted a prayer, eyes half closed. The worshippers listened intently, responded obediently where they should. Elissa felt bathed in serenity. This was where she belonged, receiving adoration, continuing her mother's legacy, and the legacy of her homeland. She finished the prayer, and lowered her arms. The large, dimly lit room was silent, expectant. She drew out the tension skilfully, inhaling a deep breath through her nose, then exhaling gradually. Her gaze swept over the ranks of the worshippers. She marvelled at the stew of Roman life she saw before her, old and young, angry and scared, destitute and comfortable, slave and free. While those at the front were silent and rapt, a few at the back were muttering to each other.

She set her gaze on one man with hair like an untended bush, who was more vocal than the others. He stopped talking when he realised he had become her centre of attention.

"The Lord and Lady are almighty," she said, her voice penetrating the quiet. "Do any here doubt it?"

No one spoke up, the man she had singled out dropping his gaze sheepishly. Several shook their heads.

"Rome is rotten. Do any here doubt it?"

Quietly, many of the followers mumbled, "No."

Her gaze pierced into the man's eyes she had singled out, and saw him start to tremble. She raised her voice, loud and clear.

"The Lord and Lady are coming. Rome will belong to them. Do any here doubt it?"

"No," shouted her followers. She saw tears trickling down the face of the wild-haired man and smiled inwardly.

"Tonight," she said, her voice quieter now, "I am introducing to you a special new member of our family. Metella, please come here." She extended a hand, and Metella, who had been kneeling in the front row, rose gracefully with a smile, and stepped forward.

"Children, this is Metella. A noble woman, from a powerful and famous family. But even her power and wealth could not prevent tragedy from striking her. Her beloved husband, cruelly murdered by unknown criminals. And does the mighty city of Rome care? Will it give her redress, aid her in finding the culprits? No, it turns its back on her in her hour of need.

"But we do not turn our backs on one who comes to us for succour, not if they renounce the evil Roman Empire and the oppression it stands for."

A murmur of approval ran through the worshippers.

"Metella, you have been initiated into the worship of the Lord and Lady. You are ours, and we are yours."

"Thank you, mother," said Metella, a tremor in her voice, her eyes moist. "Thank you all of you, for accepting me."

She bowed her head, and several of the worshippers from the front row, including Glaukos and Shafat, got up and congratulated her. They led her into the congregation, and started to introduce her to prominent members. Elissa smiled in satisfaction. Metella would be an invaluable asset.

Especially once she had changed her will in favour of Elissa.

A short man, with a weathered face approached her. She frowned, trying to place him. He wasn't an initiate, so she decided he must be one of the curious newcomers that the cult increasingly attracted.

"The Lord and Lady's blessing on you, child," she murmured, benignly.

"Oh, they have blessed me, in their way," he said. She looked at him more closely. Something about him was familiar.

"You don't remember me, do you, Elissa?"

"No, I…"

His accent. African? Punic?

The man looked around him. "You have a wonderful following here. And now some powerful, dare I say rich, adherents. You have come a long way."

"A long way from…?" Elissa hated being off balance, but a dreadful realisation was dawning on her.

"When I heard there was a cult reviving the old gods of Carthage, my curiosity was piqued. When I heard the High Priestess was called Elissa, well how could I stay away? Elissa, the sole survivor of the slaves of the household of Proculus. Apart from me."

"Tegius?" she gasped.

"How soon you forget? I know I have lost some hair since you last saw me. And some teeth. Still, I'm hurt. You were just blossoming when… when it all happened weren't you? I had plans for you."

"How did you survive?"

"I was the steward of the household. The most valuable slave. Proculus was reluctant to get rid of me, at least at first. Besides he needed someone to oversee the whole affair."

"You organised it?" Elissa said in horror.

"Organise it or be part of it. That was my choice."

Elissa swallowed. Their hushed conversation was drawing curious looks from some of the members of the congregation.

"What do you want of me now?"

"Just a little talk, I think. See if there is maybe a way that a rich lady like yourself can help out on old compatriot. I get lonely here in Rome, lacking the company of other Carthaginians. Sometimes I seek people out, just to talk, reminisce. Chat about things that happened in the old country." He looked at Elissa pointedly. "But I'm guessing you would rather I didn't do that?"

Glaukos walked over. "Are you well, mother?" he asked. Elissa realised she was trembling, and fought to control herself. "Quite well, thank you Glaukos. I was just talking to this new follower. Tegius wasn't it? We shall continue our discussion. Tomorrow evening? Please dine with me."

"It would be my honour, Mother," said Tegius. He bowed, a sneering smile on his face, and left. Glaukos looked at her curiously. Elissa looked away, then turned back to him, searching his face. She was satisfied with what she saw there.

"Glaukos, dear friend and faithful follower. I may need your help."

Chapter III

The early afternoon sun made Carbo blink as he entered the street. He paused to get his bearings, then retraced his steps from the night before. He walked back up to the third floor of the *insula* he had grown up in, and knocked on the door. It was opened cautiously by Gnaea, who looked at him with a mix of suspicion and sympathy.

"Carbo," she said guardedly. "I didn't really expect to see you back."

"I won't bother you for long. I just need to ask you a question, I should have asked last night. My mother, Atella. Where is she buried?"

Gnaea looked uncomfortable. "Atella wasn't a member of a *collegia*, and she had no money and no family members to look after her when she was gone." She shifted from foot to foot. "I mean, no family in Rome. She was cremated, and her ashes were going to go to one of the mass burial pits outside the city. But Lucius, he knew her and had a soft spot for her, so he pulled some strings to get her a place in his *collegia's columbarium*."

Carbo was quiet for a moment, then nodded. "I understand. My thanks to you both."

After getting more detailed directions to the tomb, just outside the Esquiline gate, he took his leave. He traced his steps through the crowded city streets until he reached the place Gnaea had described to him, pausing on the way only to purchase a small meal as a sacrifice from one of the opportunistic vendors working near the tombs. The *columbarium* was a rectangular brick building, with niches set within the facade in the manner of a dovecote. The particular one that Gnaea had told him housed Atella's remains was one of the larger ones, three storeys tall, with dozens upon dozens of niches, most of them containing urns of varying degrees of ornateness. A small garden in front of the tomb was occupied by a handful of people paying their respects. One small family group, a young mother and several small children, clothes tattered and dirty, body condition lean, sat on the grass. They ate a meal composed mainly of bread, presumably from the grain dole, and a few garden vegetables. The children seemed distracted and bored, not noticing the tears that intermittently overflowed from their mother's eyes.

Carbo counted across and up from the bottom left, until his gaze came to rest on a plain pottery urn. He walked up to it, and touched it with his fingertips, then lifted it down. The urn was enclosed, and he thought about opening it, but knew there would be nothing of solace to see. Instead he kissed it and placed it back gently. He unwrapped the meal he had purchased, made from milk, oil, honey and the blood of a sacrificed goat, and ate a small amount, placing the rest in the niche with the urn. He then poured a small amount of wine from the tavern's stocks onto the ground. He hoped it would be enough for the *manes*, the spirits of the dead.

Rufa examined the garden vegetables on the market stall, testing them for ripeness, turning them for signs of rot.

Shafat would beat her if the produce was substandard. The vegetable seller complained at her handling of the goods and harangued her, but she refused to be hurried, and when she had picked a satisfactory selection, she haggled the seller down to a price which wouldn't get her into any further trouble.

Task completed, she made her way back to the house of her mistress, Elissa. As she approached it, she felt her legs weakening, a terrible sense of foreboding descending on her. She ran through the events of the previous night in her mind for what seemed like the thousandth time. But try as she might, she could only come to one conclusion.

Surely, she had misunderstood. This was Rome in the reign of Tiberius. Human sacrifice hadn't occurred here for centuries.

Yet she couldn't forget the mark on Fabilla's forehead, and the fact that Glaukos said he had marked the sacrifice. She reached the house, and hesitated. Only the fact that her daughter was inside stopped her from turning and fleeing.

But if she was right, if this insanity was true, what could she do about it? She was a slave. She had no one to turn to and nowhere to go. She knocked on the door. As she waited for the porter, an image returned to her, of Fabilla's doll, Arethusa, being fed to the flames.

Elissa stood in her study, staring down at a map of Rome, spread over a table. Glaukos and Shafat stood around the table, following her fingers as she traced the streets.

"It will start here," she said tapping at one point on the map. "From here it will spread uncontrollably."

Shafat nodded thoughtfully. "With half of the population at the games, and the cohorts and *vigiles* involved in crowd control, there will be no one to stop it. It will spread throughout Rome, destroying every building in its wake."

"But is that all we want to achieve?" asked Glaukos.

Elissa looked at Glaukos sharply. "All?" she asked, archly.

"Rome's power is not in her buildings. It is in her people. Look at their history - Romans never surrender in adversity. Even when defeated by Pyrrhus or Hannibal, they kept fighting when anyone else would have surrendered. If we destroy their city, they will rebuild it, and it will all have been for nothing."

"You say this now?" said Elissa coldly. "After all our planning? You think our mission is worthless?"

Glaukos shook his head. "No, mother, not at all. I have been thinking, we need to destroy more than the buildings. We need to destroy the Roman people. Their families, their freedmen and subservient slaves. Annihilate them so totally, that those few remaining will have neither the numbers nor the will to rise again. Without Rome, their whole Empire will disintegrate in months."

Elissa looked curious now. "Go on. How will we do this?"

Glaukos smiled. "We use the Roman's own contempt for their lower classes. The shoddy, tottering buildings can be used to create chaos."

Elissa looked doubtful. "I want to know this works before we commit too many resources to this."

"Of course. Give me a little while, I will instruct a few of our followers, and then give you an unforgettable demonstration." He grinned like a gourmet about to embark on a banquet.

Carbo sat before the tomb for most of the afternoon, indulging in painful nostalgia as one childhood memory triggered another. Games with wooden soldiers with his childhood friend Sextus, scoldings and beatings for misdemeanours, births, marriages and funerals, all spun through his mind. As the sun started to dip in the sky, and the bright early afternoon light was replaced by an orange glow, Carbo took a deep breath, and stood. The family was long gone, no doubt wanting to be shuttered in their dwelling well before night fell, assuming they weren't one of the many who lived on the city streets. He walked slowly, lost in his thoughts, and it was nearly dark when he arrived back at his new home.

The tavern was over half full, and Marsia and Philon appeared to be coping admirably. Carbo suspected that Publius had often left them to it, and so he had no qualms about doing the same. He entered quietly, slipping in behind the bar to appear at Marsia's elbow as she was pouring wine from a jug.

"Everything going well?" asked Carbo. Marsia gave a little start, but didn't spill a drop. Her voice was steady as she replied.

"Of course, Master. You can rely on us to keep things in line here."

Carbo smiled. "I'm glad to hear it," he said as he surveyed the room. The atmosphere was pleasant, if loud and a little raucous, with at least half the clients happily inebriated. Vatius sat in his usual chair, feeding Myia crusts of bread. Three men caught his eye, sitting around a table in a corner, sipping slowly from their cups, and saying little. The eldest of the three, a short, stocky, grey-haired man, sat very still, but his eyes darted around the room, fixing a gaze momentarily on each dropped plate, each raised voice, seeming to assess a threat before moving on.

Carbo walked over to their table. They looked up at him but didn't stand. Carbo weighed them up, then pulled up a stool to sit with them.

"Gaius Valerius Carbo," he said, holding out a hand.

"Lucius Vedius Vespillo," said the older man, taking it and shaking it, firmly enough to show some strength, but not so strong as to seem to be trying to prove something. "My colleagues," he said, gesturing to the other two men, who nodded and also shook Carbo's hand.

Vespillo looked at Carbo appraisingly. "A veteran, am I right?"

Carbo nodded. "Is it that obvious?"

"Twenty five years in the army changes men in ways that it is usually easy to pick up. Physique, bearing. Calluses on your sword hand. The nervous tick."

Carbo smiled. "You served?"

"Twenty five years in the XXth Valeria Victrix."

"The Pannonian War?"

Vespillo nodded, his mouth tightening at the mention. "You?"

"I was with the Ist Germanica when I retired."

"You served under Germanicus?"

"I did, his memory be blessed. What a loss to Rome he was. And we are left with Sejanus, the man who likely sent him to Hades, in charge."

Vespillo sucked air in through his teeth. "Beware what you say in Rome, man. This isn't the army, all loyal brothers. Around every corner lurks an informer, willing to sell their grandmother for a few *denarii*."

Carbo held his gaze for a short while, and nodded. He opened his mouth to speak, when the tavern door was flung open with a crash. Carbo groaned as the crack in the masonry, created just this morning, widened a little. He stood to admonish the culprit, and found himself face to face with three angry men, armed with cudgels and knives. Carbo sighed as he recognised the man he had expelled that morning. Next to him was an older man, still imposing in bulk, whose facial features showed a family resemblance to Cilo. Another man, even bigger, a little older than Cilo and again similar in appearance, but with a slack-jawed expression, stood to the other side.

Cilo pointed at Carbo. "That's him, father."

Carbo winced inwardly. He was outnumbered this time, and what's more he was unarmed, with his antagonists between him and the bar, where his *gladius* lay. The elder man regarded Carbo steadily for a moment. "I'm Manius Gellius Cilo, and I'm this boy's father."

Manius looked around him. "So, old Publius Sergius sold you this place and fled?" He glanced at his son. "I did warn you not to squeeze too hard."

He turned back to Carbo. "I have no doubt that my impetuous son deserved to be thrown out of your fine establishment." Cilo scowled but said nothing, and his father carried on.

"Nevertheless, there is a way of doing things around here. I run this district, with the help of my friends and my sons, Cilo and Balbus here." He indicated Cilo and the other larger young man. Then he picked up a stool and hurled it across the room. It crashed into a table, scattering plates and wines and causing the men sitting there to jump back, startled.

"People must show me respect," continued Manius, calmly. "And if someone doesn't show respect to a family member something has to be done. Otherwise no one would respect me. Then where would I be?"

"Am I supposed to care?" asked Carbo.

Manius shook his head. "It doesn't really matter whether you care or not. It only matters that you show me the deference I am owed, or your bloodied corpse will serve as a reminder of what happens around here when respect breaks down." He nodded to the men behind him, who stepped forward.

A voice came from behind Carbo. "It's illegal to bear arms in the city of Rome, friends."

Manius paused and looked over Carbo's shoulder at the speaker. Carbo didn't turn, keeping his eyes fixed on Manius, but recognised the voice of Vespillo. He saw Manius assessing the source of the interruption, then smiled humourlessly.

"I've heard that, friend," he replied, emphasising the last word ironically. "It seems to be a custom honoured more in the breach than the observance, wouldn't you say?"

"Even so," said Vespillo. "It is the law and tradition that arms are not carried within the sacred boundary of Rome. Please put your weapons away, and leave in an orderly fashion."

"By Pluto's balls, who are you, to command me to do anything?"

"Lucius Vedius Vespillo. Tribune of the *Vigiles*."

Now Manius laughed out loud. "The little bucket fellows? Sons, either of you on fire?"

Cilo smiled and Balbus let out a mocking laugh.

The scrape of chairs from behind Carbo told him that Vespillo and his companions had stood, and he now risked a look behind him. Vespillo had drawn a *gladius* style sword, and the others had produced solid-looking clubs. The expressions on their faces suggested they didn't appreciate being addressed that way.

Manius' eyes narrowed, and Carbo saw him recalculating the odds. He stepped up close to Carbo, so their faces were inches away from each other. Carbo could smell fish sauce and onions on his breath.

"You don't seem to understand. All this around here, it's mine. The houses, the businesses, the citizens, the slaves. They all owe me honour, duty and taxes. I am their *paterfamilias*, and like the father of the household, I have the right of life and death over everyone here."

"Not me," said Carbo. Balbus and Cilo had stepped up close behind Manius, and now Vespillo moved to just behind Carbo's shoulder. "Leave my tavern. You are not welcome here. Don't come back, or we will have a problem."

Manius' eyes flicked from Carbo's to Vespillo's. "We already have a problem. And we will be back. Just remember, when the time comes for you to regret your attitude, that I gave you a chance."

Behind them, Marsia moved to the door and held it open for them, her features set firm.

Manius spat on the floor, the spittle hitting Carbo's shoes. He spun abruptly and walked out. Cilo and Balbus followed. As Cilo passed Marsia he squeezed her buttock painfully, and winked at her. "I'll be back for you, beautiful."

Marsia slammed the door behind them, and composed herself. Carbo gave her a moment, then said, "Tidy up, Marsia."

She nodded, then directed Philon to right the upended furniture, while she produced a mop and a bucket to clear up the spillages.

"First though, Marsia, a drink here for my new friend, Vespillo. Anything you like, on the house."

"Falernian?" said Vespillo with a wry smile.

Carbo laughed. "Well, I haven't had time to assess my stock yet, but if Publius was telling me the truth, Falernian is a little out of our league. This isn't the Palatine you know."

Vespillo laughed. "I had noticed. Whatever you have will be fine."

Marsia went to fetch a cup of wine, and Carbo directed Vespillo to a seat.

"Thank you. That was…unexpected."

Vespillo looked embarrassed. "Just doing my job."

"And what job would that be?"

"As I said, I'm tribune of the IInd station of the *vigiles,* on the Esquiline. "

"And who are the *vigiles* exactly?"

"Who are the *vigiles?* Where have you been for the last twenty one years?"

"Germany. As I said. For the last twenty five years as it happens."

Marsia returned with a cup of wine for Carbo and Vespillo, then returned to restoring order in the tavern. Vespillo took a deep draught of the wine, and swallowed.

"Not bad," he said. "So you served your full tour of duty then."

"As did you in the XXth."

Vespillo nodded. "I've been retired a lot longer than you, though."

Carbo noted Vespillo's head, full of hair but shot through with grey, and an almost entirely white, short-trimmed beard. "I can tell."

Vespillo chuckled. "Cheeky bastard. Well, the *vigiles,* the watchmen, were set up by the divine Augustus in the year of the consuls Lepidus and Arruntius to fight fire, after a particularly bad blaze took out a large chunk of the city. There are seven cohorts each commanded by a tribune. Overall command is with an equestrian, currently Quintus Naevius Cordus Sutorius Macro."

"What's he like? Usual clueless political appointee that we get in the army?"

"He's a good man, on the whole. Takes the job seriously."

"And that job involves putting out fires. That's why Manius called you a little bucket fellow."

Vespillo grimaced. "The name isn't the most flattering. It's been following the *vigiles* since they were formed, and it rankles. But we have all been called a lot worse. Besides, fire fighting is only part of our job, admittedly a big part. Tall, poorly built wood-timbered buildings, indoor cooking and open braziers to keep warm, warehouses with wood, lumber and grain, narrow streets allowing blazes to spread easily - this all means several fires each night, of a greater or lesser extent, just in our district."

"So what else do you do?"

"Well if you put a bunch of men out on the street at night, organise them into cohorts and centuries, and give them axes, saws and ropes, it's inevitable they will be given other tasks. So, quickly the *vigiles'* role evolved into a night watch, keeping the peace when those lazy bastards in the urban cohorts are in bed. We catch thieves and muggers, break up fights, apprehend runaway slaves and make sure that the citizens are taking the appropriate precautions to prevent fire - keeping a bucket of water and vinegar soaked blankets on the top floor of the *insulae* for example. Sometimes repeat offenders need to be taken into the street and shown that their negligence can have consequences."

"I presume your men enjoy administering the odd beating then."

Vespillo sighed. "They can be rather enthusiastic sometimes. They are all freedmen, so were never going to get a chance to join the army, not unless there was another national disaster on the scale of Cannae. Discipline can sometimes be an issue. But they are a good bunch. And they are my men, so I won't have a word said against them."

Carbo nodded, understanding the kind of loyalty a man had for his comrade in arms, whether they deserved it or not. "So how does a veteran like you come to be in charge of a group of freedmen? Surely you could have found more lucrative work as a bodyguard, or even just retire on your pension to some peaceful farm in the countryside?"

Vespillo looked into his cup and was quiet for a moment. "That's a story for some other time," he said. Then he looked up. "You should visit the station, meet the men. They would love to meet a hero from the German campaigns."

"I'm no hero," said Carbo, flatly, then caught Vespillo's frown. "Still, I would like that. Thank you."

"We are based at the IInd station of the *cohortes vigilum,* just outside the Esquiline gate."

"So how come you turned out to be here at the right time and place to be my saviour today, Vespillo?"

Vespillo laughed. "I have my ear to the ground. When I am told that a newcomer has barred the local gang boss's son from his tavern, it doesn't take a genius to work out that retribution is likely to come swift and hard. Besides, I wanted to meet the man who had the balls to stand up to Cilo and Manius."

"Well, I thank you again for your help."

"One veteran to another, it's how it should be. I shall make sure my men visit regularly, to keep trouble from your door."

"Would the promise of drinks on the house make it less of a chore?"

"I'm sure," said Vespillo, smiling. "Just don't let them get completely hammered when they are on duty. They may still be needed to put out a fire."

Carbo shook Vespillo's hand, and watched his unexpected new ally depart. Then he turned to help Marsia clear up the mess.

Tegius reclined in the *triclinium* on the couch on Elissa's left. The couch to the right was empty. Shafat hovered, making sure their plates and cups were full. Elissa waved him away, and he bowed and withdrew.

Elissa regarded Tegius with a cool stare. She had had time to recover her composure.

"It has been a very long time, Tegius. How did you come to Rome?"

"After it all happened, the master rewarded me for my … loyalty… at such a trying time. I think maybe he didn't want to be reminded of what had happened every day by seeing me around. To him, the cost of a household of slaves was a relatively small sum, not completely trivial, but nothing to lose sleep over. So he decided to start from scratch. He emancipated me, and bought a new steward, and a whole new household of slaves."

"Yes, your loyalty was paid back handsomely," said Elissa flatly.

"Oh, it wasn't all roses. I could write and add, and manage a household. But there was a certain level of disgust at both the crime, and the punishment. Of course, none of it was my fault, but I was tainted by it. Slaves and freedmen shunned me, and the higher levels of society held me in contempt. I was actually reduced to begging for a while. I thought I wouldn't survive that first winter.

"I'm a resourceful fellow, though. I found a young nobleman who was in trouble with his gambling debts. I quietly helped re-organise his finances, and he paid me well. Well enough to leave Carthage, and make a new start."

"So you came to Rome."

"Not at first, no. I spent some time in Egypt, and found work in various places. About a year ago, though, I had an unfortunate incident with the wife of a rather rich and violent equestrian, and the time had come to move on. I took ship to Rome, fairly hastily, just as you did, in fact."

Elissa didn't comment, and he carried on.

"I have enough to get by, but little extra. Then, as I was drinking in a particularly grim little tavern, I overheard a conversation about a new cult in Rome. I say new, but of course we both know that it is very old indeed. It involved the worship of the old Carthaginian gods, Ba'al Hammon and Tanit, and the High Priestess was called Elissa.

"Surely that couldn't be a coincidence, I thought. There couldn't be another Elissa who was a hereditary Priestess in the service of the Lord and Lady. So I came to your meeting to find out for myself. You have changed, grown into a very beautiful woman, might I say. But I recognised the young

Elissa, who fled Carthage in the nighttime all those years ago. Leaving behind her friends and family to die."

Elissa tried to retain her composure, but she felt the little tremble coming back. She had become happy, confident, powerful. Now this odious man from her past was stripping it all away, reminding her of the most horrific time of her life.

"What happened that night, Elissa? Your father never said. All we knew was that the Master's guest, Gnaeus, was killed by your father. That he was found with the body and the bloody knife. He made no attempt to disguise his guilt, but offered no explanation."

Elissa's hand went to her neck. Around it hung a small charm, in the stylised shape of a figure, a round circle on a cross. Her father had given it to her that night. It had belonged to her mother, was the symbol of her priestesshood. She wondered why he had chosen that night to pass it on. Maybe he had some sort of premonition.

Tegius cocked his head on one side. "It was Gnaeus wasn't it? He asked for the Master's indulgence to make use of you. You, a young virgin, barely started your first flow, I'm guessing. He was a particularly repulsive individual too wasn't he? Obese and warty. I wonder what he looked like naked? Was he very rough with you, when he took you? Was it very painful?"

"Stop," said Elissa, her voice a whisper.

"I bet you cried out, I bet your father heard. Do you realise if you had remained silent, nearly a hundred men, women and children wouldn't have been crucified? I helped the soldiers, you know. Identified all the slaves. Helped group them by family, as they nailed them out. The little ones died quickest. Some of the women wouldn't stop screaming. Most of them just hung there, waiting for the crows to come and start pecking at them, hoping they would die before the agony became too much to bear."

"Please, stop," said Elissa.

"Of course, of course, my apologies. It must be painful to be reminded. Maybe my presence itself is a sad reminder of your past. Of the guilt you bear for all those deaths. Maybe I should leave Rome, for your sake. That would be expensive, though."

"Do others know what you know?"

Tegius smiled. "I have only just confirmed for myself it was you. There is no need for anyone else to be told. Not your followers, about your past shame. Or the authorities, that you are a fugitive slave. I just need some money, and I will be gone forever, and you can continue your privileged existence here, and forget all about that terrible time."

Elissa bowed her head, and Tegius smiled triumphantly. She looked up to where Shafat was waiting, out of earshot, and gestured to him. He nodded, and hurried out.

Tegius took a deep draught of his wine, then picked up some chopped morsels of liver, slid them into his mouth and swallowed with an appreciative noise.

"You dine well, High Priestess. I am glad you have seen sense. It is best for both of us."

Behind him, Glaukos appeared, his steps quiet despite his stature.

"Mother?" asked Glaukos.

"It is as I thought, Glaukos." Her voice had steadied again, and there was iron in it now. "Tegius here has asked for my assistance in return for a favour. Please compensate him as we discussed."

Glaukos gripped Tegius' head on either side, and before the surprised man could cry out, Glaukos snapped his neck.

Chapter IV

Carbo eased himself into bed with a groan. As well as the main bar area, the tavern had a small side room, a back room which served as a kitchen and sitting area, and on the first floor two rooms, one of which served as a bedroom for the Master and slaves, and one a general purpose dining, sitting, eating, sleeping and working area. Above that, accessed from a communal stair well which led to a back door to the property, were two more storeys, each storey housing two families. Marsia had told him what the rental arrangements were, and Carbo had left it to her to continue to collect, as she had for Publius Sergius.

The bed he now arranged himself in was wooden, with a feather mattress, a luxury that showed that Publius hadn't always been on the breadline. With the aches of injuries both ancient and freshly sustained, Carbo appreciated the soft feel as it gave around him, and he pulled the blanket over him. Philon was already asleep on a straw mattress in a corner, and Marsia remained downstairs, tidying from a good evening's business, and locking and barring the doors. He closed his eyes, suddenly realising how exhausted he was, and sleep came quickly.

His dreams took him to the aftermath of a battle, as they so often did. He was naked and bloody, hands tied behind his back, secured to a stake. Long-haired warriors drank and celebrated around him and the other, pitifully few prisoners.

Intermittently, they would strike him around the head or torso with the butts of their spears, opening up wounds or making new ones, to the cheers of their comrades. Women gathered round and laughed at his manhood, one of them even picking it up and threatening to cut it off with a knife, causing it to shrink even more in Carbo's terror, much to the hilarity of the onlookers.

Carbo woke and sat up straight, gasping for breath. Marsia was instantly at his side.

"Master, are you well?" she asked.

He struggled for control, then gave her a weak smile, and nodded.

"Of course, just a dream."

Marsia put a hand on his shoulder. "Would you like me to take care of your needs? It will help you relax, and make sleep come easier to you."

Carbo frowned. "No, slave, I do not want that from you."

Marsia looked confused. "But the old master, always expected me to…"

"I'm not your old master. Go back to your bed."

Carbo turned his back on Marsia, and feigned sleep, while visions of emasculation taunted his mind.

He woke in the morning to find Marsia and Philon already up and about, doing their chores to prepare the tavern for opening. He stretched, pulled on his tunic and wandered down into the bar. Marsia was cleaning the jars that sat in holes in the counter, containing nuts, the remains of last night's stew and a particularly ripe *garum*.

Intermittently, she harangued Philon, who was unenthusiastically mopping the floor. Carbo grabbed a handful of nuts and a small chunk of bread, ate them quickly then announced he was going out.

"May we know what time to expect you back, Master?" asked Marsia.

Carbo shook his head dismissively, and strolled out into the street. The early morning sun filtering down between the tall buildings made him blink. Rome was waking up, and he watched for a moment. The last of the ox and donkey carts were making their way out of the city or back to their warehouses, to much abuse from pedestrians who yelled that they should have been gone before sun up. Men hurried in various directions to see their patrons, and some of the keener businessmen were opening the shutters on their shops, starting the job of selling anything edible, native and exotic to Rome, as well as jewellery, ornaments, pots and pans, children's toys, perfumes. Sweet and pungent smells filled the air - perfumes and spicy foods, mingling with the stench and rot of the foul streets. Anything a Roman could imagine, and many things he could not, were for sale in the shops that lined the streets and alleyways, and Carbo enjoyed a slow walk through the city.

Finding himself suddenly needing to relieve himself, he located the nearest public lavatory, paid the attendant a small coin, and settled himself on the wooden seat with a hole in, situated above running water. To his left, a man was sitting with his tunic around his waist, reading one of Cicero's speeches. He appeared to have settled in for the morning. The man to his right gave a groan as he strained, then looked satisfied at the loud volume of the splash that followed. He looked at Carbo.

"That was a good one," he said.

"It sounded impressive," replied Carbo.

"Bit cold this morning," said the man.

Carbo grunted, then agreed.

"Enjoying the games?" asked the man.

"I've been away for a while. Tell me about them?"

"You must have been gone a long time. The legions? Everyone is talking about the *Ludi Romani*."

"In honour of Jupiter Optimus Maximus, right?"

"That's right," agreed the man. "Best party of the year, except for maybe *Saturnalia*. The Urban Praetor is planning to make the closing day a real blow out this year. Chariot racing, tigers, executions, gladiators. He is promising it will be the best finale for years."

Carbo smiled, while inwardly sighing. He had seen enough bloodshed to last a lifetime, and the execution of the defenceless held no appeal to him. He had to confess to a professional interest in a good gladiatorial combat however, and the chariot races were often worth a gamble.

"When is it?"

"The thirteenth day before the Kalends of October. The first festivities have already started, if you like religious processions and poetry readings, but I know what I am looking forward to."

Carbo beckoned the attendant for the communal sponge. The attendant picked it up by the stick it was attached to, rinsed the worse of the faeces of the previous user off in a bucket, and passed it to Carbo. Carbo gave his backside a scrub, handed it back to the attendant, and rearranged his tunic.

"Which baths would you recommend, friend?" asked Carbo. "I feel the need for a rub down and a soak."

"You still can't beat the Baths of Agrippa. The first great Baths in Rome, the biggest, and still the best in my opinion. They do get crowded though, being so near to the Campus Martius."

"Thank you. Good day to you."

"Good day to you, too," said the man, then grimaced as he strained again.

Feeling a little more comfortable now, Carbo continued through the city to reach the Baths of Agrippa, situated just behind the Pantheon, near the Campus Martius as his recent companion had said. The imposing Aqua Virgo, a huge aqueduct, supplied the large volumes of water the baths required, and had been built, Carbo recalled, specifically for this purpose. The huge building was covered in white marble, which shone brightly in the morning sun. He approached the front doorway, but the bath attendant informed him that it would be another hour before opening time, so he wandered for a while among the street sellers. He bought some bread and mackerel *garum*. When he had finished, he used his bread to mop out the bowl. He may be comparatively rich by many Roman standards, he thought, but that didn't mean he was going to waste a thing.

A group of young boys and girls sat on the floor nearby, working out maths problems their teacher gave them on their abacuses. Frequently sharp raps across the back of the hand punished mistakes. One particularly slow boy was bent over the teacher's stool and given six hard stripes across the backside, accompanied by much screaming and wailing.

Carbo spied the doors to the baths opening and wandered over. He tipped the bath attendant a copper coin, and walked through into the changing room. A trickle of people of both sexes and all ages accompanied him in, wanting to make use of the facilities before the main flood of users came along in the afternoon. Carbo undressed and tipped a slave to watch his clothes and purse, moved through into the main central area, and tipped another slave for a massage and rub down with oil. Rough fingers kneaded his back and legs, and he winced where they touched the bruises from the night before. The masseur found the old injury to his thigh, with its puckered scar, and worked around it with a tenderness that surprised Carbo, and actually eased the perpetual ache there a little. As he worked, the masseur tried to engage Carbo in conversation.

"From the legions, sir?"

"Can everyone tell?" growled Carbo.

"No offence sir, but you have scars from wounds that you see caused by spears and swords, not clubs and knifes. These injuries weren't inflicted by street brawls."

"You are observant."

"I was slave to a *medicus* in the legions for many years, sir. I have seen all types of wounds, and have a good eye for what caused them and how much disability they cause. This one on your thigh for example, is a spear thrust, downwards that sliced the meat open, and was sewn shut in a hurry. The skin has healed badly, although long enough ago that the healing is complete. It looks like it probably took some infection too. This wound will still cause you considerable pain, I think."

Carbo grunted. "It's not so bad. Bearable, most of the time."

"I do have some ointment that you could try, sir."

Carbo had been given all sorts of quack treatments by the *medici* and doctors in the army, and was sceptical about all of it. But this slave seemed genuine, and there was no harm in trying. He nodded his assent, and the masseur took some thick white ointment from a pot and smeared it over the scar tissue. For a moment, Carbo felt nothing, then a deep warmth suffused his muscles. The pain that was always with him to a greater or lesser extent receded, not disappearing completely but easing. Carbo sighed.

"How much for the pot?"

"Three *denarii,* sir," said the masseur. Carbo winced, that was three day's pay for a legionary, but he summoned the slave guarding his clothes and purse, and paid the masseur what he asked for. The masseur then produced the strigil to scrape the oil from his body.

When he was finished, Carbo rose from the massage table, feeling relaxed. The baths were considerably busier already, and certainly much noisier. In the gymnasium slightly offset from the main room were a group of naked bodybuilders, lifting lead weights with loud grunts. Three young women dressed only in loin cloths and breast bands sat and pretended not to watch them, but occasionally whispered remarks to each other and giggled. At the other end of the room, a handful of men were playing a ball game, which involved a lot of running and shouting. Masseurs, barbers and hairpluckers all shouted to advertise their services, and more noise still came from their customers, in the form of moans and shrieks of pain. Beauticians, hairdressers, sellers of bread, cheese, sausages and wine all competed with each other to be heard.

Carbo moved through to the warm bath, the *tepidarium*, and groaned in pleasure as he eased himself into the water. There was a thick sheen of oil on the surface, but generally the water seemed clean, especially compared to many provincial baths he had seen where it wasn't uncommon to find accompanying you in your bathing a dead rat or a floating turd. In the warm bath with him were a couple of middle aged women, heavy breasts bobbing in the water, and two old men, deep in discussion. He heard snatches of what they were saying above the noise, but found it too difficult to work out the full gist of the conversation. When one of them uttered the name Sejanus and laughed uproariously though, the other looked around anxiously, falling momentarily quiet, then angrily chastising his companion. Carbo eased a little closer and found he could hear slightly better. The angry man was still chiding his friend.

"How can you be so flippant about the commander of the Praetorian Guard, the man who rules Rome while Tiberius is in self-imposed exile? You know what the man is like, and the city is full of informers, ready to denounce anyone who says anything the remotest bit derogatory about him."

The flippant one shrugged. "I'm an old man, I've lived a long life. If my time comes because our ruler can't take a joke, then so be it."

"And your son, will he have to suffer too for your sense of humour?" This made the joker's smile disappear. "Don't think your equestrian status will protect you or your family. On the contrary, your riches make you an even more tempting target for proscription. It is only the divine Augusta that keeps his power in check, and who knows how long will she be around for, the gods bless her?"

"I'm sorry, you are right, friend."

The angry man seemed to notice how close Carbo was for the first time. "See," he said, gesturing at Carbo as he addressed his friend. "This man here has heard everything. For all you know he is one of Sejanus' spies." He looked at Carbo. "Are you?"

"You have nothing to fear from me. I am newly returned to Rome and know nothing of its current intrigues. Besides, I didn't even hear the joke. Would you care to repeat it?"

Before the angry man could stop him, the joker repeated his joke for Carbo's benefit. "Apparently there was a man came up to Rome from Capua, and he looked for all the world just like Sejanus. So Sejanus summoned him, and said, 'did your mother ever come to Rome?' And the man replied in all seriousness, 'No, sir, never, but my father was here often.'"

The man burst into laughter again, and Carbo couldn't help but chuckle himself. His friend threw his hands in the air, and then joined in the laughter. Carbo shook their hands and moved on to the hot air room, and from there to the *caldarium*. This was hotter than he was used to, and he could only stand it for a short while, before moving rapidly on to the *frigidarium*. The freezing water shocked him as he jumped in, and he briskly extricated himself, taking a woollen towel off an attendant and rubbing himself dry. He returned to retrieve his clothes and walked out into the noon sun.

He took an ambling walk home. The clean, large buildings and well-repaired streets gave way, as he approached the Subura, to cracked cobbles with no side walks, meaning that he was forced to walk in the sewage and litter. Narrow alleys flanked by tall buildings frequently occluded the sunlight, making the place feel gloomy even at midday. Some of the shops, barely more than cubicles on the front of houses, which had still been shuttered up when he had left in the morning, were now open, and a good number of these contained prostitutes advertising their services.

As Carbo turned the corner, into the street on which he now lived, he nearly tripped over a woman sprawled on the floor. She was a *Doris*, one of the class of prostitutes that were so stunningly beautiful that they eschewed the florally patterned toga that most prostitutes wore, and simply sat nude before their stall, advertising their services cheaply and effectively, if unsubtly. This particular *Doris* had long dark hair, a slim, toned, slightly boyish body accentuated by her small breasts, and full lips. Her eyeliner was smudged with tears, dark tracks running down both cheeks, and her naked body showed off a multitude of bruises, some older and turning yellow, some fresh and dark, and some bright red where they had only just been inflicted. Over her stood a fat, sweating man, who Carbo assumed was her *leno*, her pimp. The *leno* held a thick club, and as Carbo watched, he brought it hard across her arm, making her scream.

"Useless whore," he cried. "May Venus curse you. How dare you turn down a client." He flicked the cane down again, eliciting a cry.

"Please, Master," sobbed the girl. "He hurt me last time. And he threatened me, said that next time he would leave me so no man would want me again. Then I wouldn't be able to be of service to you."

"It is not for you to decide who you will and won't serve." The cane descended again. "You answer to me and me only. Next time Cilo comes calling, you will let him do whatever he wants, even if he desires to cut your tits off!"

"Cilo, you say?" asked Carbo, keeping a neutral tone to his voice. The *leno* looked at Carbo suspiciously.

"Yes, Cilo. This stupid she-wolf turned him down late last night. He was in a foul temper after some run in in the tavern, and when she put up a fight he stormed off. But now him and his father will have it in for me. I will have to let them have free use of my girls for a month, just to avoid them setting their thugs loose on me."

"I think you have less to fear than you think, friend."

"Oh, and who are you to tell me who and who not to fear?"

"The one who had the run in with Cilo."

The *leno* paused, and let his arm drop to his side. He appraised Carbo with a searching stare.

"So, you are the one with the death wish. You are to be praised for your bravery, and avoided, in case association with you brings down your fate on others."

"As you wish. But my establishment is free of intimidation now. You are welcome to drink there, and tell your friends the same. Cilo will not cause trouble there as long as I draw breath."

"However long that is," said the *leno*. "Now if you will excuse me, I am in the middle of something here." He raised the club again and brought it into the girl's side. Ribs cracked, and Carbo winced.

"Isn't this poor business?" he said to the *leno*. "She won't be able to command as high a price if you damage her."

"This doesn't concern you. The message this sends to her and to my other girls will save me a lot of trouble in the long run. If they think they can disobey me with impunity, where would I be? No, this has to be done. Once I've beaten her, I'm going to have her flogged with a barbed whip. If she survives, she will be too disfigured to be a *Doris* anymore, but she can serve in a dark back room somewhere."

Carbo looked down at the girl at his feet, shaking violently, curled in the foetal position. She looked up at him, eyes begging. Carbo shook his head. This really wasn't his problem. Her Master had every legal right to treat her this way if he wanted. He turned his back on her and walked to the tavern, hearing the girl cry again as the club descended once more. At the tavern door, Marsia stood, arms folded. She blocked his entrance and looked at him with an icy stare. Carbo hesitated, then roughly pushed her out of his way and walked inside.

Fabilla had been inconsolable since she had lost Arethusa. Rufa had tried everything, hugs, games, even spending one of her very few coins, which she was over-optimistically saving to buy her emancipation, on a cheap beaded necklace for her daughter. Fabilla had merely smiled at her mother dutifully, then sat, sullenly, playing with the beads.

"She'll be in trouble if she doesn't snap out of it," said Natta to Rufa as they scrubbed a mosaic floor together.

"She's upset," snapped Rufa.

"I know that," said Natta. "Do you think they will care?" She nodded towards the *peristylium*, where Elissa, Glaukos and Shafat sat, deep in conversation.

"You're right, I'm sorry," said Rufa. "I just don't know what to do."

"You're sure you've looked everywhere for that silly thing?"

Rufa bit back another angry retort. Natta was only trying to be helpful. Of course, she didn't know that Rufa had witnessed the doll being ritually sacrificed, and Rufa didn't know how she could tell her. Natta would think she was mad. Or maybe Natta was part of the cult, and would go straight to Elissa.

Rufa shook her head. She was getting paranoid. But since that evening, she had started to ask herself questions. Remembering strange comings and goings, secret meetings, and a predatory expression that came over Glaukos' face whenever he looked at her or Fabilla. She knew that her mistress was a priestess in some sort of cult, but hadn't really interested herself in it. The household slaves had not been invited to join, apart from Shafat. She wasn't sure why, maybe Elissa didn't trust people that physically close to her. She had never wasted thought on it before - she was a Roman, and worshipped the pantheon dutifully, if unenthusiastically.

Now she felt, no, she knew, that there was more to the cult than some eccentric belief in long dead deities. Something deeper was happening, and it involved her and her daughter, and it scared her to her marrow.

"Did you hear about that fight in the Subura?" asked Natta conversationally, changing the subject.

Rufa shook her head, only half-listening. She felt so trapped. Obviously, she was a slave, being restricted was her lot in life. But she had never felt in danger before. As long as she did her duties faithfully, she would be fed and clothed and sheltered in return. That was the deal that kept the massive slave population in Rome pacified. Now, though, with increasing intensity, every instinct in her body was telling her to run. Unfortunately the instincts didn't tell her how, or to who.

"It was at the tavern with the sign of the cockerel. The one owned by Publius Sergius."

Rufa was aware of the place, though she could never afford a drink there, even on the rare occasion she was allowed out.

"A local thug was harassing poor Publius, apparently, when this guy steps in. Big lad, a veteran. Faces the thug down, then buys the tavern! I'm not sure how long he will last, but still, it's nice to see someone standing up to those bullies. What was his name now?"

Could she smuggle Fabilla away, arrange for her to be sold to someone else? Maybe stay behind to take the punishment herself? It would mean death for her, for sure. And who would buy an escaped slave child?

"Carbo, that was it. I think we might be hearing more of him."

Fabilla looked up at Natta sharply.

"Carbo?"

Inside the tavern, the lunchtime atmosphere was jovial and calm. Philon was receiving lots of attention, pinches, surreptitious feels and blatant gropes from men who were inclined to pretty boys. One who was better off than his colleagues paid for a quarter of an hour with the slave in the cubicle behind the curtain, and Carbo tended the bar while he was occupied. At this time of day, no one was too drunk, and no one seemed to be worried after the previous fight. If anything, they seemed more relaxed, and Carbo hoped that word had got around that the tavern was under the protection of both Carbo and the *vigiles*, and so was a safe place to drink and eat.

As he thought of the *vigiles*, he realised that one of the group of three men gaming at a table was with Vespillo the previous night, and he saluted him, and took over a free glass of wine. The man thanked him, and introduced his friends as fellow watchmen, so Carbo fetched them all drinks as well. He wondered briefly how badly a free drinks for *vigiles* policy would affect his profits, but business had seemed good so far, and he was sure the policy would be worth it. He pulled up a stool and joined them at the game.

A glimpse of the first star shining in a dark blue sky showed Rufa that dusk was falling. Her day had been spent performing her usual tasks, cleaning, cooking, a little sewing, while her stomach churned with anxiety. She didn't want to let Fabilla out of her sight, but Fabilla had her own chores to do, and besides, she didn't want to do anything to arouse suspicions by deviating from her normal routines. So she had stitched and scrubbed and stirred, keeping her face blank, obeying commands and joining conversations as if today was simply another day in servitude.

Rufa went back to her bedroom, and found Fabilla waiting for her. Her daughter had been inconsolable last night, when Rufa had told her that she thought Arethusa was lost. As she had held her daughter, she went over and over in her mind what she had heard. There was no room for misinterpretation. They had chosen her daughter for a sacrifice in some strange ritual. Rufa trembled in terror at the thought, but gradually a mad plan began to appear in her mind. It was only half formed, and it was ridiculously risky, but what else could she do? She would give her life for her daughter, do anything to keep her safe.

So now, with night coming, and her duties for the day completed, as the Mistress was not entertaining today, she picked up the purse that held the few small coins she had managed to save, took Fabilla's hand, and opened the door of the bedroom.

"Where are you off to?" asked Natta, from the bed where she was cuddling her children.

"Errand for the mistress," said Rufa, and walked out to forestall further questioning. She led Fabilla briskly to the *atrium* and the little girl skipped to keep up.

"Mummy, where are we going? Isn't it bedtime?"

"Hush, daughter. I need you now to be very grown up. We are going outside for a little walk, and I need you to be extremely quiet. Demosthenes will ask where we are going. I will answer, and you must say nothing. Do you understand?"

"Yes mummy, but why? Are we having an adventure? Will the Mistress be cross with us?"

"You just need to trust me, daughter. You do trust me, don't you?"

"Yes mummy," said Fabilla.

They reached the *atrium*, the entrance hall where visitors were received, decorated with bright frescos and marble and bronze statues. Demosthenes stood by the entrance with arms folded. As he saw Rufa and Fabilla approaching, he stepped in front of the door, and looked at them silently.

"Demosthenes," said Rufa. "We need to go out."

He regarded them steadily.

"It's late," he said.

"Yes, I know," sighed Rufa. "The cook is running low on *garum*, and he needs it for the meal he is preparing for the mistress tonight."

"Market will be closed," said Demosthenes.

"I know, I know, it's all very inconvenient. Fortunately, cook knows the name of a man whose shop is open late. It is a bit of a walk, so I might be gone a while, but cook says he makes the best mackerel *garum*, and nothing else will do."

"Why the girl?"

"She had a nightmare when she was alone last night, so I wanted her to come with me. Besides it will be good for her to see some of the city."

"Should check with Shafat."

"Oh Demosthenes, don't be such a stickler. Shafat said it was fine."

Demosthenes looked doubtful. Panic starting to rise within Rufa, she stepped forward and pressed her body up against the large doorkeeper. One hand moved to his groin, and she felt him stiffen a little under her touch. She whispered into his ear.

"Demosthenes, I must hurry to carry out Shafat's commands. So if you let me go right now, I will show my appreciation for you when I come back." She gave his manhood a little squeeze, and was rewarded with a slight twitch from under his tunic. He grinned, then stepped aside. Rufa gave him a bright smile, and stepped outside with Fabilla in tow.

The population of the darkening streets was changing from the day shift to the night shift. Shoppers, artisans, workers and those of no particular occupation gave way to groups of drinkers, partygoers, thieves and cutpurses. For a moment she was paralysed. If she walked away from the house now, she was an escaped slave, with all the consequences that entailed. If she stayed, she was going to lose her daughter in unimaginable circumstances. She gripped Fabilla's hand tight, and marched off in what she hoped was the right direction.

The journey took her over an hour, with various dead ends and wrong turnings. The area looked very different at night, with the usual landmarks hard to make out. Once she summoned up the courage to ask directions from a kindly looking couple, and fortunately they were helpful and not too inquisitive. Another time, she pulled back into the shadows when a detachment of *vigiles* ran past, carrying their buckets and pumps. A glow from a building in a neighbouring street and the smell of smoke suggested they had urgent business, but Rufa knew that one of their jobs was to catch escaped slaves, and she didn't want to chance a meeting.

Eventually she came to the street she was looking for, and then the tavern with the sign of the cockerel on the wall. She paused now, fear overtaking her again. Her legs felt weak, and her bladder relaxed, and she had to clench to avoid an accident. Judging by the light from oil lamps leaking out from the crack beneath the door, and the sounds of singing and laughter from within, the tavern was still open. She considered waiting till it was quieter, but that meant her staying out on the streets for longer, which was risky. She still hesitated. What if this was the wrong tavern? Maybe the wrong Carbo? Or maybe the right Carbo, but a Carbo who didn't remember her, or whose love and loyalty had eroded over the years.

She pulled her tunic up to hide her face as best she could, eased the door open and was assaulted by the noise, the heat of packed bodies, the smell of spicy food and sweet wine. She dragged a fascinated Fabilla through the tavern, ignoring the curious eyes on her, and made her way to the bar. Behind was a tall, dark-haired, thick-set woman.

"What can I get you?" asked the barmaid, her accent reminding Rufa of the locals she grew up around.

"I'm here to see Carbo," said Rufa in a small voice.

"Say that again," said the barmaid. "It's noisy tonight."

"I'm here to see Carbo," she said, louder this time.

The barmaid looked at her suspiciously. "And who should I say is asking for him?"

"A very old friend," said Rufa. The barmaid nodded, and gestured to another slave.

"Go and get the Master, Philon. Tell him there is a girl here for him, who says she is an old friend."

Philon stomped off, reluctant as ever to be ordered around. Marsia regarded Rufa steadily, and Rufa kept her eyes cast downwards. Fabilla on the other hand looked all around her, returning unblinking the gazes of the surprised customers. Shortly, a door behind the bar opened, and a tall, muscular man with black hair stepped out. Rufa raised her head and looked him straight in the eye. A moment passed, and she watched the man struggle to place the familiar face.

"Gaius Valerius Carbo. It's Rufa."

His face showed open shock.

"Rufa? Is it really you?" He stepped forward and wrapped his arms around her.

Rufa put her head on his shoulder. "I need your help."

Before he could speak, Rufa pressed a finger to his lips.

"Can we go somewhere to talk in private?"

Carbo nodded. "Stay here and look after the customers," he said to Marsia and ushered Rufa and Fabilla out of the back door. He looked back, and Marsia held his eye for a moment, a questioning look on her face, before he shrugged, turned round and followed Rufa and Fabilla through into the kitchen.

Chapter V

Carbo ushered Fabilla to a chair, and passed her some nuts to eat. Rufa bent down to her.

"Fabilla, I need you to be very good. You must sit still, while I talk to this man. He is going to help us."

"Who is he mother? And why do we need help?"

"He is a very old friend. And you do not need to worry."

She stood and moved to Carbo, who took her hand and smiled at her.

"It's wonderful to see you, Rufa, after all these years. She is your daughter?"

Rufa nodded.

"Of course," said Carbo. "Who could mistake the hair? You know, you weren't many years older than her when I last saw you. So you are married now? Some honest Roman tradesman?"

"No," she said, her voice a whisper. "I'm a slave."

"A slave?" he gasped. "What happened, Rufa?"

Rufa shook her head, words not coming easily.

"Well, who is your master?"

"I don't have a master, I have a mistress. But I... I..." She bit back a sob. "I ran away from her."

Carbo took a step back. "You did what? When? Can you go back before you are discovered?"

"No, Carbo, I can't, I can't."

"An escaped slave, Rufa. Are you mad? You know what they can do to you?"

Tears started to roll down her face.

"Carbo, she means to kill my daughter."

Carbo stared, one shock after another making him dizzy. He looked over at Fabilla, who seemed torn between eating the nuts and using them to make pretty patterns.

"Why? It doesn't make sense."

Rufa looked pitiful, her face painted with misery, her tears washing paler lines through the dirt on her cheeks. She too looked over at her daughter, the sight of the child concentrating hard on her play only seeming to increase her anguish. The kitchen was a small room, cramped by a couple of stools, the pots and amphorae and a glowing cooking fire. Carbo could tell that Rufa was reluctant to speak in front of Fabilla. He poked his head through into the bar, and summoned Marsia.

Marsia came into the kitchen, not speaking, but curious gaze flicking between Carbo, Rufa and Fabilla.

"Marsia, please care for this child for me. Philon can look after the bar. I need to speak to her mother alone."

Marsia looked at Fabilla anxiously. "Master, I don't know how to care for a child."

Carbo frowned. "Just make sure she has some food and water, don't let her run off or set herself on fire, and if she needs a shit or a piss, make sure she does it out of the window."

"Yes, Master."

Carbo took Rufa's arm and led her upstairs to the small living room. He ushered her to a couch, and perched himself on a stool opposite her. She sat with head bowed, saying nothing.

"You do know what they do to escaped slaves, don't you?" he said again. She didn't reply.

"If you are lucky, they will brand your forehead with the word 'Fugitive', whip you, and place an iron collar around your neck with instructions to return you to your Mistress. If you are unlucky, they might break your bones, or hang you up by your wrists with weights tied to your feet, or send you to the salt mines, or crucify you..."

"Stop, please, stop," sobbed Rufa. "I know all this, I know. But my daughter, I can't let them hurt my Fabilla."

"But why would they want to?"

She shook her head. "You will think the gods have taken my senses."

Carbo passed her a cup of water and waited for her to sip. "Try me," he said.

With an effort, Rufa got her sobs under control.

"Fabilla and I were bought by our Mistress, Elissa, about six months ago. Our last master was moving to the country, and didn't want to take all his slaves with him. We were taken to the slave market, the one behind the Temple of Castor in the Roman Forum. Have you ever been to a slave auction, Carbo?"

Carbo nodded his head. "I've been in the legions for twenty-five years, Rufa. I've seen a lot of the world."

"The slave dealers made us bathe, put us in clean clothes, put make up on to hide blemishes and pock marks on our skin, and then we were placed on a platform. We had signs hung around our necks saying we were house slaves, and mother and daughter, and that we were hard workers and healthy. The buyers walked around us, poked us, and stripped us naked to examine us. One man who had already bought three young girls wanted to buy Fabilla and not me. I was so scared he was going to take her away from me, and I didn't know what he might have planned for her. But the auctioneer thought he could get more money for us as a pair, and he turned him down. Then Elissa, my Mistress came along. She spoke to us softly, offered a good price, and took us home.

"We have worked hard for her. Fabilla does her chores, and never causes any trouble. I do everything asked of me. We are rarely punished. Elissa seemed a kindly Mistress, and we were as happy and well-looked after as slaves can be. Some things seemed strange. Elissa had many visitors, but they didn't seem to be friends. She never talked to the slaves about it, but from the things we overheard and saw, she seems to be some sort of priestess.

"Then last night, she had dinner with two men and a woman. After, I was in the *peristylium*, and they started talking."

Rufa related the events of the night before. Carbo listened in silence, eyebrows raising at the description of the sacrifice of Arethusa, the little doll. She described her flight with Fabilla, her arrival at the tavern, and then her voice trailed off.

"How did you know where to find me? How did you even know I was in Rome?"

"The slaves were talking about this veteran called Carbo who had taken over a tavern in the Subura and had faced down thugs who tried to muscle in on his business. It sounded like a Carbo I knew."

Carbo smiled, despite the tension in his guts.

"I remembered your promise to my father," continued Rufa. "That if he was not around, you would always look after me."

"You were a child then, and free."

"You didn't say there were conditions on your promise."

Carbo shook his head. "If I helped you, I would be guilty of theft. Harbouring a fugitive slave is considered stealing their property."

Rufa said nothing.

"I would be punished."

Rufa remained silent. Carbo sighed. His gaze shifted to the wall, as he recalled the occasion he had made his vow.

"Your father must have had some sort of premonition. There had certainly been a poor augury, and your father always put a lot of store in what the priests had to say. Do you remember the day we marched out?"

Rufa nodded. "Eighteen years ago, when I was eight years old. Like it was yesterday. My father, the first spear, and his three most senior centurions. My mother had died so long ago, I barely remembered her, but you were all like family to me. You all looked so handsome, your shields so shiny, helmets polished. I was so proud of him, of you all."

"He gathered us round you, the three of us, and him. He made all three of us promise on our ancestor's shades that we would care for you if anything happened to him. What else could we do? We loved that man, and we loved you like a daughter. We made our vow, and marched off into the forest. I was the only one that came back."

For a moment, Carbo's eyes narrowed as images of battle, bloodshed and horror filled his mind. Rufa touched his knee, bringing him back to the present.

"You are right, Rufa. I made my vow. Time does not change that. You can stay here for tonight. The *vigiles* and the *fugitivarii* will be looking out for you. I will think about what we can do next. Maybe we could get you out of Rome, then sell you to a good master."

Rufa bit her lip at that, but inclined her head and said, "Thank you, Carbo."

Carbo put his head on what side. "So what happened? When I finally got back to camp, they said you had returned to Rome, that relatives had adopted you."

Rufa nodded. "My uncle, my father's brother, sent word from Rome, as soon as they heard of the disaster, of my father's death. They had children of their own, but my uncle felt it was the honourable thing to do. He treated me well enough, but my aunt hated me. Maybe she saw me as a threat to her own children, two daughters. They were younger than me, and with me being legally adopted, and no male heir, I stood to inherit the most, even if it would just go to my husband on my marriage.

"My aunt tried to turn my uncle against me. She made up offences she pretended I had committed, spread gossip about me, put wicked words in my mouth. He was a weak man, prone to drinking and gambling, but he did his best to resist, and stand up for me. My new sisters hated me, but I learnt to look after myself, and I never made trouble.

"Then one day, my uncle came home completely drunk. That in itself wasn't unusual, but this time he was shouting and breaking things, and then had a huge row with my aunt. I hid myself away for the rest of the day. That night my aunt came to me in my bedroom. She told me, in a very matter of fact way, that my uncle had lost an enormous amount of money in a dice game, more than he could afford. They were in danger of losing the house, so to pay the debt I was to be sold into slavery."

Carbo said nothing, but his face betrayed his anger. He knew at an abstract level that it was a common enough situation, a child sold into slavery to pay a debt. The alternative was the debtor himself being sold into slavery in many cases, and the loss of a child was thought to be the lesser evil, especially if there were other children already in the family. Usually the mothers protested, but the head of the family, the *paterfamilias*, had absolute right of life and death over every member of the household. So the adopted child in the family was the logical choice to be the one sold to pay the debts. But this was little Rufa, the only child of his mentor, Fabius, the girl he had sworn to protect. He had thought his oath discharged when she had returned to Rome into the care of a family who, while by no means rich, had enough income to support her.

Of course, gambling could bring down even the richest person. Carbo cursed himself now for not keeping track of her, writing to her, making sure she was safe and happy. He knew that deep down the reason was that she belonged to a time in his life that he was trying to forget, although the way it intruded into his dreams made a mockery of that. It was no excuse though, he should have looked out for her. He looked at her now, a woman with a child, old enough to be the matron of her own household if she had remained free and married well, but in reality a scared, grubby, fugitive slave, and guilt gripped him.

Carbo cleared his throat. "So, you were sold?"

"Yes, a private sale, to an equestrian, a lovely house on the Palatine. I was a serving girl, but of course, as soon as I was old enough to bleed, I was used for pleasure as well. At first it was very infrequent, but as I blossomed into a woman, I became my Master's favourite, and I often shared his bed. He treated me well enough, for the most part, but his wife became more and more jealous. When I became pregnant with Fabilla, his wife insisted I was sold. Being pregnant reduced my value a lot. I guess it's a risk for a buyer - if they are lucky they get a second slave to own a few months later, even if it's one who won't be much use for a while. If they are unlucky, their new slave dies in childbirth and they are left with nothing."

Carbo nodded. He remembered friends of his mother who had died during labour, and it was even more common amongst the whores and other camp followers that were the recreation of the legionaries. Rufa was probably lucky not to be very fertile - to have produced only one child by her age was uncommon amongst slaves and the poor.

"So I was bought by a tradesman, a fuller. I used to help him with his chores. I collected the urine from the public toilets in jars, and I helped him with the laundry. I have never felt free of that smell since. The fuller wasn't married, and had a temper. He used me for his pleasure, and he beat me, and seemed to get pleasure from that too. He never touched Fabilla though, thank the Good Goddess. Once though, when he was… using me roughly, I lashed out in pain, instinctively. My nails scratched his face, made him bleed. As a punishment, he branded me."

Rufa rolled up the sleeve of her dress, so he could see the branded scar indented into her upper arm, paler than even the pale skin that surrounded it. It read "Bad Slave."

"And then a few months ago, the fuller decided he had had enough of Rome. He had saved a little money, and made some more selling his business, and selling Fabilla and myself, so he could move to the countryside and buy a small farm, growing cabbages he said."

Carbo laughed. "Each to their own. I can see the appeal. You would certainly get more intelligent conversation from the cabbages than some of the people I have met in Rome."

Rufa gave a half smile.

"So that's how I ended up at the slave auction, and the slave of Elissa. And the rest you know."

Carbo looked puzzled. "I've no idea what your Mistress Elissa is up to. It's nothing to do with me though. I'm not in the Urban Cohorts, and I'm not in the *vigiles*, and I'm no longer in the legions. I look out for myself, and I look out for my slaves and other property and I will look out for you two for now. That's all. Now you can rest here tonight. You and Fabilla take my bed, I will take the floor with the slaves."

"What will you tell your slaves about me?"

Carbo raised an eyebrow. "Why would I tell them anything? They are just slaves."

Rufa's face fell, and she looked at the floor and said nothing. Carbo realised what he had said, and felt confusion. A slave was just property. To be cared for, for certain, like a valuable horse, or even a loved pet dog. But slaves weren't Romans, they weren't citizens, they didn't have rights. Yet here was Rufa, a slave, but in his mind still the free child he had left all that time ago.

"I'm...sorry," he said falteringly.

"Why should you be sorry? You are right. Slaves are just that, slaves. You wouldn't be helping me at all, if it wasn't for a promise you made to a free man about a free girl."

Carbo opened his mouth to reply, but closed it as he realised she was speaking the truth. He stood.

"I'll get Marsia to bring up Fabilla. You two get some rest. We will work out a plan tomorrow."

Carbo went downstairs to the kitchen, to find Fabilla engaging Marsia in a deep conversation about hairstyles. Obviously a follower of fashion, Fabilla was describing with a child's frankness how Marsia could improve her appearance with new makeup and a more up to date hairstyle. Marsia was taking the advice with open-mouthed horror, to which Fabilla seemed oblivious as she continued to eat nuts and expand on her style theories. Carbo watched for a short while, smiling at the little girl's innocence.

He cleared his throat. "Marsia, take Fabilla upstairs to her mother."

Marsia turned, her face showing relief.

"Yes Master. They are staying tonight?"

"They are. Fabilla and Rufa will take my bed. Make up a mattress for me on the floor with the slaves."

Marsia looked at him with a questioning expression. He hesitated, wondering if he should share some more information with her. Slave or not though, he still barely knew her, and he didn't know whether he could trust her with that sort of secret. So he simply said, "You are not to speak to anyone about Rufa and Fabilla. Do you understand?"

"Yes, Master," said Marsia, and led the still chattering Fabilla up the stairs.

Carbo sat alone in the kitchen. His gaze wandered over the kitchen utensils, the pots and pans and jugs and ladles and knives, while his mind spun. What was he to do? What could he do? He was newly back in Rome, with few contacts, few resources, no influence with rich or poor. He didn't know how to keep his ancient promise, or even whether he should feel obliged to. She was an escaped slave, and if there was one thing the might of the Roman authorities would not tolerate, it was rebellious slaves. Although there was almost certainly no one alive now who was even born when Spartacus' revolt, the third Servile War, ended, nearly a hundred years before, the fear of the mass of enslaved humanity that thronged Rome rising up and slaughtering their Masters was ingrained deep into the Roman psyche. Even the concept of slaves wearing a uniform to identify them was forbidden, to prevent the slaves realising how numerous they were.

This was of course to Rufa's benefit - she had been able to move through Rome that night like one of the poor free citizens, with no one the wiser. Some slaves were tattooed, some branded, although usually this was reserved for previous runaways or other miscreants, but Rufa had no visible slave markings.

So Rufa could pass for a free woman, especially with her ethnicity being Roman in origin. The problem would arise from being recognised personally as the property of Elissa, by one of her other slaves for example, or the *fugitivarii,* the slave hunters, which no doubt Elissa would unleash to track Rufa down. Rufa's bright red hair was hardly inconspicuous, although maybe some sort of headwear would help with that. Of course Rome was huge, the biggest city in the world with a million inhabitants, or so it was said, which also helped someone who wanted to disappear. Yet Rome was in many ways also surprisingly small. The large population, especially the poor part of it, was crammed into tall *insulae* in choked and cluttered residential areas. It was impossible for everyone not to know their neighbour's business. Word spread as fast as the regular fires that ravaged the poor districts - how quickly Rufa had heard of his fight with Cilo was an illustration of this.

Carbo sighed. He supposed he would have to get her out of Rome. What he would do with her then, he had no idea. He thought back to her expression when he had suggested finding her a good Master. She hadn't been pleased. Maybe she had expected him to keep her as his own slave. That was clearly impossible, if he wanted to remain in Rome and run his new business. Or maybe, had she thought that having run away, she would become free.

Carbo mused on this. What slave would not aspire to that? Well, the elderly, the infirm, the children, who would likely die of starvation if they were cast out of their Master's home, as in fact often happened. For all the rest though, who were able bodied enough to make their own living, freedom was surely preferable. Carbo could not imagine living the life of a slave, at the whim of every command and desire of another man. Yet was it so different to life in the legions? Here was he, suddenly free from the chains of command, and he had to admit that he felt lost, bewildered by the lack of structure and direction that his life had previously held. He missed the legions, he realised. Could a slave of many years feel the same?

Marsia returned, and stood looking at him, hands on hips, saying nothing, but a question in her expression. Carbo hesitated, the desire to share his problem almost overwhelming his sense of discretion. Then he thought of another, a man he didn't know well, but thought he could trust. Tomorrow, he would seek advice. He stood.

"I'm going to bed. Ensure there is no one passed out under the tables before you lock the doors for the night."

"Yes, Master. Good night."

Rufa lay awake, thoughts in turmoil. She wasn't sure what she had expected from Carbo. He had at least sheltered her for the night. But if that was as far as his protection went, what hope was there for them? An escaped female slave with a young child, having to fend for herself, inside or outside Rome. Yet what choice had she had? She had no idea what was going on in her Mistress' house, or her mind, but she knew something was very wrong. She knew too that it involved Fabilla, and there was nothing she wouldn't do to protect her only child.

Fabilla stirred in her sleep, rolled away from Rufa. Nothing she wouldn't do. She looked across to where she could just make out Carbo's still form. He was undoubtedly attractive, she thought, but passion was the last thing she wanted right now, with her stomach churning in anxiety. Nevertheless, she needed his help. And what did women of her station in life do when they wanted the help of a man? What had they always done?

She crept over to Carbo and put a gentle hand on his arm. He started awake, but she put a gentle finger to his lips before he could cry out.

"Rufa?" he said in confusion. "What is it? Has someone come for you?"

Rufa shook her head. "Don't speak," she whispered, then kissed him softly on the lips. Carbo stiffened in surprise, then relaxed as her mouth worked against his. Still half asleep, he put up little resistance as she pushed him backwards and straddled him. Nervously, but as seductively as she could, she lifted her tunic over her head, her bare breasts swinging free. Carbo gaped at her.

Rufa gave Carbo an encouraging smile, then reached down beneath her for Carbo's shaft. It was limp, and seemed to shrink at her touch. Her surprise must have showed in her face, and she saw Carbo's expression fall. Abruptly, he pushed her off him, and she sprawled heavily across the floor.

"What do you think you are doing?" Carbo yelled.

Rufa blinked in confusion. Marsia, Philon and Fabilla woke up. Marsia fumbled with an oil lamp, and the room sprung into a dim flickering light. Rufa looked around her in sudden shame and grabbed her tunic, clutching it to her bare torso.

"I take you in for one night, and you think you can climb into my bed?" Carbo roared. "Do you think I succoured you just for your body? That I would go to this trouble and risk for a fuck with a slave?"

Rufa stared at Carbo as he towered over her, fists balled, and she went cold. Fabilla started to cry. Marsia and Philon looked on in shock.

"Get out," said Carbo in a low voice.

Rufa's mouth dropped open. "Carbo," she whispered. "Master, please."

"Get out," said Carbo again, voice terrifyingly steady. "Take your slave daughter with you, you whore."

Rufa hesitated. "Now!" he roared. Rufa leapt to her feet, threw on her tunic, and grabbed Fabilla's hand. Carbo took Rufa's arm and dragged her to the door, pulled her down the stairs, Fabilla in tow. Marsia followed.

"Master, maybe you should reconsider," said Marsia. "It's the middle of the night. The streets are dangerous…"

"Silence, slave, unless you want a beating."

Marsia looked like she was about to say more, but the expression on Carbo's face made her think better of it. Carbo opened the front door of the tavern, and pushed Rufa and Fabilla outside. Fabilla stumbled onto her front, and started to wail. Rufa picked her up, and stared accusingly at Carbo. Carbo merely folded his arms.

Rufa held Fabilla close to her, then turned, straightened her back, and walked slowly away.

Marsia stared at Carbo, her face white with anger. Carbo defied the stare for a moment, then relented.

"Speak, then, slave. I can see you must."

"You commanded me to silence," said Marsia sullenly.

"And now I'm commanding you to talk," said Carbo, exasperated.

Marsia drew breath, choosing her words.

"Why did you save me from Cilo?"

Carbo had wondered the same. He had been bored, lonely, terribly anxious and in need of distraction. And he had seen enough bullies in the legions to have learned to detest them. He shrugged.

"I don't know," he said.

Marsia tilted her head on one side. "I think you do. I think you know what is right. I think you are someone who understands there is more in the world than his own self interests. I think you are a brave man. I also think you are a coward."

Carbo's jaw dropped, then his face twisted in anger.

"I have fought in battle after battle with the legions. I have faced down screaming German warriors and drunken brawling legionaries. I have travelled alone from Germany to Rome despite hostile locals, robbers and bandits, " Carbo roared. "How dare you call me a coward!"

"It is the simple truth," said Marsia, unflinching in the face of his rage. "All men are. Bravery is doing the right thing, despite your fear. Something in you is scared. Maybe something from your time in the legions, I don't know. But inside, you are like a lonely child. Maybe it was your fear of being alone that led you to help me, to buy the tavern. It is your fear now that is driving Rufa away."

"I'm not scared of the urban cohorts."

"No, I think you are scared of Rufa."

Carbo gaped at her. The damned slave was seeing right into his soul. From the moment Rufa had arrived, he had been wondering how to get rid of her. She was a reminder of his terrible past, but she was also someone he had cared deeply for. He didn't want that responsibility, didn't want to care for her again, care for anyone, because people could die, and that was too much to bear.

Marsia said nothing else. Carbo turned to look down the dark street, where Rufa and Fabilla, heads bowed, were just turning a corner. He let out a curse, and ran after them.

Chapter VI

Elissa woke as light from the open roofed *peristylium* flooded through the window of her bedroom. She kept her eyes closed, momentarily reliving her successful gathering. Metella was committed to the cause now, which meant funds were no longer a problem. And the sacrifice, so necessary to receive the blessing of the Lord and Lady, had been selected. The necessary tools and equipment were coming together. She smiled, excitement in the pit of her stomach.

She opened her eyes. One of her slaves, a tall Greek boy called Stathis, waited patiently at the foot of her bed, holding a cup of water and some bread for her to break her fast with. She sat up, the bed clothes falling off her naked torso. She noticed the slave boy's eyes widen at the sight of her small breasts, his eyes lingering just too long before being averted. She thought about punishing him for his impudence, and his impiety - he was after all one of her followers as well as her slave. Then she thought about having him make love to her. She pondered for a moment. It had certainly been a very long time since she had allowed a man inside her. She had a mission, after all, a divine calling which she must not be distracted from. Besides, as the high priestess of Ba'al Hammon and Tanit, was she expected to be pure as a Vestal, or to allow her body to be used like a temple prostitute? It was not something she had ever been taught by her mother, although clearly her mother was no virgin.

She ran her fingers in a little circle around her breast, noticing the nipple becoming erect. She looked at the boy. He had blonde, curly hair, and a lightly muscled, hairless chest. She presumed he was around eighteen or nineteen years of age. His eyes came up from the floor to meet her gaze, and this time he stared in fascination, watching with mouth slightly open as she caressed herself. He wore only a loin cloth, and she could see the bulge underneath betraying his excitement. There had been a time when the thought of an erect man would have caused her to collapse in anxiety. She had rid herself of those internal demons when she had taken a male slave, tied him up, beaten him, and then used him for her pleasure. Seeing that large, brutish man, begging for mercy from her beatings, then begging for release from her attentions, had showed her just how deserving of contempt men could be. Sometimes useful, sometimes ornamental, but always at the mercy of their urges, however disciplined they claimed to be.

"Put that down and come here," she commanded. A lifetime of obedience showed, as he immediately did as he was told, depositing cup and bread on a table, then walking to the bed. Elissa sat on the edge of the bed and pulled away his loin cloth. His erect penis sprang out, and she smiled and took it in her hand. She looked up into his eyes, and he remained silent as she gently stroked it up and down. She lay back on the bed, spread her legs, and directed him to use his mouth on her. As he did as instructed, she sighed with pleasure. He had obviously done this before. Clearly he had a girlfriend, or more than one, among the other slaves. Maybe it was because he was Greek that he was willing and happy to do this. No Roman, slave or otherwise, would happily perform cunnilingus, demonstrating as it did passivity and submissiveness. A real man should be active in bed.

Elissa groaned at the sweet sensations, feeling her excitement rising. She pushed Stathis onto his back, and straddled him. Taking his penis in her hand, she slid it into herself, and started to ride him. Neither of them lasted long, Stathis because of his youth and Elissa because it had been so long since her last time. Elissa's orgasm washed over her, and then just as she saw the boy groan, she dismounted him, his seed spurting over himself, a look of combined pleasure and frustration on his face.

Elissa instructed the slave to leave and clean himself up, and lay on her back on the bed, a slight sheen of sweat making her skin glisten. Her racing heart and breathing gradually slowed, and she closed her eyes, relaxed and content. There was a loud knock at the door, and before she could call out, Shafat burst in.

"Mistress," he said, his voice breathless as if he had been running. He registered Elissa's naked body and furious expression and quickly turned his back. Elissa could see the blush on the back of his neck.

"How dare you barge in here, Shafat," said Elissa in an outraged tone. "Explain yourself."

"Mistress, please forgive me. I meant no disrespect. But it's important."

Elissa's eyes narrowed, the relaxation in her body fleeing from her like a startled bird, to be replaced by a gnawing, anxious, uncertain feeling.

"What is it?"

"The red-head and her daughter. Rufa and Fabilla. They are gone."

Elissa sat bolt upright. Her voice was unsettlingly soft, threatening.

"Turn round and explain yourself."

Shafat turned, but kept his eyes cast to the ground, trying to avoid looking at her naked body. He spoke with a tremor.

"They didn't report for their duties this morning. Rufa has always been an obedient slave, so it was very out of character. I went to her quarters, but she wasn't there. Her belongings were gone as well."

"When did she run?"

"Natta says she hasn't seen her since yesterday evening. Apparently, Rufa said she was running an errand for you. She gave the same story to Demosthenes, the night porter."

"He didn't query why she was taking her daughter with her?"

"He says she claimed she was having bad dreams and wanted to keep her close."

"Take Natta and Demosthenes to the *peristylium* and have them stripped and bound. Call for Glaukos.We will find out if they are hiding anything."

Shafat bowed and departed to carry out her instructions. Elissa yelled for a slave to help her dress. Her chamber slave, an elderly woman who Elissa decided was rapidly getting past a useful age, came over as fast as arthritic limbs would allow, to help Elissa into a long *stola*. The slave started to fuss with Elissa's hair, but Elissa shrugged her off, pulled a comb through it briskly herself, splashed on a little perfume and then marched from the room.

She arrived in the *peristylium* in time to witness Demosthenes and Natta being bound by two of the day porters, their arms stretched around columns as if they were hugging them. Demosthenes seemed groggy, obviously roused from his sleep after his night shift, already tied tight. Natta was trembling and sobbing as the ropes were secured around her wrists and stretched around her column. Glaukos walked to Demosthenes, and ripped his tunic away, revealing a muscular back. He did the same with Natta, showing the woman's pale skin and saggy midriff and buttocks. The stripping increased the moans and sobs coming from Natta's throat.

Looking around, Elissa could see that a crowd of the household slaves was gathering. She considered sending them to continue with their work, but then decided this would be a valuable lesson for them to witness. At the far side of the *peristylium*, Natta's partner, Cossus, was looking furious. Another slave had a hand on his chest, talking gently to him, while yet another was guiding Natta's children away from the scene.

Glaukos, a leer on his face, held two whips, which he showed to Elissa. In one hand was a *scutica*, with its twisted leather thongs, capable of inflicting more damage than a simple strap or cane. In the other hand was the *flagrum*, a short whip with pieces of bone at the tip. This one could flay the skin off the victim, down to the very bone. Elissa indicated the *scutica* and pointed to Natta. Glaukos bowed and stood a short way behind the naked slave, spreading his feet slightly to maintain his balance during the strokes. He looked to Elissa for confirmation and she nodded. Glaukos drew the whip back and flicked it forward with all his strength.

The crack of the whip through the air and the thump of the leather against the woman's back were followed almost immediately by a high pitched, sustained scream. Glaukos pulled his arm back and administered another stroke. Natta's first scream had not finished when the whip landed a second time, and the impact changed the pitch but not intensity of her cries. Glaukos paused to let the noise to die down, Natta drawing breath, choking and sobbing. Then he carried on, varying the timing of his strokes so Natta had no way of predicting when the next one would land.

Elissa looked round at the gathered slaves. They stood silent, eyes narrowed, expressions set, flinching with each blow and scream. Some kept their eyes averted, some seemed unable to turn their gaze away. No questions had yet been asked, following the traditional wisdom that one couldn't believe a slave unless they had been tortured first. Elissa mused on this as she watched the whip falling. Of course, she had been a slave once herself. Should she therefore treat slaves differently than someone who had always been free, who had never experienced the shame, the cruelty, the dehumanisation of the slave state? Wasn't it different for her though? She had been freed by her father's actions, he had liberated her from slavery, and then her own actions had brought her to Rome, to freedom from poverty, and the opportunity to fulfil her destiny. These slaves were just pawns in the Lord and Lady's will, and it was right that any methods necessary were used to bring the gods the respect and glory that had been denied to them for centuries.

Natta's back was red and purple from the beating, with blood trickling out from small open wounds. She was sagging against the column, her cries a continuous but weaker wail. Elissa licked her lips, and a frisson of excitement ran through her. *Take this offering of suffering, my Lord and Lady,* she prayed silently. *As a foretaste of what is to come.*

After twelve strokes, a relatively small number, Natta was becoming noticeably weaker. Glaukos, though clearly enjoying himself, looked at Elissa questioningly, and she held up a hand.

"Bring her to me," she said. Two slaves untied Natta, and brought her, half walking, half dragged to where Elissa stood, and threw her at her feet. Glaukos lifted the slave woman's chin so she was looking up at her mistress. Tears and dust stained her face, and there were livid indents where her cheek had been pressed against the stone.

"Tell me where Rufa and her child are."

Natta stared at her piteously. "Mistress, I don't know. They left yesterday evening. She said she was running an errand for you."

Elissa regarded her for a moment. "Tie her up again," she said to Glaukos, who indicated that she be bound to the column again.

Glaukos then turned his attention to Demosthenes. The big man was no braver, his cries deeper and louder than

Natta's as the *scutica* rose and fell. He was stronger though, and Elissa allowed thirty lashes before she had him brought to her. She asked the same question.

"Where are Rufa and the child?"

"Mistress, I don't know. She said she getting *garum* for cook."

"And why did you decide you didn't need to check with Shafat?"

"I'm sorry, mistress. Why she lie? Why she run? Where can escaped slave go, in Rome?"

Elissa sighed and ordered him tied up again. She took the *flagrum* from Glaukos and walked slowly over to the two bound slaves. She stroked the whip with the sharp bits of bone tied into the end. She could tell from the slaves' reactions, eyes wide, low frightened moans escaping, that they knew what it was capable of.

"Tell me. Spare yourselves the misery. Where is she?"

Demosthenes started to babble, crying that he didn't know, and begging for mercy. A trembling Natta seemed too frightened to speak. Elissa passed the vicious whip to Glaukos and walked away. It seemed likely they were telling the truth, but she would allow the interrogation to run its full course, just in case there was any chance one of them was hiding something from her. She wondered if she should put the rest of the household to torture, in case someone else knew anything. Maybe someone had helped the slave to escape. And how did she know to flee in the first place? But she wasn't so wealthy that she could afford a whole new set of slaves. Regardless, how she escaped no longer mattered. What was of importance was finding her.

The girl was the chosen one, selected by the rites to be the one that would summon the Lord and Lady to this earth, to dance in the middle of the destruction of Rome itself.

She walked back towards her bedroom, to finish readying herself for the day. She would need to summon some help, she decided. Behind her, the barbed whip started to fall, and Natta's pitiful cries rang around the *peristylium*. She wondered idly whether she would die directly from the whipping, or in a few days from her wounds.

Scrofa was waiting in her atrium, when she arrived there with Glaukos and Shafat in tow. The fat man's face was ruddy and he was breathless, obviously having made haste to have come promptly. He bowed deeply as she walked in. She let him hold the obeisance for a long moment before indicating for him to rise.

"I came as soon as I received your command, Mistress."

Elissa nodded, and gestured to him to sit. She dismissed the porter, and Glaukos took his place, standing guard by the front entrance.

"There has arisen a small problem," said Elissa.

Scrofa was silent as he waited for her to elaborate.

"The chosen one has absconded."

Scrofa looked unsettled. "I'm sorry to hear that, mistress."

"You understand the implications?"

Scrofa put his head on one side. "I believe so, Mistress."

"That girl was chosen by the Lord and Lady, as their moloch. I saw it. I was granted a vision of the girl with a head of fire, who they required in order to give their blessing to our enterprise. Through her, they told me, when they spoke to me, Rome would be destroyed and the Lord and Lady would return to our world to rule over us."

Scrofa nodded. "I know her importance, Mistress."

"So tell me how we find her."

Shafat interrupted. "She is an escaped slave. We use the correct authorities to help us find her. They have resources we don't."

"The *vigiles*?" scoffed Glaukos. "Those bumbling fools will never catch her."

"No, the urban cohorts," said Shafat.

Scrofa spoke. "That isn't really their job. The cohorts are for crowd control."

Elissa looked interested. "But you have influence in the cohorts. I'm sure that we could get them to re-allocate some resources."

Scrofa nodded uncertainly.

"Should we torture the rest of the slaves?" asked Shafat. "See if any of them have any knowledge as to where she might have chosen to hide." Glaukos looked eager at the suggestion.

"That shows commendable commitment to the cause, Shafat, seeing as you yourself are a slave."

Shafat paled and stuttered. "I didn't mean…"

Elissa waved a hand. "I hope it won't be necessary. We will see what the efforts of Scrofa and our fine men in the cohorts are capable of."

Shafat nodded gratefully.

A loud knock at the door surprised them. Shafat did the dismissed porter's job, and a slave announced the arrival of his mistress, Metella.

Shafat ushered Metella, who watied with two bodyguards, into the atrium, where the Roman matron bowed to her Mistress. Elissa offered her a hand to help her to her feet, and guided her through to the *peristylium.* Shafat, Scrofa, Glaukos and Metella's personal slave followed behind respectfully. A calm had descended on the place after the distressing noises and sights just moments earlier. Two slaves were sullenly cleaning blood from the pillars. Metella paid them no attention. Metella's bodyguards stood at a respectful distance, faces impassive.

Elissa guided Metella to a stone bench, and sat beside her, taking her hand.

"How are you, my child?" asked Elissa in a soft voice. Metella was about the same age as Elissa, but their relationship, especially since the initiation, was clearly not one of equals.

"Sadness is my lot in life. I loved him, you know, Mistress. It may not be the usual state of affairs in marriages within my class. My friends, virgin, married and widowed alike, don't understand my grief. But, he was not your typical Roman."

"You say that like it is a bad thing?"

Metella gave a wan smile. "I know how you feel about Romans. I have come to share your feelings. Most Romans would consider my husband's virtues - his tenderness, his respect for his slaves, his refusal to divorce me when it became obvious I was barren - to be weaknesses. Maybe this is why he wasn't promoted to senatorial rank. He had the property qualifications. But these so-called weaknesses, they made me treasure him. I don't think I will ever stop missing him."

"Have you heard anything more from the Urban Praetor's office?"

Metella shook her head. "I tried to visit yesterday. They wouldn't even admit me. They treated me like one of the head count. They even…" She stopped, a tremor in her voice, followed by a little sob. Elissa put a comforting arm around her shoulder.

"Go on," said Elissa.

"They laughed at me. The common soldiers of the urban cohorts, they told me I was a nuisance, that I was wasting their time. Then they said that I should find myself a new husband, and that if I was lonely at night, they would…"

This time she did break down, heavy sobs wracking her frame. Elissa held her head against her chest, while she looked at Glaukos. The big man looked away, face neutral. Scrofa looked uncomfortable and seemed about to speak, but Elissa shook her head, warning him to keep silent.

The sobs eased, and she dabbed her eyes and nose on a cloth offered by her slave.

"I do apologise, Mistress. You have more important things to do than hear my woes."

"I always have time for my loyal followers. But I must admit, the calls on me are pressing today."

"Of course." Metella composed herself. "I shall take up no more of your time. I thank you for your kindness,

Mistress. It seems to be a rare thing in Rome these days."
She rose, and Elissa stood with her.

"You will attend the next meeting?"

"I will, Mistress. Now I am given to the Lord and Lady,
I want to show them my loyalty and obedience."

"I am pleased," said Elissa. "I am sorry they are such
lowly affairs. Few of our followers are people of means, and
we have little money to worship them as they deserve."

"Oh," said Metella, sudden remembrance on her face.
"My visit was not just social. As you know, I am a wealthy
widow, with no heir. I am of course glad to donate to the
worship of Ba'al Hammon and Tanit." She gestured at one
of her bodyguards, who produced a heavy bag of coins that
had been skilfully hidden beneath his clothes to protect it
from casual thieves on the streets. She took it from him and
handed it to Elissa.

"Please accept this gift on behalf of the Lord and Lady."

Elissa's smile was suitably solemn. "I accept on their
behalf. I am most grateful. This gift will help glorify their
worship."

"If you find yourself needing more, please let me
know."

"Thank you, child. The Lord and Lady would not want
to see you go short yourself. But maybe you could consider
changing your will to their benefit. Just in the sad event that
you do not remarry, and remain childless, of course"

Metella nodded. "I will get my lawyers to prepare the
documents straightaway." She bowed and bid goodbye.
Elissa watched her leave with her slave, waiting till she was

gone before turning to Scrofa, Glaukos and Shafat, speculatively weighing the heavy bag of coins in her hand.

"Our investment is starting to pay off. These funds will be important in our preparations."

Glaukos grunted. "So can I have her now?"

"No, Glaukos. At least not until she has changed her will."

"Before I slit her effeminate husband's throat, I whispered in his ear that I was going to fuck her and kill her."

Elissa sighed. "That is a promise you will have to wait to keep, until she is no longer useful to us."

Glaukos grimaced but said nothing.

Shafat ventured cautiously, "But isn't she one of us now? A follower of the Lord and Lady?"

Elissa spat on the ground, her face suddenly contorted by a vicious expression. "She is a Roman. For now, she is a useful pawn. But when the time comes, when the Lord and Lady return, she will die, like all the Romans with their pride and their aggression and their false gods. Then, Glaukos you may have her."

Glaukos smiled.

"In the meantime, Scrofa will keep making sure her entreaties to the Urban Praetor's office fall on deaf ears."

Scrofa nodded his agreement.

"Now, beloved of Ba'al, go. Go and find our moloch, and bring her back to us. The time of our glory is approaching."

Glaukos balled his fists, a set expression on his face, and started to leave.

"Glaukos!" called Elissa after him. He stopped and turned.

"No harm is to come to the girl."

Glaukos hesitated then nodded. "And her mother?"

Elissa just shrugged.

Chapter VII

Carbo woke as the first light of sun streamed through the bedroom window, and took a moment to remember why he was on a mattress on the floor. He sat up and scratched where sharp pieces of straw from the mattress stuffing had poked into his skin. He spotted a couple of new bites from fleas and bed bugs, and scratched them too, while trying to ignore some of the older bites that were oozing. Next to him, sharing a mattress designed for one were Philon and Marsia. Philon was snoring and Marsia just starting to stir. On the bed, Rufa was sitting up, stroking Fabilla's hair, the sleeping young girl resting her head in her mother's lap. Carbo caught her eye, and she made to move, but he motioned her to stay where she was.

Carbo looked around the room. Five people occupied a room about twice as wide as a man is tall at its longest dimension. He knew it was common for the living space of an entire extended family to be a similar size. Fortunately, with Rome's benign climate, a Roman could spend most of his life outdoors, retreating home only for sleep. Still, he wondered about the occupants of the rooms upstairs. Their rent was due today, and he recalled Marsia telling him about one perennially late payer. He resolved to accompany her when she went to collect the rent that morning.

Marsia rose now, folding back her blanket and standing, naked. Carbo had a moment to admire her figure, full breasts, broad-shoulders and toned muscles developed in a barbarian lifestyle in the forests of Germany and maintained in good condition by physical labour ever since. She shrugged her plain dress over her head, then noticed Carbo looking at her and held his gaze. She smiled at him and bade him a good morning. For a moment, Carbo felt embarrassed to have been caught looking. Then he remembered their respective positions.

"Good morning, Marsia. Get Philon up, then go and find me something to eat."

Marsia dipped her head briefly, then gave Philon a kick, who woke with a yelp.

"Up, lazy head," she said sharply. "I'm not doing your work for you."

Philon rose, grumbling and cursing. Soon though, the slaves were downstairs, starting their chores, and getting on with the business of preparing the tavern for the day ahead. Carbo waited until they were alone, then looked at Rufa.

"How did you sleep?" he asked.

She smiled a little sadly.

"I would believe that I hadn't slept at all, if it wasn't for the bad dreams I can recall."

Carbo couldn't think of anything to say for a moment. Fabilla woke and stretched.

"Where are we, mother?" she asked.

"Staying in my friend Carbo's tavern. You remember we came here last night?"

"Oh yes." She smiled brightly. "When are we going home?"

Rufa looked across at Carbo, who avoided her gaze. Her face fell momentarily, then hardened.

"We aren't going back to that home, Fabilla. I will find us a new home."

"So we will have a new Mistress?"

"I...don't know."

"Did the Mistress sell us?"

"No, Fabilla, she didn't."

Fabilla's eyes grew wide. "Did we...did we *run away*, mother?"

Rufa looked helplessly to Carbo, her mouth open, fear and misery clear on her face. Carbo intervened.

"Fabilla, why don't you go downstairs and ask Marsia for some breakfast. I think there are some dates somewhere. Then maybe you could ask if she needs any help. You look like a very helpful young lady. Would you like to help Marsia?"

"Yes, Master, I would."

Carbo smiled. "I'm not your Master, Fabilla. You may call me Carbo."

"Thank you. Carbo." Fabilla smiled impishly, then flitted off in search of Marsia.

There was a moment's silence, then Carbo and Rufa tried to speak at the same time. They laughed, and Carbo indicated for Rufa to continue. She spoke in a careful, measured tone.

"You have been most kind in putting us up last night. We will be gone this morning. Thank you for your help."

Carbo looked at her steadily. "Where would you go?"

"We would leave Rome. Find work in a tavern in a provincial town."

"Somewhere they don't ask questions? Where they aren't suspicious of a young mother and her daughter turning up with no family, no man to look after them? Somewhere where the urban cohorts and the *vigiles* and the *fugitivarii* won't find you? Assuming you make it there, a young woman and a young girl, travelling through bandit ridden country alone."

Rufa's gaze was defiant, but she said nothing. Carbo shook his head.

"I told you last night that you could stay. That I would help you."

"But your vow. I mean…It was so long ago. I came to you because I had nowhere else. But I was just a child when you last saw me. I have been thinking about this all night. Why would you help me now, after all this time? What do you owe my father any more?"

A darkness passed over Carbo's face, and momentarily Rufa drew back in fear. Carbo stood, naked apart from a plain loincloth, tied at one side. He stepped forward and took her hand. Then looking into her eyes, he cupped his genitals in one hand in the traditional manner of someone making an oath, and said, "I swear to you, Rufa, by the ashes of my ancestors, by Jupiter and by Mars, that I will do my utmost to protect you and your daughter. May the gods take my balls if I lie."

Rufa gripped his hand tightly, tears of gratitude in her eyes, and they were silent for a moment. Then she put her arms around him, and started to sob heavily, suddenly unable to control herself after the anxiety and terror she had been experiencing from the moment she found out that Fabilla was in danger. Carbo held her to him, surprised to find he was enjoying the sensation of her warm body, still in the grubby dress in which she had fled her home, pressed against his bare chest. His arms stroked her back and hair gently as she cried.

Eventually, the sobbing slowed, and stopped. He tilted her chin up to look at him and found her face a mess of tears and snot. He looked around him, and found a rag on the floor, which he offered to her. She looked at it suspiciously for a moment, with good reason, he reflected - he had no idea whether the rag was a duster, a dish cloth, or the rags that Marsia had to clean and bleach after tying them between her legs once a month.   Nevertheless, she wiped her face, and blew her nose on it, before passing it back to Carbo. He held it up between finger and thumb, looking at in distaste, before hurling it over his shoulder. Rufa burst out laughing in a release of tension. Carbo laughed too, and held her hand.

"I will keep you both safe," he reiterated. "I just have to work out how. I am new in Rome, I don't have allies or patrons or family or friends. Well..." he paused thoughtfully. "Maybe there is someone."

Rufa cocked her head on one side, curiously.

Carbo strode east down the *clivus suburanus*. The late morning weather was pleasant, the sky cloudless. Carbo's height and bulk allowed him to part the crowds more successfully than most, but progress was still slow without some burly slaves to clear the way. Once, he tripped over a dead body, a middle aged man clothed only in a tatty loin cloth. The late summer heat had speeded the initial process of decomposition, and though it might not have lain there for very long, Carbo felt no real sympathy for the deceased. Death on the streets was common enough for the homeless, and besides, he had seen enough death in the legions to numb him to most sights. However, he was annoyed that no one had cleaned the corpse away yet. In the legions, such sloppiness would have been harshly punished.

He squeezed through the crush at the Esquiline gate of the Servian walls and found his way to the IInd Station of the *Cohortes vigilum*. There was a tired looking watchman on guard outside the door, lounging against the wall.

"I want to see your commander, soldier," said Carbo.

Carbo's commanding tone and military bearing had an immediate effect on the watchman, causing him to stand upright and attempt a sloppy salute.

"Sir, I don't think…"

"Now, soldier."

The watchman went into the station, and shortly afterwards, a short but muscular man with a furious expression on his face emerged.

"What in the name of all the gods do you want?"

"I'm here to see Vespillo."

"Vespillo isn't here, I'm in charge right now. Say your piece or get lost."

Carbo surveyed the man calmly. "What's your name?"

The deputy drew himself up to his full, short height and puffed out his chest. "I am Sextus Horatius Taura, second in command of the IInd Esquiline Fire Station. For the last time, who are you and what do you want?"

"I'm Gaius Valerius Carbo."

Taura's eyes narrowed. "Ah. You. Vespillo did mention you."

"In glowing terms, I hope?"

Taura frowned. "You're going to bring trouble. On yourself. On the people round you. And on the *vigiles.*"

"It's not my intention. I've had twenty five years of trouble. I just want a quiet life now."

"Well you aren't going about it in a very sensible way." Taura sighed. "Why do you need to see Vespillo anyway?"

"I… need some advice."

"Go to an astrologer then, or a philosopher."

"I don't want my fortune read, or be sold platitudes about life. I need something more practical."

"And it can't wait?"

"No."

Taura considered for a while. Then he came to a decision. "Vespillo seemed impressed with you. You don't do anything for me. Nonetheless. Vespillo will be pretty angry to be woken, but I'm thinking that's your problem." Taura told him where Vespillo lived, an *insula* two streets away. Carbo thanked him, and offered him a small coin. Taura looked at it with contempt, shook his head and walked back inside the station.

A tall, dark-skinned slave answered the door of the ground floor apartment to Carbo's loud knock.

"Fetch your Master, Vespillo," said Carbo.

"He is sleeping. He is not to be disturbed. Come back at sundown."

The slave started to close the door, but Carbo pushed it back open forcefully.

"Wake him," said Carbo, firmly. "If he says he doesn't want to see me, I will leave."

The slave stared into Carbo's piercing eyes, and decided to do as he was told. Carbo waited at the door. A few minutes later, Vespillo appeared, eyes a little red, sleep in the corners, hair dishevelled, a tunic hastily and untidily thrown on.

"By Mars' hairy arse, what is so important that you disturb my sleep?"

"I need your help."

Vespillo sighed. "More trouble with the local gangs? Maybe you need to buy some burly bodyguards."

"No, not that."

"What then?"

Carbo hesitated. "Is there somewhere we can talk in private?"

Vespillo looked backwards into the house. Carbo looked over his shoulder. The bright daylight outside meant that he could see little of the inside of Vespillo's apartment, but he got an impression of a well cared for home.

"Come with me," said Vespillo, and closed the door behind him. He led Carbo to a small, cheap restaurant on a street corner. They took a couple of chairs at a table on the street, and asked the serving slave for some bread and garum, and some watered wine. Carbo paid for them both, and waited until it had arrived.

"Out with it then," said Vespillo. "What is so damned important?"

Now that the moment was upon him, Carbo paused. He felt his heart beat accelerate. What was he doing? This man was a commander of the *vigiles*, one of his jobs was to catch escaped slaves. But who else could he turn to?

"I have a problem. Could you give me some advice? About a hypothetical matter?"

"A hypothetical matter? I'm not much good with them. I deal with what's in front of me. Fires. Cutthroats. Fugitives."

"Please indulge me," asked Carbo.

Vespillo nodded. "Very well. Go on."

Carbo thought for a moment about how to broach the subject. He looked at Vespillo's grey-bearded face, the visage forged in battle.

"In the legions, your comrades are like your family."

Vespillo inclined his head in agreement - Carbo was stating a fact, not asking a question.

"You eat with them, sleep with them, fight with them, and some of them die by your side. Someone who has not been in the legions cannot possibly understand the bonds that form between you. So you look out for each other. And each other's families."

Again Vespillo nodded, his steady gaze not wavering.

"Those bonds, those obligations, extend beyond our time in the legions. Even beyond death. Don't you agree?"

"Of course." Vespillo showed no sign of impatience, yet.

"Do you take an oath to the gods seriously?"

"I do not give my word lightly, whether I swear by the gods or my honour."

"Then how greatly would you feel obliged to the daughter of a comrade from the legions, a man who died in a battle that you survived, to whom you had sworn an oath to protect her?"

"That seems to me like a very serious obligation. Little more serious."

"And what if that girl, that you had sworn to your dead brother-in-arms to protect, sworn before the gods, was now a slave?"

"Ah." Vespillo looked away for a moment. He took a sip of his drink. Carbo looked around. No one seemed to be listening to their conversation. A scruffy dog cocked its leg against a fruit seller's stand and had a mouldy apple thrown at it by the yelling stall holder. From a nearby second floor window, a woman harangued a man, presumably her husband who was on the street outside. He seemed to be asking to be let in, and she was screaming he should run to his whore. Vespillo put his drink down.

"A legionary, current or former, owes a loyalty to the Emperor, and to his laws," said the *vigiles* commander. "I suppose, I would feel I had let the girl down, that she had been enslaved. But once it is a done deed, there is really nothing to be done. Maybe I would visit her, make sure her Master or Mistress was treating her well. Beyond that though…" Vespillo shrugged.

"What if you found she wasn't being treated well?"

"I would speak to her owner. If it was within my power, I would persuade, or threaten them to be a kind Master or Mistress."

"And if it wasn't in your power?"

Vespillo hesitated. "I… don't know."

"Now what if that slave, who you hadn't seen since she was a little girl, turned up in your house, a runaway, claiming her Mistress was threatening her life and the life of her daughter. Where then stands your loyalty to the Emperor, and your loyalty and oath to your comrade?"

Vespillo's mouth dropped, his eyes widening. "This has gone way beyond the hypothetical, Carbo, hasn't it?"

Carbo said nothing.

"Why have you come to me? Knowing what I do?"

"Because you were in the legions. I know you understand. Also, I think you are an honourable man. And… I have no one else. I've left the army, I've arrived back in Rome after twenty five years, knowing not a soul. I have no friends, no family, no patron."

"Let me get this straight, Carbo. You are asking for me to help you in giving shelter to a runaway slave? The commander of the local *vigiles*, one of whose jobs it is to apprehend fugitive slaves? Are you mad?"

Carbo's face hardened. He pushed his hair back and stood. "I am sorry to have wasted your time. I hope you will honour the confidential way in which I approached you. I will look to my own resources. I suppose it is something I will need to get used to now."

"Sit down, you idiot," said Vespillo.

Carbo hesitated, then sat down again. Vespillo looked at him and considered. This man was making waves in the already stormy seas of Suburan life. The obvious thing to do was cut him adrift. Surely he would be dead within days without the help of the *vigiles.* But Vespillo wasn't so sure. Carbo obviously had internal resources, no weakling could rise from the ranks to be *pilus prior* of a cohort. As well, he had demonstrated guts and fighting ability already. If Vespillo didn't help him, would he have an angry, uncontrolled, dangeous man in his district to deal with? Besides, Carbo could prove to be a useful foil against the power of the gangs and brotherhoods like the one run by Cilo and Manius. He thought that he would rather have Carbo inside his tent pissing out, than the other way round.

And Vespillo had to concede grudgingly that he liked the man.

"Unfortunately for me, you seem to be a good judge of character. I'm not going to betray your confidence. I'll help you." He drained his cup. "Now buy me another drink and tell me everything."

Chapter VIII

When Carbo had finished the story, Vespillo sat in silence for a while, lost in thought. Carbo looked around him. The sun was rising to its zenith and the streets were becoming more crowded. Curses rang out as hurrying citizens and slaves bumped into each other and dropped loads. Donkeys and mules carrying overflowing baskets squashed people against the walls. Hawkers, market sellers, astrologers, philosophers, barbers and prostitutes all shouted advertisements for their services and products. Vespillo looked up at Carbo, who focussed his attention back on the *vigiles* commander.

"I don't think you should take them out of Rome," said Vespillo.

"Why not?" asked Carbo.

"Several reasons. Taking them out of the gates would expose them to the scrutiny of anyone, official or private citizen, who was looking out for them. Then you have to consider where you would take them, and how you would make sure they were cared for and protected. Mostly though, any place you take them to will be smaller than Rome, and strangers coming into a new place always rouse suspicion. People ask questions. There is no other city in the world as big as Rome. Here, they are just two in a million people. It seems to me that you couldn't really do better for a hiding place. But maybe you don't need to hide."

"What do you mean?"

"Tell me about your finances."

Carbo raised his eyebrows at the personal question, but answered anyway.

"By the standards of the Subura, I am wealthy. I campaigned for twenty five years, and rose to the rank of *pilus prior* of the second cohort. You get a fair share of the spoils at that rank. And a share of the scams that go on. You know the drill."

Vespillo nodded, smiling ruefully. "There were always plenty of men who had saved enough coin to get out of a labour duty, or to pay a fine to avoid a punishment for a minor misdemeanour. They were the sensible ones, that didn't drink, gamble and whore their pay away the moment it arrived."

"Twenty five years of service adds up. I own a small farm in Campania, that I have never visited, but which provides me with an income. I have money deposited with an *argentarius*, which earns a little interest. I have some cash I keep on me or at home. And as you know, I now own a tavern, and two slaves."

"That certainly takes you above the requirement for the corn dole," said Vespillo.

Carbo nodded. "I certainly won't starve, nor really need to work. So what's the relevance?"

"Why don't you just offer to buy this slave, this, what was her name?"

"Rufa." Carbo looked thoughtful. "I'm not sure. I don't get the impression that Rufa's mistress is poor, so the money is unlikely to be an incentive."

"But it might save face for her. It is a lot easier to explain her absence by saying she has been sold, than that she has absconded. Less likely to give the other slaves ideas."

"But if, as Rufa says, the child is somehow marked for something sinister, then surely her mistress will want her back at any cost?"

"Do you really believe that part of her story? How sure are you that she isn't just a runaway? A freeborn woman, wanting her freedom back, wanting better than slavery for her child. You only have her word for what she saw. Even if she is telling the truth, maybe she misinterpreted everything. The gods know there are a multitude of bizarre cults in Rome, all with their quirks, idiosyncrasies, and disturbing rituals. We aren't like the Jews. As long as proper respect is paid to the gods of Rome, people can follow whoever and however they please."

Carbo looked doubtful. "Maybe you are right. I wouldn't want to risk returning her to her Mistress though, in case her story is true."

"Nor am I asking you to. But buying her and making her your property would be by far the simplest thing. Then you can free her if you wish. Or keep her as your own slave, if you prefer. She is attractive?"

Carbo frowned. "I wouldn't... couldn't keep her. You are right though, if I could buy her, there is no longer a problem. The difficulty is, what if I am turned down. Then she knows the girl is with me."

"What you need is a trusted agent to act as a go between. Someone who will keep your secret, but can negotiate on your behalf."

Carbo looked at Vespillo steadily. Realisation of what he had said dawned on Vespillo's face.

"Hercules' prick," he swore. "I walked into that one." He sighed. "Tomorrow, then."

Elissa sat alone in the *peristylium*, eyes closed and head bowed. Worries and anxieties crowded her mind, too many for her to concentrate on any one of them. What if it rained that day, or the air was still? What if the fire failed to catch, or was extinguished too quickly? What it someone betrayed her, or the authorities discovered her plans somehow? And how would the Lord and Lady react if they did not receive their promised sacrifice?

Her lips moved in silent prayer.

"O Lord Ba'al Hammon and Lady Tanit, Face of Ba'al. Bless your servant, and your followers. Bless this holy task you have given me, and make me strong enough to do you honour. Make your enemies stumble and fall and let their people and armies and gods be destroyed by your fierce anger. Lord and Lady, keep me strong in your faith."

She felt a sense of calm suffuse her, spreading from her centre out through all her limbs, warming her. Her features relaxed, and their anxieties evaporated. She smiled softly to herself. She had no need to worry. The Lord and Lady would make sure all was well.

A polite cough disturbed her reverie. She looked up to see Shafat standing a respectful distance away.

"What is it?" she asked.

"There is someone here to see you, Mother."

Vespillo sat in Elissa's atrium and looked around him. The entrance hall to the *domus* was traditional in most ways. It was open to the air, with the ubiquitous *impluvium*, the marble basin that collected water, as a centrepiece. A few pot plants and statues were scattered around, and the walls were decorated in beautiful, if somewhat tired looking frescoes of pastoral scenes. A little oddly, the *lararium,* the shrine to the *lares,* the household gods, looked particularly neglected. The *lararium* wasn't just the wall niche or painting seen in poorer houses, but was a proper miniature temple, set on a podium with marble sides. Within it was a representation of the *lares,* a little silver statue of a pair of youths, dressed in the short-sleeved tunic worn in the country, holding a horn and a dish in the traditional manner. But there was no evidence of daily or even monthly libations, no wine or perfume or burnt offering. The statues themselves were tarnished, and the shrine held a sheen of dust.

Vespillo looked over at the porter, who stood against the door, shoulders slumped, head dropping. He was a short, stocky, Gallic type, and as Vespillo watched, he let out a wide yawn.

"Tired?" asked Vespillo.

The slave straightened himself and looked chastened. "My apologies, Master. I have been working nights as well as days."

"Oh? Why is that?"

The porter didn't meet Vespillo's gaze. "Another porter was...taken ill."

Vespillo continued to look at the slave, but the porter kept his gaze fixed on a point midway up the wall. Time passed, and Vespillo started to get bored. Moreover, he needed to urinate, the wine he had drunk earlier starting to make its effect felt. He knew, though, that it wasn't his place to ask to use a toilet within the *domus*, and he didn't want to miss his appointment with Elissa by nipping out to piss in the street. He stood, trying to distract himself, but found he was shifting uncomfortably from foot to foot.

"Vedius Vespillo?" The enquiring voice had an eastern accent. Vespillo turned to see a tall, thin, balding man with a Syrian appearance. "I am Shafat, Mistress Elissa's steward. She will see you now."

Vespillo was ushered through to the peristylium, where he was shown to a pale, willowy woman, clothed in a white dress and plain jewellery, who sat on a stone bench near the fountain. To her right stood a scarred giant of a man. Her gaze was fixed on a bronze statue, with its arms outstretched. Vespillo recalled the statue being mentioned in Carbo's retelling of Rufa's story. As Shafat announced Vespillo's name, the woman looked up, a faint smile briefly moving across her face. She didn't stand, but waved Vespillo to a bench at right angles to where she sat.

"Vespillo," she said, regarding him steadily. "Tribune of the *vigiles*. Second station? Am I right?"

Vespillo was taken aback. "You are very well informed, my lady."

"You have met my steward, Shafat." She gestured to the giant. "This is Glaukos, a… friend." She gave another half smile. "So to what do I owe the pleasure of this visit? Have we infringed one of the fire laws?"

"No, mistress. In fact I am not here in an official capacity."

Elissa's expression held only faint interest.

"Then please go on."

Vespillo cleared his throat. He felt oddly intimidated by this slight woman, an unfamiliar feeling for the veteran of the legions, and currently commander of some of the roughest men that Rome kept under arms.

"I understand you have lost a slave," he said, tentatively.

Suddenly Elissa was alert. Although she only betrayed the subtlest outward changes in demeanour, a slight widening of the eyes, a straightening of her back, Vespillo did not miss the signs. If he had been in a bar in a garrison town, facing a legionary, he would have been reaching for the reassuring handle of his *gladius*.

"You have information for me?" asked Elissa, quietly.

"In a manner," said Vespillo. "I am acting as an…agent, on behalf of one who has knowledge of a slave that he has reason to believe was once your property."

"Once my property? I can assure you, commander, that I have not relinquished any rights over my property."

"Of course not, mistress," said Vespillo quickly. "My point was that it was uncertain whether this slave was indeed the same as the one you had lost."

"Then describe the slave to me."

Vespillo hesitated, trapped. Describing Rufa and Fabilla to Elissa would make it clear that Vespillo had information about her lost slave, implicating him in Carbo's failure to return Elissa's property.

"She is a young woman, whose most striking feature is her red hair. She has a young daughter, aged around seven years, who has similar hair."

Elissa nodded. "They are mine. Where are they?"

Vespillo spread his hands. "Unfortunately, it isn't quite that simple. The man on whose behalf I have come to you has taken rather a liking to them. He has asked me if you would consider selling them to him."

"No," said Elissa, simply. "Now, if you would make the arrangements for their return, I would be most grateful."

"He has authorised me to offer you a considerable sum of money for them."

"They aren't for sale."

"He mentioned the sum of two hundred *denarii*."

Elissa did not blink at this exorbitant sum of money for the two unskilled female slaves.

"You seem to be having trouble understanding my words, Tribune. You are familiar with Latin?"

Vespillo's eyes narrowed, unaccustomed to being insulted.

"You could buy half a dozen new slaves for that sum, of high quality. May I ask why these two are so important to you?"

Elissa opened her mouth, looking like there was a sharp retort on the tip of her tongue. Then, with a visible effort, her features softened. She looked down, becoming almost coquettish as she glanced back up at him from beneath fluttering eyelids.

"The woman," said Elissa. "She is…special to me."

"Special?" asked Vespillo.

Elissa placed her hand to her throat, stroking it gently, letting her hand trail over her breast, before letting the hand fall back to her lap. The simple movement, so discordant with her previous behaviour, startled Vespillo. He was uncertain whether to be aroused or disturbed. Elissa was undoubtedly beautiful, and the simple erotic gesture stirred him, but he felt a deep distrust of this woman. He had to concede to himself that the distrust stemmed almost entirely from Rufa's story. Now he started to doubt himself. What if Rufa was actually running from Elissa's unwanted amorous advances? He was a man of the world, he was aware that women had needs as well as men, and that they sometimes sated their lusts with female as well as male slaves. It might be said that female slaves offered some advantages, not having similar problems with unwanted pregnancy, or indeed the occasional failure of a male slave to rise to the occasion, terrified of punishment for poor performance.

"I understand, mistress," he said. "Is this your final answer?"

Elissa sighed. "Matters of the heart are rarely overruled by the head. Although I can see the generosity of the offer, I must decline, and ask that my property is returned as soon as possible."

Vespillo considered whether he should change his advice to Carbo. Why risk so much for a woman that could be lying? Slaves lied all the time. That's why their testimony was inadmissible in court unless they had been tortured to get to the truth. He looked down. Beneath his seat, something caught his eye. Something small and dark. He couldn't quite make out what it was.

Shafat appeared behind them. "Apologies, mistress, but you asked to be informed as soon as Pavo arrived."

"Thank you, Shafat, please show him in."

A portly man in his forties entered, flanked by two soldiers of the urban cohorts. He strode straight to Elissa, taking her hand and giving a slight bow. As Elissa greeted the man, her attention off Vespillo momentarily, Vespillo reached down with one hand and retrieved the object from beneath his seat. He looked at it, trying to make sense of what he was seeing. It seemed to be made of cloth, but had been mostly burnt. Parts of it crumbled at his touch, leaving ash on his fingers. Suddenly he realised what he held. It was the cremated remains of a rag doll.

"Mistress Elissa. You asked for my attendance," said the newcomer.

"Thank you so much for coming, Tribune Pavo. Please take a seat. Do you know Lucius Vedius Vespillo?"

Pavo gave a Vespillo a brief glance. "No."

"He is a commander in the *vigiles*."

Pavo laughed. "I understood you wanted the help of the urban cohorts in retrieving some lost property. I don't think you will need the little bucket boys to assist you."

"No, no, Pavo. Vespillo is not here in an official capacity. He has information on the whereabouts of my missing slaves. He was, I believe, about to arrange for their return. I fear you may have had a wasted journey."

Pavo turned towards Vespillo, a look of contempt mixed with resentment on his face.

"A visit to you is never a wasted journey, mistress. But if the matter is successfully resolved in your favour, I am most happy. I am sorry to have interrupted. Please, continue, Vespillo."

"Unfortunately, I don't think things will be that simple. The man on whose behalf I am acting has become very attached to these slaves, and I think will not lightly give them up. I was trying to come to a financial compromise with the mistress here."

"Which I rejected, as you will recall Vespillo. So if you could give the details of their whereabouts to your superior here, the matter can be concluded."

"Pavo does not outrank me," said Vespillo, defensively.

"Nevertheless, I am your superior," said Pavo, pompously.

Vespillo suppressed a flush of anger. He was proud of his men, whatever people called them, however they were regarded. There was no gain though in arguing their position in this situation. He knew that Pavo undoubtedly received the same disrespect in the presence of an officer of the Praetorians. Unless you were Emperor, there was always someone above you.

"The man who sent me is not going to return the slaves, I fear."

Pavo shrugged. "No matter. Just tell me where they are and we will go and get them."

"I don't know the location of the slaves," said Vespillo.

"Then give me the name of the man. We will get him instead, and he will soon reveal where he is keeping them."

"I can't give you his name."

Pavo looked at him sharply. "Why ever not? You do know the penalties for aiding the escape of a slave."

"Of course I do," said Vespillo. "Like you, my job is to uphold the law. Maybe more so. We keep the streets safe for everyone. Your job is largely to maintain civil order, for the benefit of the rich."

Pavo stood, anger on his face. "Tell me his name, you pathetic little bucket boy."

Vespillo stood, too, and moved closer to Pavo, obviously shorter than him, but stronger and fitter. The two soldiers moved up behind Pavo. Vespillo calmed himself with a physical effort.

"I can't give you his name. I don't know it."

"Pah," spat Pavo. "How is that possible?"

"He approached me in a tavern, paid me some coin to convey his message."

"Then you are to meet him again, to give him your reply? We can intercept him then."

"No. Those of us who work the streets at night have a reputation to keep up. We have informers working for us. The *delatores* come to us. Slaves and citizens bring us information. If I give my word to act as an honest broker to a man, and betray him, it will damage our relationship with those we walk the streets with at night, who we live alongside, eat and drink with. I cannot allow it."

"Cannot?" roared Pavo. "I am your superior."

"So you say," said Vespillo. "But you are not my ranking officer, nor do you command me."

Vespillo turned to Elissa. "If your position remains unchanged, I think we are finished here."

Elissa's eyes showed her fury, but she remained composed. Beside her, Glaukos kept a steady, menacing gaze on him. The combination was completely unnerving.

"Think carefully what you are getting yourself into, commander. I will recover my property, by whatever means necessary."

"Good day to you, mistress. And to you, tribune."

Vespillo offered Elissa his hand. It seemed she wouldn't take it, then she looked at it more closely, taking it in delicate fingers and pulling it closer for inspection. There was ash on his fingers, and it transferred onto her. She rubbed at the ash on her pale hand, then looked up at him.

"Apologies, mistress," said Vespillo, insincerely. "Hazard of my job."

He strode towards the exit. The two soldiers of the urban cohorts barred his way temporarily, but an unwavering stare from Vespillo cowed them into parting for him. As he left the *peristylium*, heading out through the *atrium* to the street outside, he heard Pavo shouting.

"Your commander will hear of this!"

Vespillo smiled to himself. They would have to find whichever tavern or whorehouse his commander was holed up in first. He paused outside the front door, suddenly remembering his bladder. He pulled up his tunic and urinated against Elissa's front door.

Inside the *peristylium*, Elissa ignored Pavo's ranting. She looked under Vespillo's seat, and around where he had been sitting, but found nothing, except a slight stain of ash, maybe where a burnt object had sat for a while, not properly cleaned up by the sloppy slaves.

Carbo was waiting anxiously at his tavern for Vespillo's return. When Vespillo arrived, his grim expression told Carbo all he needed to know. Carbo called for Marsia to fetch them both a drink. The bar was reasonably quiet, and they took a table in the corner where they could talk without being disturbed, except by Myia who sat beneath the table and noisily scratched her fleas.

"She said no, then," said Carbo. It was a statement.

Vespillo nodded. "She spun me a story that Rufa was her lover, and she wanted her back because she was emotionally involved with her."

Carbo studied his face. "You believed her, didn't you?"

Vespillo shrugged, semi-apologetically. "I don't know Rufa. I still haven't actually met her. You haven't seen her since she was a child. Maybe she was good and honest and true as a free little girl, but people change. Slavery changes people. Now she could be willing to tell you anything for your help. You must admit, her story does seem a little far-fetched. Elissa's tale of a slave spurning a lover does seem more believable."

"And yet here you are," said Carbo. "Alone, without the urban cohorts to return the slaves to their rightful owners."

Vespillo grimaced. "Don't talk to me about the urban cohorts." He sighed. "Unfortunately, Carbo, I believe Rufa."

Carbo looked at him, surprised. Vespillo drew out a dark, crumbly, carbonised object from beneath the folds of his tunic, and gave it to Carbo. "I found the doll. The child's doll, that Rufa says she saw burnt. I don't know what's going on in that house. Maybe nothing. Maybe Rufa misinterpreted what she saw. But I believe her fear is genuine. I also believe Elissa could be a dangerous adversary. She is certainly well connected."

Carbo let out a deep breath. "So what now?"

Vespillo took a swig of his wine. "Now, I go to bed. I have maybe a few hours before my next night shift starts, and I intend to get as much sleep as I can. We can talk more soon. For the time being, keep her out of sight. Elissa has summoned the urban cohorts to help in the search."

"The urban cohorts? Is that their job?"

"No, they are more for crowd control. You haven't been in Rome for a long time, so maybe you don't remember how the law works here. It is not a military rule though. Basically, the Praetorians protect the Emperor, the urban cohorts keep the peace, and the *vigiles* fight fires and small scale crimes. But a tribune from the urban cohorts turned up at Elissa's house while I was there. Elissa obviously has some pull where she needs it, to get them involved in something like this."

Carbo looked troubled. Vespillo stood and clapped him on the shoulder. He drained his wine glass. "Don't worry. It

will all work out. One way or another." Vespillo gave a
loud yawn, then left. Carbo didn't feel reassured.

Chapter IX

Fabilla sat in the corner of the kitchen, sullen-faced. Marsia tried to interest her in a game of dolls, but Fabilla turned away in disgust, facing the corner. Marsia looked at Rufa, helplessly. Rufa sighed.

"Thanks for trying, Marsia," said Rufa. "I don't think anyone will get through to her when she is in this sort of mood."

Marsia stroked Fabilla's hair affectionately, then left her to her sulk. She approached where Rufa sat, cleaning a large saucepan that contained stubbornly congealed *garum*. "I can see her frustration. The poor girl has been cooped up for three days now. She must be bored out of her mind."

"Don't you think I know that," snapped Rufa. "Well, she is a slave. She had better get used to doing things she doesn't want."

Marsia looked taken aback by the sudden flash of anger. "I'm sorry, Rufa. If my attempts to help are distressing you, I will refrain in future."

Rufa looked like she was about to retort. Then she bit her lip, which had started to tremble. She put the saucepan down.

"No, Marsia, I'm sorry. You didn't deserve that. It's just … so difficult. We are here in hiding, not able to risk showing our faces in case an informer recognises us, or the urban cohorts drag us back to Elissa. I don't know what the future holds. Might we end up back with Elissa, to die at her hands? Or captured and punished as fugitives, whipped, branded, even crucified?" Her voice shook, and she dropped her face into her hands. Sobs racked her body. Marsia put her arm around her shoulder, and held her, unsure what else to do.

A small body interposed itself between the two women. Rufa took her hands away from her face to find Fabilla's arms around her, the child wearing a confused and concerned expression.

"I'm sorry, mother," said Fabilla. "I didn't mean to make you cry." She looked at Marsia seriously. "I'm sorry too, Marsia, for my rudeness."

Rufa smiled at the formal apology, and hugged her daughter to her, tight. The tears continued to flow, the anxiety and depression remained, but the feeling of the warm little girl who was the centre of her world, clutched against her, gave her some sensation of relief.

"Carbo is a good man," said Marsia. "Also, brave, and strong. Trust him."

Rufa nodded uncertainly. Carbo had told her that Elissa had refused to allow him to buy her, although he didn't go into any detail of how the conversation had gone. She got the impression that it wasn't actually him that had visited Elissa. Since then, Carbo had gone about life as normal, helping out in the bar when Marsia and Philon were too busy, going to the bath and the markets, and sleeping in the room with Rufa, Fabilla, Marsia and Myia. Carbo's sleep remained badly disturbed, and his nightmares woke them all. He refused all comfort however, from Marsia or Rufa.

Rufa had noticed though, that when Fabilla saw him upset, and gave him a hug, he did not push the young girl away.

"I do trust him. I just wish I knew what he had in mind."

Philon burst in from the direction of the stairs Myia nipping excitedly at both their heels, yapping and running in small circles. Philon kicked the little dog away.

"Why do I have to sleep on the top floor?" asked Philon, in a loud whiny voice.

Marsia's glare pierced Philon. "Because we have guests that need the space. And because the Master wills it."

"But Marsia, the stairs are so tiring. I have to carry the chamber pot down four flights every time I want to empty it, just because you won't let me tip it out of the window. And everyone knows that if there is a fire, the ones on the top floor are less likely to make it out alive. Why does it have to be me anyway? Why not the newcomers that have caused us all this inconvenience? Not to mention danger."

"Danger?" asked Marsia, her voice low. "In what way are they dangerous?"

"It's obvious they are fugitives from something. Escaped slaves or criminals. Appearing unannounced one night, then hidden away by the Master, never going outside. If they bring prosecution to this household, then you know the slaves will be tortured first before any trial even starts."

Marsia's voice was calm, but her flashing eyes gave Philon pause.

"I suggest you keep those thoughts to yourself, Philon, or you will have the Master to answer to. And worse, me."

Philon looked down, the temper draining from him quickly. Rufa was staring at the floor, her face pale. Fabilla was regarding him curiously. Myia was still wagging her tail.

"Now go and get the tavern ready to open, then get yourself presentable for any clients who want your services."

Philon slouched back up the stairs, scuffing his feet on the steps in a disgruntled manner as he went.

"Are we a danger to you?" asked Rufa, softly. "Is that how you feel?"

Marsia shook her head firmly. "Listen, girl. My loyalty is to the Master. If he wants to show you kindness, then I will extend the same to you. So will Philon, or there will be trouble."

Rufa smiled, her vision still misted by tears. She squeezed Marsia's hand tightly.

"Thank you, Marsia. I mean that."

Marsia nodded curtly, then extricated her hand from Rufa's grip. "Just remember, the Master knows what to do. Now, those saucepans won't clean themselves."

Rufa picked up the *garum* pan, and with one last grateful glance at Marsia, went back to cleaning it.

Carbo lay back in the hot pool in the *caldarium* of the baths, letting the stinging heat that penetrated his flesh ease the stiffness of his joints, and the tightness in his scars. He wondered what to do. Vespillo's advice to remain in the city was sound for the short term, he knew. Rome was a city of a million people, but packed into a small space. It would be unlucky to bump into someone who knew Rufa. It was possible, however, especially in some of the more public places - the temples, the forum, the theatre, the market. What sort of life would it be for her, constantly looking over her shoulder, in fear of recapture, torture, death, for her and her daughter?

In one corner, two men grunted, lifting heavy weights. Their muscles were well-developed, showing they were probably regulars. He watched them for a moment, speculating idly whether their physical closeness was a result of friendship or love. If the latter, which was the giver, and which the taker? He wrinkled his nose at the concept - unlike many of his army colleagues, neither role appealed to him.

His thoughts drifted back to Rufa. She had undoubtedly grown into a beautiful woman in the many years since he had last seen her. Maybe that made it easier to care about her fate, and that of her endearing daughter, who in many ways reminded Carbo of Rufa herself at the same age. His oath would have stood fast though, he realised, whether she was a beautiful slave, a foul-mouthed market trader's wife or the lowest street whore.

She was finding her way into his thoughts often, and he knew that he was becoming attached to her in her own right, not just because of some abstract concept of honour and duty. It surprised him. He had never paid much attention to slaves before. Growing up, his family had been too poor to own any. In the legions, the only slaves belonging to legionaries and centurions were those captured in war, who were usually sold on at the first opportunity.

Generally though, his attitude to slaves was that of the general populace. They were the lowest of the low. The poorest free citizen, or even the former slaves known as freedmen and freedwomen, liked to have someone else to look down on, and the slaves fulfilled this valuable role. Of course, everyone heard of the poor fools whose heads were turned by a pretty male or female slave, and who freed them in order to take them as wife, lover, concubine or catamite. Carbo had always viewed that sort as weak and easily manipulated. Now, was he being the same? No, it was different, he told himself. He had known Rufa when she was free. Besides, there was always his obligation to her.

He was over-analysing, he realised, and it was giving him no help with the decision he had to make. A plump youth, from a rich family to judge by the size of his attending retinue of slaves, jumped high, tucking his legs under him, and landed in the pool with a large splash that covered Carbo and a number of other bathers. When the boy surfaced, he got some filthy looks, but no one dared to say anything to him. Carbo considered whether it was worth the effort of making a scene, but his relaxed muscles begged him not to move, so he closed his eyes and continued to think.

He considered the consequences of ignoring Vespillo's advice against moving Rufa and Fabilla out of Rome. Practically speaking, although there were some risks in getting them out of the city gates, they would not be large. With the volume of wheeled traffic entering and leaving the city after nightfall, it would be a simple matter to conceal the female slaves in an empty cart for the transit through the gates and beyond the walls. After that, it was just a matter of deciding where they would go. The first place would be

Carbo's farm in Campania. After that, Rufa could decide her own fate. She would need some help though. A single mother and daughter would not last long in the countryside without a family to protect her. They would quickly end up at the mercy of bandits, robbed, raped, enslaved, murdered.

So just relocating her would not end his obligation. He would have to find her a husband, a task he had no idea how to go about. Alternatively, he could set her up with a small property, some money and some slaves of her own, for protection and income. That would eat significantly into his own wealth, however. Not that that course of action was out of the question. Carbo just didn't want to start working for a living, at his age, his body worn out by twenty five years of active service.

Briefly, it occurred to him that he could take her for a wife himself. She was beautiful and obviously fertile. Was there much more that any man needed? Then, as his thoughts drifted to a life of matrimony with Rufa, and to the marriage bed, decades old images flashed into his mind. He could see, so clearly, the priestess standing in front of him, brandishing the small knife. He felt his hands bound behind him, wrapped around a tree in a glade. The screams of the victims of the depilator in the baths sounded to him like the screams of his comrades as they bled out through unstaunched castration wounds. The laughter of the athletes practicing sounded like the mocking laughter of the German warriors as they watched the fear in his eyes, pointed at his naked body, the way his manhood shrivelled in fear, then leaked urine uncontrollably.

Carbo's heart started to pound, loud and fast, the blood rushing in his ears. He felt dizzy, his stomach tensed, his chest started to get tight, and he couldn't seem to take a deep enough breath. His fingers started to tingle as panic rose inside him. He started to look around him wildly, searching for a way to escape.

A huge splash into the pool drenched him again, and broke the attack he had been seized by. He took some deep breaths, feeling his heart slow, his muscles relax. The rich youth swam back to the side, a self-satisfied grin on his face. Carbo reached out with one hand and pushed the boy's head under the water. Fist clenched in the boy's hair, Carbo held him under for a count of ten, before pulling him up to the surface.

The boy sputtered and coughed for a moment, then screamed at Carbo. "How dare you assault me!"

Carbo let him go. "Be more considerate of other users of this place in future."

"I will do as I please. I am the son of an equestrian!"

Carbo ducked him again The boy's attendants now stepped forward in alarm, but Carbo held up a threatening hand. "Don't come any closer," he told them, "Or the boy drowns."

They hesitated, while Carbo counted to fifteen, then let the boy surface. This time the boy took longer to get his breath back. He turned to his slaves, and yelled, "Don't just stand there. Beat this man!"

The slaves did not look like they were used for any physical labour. The most senior of them was an elderly man who probably served as a scribe or bookkeeper for the boy's father. He sized up Carbo's muscular, scarred torso which was visible above the water, then reached a hand down to the boy and pulled him from the pool.

"I think," said the slave, "It is time to get you home to your father. I think it best we don't tell him about the scene you made here. You know how he feels about being publicly embarrassed."

The youth blanched at these words. He looked at Carbo from the side of the pool, his pride and fear at war. Fear won, although Carbo could not say whether it was fear of Carbo himself, or the boy's father. The slaves dried the boy off with a woollen towel, rather roughly, then helped him dress in tunic and jewellery, before ushering him out of the building.

After the youth had gone, a couple of the other bathers laughed, and clapped Carbo in a congratulatory manner on the shoulder. Carbo was pleased the distraction had dispersed most of his panic. He was left with a feeling of unease in the bottom of his stomach though, and sighed at the loss of the relaxed state he had achieved. He pulled himself out of the pool, dried himself, dressed, and walked out into the street.

He stopped at the stall of a food seller, and bought a hot sausage, topped with cheese and *garum*, with some bread. He ate pickily, appetite a little reduced by the anxious feeling that lingered, but the spicy sauce just maintained his interest in the meal. The attack reminded him why he was single, why he wasn't looking for a woman. Marrying Rufa was clearly out of the question, if the mere thought of it made him feel like that. Finding her a husband would be difficult given his tiny social circle. Finding one who didn't ask questions about her past would be impossible, especially with her brand. Setting her up somewhere on her own was a possibility, although he feared for the safety of any young woman without a male protector, be it father, brother or husband, in city, town or countryside.

The only answer seemed to be to resolve her slave status. Have her lawfully free, and he could then protect her as long as it was needed for her to get on her own feet, find herself a husband, and start the life most Roman women aspired to, matron of her own family. Yet if Rufa's mistress, Elissa, had rejected a financial offer, what other recourse did he have to persuade the woman to free her? He wondered about the strange ritual that Rufa had observed, the strange threats she had overheard. Rufa was sure she had heard the phrases "Rome's punishment" and "the day of retribution." They sounded like the ravings of a cultist, praying to their gods to rain vengeance down on their enemies. Still, the authorities tended to frown on that sort of behaviour. Keeping the peace among the masses of Rome was paramount. The carrots they offered were the corn dole and the free entertainments such as the theatre and the games. The stick was often literally a stick, usually wielded by a member of the urban cohorts who enjoyed his job too much.

Maybe if Carbo found out more about Elissa's cult and her plans, he could find some leverage to persuade her to give Rufa up. He finished off the last of his sausage and stood. The knowledge that he had decided to take action eased the remainder of his anxiety, and he even smiled a little. He took a slow walk back to the tavern, his mind working out a plan.

Chapter X

The tavern was full, business brisk. Carbo sat on a stool outside, enjoying the cool early evening air, lost in his thoughts, only vaguely aware of the noisy throng of people crowding the streets, some trying to finish their chores before the dangers of being out at night caught up with them, the braver and burlier ones just starting the night's revelry. Marsia was serving a hot trade of drinks, sausages, soup, and lashings of *garum*. Philon waited on the customers, clearing up, topping up empty cups and glasses, and as required, taking them into the cubicle and attending to their other needs.

Marsia noticed a young man with a severely pox-scarred face sitting alone without a drink. She carried a jug of wine to him and smiled.

"Can I help, sir?"

He looked up at her. "Mend a broken heart?"

Marsia glanced around her. Philon seemed to be coping, so she pulled over a stool and sat with him.

"I can only offer wine I'm afraid, and a friendly ear. Do you want to talk about it?"

She poured him a cup of wine from the jug. He took a deep drink, wiped his mouth, and looked at her steadily. Something in her guileless face seemed to open him up.

"I'm sure it's a story you have heard a thousand times before. I spend my days keeping the peace on Rome's streets. In the evenings I return home to the family I support with my meagre wages."

"You are in the Urban Cohorts?" asked Marsia.

The man nodded. "These last five years. It keeps a roof over our heads, food in our bellies, and the bailiffs away from the door."

Marsia nodded, listening attentively.

"I've been married for four years, to the daughter of a freedman. Frankly, she married above her station. But I found her pretty, funny. Ran a good household. Fantastic when the lamps are blown out, if you get my meaning."

Marsia smiled knowingly.

"Life was good I thought. I loved her. We have a baby son. Then today, I injure my ankle on the training ground, so the centurion sends me home early. Fourth floor of the *insula*, I limp to the top, and walk in on my darling wife on her back, with the son of the fishmonger from the shop below in between her legs. My baby son was there, in his basket, while she fucked a spotty kid who smelled of *garum*." He frowned. "At least, I think the baby is mine."

Marsia took his hand, tenderly. "What did you do?"

"Walked straight back out, before she said anything. Came straight to the nearest tavern. And here I am, trying to get drunk. I'm on my fourth though, and it doesn't seem to be working yet." He took another swig.

"I'm Marsia."

"Gaius Ambrosius Barbatus," said the urban cohort legionary.

Marsia gave him a sympathetic look and squeezed his hand. "What do you intend to do?"

"Tonight? Just carry on getting drunk. Pass out in some back alley."

"And tomorrow?"

"Who knows? I'm *paterfamilias*. I could beat her. I could throw her on the street. I could kill her."

"Will you?"

Barbatus shook his head. "That's a decision for tomorrow."

"Maybe you should find some company for tonight then, sir."

Barbatus hesitated, then sighed.

"I can't say I'm not tempted. You are very beautiful. But thank you, no. I think I would find it… painful."

Marsia smiled. "I didn't mean me anyway, sir, I don't serve in that way." She patted his face. "You have my sympathy, Master.

Barbatus smiled and returned to his drink. Marsia walked over to the bar to replenish her serving jug. Philon put a hand on her arm. "What's his story?"

Marsia shook her head. "He's a legionary in the Urban Cohorts. Just caught his wife cheating on him. He wants to drown his sorrows."

"His purse looks full. He doesn't want a roll on the mattress?"

"I suggested he should find a girl. I think he is just too sad."

Philon looked speculative. "Maybe he wants something different?"

Marsia glanced at him. "I think he just wants to be left alone. But you are welcome to try."

Philon picked up a jug and walked over to Barbatus' table.

"Would you like a refill, sir?" asked Philon.

Barbatus nodded and held up his cup. Philon poured.

"Marsia told me your sad story. May I sit, sir?"

Barbatus grunted unenthusiastic assent, and Philon sat next to him.

"My girl says she would marry me,
Though Jupiter himself came calling,
But what a woman says to her passionate lover,
Should be written in wind and flowing water."

Barbatus looked at him. "What?"

"It's Catullus, sir."

"What is?"

"That quote. It was written by the poet Catullus, when he was rejected by his lover, Lesbia."

"Never heard of him," said Barbatus.

"He speaks of the faithlessness of women."

Barbatus laughed mirthlessly. "Well, he has that right."

"I think the company of other men is far preferable to that of weak, cheating, unreliable women, don't you?"

Barbatus eyed him suspiciously. "I think the only person anyone can rely on is himself. And even then, only with caution."

"Many of the greatest warriors of my race would rather be with a man than a woman. Achilles and Patroclus. Alexander with his eunuch, Bagoas."

Barbatus studied Philon's round features, plump figure, smooth skin. "You are a eunuch yourself aren't you?"

"I am, sir. It makes me the ideal male companion to one seeking comfort and solace."

"A eunuch. Lucky you. You experience the pain of castration in one go, then it is forever behind you. I envy you. Me, I will have to go on living with this pain."

"I would like to help you sir. I am very experienced, I know how to make a man feel pleasure, ease his pain."

"I told your fellow slave, I'm not interested tonight."

"I see," said Philon, looking crestfallen.

Barbatus clapped Philon's shoulder.

"Don't worry. You are a pretty boy, I'm sure you will find plenty of takers. Even if you don't, at least you will sleep under a roof tonight, fed and clothed, unlike the homeless and runaways. You know, yesterday, we were told to keep our eyes open for a fugitive slave. Us, the urban cohorts! Who do they think we are, *fugitivarii or* the *vigiles*?"

"What was special about that slave then, sir?"

"Buggered if I know. Nothing as far as I could tell. Except we are told she has vivid red hair. She is hardly the only one in the city though. Whole thing is a wild goose chase."

Barbatus drained his cup and stood, swaying a little and putting one hand on the table to steady himself.

"I'm going for a walk to clear my head. Then to another bar. And another one. Then I'll either pass out in a back alley, or throw myself in the Tiber. Haven't decided which yet."

Philon nodded, distracted. "Have a good evening, sir."

Barbatus staggered out into the street. Philon looked towards the back door to the kitchen, where he knew Rufa was busy cooking and washing up. He sat in quiet thought for a moment, then carried on with his work.

It was early evening, dark not long fallen. Carbo looked around the headquarters of the second cohort of the *vigiles urbani*. The building looked like it was once the domestic dwelling of a reasonably well to do family. Frescos of tranquil pastoral scenes covered the walls, and some of the original furniture remained. They were in what Carbo presumed was originally the *tablinum*, which Vespillo had turned into an office. Nearby hovered a slight, youthful member of the cohort that Carbo supposed served as Vespillo's secretary, judging by the way Vespillo occasionally barked orders at him. Taura, the senior centurion of the cohort who commanded the first century, and was Vespillo's deputy, was sitting at a desk, laboriously writing a report, with much cursing and scribbling out of mistakes. Taura had given Carbo a grumpy greeting when he had arrived a short while earlier, remembering him from his previous visit, and now shot him filthy looks from time to time. Occasionally, Carbo heard him muttering words he was sure he was supposed to overhear, like "cursed civilians," and "hanging around like a bad smell."

Carbo was sitting on a stone bench, while opposite him, with his feet up on a stool, Vespillo lounged on a cushioned wooden chair. Carbo asked him what had happened to the former owners of the house.

"Not a clue, this was already requisitioned as the cohort headquarters a long time ago. I was only appointed tribune a few months ago. Plancus, do you know?"

The secretary spoke up in a thin, slightly nervous voice. "The records show that the current headquarters of the second cohort of the *vigiles urbani*, belonged to one Gaius Volumnius Ambustus."

Vespillo laughed, and Carbo looked at him curiously. "Ambustus? How ironic, that the fire station should once have belonged to someone whose name means burnt."

Carbo smiled, and opened his mouth to change the subject, but Plancus continued.

"The house was requisitioned fifteen years ago, as part of the development of the *vigiles*. The owner was compensated, and moved out. Initially this place was the headquarters for only two hundred men, mainly due to trouble recruiting. After the *Lex vesillia* was passed three years ago, which decreed that any freedman who had completed six years of service in the *vigiles* would be granted full citizenship, recruitment became easier, and the cohort grew to its present size of seven centuries, each of around eighty men when at full strength with no illness or injuries."

"Is he always like this?" asked Carbo.

"He used to be secretary to an equestrian who fancied himself a historian. It seems to have rubbed off on him. His master died without ever publishing anything memorable, but he freed Plancus in his will. How far are you through your six years of service. Before you become a citizen?"

"Just a year, so far, sir."

"How old are you, soldier?" asked Carbo.

Plancus drew himself up a little taller at being addressed like a legionary. Carbo realised that the *vigiles,* drawn from the ranks of freedmen, considered the lowest of all the men under arms within the Empire, must have some serious issues with self-esteem.

"Seventeen, sir."

"You look like a fine member of the cohort, soldier."

"Thank you, sir," said the boy, beaming.

Vespillo shook his head at Plancus' enthusiasm.

"May we talk privately?" asked Carbo.

Vespillo nodded. "Plancus, Taura. Would you mind?"

Plancus gave an enthusiastic salute and hurried from the room. Taura appeared to glare at the writing on his desk for a moment, then slowly stood and left.

"Grumpy bastard that one, isn't he?" said Carbo.

Vespillo laughed. "He does his job. Keeps the men in line too. Discipline is a constant problem in the *vigiles.* Despite how you addressed Plancus, these men aren't soldiers. They are a motley crew of clueless ex-domestic slaves like Plancus, cutthroats who would probably be rotting on a cross if they weren't serving in the cohort, homeless down and outs who would starve if they didn't serve here, and wannabe legionaries who like to boss the civilians around, pretending to be Praetorians or members of the urban cohorts or something."

"How did you come to be tribune of this lot then? Surely someone with your military experience would be better serving in a regular unit like the urban cohorts. Or just retiring with your pension?"

Vespillo grimaced. "That's a long story. You want to talk about your problem I take it?"

Carbo noted the abrupt subject change and decided not to pursue it.

"Yes, I wanted some more of your advice. Maybe your help too."

"Go on."

"My options are limited. I don't think helping her escape from the city, nor hiding her within the city are solutions. With her hair, although she isn't unique, she is quite distinctive. The city is full of informers looking to make a quick *denarius*. And finding her somewhere to live in the countryside, well that leaves her open to the slave hunters and the bandits."

"You have thought of finding her a husband?"

"I have," Carbo said. "She has a brand. He would have to be complicit, and who could I trust that wouldn't rather take the reward for her return than keep her?"

"So manumission is the only solution?"

"The only one that I can think of. But her Mistress seems unmoved by financial incentives. What are the other options to persuade this woman to free her?"

"Physical threats. Intimidation. Blackmail. Murder?" he said, matter of factly.

Carbo frowned. "Aren't you supposed to be upholding the law?"

Vespillo shrugged. "Just stating the facts. Doesn't mean I condone any of those, but you asked for the options."

"Well I'm not going to go in there and kill her. I don't want to have my head cut off or be thrown in the Tiber.

Physical threats and intimidation, maybe. I'm not one to shrink for a fight, but would she be intimidated by one man, when she has a house full of slaves to protect her?"

"Blackmail, then?" suggested Vespillo. "We do keep coming back to this odd cult that seems to be at the centre of her strange behaviour."

"I need to find out more about it, don't I? But where do I start? I know nothing about cults."

"Me neither," said Vespillo. "But I know a man who does."

Carbo raised his eyebrows, curious.

"I am going out on patrol soon. I'm not the type of commander to sit behind a desk all night."

"I noticed," said Carbo with a smile, remembering their first meeting.

"We can take the patrol past the house of Kahotep, and pay him a little visit."

Chapter XI

Carbo and Vespillo walked through the Vth Esquiliae district, one of the fourteen administrative regions into which Augustus had divided the city, over thirty years before. The sky was clear and starry, but the moon was hiding behind the buildings, and the tall *insulae* lining the streets allowed almost no light to filter down to ground level. The doors to the houses and shops were boarded up as tight as the Mamertine prison, the windows shuttered or secured by iron railings. Within the larger dwellings, a porter would be awake, sometimes chained in the atrium to make sure he did not desert his post. Beware of the Dog signs were common.

They were accompanied by fourteen men from one of the centuries of the *vigiles*. Each man carried an axe, a pick, or a hook on a rope, to help pull down burning buildings, and a couple carried torches to light the gloom. Carbo noticed that his companions were alert but relaxed. The terror that the night streets of Rome held for ordinary citizens was laughed at by these men, who spent half their waking lives patrolling after sun down.

Vespillo intermittently tutted and grimaced as he looked at the closely packed, flammable buildings.

"You know, a fire in the wrong place, on a windy, dry day, and all this could go up. One of these days, the whole of Rome will burn, you mark my words."

Carbo looked at him sidelong. "You're cheery."

Vespillo shook his head. "It feels like being in a fight against barbarians, outnumbered, waiting for the inevitable. Recruitment is hard. It's not a glamorous job, it's dangerous and poorly paid. Even with the *Lex Visellia,* we are far from full capacity. Then we keep getting pulled away from our duties to help out with crowd control, as we are at the moment with the *Ludi Romani* in full swing. We will be really stretched on the last day of the Games when the whole city will be out. The Gods protect Rome from fire that night."

A cry for help came from a tiny side street. Vespillo nodded to two of his men, and they set off at a run. Carbo followed a little slower, cursing at the stiffness in his leg, courtesy of his old wound. Turning the corner into the little dead end street, they came across a man lying on the ground, toga in disarray, curled up in a foetal position as two men laid into him with feet and sticks. Standing on the far side of them, a smaller man carrying a knife watched the assault with a grin on his face. He hefted a purse in one hand, presumably belonging to the prostrate victim.

"Halt," yelled Vespillo. The man with the knife and purse looked up, and rushed at the watchmen, brushing them aside as he headed for the exit to the alley. He reached what he presumed would be safety just as Carbo turned the corner. Carbo stuck out a straight, stiff arm, and the fleeing man ran full into it, head snapping back, feet continuing running, so he slammed into the ground with the full weight of his limp body. Carbo kicked him in the head to make sure that he wasn't getting up again, then retrieved the knife and purse.

The two muggers still in the alley were slower to react. Vespillo drew his sword, and his two men hefted their axes menacingly. One of the muggers charged them with a roar, wielding a thick club at the tribune's head. He ducked the clumsy blow and slashed his sword backhand across the back of the man's legs, hamstringing him in a single stroke. The man's legs stopped functioning and he tumbled to the ground. The other mugger dropped his club and fell to his knees in supplication. Vespillo's men led the two muggers away, one walking, one unable to walk and being dragged by the collar of his tunic, crying in pain and pleading for mercy.

Vespillo knelt by the injured victim, who was hugging himself and moaning softly. Carbo appeared by his side, the mugger he had dealt with slung over his shoulder. Vespillo looked up at Carbo.

"How are your healing skills?"

"I'm no *medicus,* but my skills are probably as good as yours. You pick up a few things when you have been in battle a lot."

Carbo dumped his unconscious load, and crouched down by Vespillo.

"Can you tell us your name, citizen?" asked Carbo in a loud voice. The man made some indistinct noises. Carbo ran his hands over the man deftly, provoking more groans when his fingers probed injuries.

"Head injuries, but I can't feel a skull fracture. Bleeding from his nose and mouth, but not from his ears. Some broken ribs, but I don't think his lungs are punctured, his breathing seems ok. Limbs bruised but not broken. Might be bleeding internally, might not. I guess that will decide whether he lives or dies."

Vespillo nodded agreement. "We have four *medici* stationed permanently at the station house. They can do their best for him."

"Four?" Carbo raised his eyebrows. "That's a lot more than in the legions."

"No offence, Carbo, but battles aren't that common in the legions. The *medici* there mainly stitch up wounds from bar room brawls. The fires and the criminals keep our *medici* pretty busy every night."

The rest of the patrol had now arrived, alerted by their colleagues escorting the arrested muggers away that more help might be required. Vespillo allocated two to carry the victim back to the headquarters, two to carry the mugger that Carbo had knocked out, and four to escort the two conscious thieves back to the holding cells.

After they departed, the street became quiet again, although the sounds of the night carried to them from further away - the revellers, the rumble of wheeled traffic on the main roads and the sound of the hooves of the horses, mules and oxen. The smell of the night was subtly changed as well, the dusty odour replaced by something a bit damper and more cloying. Dogs barked incessantly, sensitive to any sound that might threaten their Master's home. Calls rang out from those who couldn't make a living during the day or found it more profitable to work at night. The wine sellers, the snack merchants, the older prostitutes, all tried to outshout each other to advertise their wares to the nocturnal denizens of the city. In this little back alley though, the doors and windows remained shuttered, the inhabitants not daring to peek out.

The depleted group carried on their patrol, six watchmen with their commander, and the strange experience of having a guest patrolling with them. Carbo caught the odd muttered comment from the men behind him, speculating, making barbed comments about his limp. He was used to ignoring minor insubordination from the ranks, though. You had to pick your battles. In his time as a leader of men in the legions, he had slapped down anything overtly disrespectful. Anything else was just blowing off steam. Vespillo wasn't so tolerant, and when he overheard one snide comment, he halted the patrol, took the offender aside and gave him a stern verbal dressing down.

Carbo was impressed with the controlled way the commander disciplined the man, a thuggish looking Gaul. The tall, well built young man with long blonde hair towered over Vespillo, but he bowed his bed as he took the reprimand. When the patrol continued, the *vigiles* were quieter and more respectful.

Vespillo pounded on the wooden door at the end of a dark street. A hulking bodyguard slave, armed with a club, lounged sullenly against the wall, eyeing them suspiciously. A sign painted on the door outside showed a collection of astrological symbols. Carbo thought he recognised a ram and a crab, and some others more obscure. The door was opened by a beautiful, dark-skinned slave with a beatific expression, dressed in a simple white robe. A waft of sweet perfume and incense accompanied her.

"We are here to see Kahotep," said Vespillo.

The slave's voice was soft, with a strong Numidian accent. "He is performing a ceremony at the moment, Master."

Vespillo pushed the door open and gently eased the girl out of the way.

"I'm sure he won't mind us waiting."

The watchmen remained outside, and Carbo and Vespillo entered a small atrium. Further inside, in the *tablinum,* they could see two figures seated on cushions. The nearest, with their back to them, was a middle aged lady. Her elaborate hairstyle and gold jewellery marked her out as a matron in a well to do family. Facing them was a round-faced man with narrow set eyes, a pointy nose and a completely bald head. His eyes were closed, and he held the woman's hands, palms upwards, lightly in his own. He was chanting, a language Carbo didn't recognise, his voice rising and falling theatrically. An incense burner spewed out large quantities of sweet smelling smoke.

Vespillo folded his arms and leaned against a wall, a smirk on his face. Carbo looked across at him, then copied him, waiting patiently.

Eyes still closed, the bald man started talking in Latin with a heavy Egyptian accent, his voice slow and soft. "The gods are listening now, Mistress. Speak. Ask them what you want to know, what boon you desire."

The matron spoke. "O gods, tell me, I humbly beseech you. Answer my question."

There was a pause. The silence became prolonged and the woman began to fidget on her cushion. She started to speak again, but was interrupted by the bald man. His voice was high pitched, but powerful now, the words loud and slow.

"I am Isis. Who calls on me?"

The woman started to shake. Her voice was quiet now, trembling. "O Isis. I, Dullia Crispina, ask you this question. Is my husband true to me? Does he honour me? Or does he betray me, with the slaves, the prostitutes, the neighbours?" She hesitated and her voice became a whisper. "My sister?"

Another pause. Despite himself, Carbo could feel a tension rising inside himself, waiting for the answer.

"Your husband…" said the bald man in the high voice. The woman was stone still now, her full attention fixed on the man. "Your husband…" His voice trailed off. Then he spoke in his normal voice. "I have lost the connection with her," he said, sounding deflated.

The woman let out a little moan. The man laid a hand on her knee, reassuringly. "Let me get my breath back," he said wearily. "It is draining on my spirit. I will try again momentarily. We did discuss my fee didn't we?"

The woman nodded. "Two *aurei*, we said."

"We did, we did," agreed the man. "I wonder though, if the goddess feels the sum is a little, ahem, paltry."

"Paltry?" said the woman, her voice rising.

"Oh, it is more than adequate for my humble services, Mistress," said the man. "But the money all goes towards the honouring of the goddess. Maybe she feels dishonoured."

The woman seemed doubtful. "How much do you suggest?"

"Oh, it is not my place to suggest a donation to the goddess."

The woman reached into her purse and counted out four golden coins. The man looked each one over carefully, tucked them into a fold in his tunic, and then took her hands again. Eyes tight closed, he spoke again in the high voice.

"I, the goddess Isis, am here, Dullia Crispina. You ask, is your husband true? Does he betray you, with the slaves, the prostitutes, the neighbours, or your sister? The answer is..."

Dullia Crispina leaned forward, quivering slightly.

"The answer is, your husband is true." The woman's shoulders slumped in relief. The man moaned, and fell to one side, limbs rigid, twitching and thrashing. The woman looked at him in alarm. Carbo started forwards as well, but Vespillo laid a retraining hand on his arm. The twitching and thrashing subsided. Slowly, the man sat upright again.

"My apologies, Mistress. When the goddess leaves me, I am sometimes taken by a seizure. It is a curse of my calling, but one I bear willingly. Did you get your answer?"

"Yes," said Dullia Crispina, her voice still a little shaky. "Thank you. Thank you Kahotep, so much. You don't know how much the reassurance means to me."

Kahotep smiled softly. "I am but a vessel for the gods and goddesses. Do them honour and that is thanks enough for me." He noticed Carbo and Vespillo now, lurking in the shadows of the atrium, and his eyebrows went up. "And now, Mistress, would you please excuse me? I see the next seekers of answers and enlightenment are waiting for my humble skills."

"Of course, Kahotep." She stood, and Kahotep stood with her, and bowed, then ushered her out, casting Vespillo a filthy glance as, with the help of his slave girl, he showed her to the door.

"A good evening to you, Dullia Crispina. Make sure your slave conveys you straight home. The streets of Rome are such a worry at this time of night."

"No one scares my slave, Kahotep." She laid a proprietary hand on his arm, and the look she gave him made Carbo wonder if she was being true to her husband.

"Thank you, Kahotep, for everything."

"My pleasure, Mistress," said Kahotep, bowing again. He closed the door behind her, then turned to Vespillo, the smile that had seemed frozen to his face dropping away instantly.

"Vespillo, you cock sucker," he said, his accent suddenly becoming the vulgar Roman of the streets and *insulae*. "What are you doing here, by Juno's dry cunt?"

"A pleasure to see you, too, Kahotep."

"I was working!" he spat. "How dare you interrupt me?"

"Do you have a bucket of water?" asked Vespillo.

Kahotep looked non-plussed. "What are you talking about?"

"It is my right and duty, as a tribune of the *vigiles* to make sure that every homeowner has a supply of firefighting equipment. So, do you have a bucket of water?"

"No I don't have a donkey-fucking bucket of water."

"I see," said Vespillo. "Sand? A soaked blanket?"

"No," said Kahotep, angrily. "I don't have a bucket of water, a soaked blanket, a siphon, or a hundred drunk Gallic slaves trained to piss on command."

"Oh, dear. Do you know the penalty for failing to protect your house against fire? I could have you beaten. Or maybe I could fine you those four *aurei* that you took from that poor gullible woman?"

"Gullible?" blustered Kahotep. "She got an answer from the goddess."

"So she thinks. I must admit the seizure was impressive. You should be in the theatre. I presume you intend to blackmail the husband now you know she suspects him?"

"Certainly not," protested Kahotep. "I show people the way to the gods. That is all. Now what do you want, or did you just come here to harass me to get your kicks?"

"Well, maybe we could forego the fun of having you beaten, if you could give us a few moments of your time?"

Kahotep grudgingly beckoned them in, and showed them to seats.

"I'm thirsty, aren't you, Carbo?"

Carbo nodded agreement.

Kahotep tutted, then called out.

"Dahia, get something cheap for these two intruders. I mean guests." The dark-skinned slave nodded and fetched them watered wine. When they had full cups, and had taken long draughts of the drink, Vespillo leaned back.

"Why don't you tell Carbo what it is you actually do, Kahotep?"

Kahotep rolled his eyes, his Egyptian accent returning. "Who can explain the wind, dear Vespillo, the sun, the mysteries of birth and life? I have spent my life trying to understand the world, our relationship to the gods, and our humble place in the grand scheme. That small level of understanding that I have achieved, it is my duty to pass on to those who are in need. Those who need comfort, or reassurance, or want to know how best to do honour to the gods."

Carbo looked at Vespillo. "He fleeces idiots for cash, then?"

Kahotep opened his mouth to protest, but Vespillo just laughed. "Of course. But in order to be convincing, he has had to learn a lot about religion, and the cults and mysteries. That's why we are here. You didn't think we were going to have our fortunes told?"

Carbo shook his head, and looked at Kahotep, who was sitting with arms folded, mouth drawn into a tight line.

"Forgive us, Kahotep. We are mocking, and yet I have come to you for help. I need to know more about a particular religion or cult, but don't know where to start. Vespillo suggested you."

"I see," said Kahotep. "Of course, my time isn't free. Not that I need money for myself, you understand, but I got to have the resources to appease the gods, with offerings, libations, sacrifices, don't I? Even incense don't come cheap..."

"How about we see how many widows you can cheat from a cell at headquarters?" said Vespillo.

Kahotep started to bluster about threats and injustice, but Carbo held up a hand. "No, Vespillo, he is right, he should be compensated for his time." Carbo proffered a *denarius*, which Kahotep took with a suspicion. He inspected it, pocketed it and then sighed. His voice became soft and low.

"Ask then, knowledge seeker, and this humble servant of the gods will answer to the best of his poor ability."

"What do you know about Ba'al Hammon and Tanit?"

Kahotep's eyes widened, and his eyes flickered around the room, as if worried that someone would overhear.

"Why do you ask about them?"

"I have paid to ask the questions," said Carbo.

Kahotep looked thoughtful. His words when they came, seemed guarded. "Ba'al Hammon was the chief god of the Carthaginians. Tanit, the patron goddess of Carthage, was his bride."

"So they are just like Jupiter and Juno?"

"Not exactly. Ba'al Hammon has been compared to Saturn. Tanit is still worshipped openly in North Africa, where she is now called Juno Caelestis. Her symbol is still found frequently there."

"What is her symbol?" asked Vespillo. Kahotep took a wax tablet and drew an abstract figure, a trapezium, topped by a horizontal line and a circle, which looked like a child's drawing of a woman in a dress.

"So worshipping Saturn and Juno seems pretty harmless. Are their worshippers generous with their gifts, as we are during our Saturnalia festival?"

"If only it was that benign. The sacrifices these gods demand from their followers…" Kahotep shook his head. Vespillo and Carbo looked at him steadily, and he swallowed, and continued.

"If a Carthaginian wanted a favour of the gods, they would sacrifice to them. For simple things, every day requests, they would sacrifice flour, sheep, calves, doves, just like we do. But if it was something very important, then Ba'al Hammon and Tanit would demand a child."

Carbo felt a chill run down his spine and he looked at Vespillo, who returned his gaze, face set.

Kahotep continued. "There would be a statue of Ba'al Hammon or maybe the lady Tanit, in a place known as a tophet, or roasting-place. The statue was made with arms stretched out and up, and they led down to a hole and a hollow centre. A fire was built at the base of the statue, and when it was hot enough, the baby would be placed on the arms. When the time was right, it was released, and it would roll down into the fire. Loud music would be played on flutes and drums, so the relatives, who were not allowed to weep, would not hear the baby's screams, or the noises that were made as it was consumed."

Carbo saw Vespillo staring at the floor, looking sick. He looked back to Kahotep, uncertain what to say.

Kahotep sighed. "In the most ancient times of the city, the nobles would sacrifice their own children for the safety of Carthage. Diodorus Siculus' *Bibliotecha historica* tells us that in later years, the Carthaginian nobility bought and reared children to sacrifice, the way the rearers and sellers of doves in the market place do nowadays. When Carthage was defeated by Agathocles of Syracuse, the nobles feared they had displeased the gods with this practice, and sacrificed three hundred high born children who had escaped the flames because of this practice of substitution, and a further two hundred to make amends. The gods alone know how many were sacrificed during the Punic wars, when the Carthaginians rightly feared their city would be destroyed."

"But Carthage was destroyed over two hundred years ago," said Carbo. "This worship, these...practices, surely they were stamped out at the time?"

"Who can truly ever kill a belief? For certain, there are still pockets of worship of the Lord Ba'al Hammon and the Lady Tanit in North Africa."

"And in Rome?"

Kahotep hesitated. "I have no direct knowledge of such a cult in Rome."

Vespillo looked menacing. "If you have any information, Kahotep, of such a vile thing happening here..."

"No, no," said Kahotep, hastily. "I really know nothing. But... I hear things."

"Go on," said Carbo.

"I hear mention of a tophet, a moloch, a sacrifice. I hear whispers of a return of the Lord and Lady. I hear that when they come, Rome will be destroyed."

Vespillo laughed without humour. "The fantasy of every ground down minority with a grudge in Rome, and there are plenty of them."

Carbo looked into Kahotep's eyes, and saw fear there. He felt the same feeling in the pit of his stomach, and shook his head, feeling foolish that these stories to scare children would be affecting him in such a way.

"Thank you for your time, Kahotep." Carbo stood, and handed him another coin. Vespillo drained his drink, and stood too.

"Get a bucket of water and a soaked blanket," said Vespillo. "I will be back to check. And if you hear anything else on this subject, make sure you come to me."

Kahotep nodded, grudgingly.

"We will see ourselves out."

Vespillo and Carbo left, and Kahotep looked thoughtful.

"Dahia," he said. "This worries me. You have your ear to the ground. Have you heard anything of this new cult?"

Dahia looked him in the eyes and said sincerely, "No, master, nothing."

Outside, away from the thick scent of incense, Carbo took a few deep breaths.

"More evidence that your slave has been speaking the truth."

"She isn't my slave," snapped Carbo, still feeling nettled by the horrific words he had heard.

"Whatever she is then. Maybe soon we should pay Elissa another visit. It sounds like there might be more to interest me here than just an escaped slave."

Chapter XII

Vespillo and Carbo met up with the watchmen and resumed their patrol, a thoughtful quiet having descended on the pair. They hadn't gone far, when Vespillo held up a hand for the party to halt. He sniffed the air, turning his head left to right and cocking his head on one side. Carbo took a deep breath through his nose, but could only smell the usual fetid stench of a Roman street, the mingled smell of human and animal faeces, the ammoniacal smell of urine from the same sources, as well as from the fuller's shops, rotting corpses, human and animal, and the waste products of the households that lined the street.

Vespillo however, had noticed something else. He indicated a direction for the party to take, and they followed him. Shortly, Carbo started to pick out a different smell in the still air. Smoke.

Not long after, he could see a glow that flickered over the rooftops, and could hear distant shouts and screams. Vespillo and his men broke into a run and Carbo sighed as he followed, wincing with each step at the pain in his leg.

When he caught up with them, he found that Vespillo had taken charge. Another patrol had converged on the same spot, and they were all waiting for Vespillo's orders. The fire had started in the first floor of an *insula*, in a typically packed part of the city. A fat woman was loudly berating her husband for failing to extinguish their brazier before they slept.

"You oaf, I tell you every night that this could happen. We've lost everything, you useless fool!"

"I swear I put it out," he protested. "I don't know how this could have happened."

Carbo stared at the flames, his guts tightening. He stepped back uncertainly.

Vespillo directed one man to fetch the heavy fire fighting equipment from the *excubitorium*, and then turned his attention to the blaze. It had already spread throughout the apartment in which it had begun, and was working its way upwards. A small group of people stood around, watching hopelessly. Some were naked, some wearing the simple tunics or breastbands that they had worn to bed, and some clutched a few objects they had been able to retrieve. One child held a wooden doll, while she buried her face in her mother's tunic. A woman held a small collection of cooking utensils, a man carried a funerary mask, a small statue that was presumably the *lares* from the household shrine, and an ornate glass cup. Some of them stared at the blaze in silence, some shouted curses at the man whose wife had identified him as the firestarter, and one woman was on her knees, screaming hysterically, being comforted by her husband.

Vespillo looked around him, assessing the situation briskly. "The neighbouring houses will catch soon. There is no firebreak until the end of the street. Before long, this whole neighbourhood will go up. We need to take those houses down. You and you, get inside and clear them out.

You, get these people organised into a chain for water. The rest of you, get your axes and hooks and get ready to take those houses down."

Soon, bleary eyed families started to emerge from the neighbouring houses, rousted from their beds by the brusk watchmen. Most took in the situation quickly, the blaze, the crowd, the *vigiles* already taking their axes to the door, and fitting hooks around the beams, ready to tug the house's supports away to collapse it. One man, sporting a paunch and a bald pate, spotted Vespillo giving orders, and approached him angrily.

"What is the meaning of this? How dare you get me out of bed? And what are these men doing to my house?"

"We are demolishing it, sir, to stop the fire spreading."

"You most certainly will not," said the portly man. "I own the toga shop on the ground floor. This is my livelihood."

"I'm sorry, sir, but there is no choice. If we don't take these two neighbouring buildings down, the blaze could spread through the city."

"Then do your duty and put the blaze out. You little bucket fellows should do your cursed job!"

As he spoke, rope buckets sealed with pitch, filled with water from the nearest fountain, started to be passed down a line of watchmen and civilians, and emptied onto the ground floor of the fire. The inadequacy of this measure was obvious from the fact that the water hissed and evaporated the moment it hit the fire, and went nowhere near the higher reaches of the burning building. Carbo judged this building was six stories high. It was made predominantly from wood, as many of the cheaper buildings in the poorer parts of town still were, despite official recommendations to use less combustible materials for construction.

"By law, sir, there should be a gap of five feet between adjacent buildings," said Vespillo. "I see your *insula* and the one on fire share a common wall."

"But no one obeys that law," said the man. "Look around you." He gestured at the closely packed buildings all around.

"More's the pity," said Vespillo. "If they did, maybe we wouldn't be forced to take such drastic action."

Some people from nearby houses were starting to emerge onto the streets now. Some of them brought firefighting equipment with them - it was in their interests to prevent the fire spreading any further.

"Where is your firefighting equipment, sir? By law you should have a supply of water and other preventative facilities in your house."

The man stuttered a little. "I…well, I had some water, but it got used up, and I didn't get round to…"

"You realise I could recommend to the authorities that you are beaten for negligence if you haven't taken proper steps to prevent fire in your house."

The man paled at the threat.

"Now please step back, sir, and let me do my job."

Vespillo turned his back on the man, and continued to direct the *vigiles* and their civilian helpers. Some of the local civilians were supplying filled buckets, some had patchwork quilts soaked in water which were tossed onto the flames, others even had supplies of vinegar which was supposed to be effective at putting out a blaze. It was obvious though, that their efforts were insufficient, and the flames were now starting to emerge from the upper floors of the two neighbouring houses. The watchmen who had been allocated to clear those houses emerged, driving some families before them, all coughing and a little blackened, evidence that the fire had taken hold inside.

From the top floor of the house to the right of the one where the fire had started, a woman leaned out of the window and screamed for help. Vespillo looked at her helplessly. The woman was illuminated from behind by an orange glow. Her screams became desperate, and she climbed out onto the window ledge.

"Get the mattresses," snapped Vespillo. "Now!"

Two of the watchmen hurried to get the mattresses and blankets that could be used to break a fall from a height.

"Stay where you are," bellowed Vespillo up at the woman. "We are getting a mattress."

If the woman heard, she gave no acknowledgement. She edged further out onto the ledge, but the flames were starting to lick around the window frame. Vespillo looked around desperately for the mattresses. The two watchmen were nowhere in sight. A despairing wail came from the top floor, and Vespillo looked up in time to see the woman jump. An impulse seized him to try to catch the woman, but he knew that would kill him. He stepped back, and the woman's screams were abruptly cut short as she impacted the ground. She lay still at his feet, limbs at unnatural angles, blood pooling around her head, hair smouldering.

The two watchmen he had dispatched for the mattresses returned, empty handed.

"Where were you?" said Vespillo, his voice quite with anger.

"Commander, the houses at the end of the street have been collapsed. We couldn't get through."

Vespillo looked confused. "Who ordered that? That's not the right place for a firebreak."

"I don't know, Commander. But it's worse. There is a lumber warehouse down there.

Vespillo cursed. "If that goes up, it could spread through half of Rome. Find a way round to get those mattresses. We may need them yet. "

He turned his attention back to the burning house to the left of the source of the fire. "Let's get this house down."

He directed the men with hooks attached to ropes to take up the slack on the beams. The correct application of force would bring the endangered houses tumbling down. Vespillo held up a hand, ready to give the order to pull. A blackened man came staggering out of the building, coughing uncontrollably. He gasped for breath, moving towards Vespillo. One of the watchmen supported him as his strength seemed to give. Vespillo took breath to give the order to pull the ropes, but the man grabbed the hem of Vespillo's tunic.

"My…son," he croaked. "My wife. They are…" He coughed, took a breath and tried again. "Inside. The second floor. She won't leave him. He's trapped. Please. Help."

The *vigiles* on the ropes looked to Vespillo for orders. Vespillo hesitated, looking at the flames and smoke. Then he looked at the dead woman on the street, hastily covered with a blanket. He ripped a strip from his tunic, dunked it in a water bucket, pressed it over his face, and charged into the building. Carbo's jaw dropped.

"Vespillo, no!" yelled Carbo. The other watchmen dropped their ropes, and stood, making no move to assist. Carbo cursed. The stupid bastard, why was he risking his life for a family he had never met? Carbo stepped forward, feeling the heat from the house, the smell of smoke, burning wood, and burning flesh. Suddenly he was back in Germany, the smell of wood fires heavy in the dank air, scented with the sweet smell of cooking meat, that he knew from the high-pitched screams was the cooking of his comrades.

He stared into the flames, and his insides clenched. He struggled to take a deep enough breath, his heart started to race uncontrollably, cold sweat broke out all over his body, and his legs weakened. Every part of him screamed to stay put.

But he needed Vespillo. Marsia's words echoed in his mind. "Bravery is doing the right thing, despite your fear." Copying Vespillo, he ripped some cloth from his tunic, wet it, and ran into the house.

The heat was intense. The wooden beams and ceiling were blazing, the doors smouldering. The first room was the shop of the toga maker, and piles of white togas were alight. The air was thick with smoke that made him gag and cough despite the makeshift mask. He heard a scream, and caught a glimpse through the smoke of Vespillo running up the stairs at the back of the shop. Shielding his face against the heat, Carbo followed. Flames licked at him, and the wooden steps groaned as he put his weight on them. He trod carefully, but as rapidly as he could, reaching the first floor quickly. The screams were coming from higher up though, and he continued to ascend. Vespillo was faster than him, despite the greater age, Carbo's unreliable leg slowing him as usual. His face felt like it was blistering, his throat was burning, his leg screamed in pain, and his hands were scalded when he stumbled on treacherous floorboards and reached out to the flaming walls to steady himself.

On the third floor, he found Vespillo, struggling with a beam that had fallen across a doorway, jamming the door shut. Vespillo looked round at Carbo, his face registering brief surprise, before he yelled over the noise of the fire and the screaming from inside the room, "Quick, give me a hand."

Carbo stepped forward, placing his hands under the beam. He shifted his grip to find a part that wasn't alight, but still felt his hands start to burn. The damp cloth discarded, he felt as if he couldn't breathe in the thick smoke.

"On three," said Vespillo. "One, two, three, heave!"

The beam lifted a little way under the combined efforts of the two men, then a piece of ashen wood broke off under Vespillo's grip and it sank back.

"Again! One, two, three!"

Carbo couldn't speak, and he felt he would suffocate if he was there much longer. Straining every muscle he lifted and twisted the beam from where it had jammed, and together they hefted it away. Vespillo yanked the door open and they entered.

Inside, the air was clearer, the small window allowing some ventilation, and Carbo took deep breaths, still spluttering. Near the window, a young woman held a boy of three or four close to her, as far from the flames and as near the outside as they could stand. The boy had his face turned into his mother's *stola*. The woman's face was pale underneath the soot and ashes that marred it.

"This way," said Vespillo, reaching out a hand. The woman hesitated then passed the boy to Vespillo. Carbo grabbed the woman's wrist and pulled her towards the stairs. Vespillo and the boy started to descend, but had taken no more than a few steps, when Vespillo's foot went straight through the wood. He staggered, his leg tearing against the splintered stairs, and the rest of the stairway started to give way. Carbo grabbed the boy, almost throwing him back up the stairs to his mother, then reached a hand out to Vespillo. Their hands clasped, but for a moment, it seemed like Vespillo would drag Carbo down through the widening hole with him. Carbo braced himself on the most sturdy part of the stairs he could find, and pulled with all his strength. Vespillo, using his hands for purchase, clambered back up the top of the stairway. A couple of heartbeats later, the rest of the stairs gave way, and they stared at the loss of their escape route.

The woman started to howl afresh, but Vespillo grabbed her and the boy, and hurried back into the room where they had found her. He moved to the window, looking down from the third floor to the small looking *vigiles* below.

"Bring up those mattresses," he called out.

"They are on their way, commander," replied one of the watchmen below. "They will be here soon."

"Hurry," yelled Vespillo, and turned back to the others.

They stood, looking at each other. Fire was licking along the beams and the roof, and the room was filling with more smoke, despite the ventilation. The woman hugged her son tight.

"You didn't need to come in here," said Vespillo to Carbo.

Carbo shrugged. "Neither did you."

They both fell silent, while Vespillo watched for signs of progress from below. The heat started to build, and the boy began to wail. The woman moved to the window, retreating from the fire and the smoke. The pain from the heat was becoming intense, and the boy was screaming. The woman looked out of the window to the street below.

"Just wait," said Vespillo. "We can jump soon."

A roof beam collapsed in the middle of the room, sending up a shower of sparks, and a burst of searing heat washed over them. Some of the sparks lodged in the woman's flamboyant hair style, and the oil with which she had styled it caught alight. She screamed, and holding the boy, she jumped.

Carbo and Vespillo both dived towards her, but she was gone. They looked out of the window, and saw that she had landed on three piled up cloth mattresses. The watchmen were wrapping mother and son, both of whom seemed stunned by the fall, in damp cloths to extinguish the flames.

They pulled the two clear of the mattresses and yelled up to Carbo and Vespillo.

"Jump, commander."

Vespillo looked at Carbo. "Watch what I do."

He moved to the window, stood facing into the room, and let himself fall backwards, arms outstretched. Carbo watched the fall, seeing him hit the mattresses with a thump, the impact reduced by the whole area of back, arms and legs connecting with the cushioning at the same time. Vespillo rolled clear, and yelled up at Carbo to jump. Carbo moved forwards, turned so he was facing into the room, and gripped the sides of the window. He hesitated. Letting himself fall felt too unnatural.

The ceiling collapsed. Another shower of sparks raced towards him. He let go.

He knew straight away that he hadn't got it right. His head was lower than his legs. The fall, a matter of a heartbeat in length, seemed to draw out forever. Then he hit, the back of his head thumping down hard, before the rest of his body caught up and arrested the momentum. Darkness rushed into the periphery of his vision, and he lay for a moment, unable to move. Several strong hands grabbed him and dragged him clear, pouring water over him to douse any flames and remove any lingering heat, then carrying him, semi-conscious, to the other side of the road.

He lay slumped against a wall, the world spinning round him, only vaguely aware of what was happening. He heard Vespillo giving the orders to collapse the building, heard the groan of stressed timbers, then the unbelievable din of a building falling down, clouds of dust and rubble and burning timbers all crumbling in on themselves. He was aware of the arrival of the *sipho*, a fire engine pulled by two horses, with a reservoir of water and a pump. As his head started to clear, he heard another crash as the building on the other side of the fire's source was demolished. By the time he was able to get to his feet, the blaze was under control, the *siphonarius* directing the pump, the *aquarius* directing the supply of water, Vespillo pointing out places where the *vigiles* needed to beat out a flame or move some combustible material.

The building in which the blaze had started finally collapsed, its burnt out timbers giving up supporting the shoddy construction. When the last of the flames were extinguished, Vespillo turned to Carbo.

"Let's go back to the station. The *medicus* will need to look at you."

"And you," said Carbo. "What happens here now?"

Vespillo shrugged. "Clearing up to be done by the residents. No doubt some bodies to recover. Livelihoods to be rebuilt. Not our job any more though, we have done what we are paid to do."

Vespillo clapped Carbo on the shoulder and together they started limping back to the headquarters, Carbo hampered by his old war injury, Vespillo's by the new injury where he had ripped his leg on the broken floor. They clambered painfully over the ruins of the collapsed building at the end of the street. Vespillo looked back at it, frowning, then carried on back to towards the fire station.

In the shadows at the end of the street, Glaukos smiled triumphantly.

"You see, mother? If we plan this carefully, then a few strategic collapses of buildings in main roads will choke the city. The panicking people will never be able to escape. The *vigiles* will be unable to bring up their firefighting equipment. The families in the houses and trying to flee on the streets will be consumed, and even those attending the games will be caught up in the conflagration. By the time it reaches them, it will be unstoppable."

Elissa nodded. "It is good. The Lord and Lady will be pleased. Provided they receive their chosen sacrifice."

A cloud passed over Glauko's face.

"They will, mother, I promise."

Philon scurried down the alleyway, heart pounding at the thought of the terrors of the night. The times he had been out after dark before, it had been in a group, accompanying a former Master to a party, along with a retinue of other slaves and hangers on, a number of which would have clubs and knives concealed subtly about their person. Now Philon had none of that assurance and protection. He passed the open mouth of an alley, and a sudden scream made him start, his heart faltering. A small cat came rushing out, pursued by a larger tomcat. A short way down the street, the tomcat caught the queen, grabbed her by the scruff of the neck, and with a large amount of noise from both parties, mated with her.

Philon pictured himself in the place of the queen, a position he had found himself in so many times, and flushed in embarrassment and anger. The gods are cruel, he thought. Had he not been born into slavery, he would have been the master of his own fate. He would maybe have slaves of his own now, food and wine whenever he wanted, a woman, whatever that felt like. Instead he had been raised in servitude, sold away from his mother when he was only seven to a succession of Masters of varying wealth, kindness and proclivities. From a young age he had been a catamite, used for the pleasure of his Master or the guests in any way they saw fit.

Then, when his body started to change, fluffy hair started to appear and his voice started to waver, he was taken to visit a place on the Viminal. He would never forget the rising terror as he was led into a small dimly lit room, how he was stripped and held down firmly on a table, how an old man had looked down into his face, and told him not to struggle. Then rags forced into his mouth, the indescribable pain between his legs, his desperate struggle against strong arms that restrained him, more rags thrust into the void where his testicles had been, then the world swimming around him and fading to black.

When he had woken from the experience, he had still been in excruciating pain, and it had taken him days simply to be able to walk again. Within a couple of weeks though, he was resuming his duties, and those duties had changed little, in the same way his body had stopped changing.

The sex was often painful, although in later years he had taken a certain pride in his ability to pleasure a man, and since, as some eunuchs did, he had retained his ability to achieve erection, some kindly men had even seen to his own pleasure. He knew that Romans saw no shame in penetrating man or woman, but would be completely humiliated to be penetrated themselves. He even understood from his conversations with female slaves and prostitutes that Roman men viewed it as shameful to use their tongue to pleasure a woman, although some who enjoyed it would practice it in secret.

More recently, having been sold to Publius Sergius, his duties had become more varied, including serving in the bar, and menial tasks, and he had realised at that time, with an almost sick resignation, that he had come to view his work as a prostitute as less onerous than mopping floors and cleaning out cooking jars. His ability to have sex without the risk of procreation had led to him developing a small clientele of women, many quite noble born.

Then last night, he had been with a freedman. Afterwards, tired, he had lain still, pretending to listen while the man chatted. Slowly, though, he had started to focus on the man's words, as he spoke of old gods returning, of the plight of the slaves and the poor, of the destruction of the Roman Masters. He listened, and started to ask questions, and eventually the man told Philon about a meeting, this night.

After the man had left, Philon had agonised over attending. His fear of the night, of punishment from the Master, of the meeting itself, all warred with his desire to know more. Then he found the Master had gone out for the night and so he had sneaked away.

Now he arrived at the destination he had been told about. The sign that had been described to him, something called the sign of Tanit, was painted on the wall, small and discreet but easily found for someone who had been told where to look. He knocked, and waited. Down the street, he heard a group of youths, drunk, laughing, fighting among themselves, coming nearer. His stomach twisted at the thought of being caught in the open by the louts, but he was also scared of what he would find inside.

Just as he was sure the youths would see him, the door opened, a crack.

"What's the password?" came a man's voice.

"Tanit reigns," said Philon in an unsteady voice.

The door swung open, revealing a man dressed in a long robe.

"Welcome, brother," he said, ushering Philon inside.

Philon entered a large atrium, lit by flickering oil lamps. Twenty or so people of both sexes and all ages, from a couple of children to an ancient looking old lady, were seated on the floor. A small fire in a brazier at the far end also provided heat and light, the smoke disappearing up into the night. Incense burners scented the air. At the front of the room, a man in a white robe was kneeling, hands held upwards in supplication as he chanted.

A young woman with dark skin, clothed in a simple white dress, smiled at him, and shuffled along the floor to create a space for him. He hesitated, then settled himself next to her. She leaned close to him and whispered.

"Is this your first time?"

"Yes," he said, still unsure what he was doing there.

"It's my third time. I have so much to learn. I'm Dahia."

"I'm Philon. What happens here?"

"We have lessons. We pray to the Lord and Lady. Afterwards, we drink wine."

"It's like a *Bacchanalia*?"

Dahia laughed. "No. We drink in moderation, and talk to each other about our lives. About servitude, slavery, poverty, oppression by the Roman masters."

"It sounds seditious."

Dahia shrugged. "Maybe the Roman nobility would think so. Do you see any here?"

Philon looked around him. Various ethnicities were represented, the dark skin of a Numidian such as Dahia, the long blonde hair of a Gaul, the tan complexion of a Syrian. All held in common a lowness of birth or situation - there was no expensive jewellery on show, no fine clothing. Just the simple, unwashed garb of the lowest levels of Roman society.

The man at the front finished his chanting and addressed them. Philon listened intently, as he talked about the Roman Empire, its desire and ability to crush all opposition, to absorb all cultures into itself, removing individuality, self-rule, freedom. He talked of noble civilisations destroyed or conquered by the Roman war machine, the Greeks, the Egyptians, the Carthaginians, the Gauls. He talked of how the Roman pantheon ruled over all, the elder gods driven from this world. Then he talked about the return of the elder gods. How their mother, Elissa, the prophetess, had revealed to him that the Lord Ba'al Hammon and his Lady Tanit were to return, to descend on Rome, bringing destruction to the Roman rulers, and freeing the oppressed.

Philon listened enthralled. Until this moment, his resentment of his position in life had been a dull ache, not specifically directed at any one thing. He thought of being a slave to Rome in the same way he thought of an illness - a thing inflicted on him by the gods. Now, he came to understand that his lot in life had a reason, a cause, and that cause had a name. Rome. Life could be different, he could be free.

The speech ended, and the listeners were silent. The leader offered a prayer to Ba'al Hammon and Tanit, and then went among the group, handing out cups of wine.

Philon sipped, mind racing. He noticed Dahia was looking at him, a smile on her face. He smiled back. They talked, and talked more. She told him of her background, born into slavery in Rome, moved from master to master, some kind, some abusive, until she ended up with her current master, an initiator. Philon found her easy to talk to, and explained about his past, leaving nothing out. Together, they talked to others in the group, and to the group leader himself. He told them again how Rome was doomed, how justice was at hand.

The hour grew late, and the meeting started to break up. Dahia and Philon left together, their paths taking them in a similar direction through the city, and they talked more. Philon's fear of the dark had receded, his distracted mind ignoring the sounds that had terrified him on the way to the meeting.

When their paths diverged, Philon didn't want to say goodbye. Dahia looked into his eyes, then kissed him briefly on the cheek. She hurried off towards her home, and Philon watched her, trying to come to terms with the emotions that this girl, this night had stirred in him. Slowly he became aware that he was standing alone in the dark, in the Subura. The terrors started to return, and he put his head down and hurried back to the tavern.

Chapter XIII

Carbo sat with Vespillo in the tavern that was becoming locally known as "Carbo's place." It was early evening and the place was packed. Carbo's reputation for being able to keep order within his establishment had been good for business among those who wanted to be able to drink and talk and gamble without the threat of violence. Carbo made sure that his customers had no doubts about the consequences if they stepped out of line. Already this evening, two drunken members of the urban cohorts had fallen out over a game of *Tali*, one claiming he had thrown the Venus hand, the highest possible, while the other accused him of cheating. When they had started to come to uncoordinated blows, Carbo had cracked their heads together and tossed them both out, sprawling on the streets, to much laughter and applause. Vatius, drinking in his usual seat, had toasted Carbo with a full cup of wine, far from sober himself.

"Not only an old man becomes a child again," said Vatius. "But also a drunkard."

"Socrates?" hazarded Carbo.

"Plato, actually. Good guess though."

A long sleep during the day had relieved Carbo and Vespillo of some of the tiredness that the previous night's exertions had caused them, although they both still ached and stung from burns, cuts and bruises. Carbo rubbed the lump on the back of his head, where his skull had connected with the ground despite the thickness of the mattress. It throbbed, and he probed it. He was lucky not to have cracked his head open, or to have suffered after effects of the injury. He had seen more than one man die some hours after obtaining a head wound in battle which appeared from the outside not to be serious.

"Why did you do it?" asked Carbo.

Vespillo drank deeply from a cup, and wiped his grey beard with the back of his hand. He belched.

"Do what?"

"Run into a burning building."

"It was my job."

"It was the job of every man there. You were the only one to do it."

"Not the only one. Some idiot civilian followed me in. Why was that?"

Carbo shrugged. He wasn't sure himself. He knew that he liked this man, and thought that he probably needed him too. Certainly he was the only friend he had in Rome right now.

"I think it must be the military training. You follow your commander into battle, wherever he leads."

"I'm not your commander."

"I got caught up in the moment. I felt like one of your men. Why did you go in first? I wouldn't have done that."

"I wonder. I think you might. Especially if it was to rescue someone you cared about."

"That's just it though. The deaths of that family would have been a tragedy, but they meant nothing to me. I wouldn't have risked my life for them. I risked it for you. So why did you go in? What were you trying to prove?"

Vespillo swirled the contents of his cup around, looking down into it, as if they would provide him with a simple answer. Then he looked up at Carbo.

"Do you want to know my story? How I ended up a ranker in the *vigiles*?"

Carbo regarded him steadily. "Do you want to tell me?"

Vespillo paused, then said, "Yes, I think I do." He sighed.

"Pannonia was bad," he went on. "Do you remember it?"

"I was in Germany at the time. I recall that old Biberius Caldius Mero had withdrawn a lot of troops from Dalmatia and Pannonia for a campaign on the Danube." Carbo used Tiberius Claudius Nero's old army nickname, meaning drinker of strong hot wine.

"That's right. It was a mistake. Pannonia had never accepted Roman rule, and there had already been several rebellions in the past few years. As soon as our troop numbers reduced, they rebelled in strength. They killed citizens, traders, wiped out a detachment of auxiliaries. I was at Raetinum."

Carbo's eyebrows went up. "You were there at the fire? What happened?"

Vespillo's face clouded. "We made a breach in the town wall. We thought it was all over, just mopping up to do once we were inside the defences. But the rebels fired their own homes. We had already started to let our guard down. Many of the boys were in the houses, looting, pillaging, raping no doubt. You know the score. Hundreds of us were trapped in the flames. You never get used to the stench of cooking flesh, the screams of people burning to death. But that first time was the worst."

Carbo suppressed a shudder, his own memories bubbling up.

"So that's why you joined the *vigiles*?"

Vespillo shook his head. "I wish it was so noble. Truth is, the *vigiles* were the only ones that would have me. Even the urban cohorts wouldn't touch me with a *pilum*."

Carbo was quiet, letting Vespillo collect himself.

"When the war was over, we thought we would get our rewards. Land, discharge for those who had served their time. All our back pay. Then we heard about the Teutoberg disaster, and everything changed."

Vespillo noticed that Carbo had gone very still. "Were you there?" he asked.

Carbo nodded. When he remained quiet, Vespillo continued.

"I had been promoted to centurion by the time Percennius stirred things up. Protesting against the usual things, pay, conditions, length of service. The local civilians took a hammering. Robbery, rape, murder."

"Were you part of the revolt?"

Vespillo shook his head. "No."

"Good. Mutineering *cunni*," spat Carbo.

Vespillo raised his eyebrows.

"I'm sorry, friend," said Carbo. "But really, you guys did not have it bad. None of you went through, what we, what I…"

Carbo broke off, stopped talking. Vespillo waited to see if he would say more, then continued.

"Well, I was beaten by my comrades as a result of my loyalty. Although later, after Drusus had talked the mutineers down, my steadfastness was noted and I was promoted to leading centurion of the second cohort. I was posted to a border fort in Thrace. Life became simpler, and more comfortable. I met a local woman, Orphea, who lived in one of the villages near the fort. She became as near to my wife as it is possible for a soldier to have. I made her comfortable, made sure the locals knew she was under my protection, and to be left alone. She was resented, even ostracised for her fraternising with the occupiers, but she bore it well, and she loved me. Eventually, we had a son together."

Carbo looked up sharply. He had thought Vespillo was childless. Vespillo didn't meet his gaze, and continued to stare down at the table. For a moment, he didn't speak, and Carbo wondered if he had decided he had said enough. Then he went on, and this time his voice cracked as he spoke.

"Two years ago, the Thracians revolted. The recruiting officers had been through their towns and villages, enthusiastically press-ganging anyone of military age into the auxiliaries. The Thracians probably had the right of it. They were certainly suffering, and at first they made peaceful representations. The governor played for time until reinforcements arrived. A legion from Moesia, and some loyal Thracian auxiliaries answered his call, and he took the fight to the rebels. After his first victories, he moved his headquarters closer to the enemy camp, and he left the loyal Thracian auxiliaries behind to guard his previous headquarters.

"I was stationed with the governor, fortifying his camp. The Thracians were fortified in the hills, and it became something of a standoff. Then word got back to the camp of how the loyal Thracians were behaving. Apparently with the blessing of their superiors, they were allowed to plunder the local countryside, provided they were back at night to guard the camp. That included my Orphea's village."

Vespillo shook his head. "Remember, I had seen it before in the mutiny. I had seen what happened to civilians when soldiers drunk on wine and rage and battle lust were let loose on them.

"I petitioned the Governor to command them to restraint, or to send a detachment to enforce discipline. He ignored me, told me that the locals were in revolt, and they were getting what they deserved. I cursed him, and he had me removed from his presence. I was broken to the ranks, and put on sentry duty. Out of my mind with worry, I deserted."

Vespillo looked into Carbo's eyes now, searching for a reaction. Carbo stared back at him, shock written on his face.

"You did what?" he whispered. "And you have the nerve to sit here and drink with me?" His voice rose. "A deserter. A coward!"

Vespillo's expression looked drawn. He nodded.

"I deserve that, I know. But I was torn. Loyalty to the legions, or to my family."

"The legion first, Vespillo. Always."

"Really, Carbo. Are you so perfect? Do you always do the right thing, without hesitation? Besides, how would you know what it is like to have your family threatened? You, who have no one."

Carbo opened his mouth to retort, then closed it again, chastened.

Vespillo sighed and continued. "I ran through the countryside, avoiding Roman patrols, Thracian rebels and rioting Thracian loyalists. I ran past burning villages and crops, past trees with bodies nailed to them, many still alive. I skirted around groups of soldiers who had cornered civilians, an old man they were stoning, a woman they were taking it in turns to rape. When I came to Orphea's village, it was already alight. Soldiers went from house to house, as they drunk and laughed among the destruction. Orphea's house wasn't burning, and I felt a surge of hope as I rushed inside.

"Orphea was on her back on her table. A Thracian soldier was between her legs, while another jeered and laughed. I killed the spectator first with a thrust in his back, then when the other stood, I stabbed him in the heart. Then I turned to help Orphea. She was already dead, her throat cut. In the corner, head caved in, was my four year old son."

Carbo looked down at the table. "I'm sorry." The words seemed completely inadequate.

Vespillo swallowed. "There were ten Thracian auxiliaries in the village. They were drunk and slow. I killed them all. Then I returned to the governor and threw myself on his mercy. When he heard my story he put me in the front line, aiming to carry out my full punishment after the battle. I think he hoped I would die in the assault. I think I hoped I would too.

"The Thracians were desperate when they came, starving and out of water. We fought all day, and then night fell and we fought all night. In the dark, no one could tell friend from enemy. We broke. A few of us stayed and fought. Those of us left pushed the Thracians back to their hill fortress at dawn, and they surrendered.

"I was taken before the governor, ready to receive my punishment. In view of the way I had fought, and the reasons for my desertion, he took pity on me. I was dishonourably discharged, quietly and without fuss. I lost my back pay and my chance of any land on retirement. I made my way back to Rome, doing odd jobs along the way, or begging scraps of food.

"When I arrived in Rome, I was destitute. I was sleeping under the aqueducts and in the temple doorways, begging along with the rest of the poor. Some of the crippled veterans I begged with told me about the *vigiles*, how they would take anyone, so I applied. They were right. I didn't hide the truth of my dishonourable discharge, but my recruiting officer didn't care. The *vigiles* were made up of thugs and freedmen, and they were keen to have someone with experience of the legions, especially an officer.

"I threw myself into the work, and found that I enjoyed it. It's exciting and rewarding, genuinely helping the people of Rome. I could put the memories aside, and I could try to restore my pride, bury the dishonour of desertion, and of failing to save my family. My work and command experience was noticed, and I was promoted, quickly. I met Severa, who was the widow of a local tradesman, and we married. Life now is good. I enjoy my work, I command a lot of men, I have a position in the community, respect, and a wife who loves me."

"Yet still you have something to prove, don't you," said Carbo, quietly.

"Yes," said Vespillo. "And I always will."

They remained quiet, drinking together in silence, while the hubbub of the busy bar swirled around them. Eventually Vespillo looked up at Carbo.

"And you? You have a story to tell?"

Carbo shook his head. "Not today. Maybe never."

Vespillo's face showed disappointment, that his openness had not been reciprocated. But when he saw Carbo's stare into middle distance, his stillness, the tension in his jaw, he realised he shouldn't press the subject. He sighed and drained his glass.

"So, now you know all about me. Maybe you understand a bit more why I wanted to help you and Rufa. I couldn't protect the ones in my charge, but I can help you protect yours."

"Thank you," said Carbo. "For that, and for sharing your past with me."

Vespillo waved the thanks away. "So, the question is, what next? Can we do anything with the information we got from Kahotep?"

Carbo considered the question. "We need more specifics, don't we? We need to find out what Elissa is up to."

"Slaves are usually easy enough to bribe. Ask Rufa who she thinks would be the best one to approach."

"Good idea. I'll go and talk to her. Thanks again Vespillo. I'm sorry for judging you. You are a friend."

Vespillo smiled. "It seems I am."

Carbo sat in the back room of the tavern with Rufa. Her expression was tight, and she was snappy when Fabilla's childish singing irritated her. For her part, Fabilla was quick to tears at the rebuke, and it required a hug and an apology from Rufa to calm her. Carbo realised that Rufa and Fabilla had been confined to this one room and the bedroom for several days now. He reached out across the table and covered her hand with his. She looked up at him and suddenly her eyes were full with tears.

"What is going to become of us, Carbo?" she asked.

"That's what I'm working on. I need to persuade Elissa to leave you alone. Vespillo and I think we need to find out more about Elissa's activities, so we can have some leverage."

"You told Vespillo about me?"

Carbo nodded. "I can't do this alone, Rufa. It's too big."

Rufa turned away. "I'm being unfair on you, aren't I? I've come here, calling in a promise you made to a little girl a lifetime ago."

Carbo squeezed the hand. "I made the promise, and I will stick by it. Now, have you told me everything you know about Elissa and what she does?"

"I think so. She has these meetings with people who seem important, but I don't know them."

"Do you remember any names?"

She closed her eyes in concentration. "There was a woman called ... Metella, I think."

"The Metelli are a big family, that doesn't narrow it down too much."

"There was someone called Scrofa too. I overheard the mistress ask how things were in the office of the Urban Praetor."

"She isn't your mistress any more, Rufa."

Rufa looked down, then shook her head. "I'm sorry. I feel a long way from being free. I might as well be imprisoned. It's only been a few days, and already I'm chafing to see a street, a crowd."

"You know why you must stay out of sight, Rufa."

"I know, Carbo, but it's not just me. How do you explain to a seven year old child why we must remain hidden?"

"It's not worth the risk."

"Rome is a big place Carbo. With my hair under my hood, I would never be recognised."

Carbo changed the subject. "I need to speak to someone from Elissa's household to find out more. Do you think any of the slaves would talk to me? One who might have some knowledge of what goes on in that house?"

Rufa considered for a moment. "I shared my quarters with my friend Natta and her husband Cossus. He was Elissa's caretaker. He would know everything about that house. He wouldn't talk to you, though. He doesn't know you. Why would he risk punishment?"

"I can make him talk to me."

"You think threatening him will get you the information you want? He would probably just tell you anything he thought you wanted to hear, and then go and tell Elissa."

"There's no alternative."

"There is. I will come with you. He might talk to me."

Carbo shook his head firmly. "No, it's too dangerous."

"Is it more dangerous than sitting here and waiting to be found?"

Carbo thought for a while. "He could come here, couldn't he? There would be no need for you to go out."

"And how would you get him a message? He can't read. Who would you trust to talk to him? I know his schedule. He usually goes out for supplies for repairs and such like early each morning. We could wait for him."

Carbo sighed. "Are you sure you want to do this?"

"Yes. I need to. Staying here, not knowing what will happen to me, is killing me. If you think getting more information will be of use, then I can help."

"Fine. Tomorrow morning then. I'm going to get some sleep."

"I will retire too. Fabilla, bedtime."

"Mother," moaned the young girl, who had been rolling some knucklebones.

"No argument." Rufa took Fabilla's hand, and led her upstairs. Carbo poured himself a glass of watered wine and drank. Marsia entered the kitchen to fetch a bowl of soup to take back to the bar, which was still noisy.

"I'm going to bed, Marsia. Close up the bar when the last customer has gone."

"Yes, Master."

Carbo made his way up the wooden stairs to the first floor bedroom. He found that Rufa had settled Fabilla onto the mattress on the floor that Carbo had been sleeping on. Fabilla was already snoring, and Carbo marvelled at the way children could go from fully awake to asleep so quickly. He wished he had that ability. Rufa looked up and whispered, "I'm sorry, is it ok if she takes the mattress on the floor? She will sleep better if she has her own space."

"Of course." He looked around. "I suppose I will find a corner."

Rufa looked at him shyly. "You can share the bed with me." She let her dress fall to the floor, and she was wearing only a brief loin cloth and a breast band beneath. Carbo felt his lust stirring as his eyes moved over her lithe body, her smooth skin marred only by the brand on her arm. She stepped forward, and slid one arm around his waist, then slowly pulled him down to the bed, kissing him softly. His fingers slid over her skin and he sighed softly at the touch. Her hand moved down his chest, lower, light fingertips, seeking, till they reached his hardness.

For a moment, he tried not to think, tried to lose himself in the feeling. Then images started to flash in his mind. His heart started to race, he started to sweat, his breathing became tight, and his erection disappeared like a flower wilting in the heat. Rufa looked into his eyes.

"Do you not like me in that way?" she asked, her voice small.

Carbo shook his head. "It's not you, it's…" He swallowed, fighting down the familiar sensation of rising panic. Rufa watched him for a moment, seeing his anxiety. She didn't say anything further. She just slid her arms around him, and cradled his head against her shoulder. They lay together, and Carbo found to his amazement that the racing heart, the knot in his stomach, the fast breathing, all started to settle. He held Rufa close, and he marvelled at the strange sensation, one that he hadn't felt for so long, one that with his past, and with what was happening in his life right now, he knew was inappropriate. He felt relaxed. He fell asleep, holding onto Rufa.

Chapter XIV

Carbo and Rufa sat on the edge of a fountain, watching the market traders. It was a *nundinae,* a market day held every eighth day, when farmers and merchants from the country made their way into the centre of Rome to sell fresh goods. The streets were closed to normal traffic for the day, and stalls were crammed into every available space, selling the mundane such as garden vegetables as well as the exotic such as perfumes and fine wines. Slaves and housewives scoured the market for fresh goods to last the eight days until the next market came around.

Rufa breathed in the air deeply, warmed by the early autumn sun. She had been in captivity most of her life, but as a domestic slave she had been allowed to wander around the house freely, and was often given errands in the city. The last few days, during which she was terrified of capture, scared to show her face to the world, and yet bored senseless by the confinement, had been among the worst in her life. Compounding it was the problem of Fabilla, even more bored, and not understanding their situation.

Rufa felt a little guilty at leaving Fabilla behind in Marsia's care. Fabilla had wept and screamed at the injustice of her mother going out without her, but Rufa knew that it was too dangerous to risk her being seen. Rufa herself felt her heart beating fast, her stomach tightening each time she felt someone's gaze turn on her, relief flooding through her as the bored eyes scanned away. She wore a plain *stola*, neither too showy nor too tattered, which Marsia had bought for her on Carbo's instructions. Her red hair was hidden by a cloak pulled up over her head, and she drew the edges of it around her face, so there was little of her on show to be recognised.

Carbo dipped his hand into the water from the fountain and took a slurping drink from his cupped palm. "When will he come?" he asked, for at least the fifth time.

"I still don't know," said Rufa, a little impatiently, despite her fear, and the debt she owned Carbo. "He was never the most reliable slave. But he has to get supplies when the market is here, the mistress always insisted on fresh goods."

Carbo sighed, and shifted his weight. His leg ached if he sat in one position for too long, but he didn't want to leave this vantage point where their target should be visible. He scanned the crowd, pointlessly as he didn't know what this slave looked like. Rufa remained alert, her eyes darting over the faces. Her hand moved tentatively to his lap. He looked down at it for a moment, then took it gently in his own hand. She looked at him and smiled softly.

A familiar figure caught her eye. The man was dressed plainly, and it was impossible to tell from his garb whether he was slave or a poor free man. She squeezed Carbo's hand, and nodded in the direction of the figure. He was in a sea of heads, and too far away for Rufa to be sure it was him. Carbo squinted, and looked at her quizzically. The man worked his way through the stalls, coming nearer to their resting place. He turned to a trader to purchase some onions, and Rufa lost sight of him momentarily. Then he emerged, coming closer again, and Rufa clearly saw the face of Cossus, partner of Natta, the couple who shared her room during her time in Elissa's service.

"That's him," she said. Carbo nodded and stood, grimacing as he stretched out his stiff leg. He took Rufa's hand, and made his way through the crowds. Progress was slow, but his large bulk helped him to make headway, and soon he was within a short distance of Cossus. The severe crowding made a subtle approach impossible, so he hung back, watching and following. Cossus had no reason to think he was being followed, and didn't look round once as he made his way about the market place.

Fortunately he was an efficient shopper, and didn't spend too long haggling or sampling the goods. Before long he had a full bag of goods and was leaving the market. Rufa and Carbo followed at a short distance, until the crowds eased. Cossus turned down a quiet alleyway, and Carbo spotted an empty doorway up ahead. As Cossus approached it, Carbo took a couple of strides forward and with a strong arm guided him into the recess.

Cossus gasped in alarm, whirling to face his attacker. His arms came up to defend himself, dropping his sack, but Carbo pressed up against him, pinning his arms back.

"Stand still," he hissed.

"What do you want?" said Cossus. "I've spent my money on goods, there is none left."

Rufa appeared beside Carbo.

"Cossus," she said, pulling her cloak away from her face, revealing a rim of her distinctive face.

Cossus' eyes widened, then narrowed in anger.

"You!" He made to lunge at her, but Carbo restrained him. "You evil whore. You *cunnus*. I spit on your tomb." He did spit at her, hitting her on the shoulder. Rufa drew back in shock at the reaction.

"This is going well," muttered Carbo.

"Cossus, why are you saying these things to me?"

"You ran away. What did you think would happen to the rest of us?"

"What…what do you mean?" asked Rufa.

"She tortured Natta. And Demosthenes. With the *flagrum.*"

Rufa paled.

"Is she…?"

"She lives," said Cossus. "For now. Her wounds are grave. I… don't think that she will survive."

"I'm so sorry," said Rufa, almost whispering, tears filling her eyes. "I never meant for any of that to happen."

Cossus slumped, the fight going out of him. Carbo cautiously let him go, and stepped back, keeping an eye on the street. One or two passers by eyed the small group suspiciously, but no one showed any intention of intervening.

"Why did you run, Rufa? Why put the rest of us at risk like that?"

"I didn't know she would take it out on the rest of you. But I had to leave. Fabilla, she was in danger."

"What are you talking about?"

"That's why we want to talk to you," said Carbo.

Cossus turned his gaze on him. "And who are you, and why are you assaulting me in broad daylight?"

"I'm sorry about that," said Carbo. "We needed to talk to in private, away from prying eyes and flapping ears."

"I'm not interested in talking to you. Or your whore."

"Please Cossus," begged Rufa. "The mistress means to kill Fabilla."

Cossus looked defiant, then relented. "There is a tavern at the end of this alley. The wine is foul and the food is likely to poison you, so it's usually quiet. Let's go there."

Carbo nodded, and let Cossus lead the way.

As Cossus had predicted, the tavern was all but empty. The plump, bald, perspiring proprietor was slumped at the bar, chin on his hands. A small dog sat on one table nibbling its backside, and a bored, elderly prostitute seated on a couch raised her eyes briefly as the two men entered, then let her gaze fall to the floor again as she saw the attractive young woman accompanying them. They took a table in a corner, sat and waited. The proprietor sighed, struggled to his feet with a groan and walked over to them stiffly.

"What do you want?"

Carbo looked around the bar, taking in the fading frescos, the filthy, stained tables, the rickety furniture, and a couple of rats gnawing a bone in one corner.

"A cup of your finest Falernian, please," he said.

The tavern owner seemed to miss the irony completely. "Don't have any."

Carbo shook his head. "Just get us three cups of your least vinegary wine."

They waited in silence while the tavern owner huffed and puffed, making a big show of selecting a particular wine. He poured three cups and brought them to the table, slopping some of the contents over the side. "Ten *asses* for these. My best wine."

Carbo took a sip and grimaced. "You should pay us to drink this stuff. Take four and be grateful." He slipped the copper coins across the table. The tavern owner grumbled, but Carbo's expression prevented him from arguing his case. He took the coins and wandered off to his station at the bar.

Cossus took a sip of drink as well. Even the slave wrinkled his nose. Rufa left hers untouched.

"So, as the man said. What do you want?"

Carbo looked across at Rufa.

"I'm so sorry about Natta," she said. "I never meant that to happen. Never thought…"

"What did you think?" snapped Cossus. "That the mistress would celebrate your escape by giving us all honeycakes?"

Rufa looked distraught. "I had no choice, Cossus. I found something out. I saw the mistress and some others. They were performing a ceremony. They sacrificed Fabilla's doll."

"So? The mistress is crazy. We all know that."

"They marked her with a sign. They said she was going to be a sacrifice."

"It's just her talk. Her way of stirring up her followers." He looked at Carbo. "You don't believe all this nonsense, do you?"

"Tell me about this cult," said Carbo. "What do you know?"

Cossus took another sip of wine, then looked like he regretted it.

"The mistress claims she is Carthaginian. That she fled from the city as a child. That her mother was a priestess, and her mother before her, and that she herself is a priestess of the ancient Carthaginian gods. She is quite…persuasive. She has followers throughout the city, and they meet in secret and rail against the cruelty of the Roman overlords."

"She sounds dangerous," said Carbo.

"No more than any of these crazy cults that spring up everywhere. Every time I head out to the market, there is a new prophet on the corner, crying that doom is near, that we must all follow whichever god is in vogue, or we face annihilation. It's one of the few things I admire about Rome, that we tolerate these idiots. The mistress is just another prophet, albeit with a bigger following."

"What do you know about her followers?"

"Well, she certainly knows how to woo the influential. I've seen some interesting comings and goings. Wealthy merchants. Rich widows. City officials. Most of her followers come from the underclasses though. The slaves and freedmen, the poor and disenchanted."

"Why don't you join them then?"

"For what? Promise of salvation? Throwing off the yoke of the cruel Roman Masters? Pah. I have learning you know. I used to be a teacher. I know Greek. I've debated Plato and Socrates with philosophers. Why would I be taken in by a mad woman?"

"You think the cult is just for the stupid?"

"Of course. And what happens when a lot of stupid people try to conspire? Not a lot. They couldn't organise an orgy in a brothel."

Carbo and Rufa exchanged glances. Carbo wasn't so sure. Elissa had a formidable personality. Maybe most cults comprised the deluded leading the weak, but this one felt different. Somehow far, far more dangerous.

"I had better get back before the mistress realises I have been gone too long, and has me whipped." He looked at Rufa bitterly.

Carbo stood, and passed Cossus a *denarius*. "Thank you for your help."

Rufa looked at Cossus with anguish. "Please tell Natta, I'm… I'm sorry."

Cossus looked at her steadily, then turned and walked away. Rufa looked down at the table, tears welling in her eyes. Carbo reached forward and tilted her chin up with one finger so her eyes met his.

"It's not your fault. You did what you needed to do. You aren't responsible for Elissa's actions."

Rufa looked at him doubtfully, but the tears stopped flowing.

"Come on, let's go and find Vespillo. See what he makes of what Cossus had to tell us."

Rufa rearranged her cloak to cover her head again, and they stood and left. As they entered the street and turned in the direction of home, neither of them noticed the man watching them from a shadowed doorway a short distance away.

Glaukos narrowed his eyes, staring at the woman. He couldn't identify her clearly, with her cloak drawn around her, although the large man she was with was striking and memorable. As they walked away from him, he made to follow them. Both of them seemed nervous, the large man glancing around him regularly, and Glaukos had to hang back to avoid being seen. The woman kept her gaze directed downwards, making it hard to see her face, and he cursed in frustration.

The couple walked in the direction of the Subura, and the streets became narrower and the crowd thicker. Glaukos started to struggle to keep them in sight, and tried to move closer. He had to jostle people out of the way to make progress, and became more short-tempered.

A shopkeeper emerged from a doorway carrying a large jug of *garum*. Glaukos, eyes fixed on the couple he was following, bumped into the man, who dropped the jug. The pottery shattered on the floor, spreading the stinking fish guts sauce over the dusty ground. Glaukos tried to push on, but the shopkeeper grabbed him.

"Get out of my way, you clumsy fool," he hissed.

"Not till you pay me for that. That a *sextarius* of best quality *liquamen primum* there."

Glaukos tried to pull his arm away, but the shopkeeper held his sleeve fast. "Ten *denarii*."

Glaukos wasn't sure he had that much on him. Anxious to be away, he fumbled in his purse and drew out a handful of the silver coins. He thrust them at the shopkeeper, who took them with one hand, weighing them speculatively.

Reluctantly, the man released Glaukos' sleeve. Glaukos turned back to his quarry, but they had vanished into the crowd. He pushed on down the main street, but there were too many side roads in this region, and he couldn't find them.

He paused and thought for a while. His hunch had nearly paid off. Cossus and Natta were obviously close to Rufa, and so it was logical that Rufa might try to contact him. Following Cossus had made sense, and only bad luck had intervened to prevent him from being able to bring his mistress valuable information. He was sure the woman in the cloak was Rufa. He couldn't prove it, but he would soon have Cossus back in the *domus*. Then Cossus would talk to him. In fact he would beg to tell him everything.

Carbo and Rufa walked down the street to Carbo's tavern.

"Vespillo said he would drop by this afternoon. He's probably drinking in the tavern now. I wonder what he will make of all this."

Rufa nodded, eyes still downcast. As they reached the tavern, a woman stepped out of the shadows.

"You are Carbo?"

Carbo looked at her. Her accent was roughest Suburan, but her clothes and jewellery suggested some wealth. She was in her late forties or early fifties, and had a firm, handsome face out of which looked flinty eyes. Behind her stood two tough-looking men with ill-concealed cudgels beneath their tunics.

Carbo nodded. "And you are?" he asked suspiciously.

"Broccha," she said. "Wife of Manius, mother of Cilo and Balbus."

Carbo tensed, looking at the thugs behind her, instantly preparing for danger. Broccha held out a placating hand.

"I'm not here for a fight."

"What then?"

Broccha sighed. "I love my family, Carbo. They are not perfect. Who is? But they care for each other and they care for their mother."

"My mother is dead," said Carbo.

Broccha nodded. "I heard. I knew Atella. A fine woman."

Carbo inclined his head in acknowledgement of the praise.

"Atella spoke of you often, you know. She was very proud of her son in the legions, and she loved you."

Carbo gave no outward sign of reaction to the words, but his throat tightened.

"I am proud of my fine sons, and my handsome husband. They keep order here."

"That isn't their job," said Carbo.

"Then whose job is it? The urban cohorts? The *vigiles*? No one cares about this place."

"Still, their idea of keeping order is bullying and extortion."

"I did say they weren't perfect. But they are mine. So I am asking you to come to an understanding with them. You are brave and stubborn. So are they. Unless one of you backs down, this will end in death. Most likely yours, and I don't want to see that happen to Atella's son."

"It could end in the deaths of your husband or sons."

"Yes," conceded Broccha. "And I would like to avoid that possibility too. So, please. I will talk to them, make sure the tax you pay is minimal. Just a token, so that the people around here can see that you respect and honour them. They will leave you alone then."

Carbo shook his head. "I'm sorry Broccha. I understand why you want this, and I respect your wish to protect your family and keep the peace. But understand, I was a *pilus prior* in the legions. I commanded centuries. I fought barbarians for over twenty years. Do you really think I would roll over for a couple of street thugs?"

Broccha looked downcast. "No, I didn't. But I had to try."

"Go, Broccha, with my respect. Try to persuade your family to stay away."

Broccha sighed. "I was as successful with them as with you, sadly. I'm sorry for what is to come, Carbo."

"So am I," said Carbo. Broccha turned and signalled to her bodyguards, and they walked away.

Carbo entered the tavern, and found Vespillo drinking wine at a corner table. Carbo joined him and related what had just happened.

Vespillo shook his head. "Manius has been in charge around here for years. If he lets you face him down, with no retribution, his authority will vanish. He can't let that happen."

"What should I do? I can't guard the tavern all the time. Next time he may come back when I am not around, and burn the place down, or murder my slaves."

Vespillo pursed his lips. "I will leave a couple of my men here. Dentatus and Bucco. Good lads. A bit dim, but good in a fight, and they certainly won't mind the idea of guarding a tavern. Just don't let them get too drunk will you?"

Carbo laughed. "I don't think that would be in my interests. Don't worry, Marsia is plenty fierce enough to keep them in line."

He looked around the tavern. There were a few drinkers there, some playing *tali,* or board games such as *ludus calculorum*, some staring down into their cups morosely, a couple looking at Carbo and whispering.

"Go out the back again Rufa. It's not safe for you to be out here."

Rufa looked as if she would argue momentarily, then bowed her head and retreated to the back room.

"So, did you find anything out this afternoon?" asked Vespillo.

"Some. Enough to know Elissa is mad. And that she is dangerous, or at least wants to be. Whether she is just a fantasist, or she could do some real damage I don't know."

"Maybe it doesn't matter. If she thinks that she has a dangerous secret, and we let on enough to make her think we know everything, then she may let Rufa go."

Carbo thought about this. "Makes sense. So we go and see her?"

"Tomorrow, I think. Every day wasted is another day she could be discovered." Vespillo stood. "I will send over Dentatus and Bucco."

"My thanks, Vespillo. You are a good friend."

Vespillo clapped Carbo on the shoulder. "Stop it, you'll make me cry. Tomorrow, we will go to Elissa together. Maybe we can get this thing sorted once and for all."

Chapter XV

Carbo and Rufa lay together on the bed. It was still early evening, and for a change, they were alone together. Marsia was entertaining Fabilla, and Philon was entertaining the tavern guests, one way or another. Philon had already approached Dentatus and Bucco. Only Bucco had been interested, and he had insisted that he get Philon's favours for free, as part of his recompense for guard duties. Philon hadn't liked this idea, and had told him that free drink was the only thing that had been agreed.

Rufa stroked Carbo's hair, looking into his eyes. "Tell me about army life. Was it hard?"

"You don't remember?"

"Some. I was very young when father died. Besides, I only ever knew what it was to be a camp follower, and a rather spoiled one at that. Not what it's like to be a soldier."

"I don't like to talk about it," said Carbo.

Rufa placed a palm against his cheek. "You don't have to tell me the bad bits. But don't you have any good memories? The taverns. The friends. The women?"

"There were no women," said Carbo. "Not after…" He shook his head. "Friends, yes. That is one thing I think I will never stop missing. The men who you lived with day in and out, men who would die for you, and you for them, because that was the only way it could be in battle. Men you drank with, laughed with, gambled with. I miss them, the ones I said goodbye to the day I left the legions, and the ones I said goodbye to the day they died."

"Like my father."

"Especially your father."

A silence hung between them for a moment. Then Rufa craned her head forward and kissed him on the lips. He hesitated, but the softness against his mouth was like a draught of wine flowing through his body, relaxing and exciting him at the same time. He slid his arms around her and drew her close, feeling her soft body against him. Her fingertips caressed his back, and his lips moved to her neck. She tilted her head to let him kiss and nibble at the sensitive skin there.

They undressed, and he lay back on the bed. When she reached down to grasp his hardness, he tensed, felt the familiar rise of panic. But she stroked his face and kissed him lightly while her fingertips teased and stimulated him further, and miraculously, he felt the panic recede.

She straddled him and guided him inside her, and with exquisite care and tenderness, she rode him gently. The feelings intensified quickly, and in moments he had lost himself in the sensations. She leaned forward to kiss him again, her breasts grazing his chest. All too soon, he gripped her tightly as he climaxed, and she smiled down on him.

They lay together, Carbo gasping, mixed emotions running through his mind.

"You didn't need to do that," he said, when he had recovered some composure. "You don't owe me that, for what I'm doing."

"I know," she said. "I wanted to."

"But wasn't it all too… quick for you?"

"Carbo, I know you haven't been with a woman for a long time. If it hadn't been quick, I don't think I would have been very flattered."

Carbo laughed, and kissed her lightly on the cheek.

She smiled again, then her expression became serious.

"Carbo, will you tell me what happened to you? And to my father."

"I don't talk about that," he said, brusquely.

He watched her face fall, and she bit her lip and turned away. He cursed himself, and sighed.

"Rufa, I have never spoken to anybody about what happened to me then."

"It's fine," said Rufa, her tone forlorn. "You don't need to say anything."

"You will be the first person I have told."

Rufa turned back to face him, searching his gaze.

"Why me?"

Carbo struggled with the words, an old soldier who had avoided women for much of his adult life. "Because I think I…like you."

The smile on Rufa's lips, just an upturning at the corners, but with a sparkle in her eyes, told him she was pleased with the remark. She hugged him firmly.

"I like you too, Carbo. Not just for what you are doing for me. For who you are."

Carbo stroked her hair, then sighed. "What do you want to know?"

"My father and you marched with Varus, didn't you?"

Carbo nodded.

"How did he die?"

"Like a hero," said Carbo firmly. Her expectant expression told him he would need to add more detail. He steeled himself, and recalled in his mind's eye the scenes as they left camp that day, to put down a minor revolt by the Angrivarii tribe in Germania. Three legions, resplendent in battle dress, headed north-west, with Publius Quinctilius Varus, the governor himself leading them.

"You must know the story," he said. "How Varus led us into the Teutoberger forest at the urging of his German friend Arminius. How Arminius betrayed us all, organising an ambush."

"Of course," said Rufa, softly. "Who doesn't? But so few survived, so few came home. No one knows what really happened in that forest."

"Arminius knows. And I know."

Carbo collected himself, then continued.

"Varus suspected nothing, even though he had been warned of a plot. He had complete faith in his friend Arminius. We left in marching order, not battle order. You were lucky that you stayed in the camp. There were many civilians, men, women and children with us that day. Still, three legions marching in line is quite a sight. Varus was in the middle, with the best of the troops to protect him. That was where I and my men were. Behind came the eagles, legionaries marching six abreast behind them. It would have been over twenty two thousand men if the legions had been at full strength, but of course they never were.

"As the day wore on, Arminius came to Varus and asked if he could go ahead to make sure the tribes were in support, and the way was clear. It seemed like a reasonable request, so Varus agreed. We built camp that night, oblivious to the danger we faced. The next day we set off in high spirits, but the going became more difficult. It was mountainous and forested, and forward detachments had to clear us a path. The weather turned against us, rain and wind that started as a persistent drizzle and became a full blown storm. The wagons kept getting stuck in the mud, men slipped over in the treacherous footing, and we felt tired, wet and angry. After nearly a full day of this, the first attack came.

"They surrounded us on all sides, and targeted the horses with spears, which made them bolt and rear. Then they attacked. It was chaos. There were civilians in the way, falling to enemy spears and Roman *gladii* if they happened to be in the wrong place at the wrong time. We were outnumbered and disorganised.

"But we beat them off, and Varus, though shaken, and with some firm words from his officers to stiffen his nerves, ordered a camp to be built. Half of us stood guard while the rest worked in the rain and wind to put up the stockade and tents. Although everyone was rattled, we had beaten them off. Defeat was never really considered then. We were three Roman legions. No barbarian army, no matter how numerous, could seriously threaten a force that size now the element of surprise was lost."

Carbo shook his head at the hubris they had all shown.

"We agreed to strike out for the river. But first we had to march through a narrow pass. We had been harried all morning before we reached this place, and we knew that it looked dangerous, but we had no choice but to march on.

"Arminius and his men had prepared well. They had lined the pass with turf and sand walls and ramparts, and they came out from behind these, and started to cut us down. The space was too confined to form our usual defence behind a wall of shields, so most of the fighting was one on one.

"The slaughter..." Carbo trailed off, and Rufa held his hand, waiting for him to continue on his own time. He took a breath and let it out slowly.

"We fought well, but we had lost all our traditional advantages. Spears hailed down on us. Your father rallied some men, myself among them, and we charged up the steep slope.

"The going was deadly. If a legionary's footing went in the steep, slippery mud, his shield dropped and a spear would find him before he could rise again. Barely half of us made it to the defensive line. Your father was first over the wall, screaming like a demon from the pits of Hades. We followed, hacking and slashing around us, and soon we had cleared the makeshift fortress of its defenders. But there were many more, lining the pass on both sides.

"We returned to the fighting lower down, and your father performed the same feat. Three more times he gathered men about him and stormed the defences. Each time, those of us that survived came away more bloodied, more exhausted. Every one of us had blood flowing from multiple wounds, and our strength was nearly gone. You can't imagine how it feels to charge into battle, knowing your life depended on how you fought, yet barely being able to lift your sword."

Carbo's gaze was fixed in the middle distance now, the long ago scenes so fresh in his mind it was as if they were playing out in front of him.

"Still the slaughter around us continued. Your father rallied us once more, and we charged up the hill. We were too slow this time. Three quarters of us were dead before we reached the top, and we were badly outnumbered by the defenders. We fought in desperation, and the numbers shifted in our favour.

"Then your father's *gladius* became wedged in a German warrior. As he tried to pull it from the dying man, another German came at him from behind, and thrust his sword through your father's back and out the other side."

Rufa's hand tightened on his and Carbo looked into her eyes, anguish etched on his face.

"I killed the man with a single thrust under his armpit, Rufa. I avenged him."

"Thank you for that, Carbo," she said, eyes moist.

He sighed. "Suddenly there was a lull in the fighting as our men finished off the remaining Germans in the small area around us. I held your father as he died, looking into his eyes as the light went out. "

"Did he say anything?" she asked in a small voice.

Carbo shook his head. "I'm sorry. I would love to tell you that he spoke of heroism and friendship, or that his last words were of you. But death in battle seldom allows that. He moved his lips, and blood came out, and he died."

A choking sob escaped from Rufa, and she looked at him, vision blurred by the tears.

"I'm sorry, Carbo. I shouldn't have put you through this. It was selfish."

"No," said Carbo. "It feels somehow…right. Especially to be telling you, of all people."

"Do you want to stop now?"

"No. I feel like if I don't finish the story now, I never will."

Rufa squeezed his hand tight. "Only if you are sure, then."

Carbo took a breath to steady himself, then continued.

"The cavalry left us then. To this day, I don't know if they abandoned us like cowards, or retreated on the orders of Varus. Watching them go made us feel even more hopeless. The driving rain had soaked through the leather of our shields, making them a huge burden to lift. The violent wind stopped our javelins and our archers' arrows from finding any targets. The Germans, though, with their light armour could attack and withdraw at will. On top of this, the German tribes who had been scared to challenge Rome now saw we were vulnerable, and threw their lot in with Arminius. Fresh, unbloodied Germans joined the fight against legionaries that could barely lift their sword and shield. We were finished."

Carbo sighed, his slumped shoulders reflecting the sting of defeat, the shame and the terror he had felt, all those years ago.

"We all knew stories of how the Germans treated their prisoners. I had hoped they were exaggerated. It seemed unreal, to be discussing with my comrades whether we should take our own lives, or surrender to who knew what fate. Varus ran himself through with a sword. I think now he did the right thing. Ceionius, the surviving camp commander, decided to surrender. There was no escape, we were surrounded and trapped. I was scared, and I wanted to live. I surrendered with Ceionius."

Carbo bowed his head. Rufa put a hand to his cheek, and he looked up, face pale and drawn.

"Varus' body had been partially burned and buried by his officers, but the Germans dug it up, and mutilated it. I watched his head being carried off as a trophy. The three eagles were taken. One of the standard bearers threw himself into the marsh with the eagle concealed in his belt, but the Germans found it all the same.

"Then the priestesses arrived, and the horror really started."

Carbo looked at Rufa. "I'm not sure it benefits you to hear this."

Rufa returned his gaze steadily. "If you were strong enough to experience it and survive, then I am strong enough to at least hear it."

Carbo took a deep breath to steady himself. "The priestesses were robed in white. We were chained, and pushed to our knees before them. They ordered their men to start building altars. I saw a legionary have his tongue cut out, and his lips sewed together, while an onlooking German said in Latin, 'Now, snake you can't hiss.' I watched as men had their eyes put out, then their heads chopped off and nailed to trees. I saw officers burned alive on the altars. The smell, the screams…"

Carbo swallowed. "One officer brought his chains down on the top of his head so hard, he dashed his own brains out, rather than suffer the same fate. I envied him his bravery. We were imprisoned in long ditches. No one had the strength or morale to flee anyway. We just submitted meekly as they performed their atrocities. Some of my friends were taken to forked pillories. Their heads were put in the forks, and they were left to dangle, slowly strangling.

"I was taken by a priestess, a young woman. I remember looking into her face. It was pale, beautiful, hooded in white, and totally pitiless. She commanded me stripped naked, and pushed on my knees before her. She took out a curved knife. She cupped my manhood in her hands. She massaged a little. I don't know if she expected me to harden. I think it just shrunk."

Carbo let out a little laugh, but it sounded hollow, even to himself. He could feel the old panic trying to rise, but the reassuring presence of Rufa helped him to suppress it.

"She slid the knife over my chest, cutting into the muscle. I don't even remember if I cried out. I just wanted to die before the suffering became unbearable. Then she put the knife to my genitals. She started to press. I started to beg.

"An older priestess came up, and told her to stop. I could see a silent battle of wills take place between them. Then the younger one dropped her knife, and walked away. The older priestess said something in German to my captors, and they bowed to her. She looked at me, and said in Latin, 'You are to be sold to the Sarmathians. They won't want a eunuch.' They took me back to the pit.

"They didn't keep many slaves. They burnt, strangled, cut throats, cut off heads. You can't imagine…"

Carbo swallowed to keep down the rising bile. After a moment, he continued.

"The next day they took those of us that remained away, bound in chains. We had travelled maybe half a day, when the soldier behind me managed to wriggle out of his chains - he was pretty skinny and they didn't really fit him properly. He ran, and most of the guards chased him. One of those remaining came over to inspect the chains he had escaped from. No others were near. I was seized by a sudden desperate madness. I strangled the guard with the chains, took his key to undo my bonds, threw the key to the others, and we fled in multiple directions.

"They couldn't chase us all down, even mounted. I found out, years later, that about twenty of us escaped, but only three of us made it to freedom. I think it was weeks before I made it back to a Roman camp, moving at night, living off roots and bugs that I found. I was sick, thirsty, hungry, my wounds festering. It took me over a month to recover physically. But my spirit… I don't think it ever has. Or will."

"Your spirit is strong, Carbo," said Rufa, firmly, but Carbo shook his head, inwardly cursing the feeling of weakness he still carried inside him.

"I joined Germanicus' campaign, and I was with him years later when he found the site of the massacre. Bleached bones lay in the dirt where the bodies had fallen. There were broken spears, horses' legs, heads still nailed to the trees. A few of us that had survived the massacre were in

Germanicus' legions, and we showed him where their fortifications were, where Varus had died, the pits where they had held us, the pillories where they had strangled us, and the altars where they had burned us. Germanicus wept, we all did. We buried them then, my comrades. Germanicus himself laid the first turf on the funeral mound.

"I fought for Germanicus, for the legions, for Rome, for many years after that. But most of all, I fought for my comrades, the ones about me, and the ones who had fallen. Like your father."

He finished speaking. Rufa looked at him, moisture filling her eyes. She held him close, and despite his best efforts, he felt tears welling up inside him as well. He bit his lip, and held them in.

Philon gave the password again, and entered the cult meeting. He scanned the gathered cultists sitting in the dimly torchlit room, and he found Dahia. He squeezed beside her, and she turned to him with a genuine smile.

"Philon, how have you been?"

"As well as a man who is slave, eunuch and prostitute can be."

Dahia's expression was sympathetic and she took his hand. "That's why you're here, why everyone is here. Life has been cruel to us, and we look to the Lord and Lady to restore justice."

Philon patted her hand gently. "And why do you come?"

"I am a slave too, you know that. Many slaves accept their lot. Some even relish it, those with a good Master, who looks after them, shelters them, keeps them free of the peril of starvation. But it isn't right. No one should be owned by another."

"Radical words. Do you think the Lord and Lady coming to Rome will change that?"

"Yes!" she said, the word an emphatic hiss, eyes flashing. "They will not allow this injustice to continue."

Philon felt a leap of excitement and hope in his belly, even though he doubted the words. He was not so foolish as to believe the Carthaginians had any different views on slavery than Romans. Slavery was a universal situation, a way of life in every nation and every culture that had ever been. That had been drummed into him as a child, when he first learned that he wasn't as free men. As long as there were free men, there would be slaves, he was taught. Dare he hope that the coming of the Lord and Lady would make things any different?

A thin, beautiful woman entered the room, and a hush fell. "That's the Mother Elissa," whispered Dahia. Philon stared at her, captivated by her presence and beauty. She said nothing, just nodding to the worshippers, then retreating to a simple chair at the side.

The leader of the mysteries today was a plump man who Dahia said was called Scrofa. He was obviously high in the confidence of the Mother from the way he spoke easily to her. He moved to the front of the room, and raised his hands in the air. The followers all knelt, leaning forward so their foreheads touched the floor.

"Lord and Lady, hear us, your faithful servants. Bless us with your presence, your strength tonight, and keep us till the time of your return."

The followers chanted in unison. "Ha-mmon, Ta-nit, Ha-mmon, Ta-nit."

"Sit up, faithful ones."

The followers raised their heads, so they all rested with their haunches on heels, straight-backed.

"Soon, the day of freedom will come. Soon, the Lord and Lady will descend on us, rewarding us for the offering we will give. The time is nearly upon us. These are not just words. The Mistress Elissa has told us the hour and the date. We will offer them the ultimate sacrifice on the last day of the Romans' biggest games, the *Ludi Romani*. On that day, Rome will be destroyed, and the Lord and Lady will descend to reward her faithful army."

"Glory to Tanit, glory to Hammon," breathed the followers in awe.

"But before that day comes, we have work to do. Some of you have tasks already entrusted to you. I bid you carry these out diligently. The rest, be ready on the day, for whatever comes."

Scrofa paused and looked around the captivated faces.

"Elissa has also bid me to ask you all to be alert for something she has lost. Her slave and the slave's daughter have betrayed her, left the sight of the Lord and Lady. She believes they are still within the city. Mother and daughter are quite distinctive, both with bright red hair. The mother has a slave brand on her upper arm, that reads 'Bad slave'. They may be anywhere, sleeping rough in a cemetery, staying in a tavern, hiding in the Cloacus Maximus. If any of you come across a red-headed mother and daughter who are new to your area, you are to let me know."

The rest of the worship continued with ritual, chant and ceremony. At the end, Dahia leaned over to Philon. "What was all that stuff about the red-headed slaves?"

Philon didn't reply, as a sudden certainty crept over him.

He walked home from the meeting, mind occupied. Various noises, screams, laughs, roars and loud vomits still distracted him and sent shivers down his spine, but he made it home without incident, still lost in his thoughts. By force of habit, he walked in through the back door, and into the room that until recently had been his bedroom. As the door swung open and he stepped inside into the dimly lit room, he saw Carbo and Rufa, lying naked in each other's arms. He stared for a moment, then his eyes dropped to the floor as Carbo lifted his head and looked at him.

"What do you want, Philon?" asked Carbo, gruffly.

"I'm sorry, master," said Philon, voice humble. "I mistook my quarters."

"Close the door, then."

Philon bowed his head and retreated backwards, closing the bedroom door behind him. He climbed the stairs towards his own bedroom, mind in turmoil. He had seen the brand. It was her.

Philon lay in the dark, sleep far away. He was starting to feel a connection with the followers of the Lord and Lady. He thought of Dahia, a woman he could appreciate was both kindly and attractive, and he felt a pang of regret that he could not be for her what most men could be for a woman. He had thought that was something he had come to terms with a long time ago. But Dahia stirred strange unfamiliar feelings within him. As for, Elissa, she was simply mesmerising. And Elissa had given them a command, to look for the red-haired slaves.

Philon knew now that the ones she had been talking about were Rufa and Fabilla. It all made sense now, their sudden appearance in the middle of the night explained by the fact that they were fugitive slaves. But to who did his loyalty belong? His master, Carbo, who had not treated him unkindly. Or his new mistress, the mother Elissa? He squeezed his eyes shut, and prayed to the Lord and Lady for guidance.

Chapter XVI

Elissa paced round the *peristylium*, irritable and uncharacteristically anxious. The date of the final day of the *Ludi Romani* came ever closer, and while most of the preparations were proceeding according to plan, she was still no closer to finding the moloch. What would happen if she wasn't found in time? Could another be substituted in her place? The signs had been clear - it had to be her. So what would happen if there was no sacrifice, or the wrong sacrifice? Surely, the Lord and Lady would not come. Or worse, they would come and let their anger fall on her and her followers, instead of the Romans.

Glaukos had turned out to be useless. He had told her that he thought he had seen Rufa, but then had let her get away. All he had returned with was the information that Cossus had met with them. And all that Cossus had been able to tell Elissa, before he died under her ministrations, was that Rufa was accompanied by a large, rough man.

Shafat approached her, but stood a short distance away, head bowed, waiting to be acknowledged. She realised he was aware of her temper and was trying not to provoke her, but his obsequiousness irritated her further.

"What do you want?" she snapped.

"Mistress, you have a visitor."

"Who?"

"A slave called Philon."

"What is he to me?"

"He says he is a follower of yours. He says he has information about the red haired girl."

Elissa felt a tightening in her chest, of hope, and fear of false hope.

"Bring him to me now."

Shafat bowed and backed off. He returned moments later with a smooth skinned, round faced, plump young man. Shafat left them alone.

"Speak," said Elissa.

The effeminate voice that the newcomer emitted, together with his appearance, clearly marked him as a eunuch to Elissa.

"I am a new follower of yours, and of the Lord and Lady, mistress."

"Shafat said you had information for me," said Elissa impatiently.

"We were told at our meeting that you were looking for a red headed slave woman with a red headed daughter." Elissa inclined her head, but regarded him with an unblinking stare. Philon swallowed, nervous under the gaze, and continued.

"I am the slave of a tavern owner. He has a red-haired woman and a red-haired woman staying with him. They arrived a few days ago. They forced me out of my quarters in fact."

The whine in Philon's voice set off another surge of irritation in Elissa's gut, but she suppressed it with an effort, and kept her cool stare on his face. His words started to come faster now as his anxiety increased.

"I saw the woman's arm yesterday. She has a slave brand."

Elissa almost dared not hope. There must be many red-haired slaves in the city. Could these be her fugitives?

"Their names," she said, her voice not much more than a whisper. "Tell me their names."

"I was told the mother is called Rufa and the daughter Fabilla."

It was them! Not even attempting to disguise their identity. They must be with a man they trusted, and by extension they had trusted his *familia.* She sent a silent blessing to the Lord and Lady.

"Tell me where they are."

"In the backrooms of a tavern, in the Subura."

"Which tavern? What is your Master's name?" Elissa's patience was running out.

Philon opened his mouth to speak, but Shafat was back, head bowed.

"What is it?" Elissa snapped.

"You have more visitors, mistress."

Elissa considered telling Shafat to send them away, but then realised if she had done that with this eunuch, she would have missed out on this vital information.

"Who are they?"

"That commander from the *vigiles,* Vespillo."

Elissa tutted. Glaukos had told her that one of their followers, Dahia, the Numidian girl, had information that Vespillo had been making enquiries into her followers. She wondered whether he was going to be a problem, one that would need a decisive solution.

"There is another man with him," said Shafat. "His name is Carbo."

A small noise came from Philon, and Elissa and Shafat turned to him. His face had paled, his eyes wide.

"He cannot see me here," hissed Philon in a loud whisper.

"Why ever not?"

"Carbo is my master. He is the one who has your slaves."

Carbo and Vespillo waited in the *atrium*. Carbo took in the room, noting the same things that Vespillo had told him about - the neglected shrine for the *lares*, the tarnished statue inside. The doorman was uncommunicative, so Carbo just stood, while Vespillo wandered around looking at the frescoes. After a wait which was shorter than they expected, the doorman escorted them into the *peristylium*.

They were confronted first by a huge, muscle-bound man with the tanned skin of an easterner, and a deep scar across his cheek. Carbo found himself looking up into his face, an unfamiliar feeling for the tall veteran.

"What do you want?" he said, in a strong eastern accent, Galatian or Asian, Carbo thought.

"And you are...?" asked Vespillo.

"Glaukos. What is your business here?"

"We are here to see Elissa. On personal business."

Glaukos folded his arms. "You can discuss her personal business with me."

"Oh, you are her secretary?" sneered Vespillo. "You don't strike me as a man of many letters."

Glaukos took a threatening step forwards, and Carbo tensed, ready to react to any aggressive act.

"Glaukos!"

Elissa's sharp voice stopped the giant instantly. He glared at the two visitors for a moment, then his shoulders drooped and he stepped aside.

Beyond him, the priestess stood, straight-backed, clothed in a white dress. Whatever image Carbo had had in his head, he had to reevaluate at the sight of this cold-eyed but beautiful woman. He was instantly transfixed by her gaze, like a spear through his chest, pinning him in place. Her face seemed to blur, transforming into the face of a German priestess from the Teutoberg forest, disdainfully regarding her pathetic captive. He felt his heart start to race, his mouth turn dry.

Her eyes flicked to Vespillo, and her spell over him broke. He let out the breath he hadn't realised he had been holding.

"Commander," she said, inclining her head. "Have you come to purchase one of my slaves again? Shall I have them parade out here for you to choose one? I'm afraid you haven't given me any notice, so they may not be as well-turned out as I would have hoped."

Vespillo gave a cool smile. "Actually it's more of an official visit."

Elissa raised an eyebrow. "Oh? You are going to aid me in finding my fugitive? That is after all, one of the duties of you little bucket boys isn't it?"

Vespillo's expression hardened. "We prefer to be known by our official title. We are the *vigiles.*"

"Of course. And this man with you, is he a little bucket… I mean is he a member of the *vigiles* too?"

"He is… an associate."

Elissa allowed her gaze to run slowly up and down Carbo's figure, her eyes coming to rest on his face. Carbo returned her stare, trying to look impassive.

"And you aren't going to introduce me to this unofficial associate of yours, that you have brought into my house while on official business?"

Vespillo cursed inwardly. She had taken control of the conversation smoothly, left him on the back foot. He had no desire to give Elissa Carbo's name - it might lead to the woman making her own investigations. Carbo however gave a small bow.

"Gaius Valerius Carbo," said Carbo, making an effort to keep his voice steady. "Thank you for inviting me into your home, mistress."

"I'm not sure I did any inviting, Carbo. Nevertheless, you are welcome."

Carbo inclined his head. With an effort, he held her eyes, for long enough for Vespillo to start to become uncomfortable. Then, without taking her gaze off Carbo, Elissa said, "Please, both of you, take a seat. Now, Vespillo, tell me how I can help?"

Carbo was forced to break eye contact first as he looked for a place to sit, and when he had located a stone bench, he looked back up to see a faint smile on Elissa's lips. He remained expressionless, inwardly chagrined he had lost that first battle of wills. Carbo and Vespillo shared the stone bench, and Elissa sat on a small wooden stool with a cushion that one of the slaves had brought out. When they were settled, Elissa looked at Vespillo expectantly. Vespillo hesitated.

On the walk over, Vespillo had explained how he would improvise questions, try to draw Elissa out, while implying that they knew more than they really did. Now, as Carbo glanced over at him, he realised that this forceful, beautiful woman had robbed Vespillo of his usual confidence. The old army veteran, leader of the rough and ready *vigiles,* was struggling to string two words together. Carbo turned his attention back to Elissa and spoke.

"The *vigiles* are investigating some...er... concerning allegations and rumours."

"How exciting! What rumours may these be?"

"We aren't at liberty to discuss them, but we have a credible source that suggests you may have useful information for us."

"A credible source? Not a slave then. Unless you had them tortured of course."

"A credible source is all I can tell you for now."

"Well, I wouldn't want you to give away any state secrets. But I ask again, what does this have to do with me?"

"Our source suggests that you have knowledge of a conspiracy to commit a human sacrifice. And further, that you are leader of a cult that indulges in human sacrifice."

Elissa laughed, a light, tinkling laugh that contrasted with the hardness in her eyes.

"It is true I am a worshipper of gods that are foreign to these shores. And that I have some followers of my own.

That is hardly a crime is it? Or has the Senate made a new law? Are you now going to arrest all the followers of Isis and Cybele and Mithras and Jehovah?"

"Human sacrifice is murder," said Vespillo, finding his voice at last. "It will not happen in my city."

"And yet it did, didn't it, Commander? Oh, it wasn't recent, but then when was the last time Rome was truly threatened? When Hannibal had massacred your entire army at Cannae. And when all seemed lost, what did the city of Rome do. They took two vestal virgins, two girls forced to abstain from sexual relations for all their youth, just for the good of the city, and accused them of having had sexual relations. Their punishment? One committed suicide, the other was buried alive. Imagine that, being entombed until the lack of air or food or water killed you. Another time, a Gallic man and woman and a Greek man and woman were buried alive in the Forum Boarium, as sacrifices, because of words written in the Sibylline books. Yet you tell me that Rome believes human sacrifice is murder?"

Despite himself, Carbo was impressed by the woman's knowledge of their history. Vespillo's face was starting to flush, and he spluttered a reply. "Those things happened a long time ago. They were dark times."

"Aren't dark times always among us? It wasn't so long ago that the Germans inflicted a defeat on Rome that was nearly the equal of Cannae." She turned her stare back to Carbo. "I wonder how that must have felt. The proud Roman army cut down by barbarians. The survivors tortured. *Sacrificed*." The last word came out as a hiss, and Carbo felt a shiver run down this spine that he couldn't control. He felt cold, the woman's words, his memories, making his heart start to race, his skin become clammy. He swallowed hard. He would not let the terror overwhelm him!

Elissa watched him intently for a moment, something like excitement in her eyes. As Carbo mastered himself, he saw a look of disappointment come to her face. She turned back to Vespillo.

"In any case, this is academic. I worship, I have followers. There is nothing more to say."

Carbo felt disappointment rise within him. The plan to get her to confess all, and use the knowledge to force her to relinquish her claim over Rufa and Fabilla had always been a little shaky. Now he had met the woman, though, he realised the utter futility of it. He resigned himself to fleeing the city with Rufa and Fabilla, finding somewhere in the country out of reach of this mad woman.

A pounding came from the street door. Vespillo and Carbo exchanged surprised glances, but when Carbo turned back to Elissa, he noticed a strange expression of satisfaction on her face. A moment later, Shafat appeared.

"Apologies for the interruption, mistress, but the urban cohorts are here."

Elissa smiled. "Show them in, Shafat."

A broad, earnest looking man in the uniform of a centurion of the urban cohorts was ushered in, four fully armed and armoured legionaries behind him. Vespillo and Carbo stood, facing the newcomer uncertainly. Elissa remained seated.

"Lucius Mocius Poppillius, centurion of the second cohort of the Urban Cohorts, at your service, mistress." The centurion took off his helmet and gave a short bow.

"Thank you for coming so promptly, centurion. You received my full message regarding my missing slaves?"

"Yes mistress. I'm only sorry it has taken us this long to be of assistance. My men have been keeping their eyes open, but found nothing."

"Well, we know why now, do we not?" She gestured at Carbo. "This man is Gaius Valerius Carbo. He is the man who has been harbouring the fugitives."

Carbo's stomach lurched at the words. He looked across at Vespillo, whose horrified expression must have mirrored his own.

"I want him arrested, at least until my property is returned. Be careful though. He is a veteran of the legions, and I understand somewhat hard to handle."

"Not to worry, mistress. We've seen the type before, all puffed up with their own size. There's little me and the lads can't handle though." He drew his sword, the legionaries behind doing the same, and advanced on Carbo. Vespillo stepped between them.

"Hold it right there, centurion," he said, raising his hand, palm outwards.

The centurion paused at the tone of military authority in Vespillo's voice.

"Who are you?" he asked, suspiciously.

"Lucius Vedius Vespillo. Tribune in charge of the second cohort of the *vigiles,* Esquiline station. There is no evidence this man is guilty of anything."

"Vigiles?" The centurion barked the word out with a laugh. "You have no authority over the urban cohorts. Now stand aside and let proper soldiers do their work."

"Proper soldiers?" Carbo stepped up to the centurion, their faces close, so he could smell the mix of *garum* sauce and wine on his breath. "Walking around Rome, beating down disturbances amongst unarmed citizens. Your men are thugs and you know it. Try facing a horde of Germans, berserk with rage, armed to the teeth, roaring down the hillside onto your position, when all you have to protect you is your shield, your sword, and the man either side of you. Then talk to me about proper soldiers."

The centurion looked momentarily cowed, but Elissa snapped, "Do your duty man, and arrest him."

The centurion's expression was more respectful when he eyed Carbo now, but his voice was still firm. "You must come with me now. Please turn around and put your hands together."

Carbo looked at Vespillo, bracing himself for action.

"Do as they say, Carbo. They have nothing on you. I will make sure you are free before you know it."

Carbo hesitated, then nodded. He turned and felt his wrists firmly bound behind him.

"Don't worry about me," he said to Vespillo. "First, go and make sure my... loved ones are safe."

Elissa clapped her hands and laughed, again the incongruous, light laugh. "Loved ones? Oh how sweet. I presume you mean my slaves. Well don't worry about them, the cohorts are already on their way to retrieve them now. Isn't that right, centurion?"

The centurion nodded, hesitant, unsure now about the rights and wrongs of the situation. Carbo stared at Elissa in disbelief, unable to understand how she had found them so quickly. Then he roared, and charged at the centurion, head down, butting him in the stomach. The centurion went down hard, but the banded metal hoops of his *lorica* took much of the force, and dazed Carbo. He turned to confront the legionaries, and aimed a kick at the knee of another, who howled as his leg buckled. But as Carbo whirled to face a third, the hilt of a *gladius* smashed into the back of his head. He went down onto his hands and knees, stars flashing before his eyes, the world spinning rapidly around him.

"Go, Vespillo," he croaked. "Do what you can."

Vespillo, who had barely had time to move, such was the speed and ferocity of Carbo's attack, made to leave. One of the legionaries barred his way, and the centurion staggered to his feet.

"Get out of my way," said Vespillo, voice low and dangerous. "Unless you are going to arrest me too."

"Yes," said Elissa firmly. "Arrest him too."

The centurion shook his head. He turned to Vespillo. "You may go."

Vespillo shot Carbo a quick look, where his friend was breathing heavily. "I'll be back, Carbo. Don't resist any further, it will just make things harder."

Carbo tried to nod but it made the spinning worse. Vespillo turned and ran for the doorway, barging Shafat aside as he left the house.

Elissa turned her withering stare on the centurion. "Why did you disobey me?"

Popillius looked embarrassed, but kept his head high. "With all due respect, mistress, you are not my commander. We had no orders about that one, nor complaints against him." He nodded to two of his men, who lifted Carbo, with some effort, back to his feet. "We will take this one away, mistress. Hopefully my men will return your property promptly."

Elissa's eyes flashed. "They had better centurion, or your superiors will be hearing about it."

Poppillius nodded and led his men out, dragging Carbo with them.

Vespillo's lungs were burning, his legs leaden, as he pounded along the streets. Although his job kept him active, he wasn't trained or built for running a long distance, nor was age on his side, and his body yelled at him to stop, to lean against a wall and regain some breath. He carried on anyway, knowing what was at stake. The centurion had seemed reasonable enough, but he knew Carbo's words were true. The urban cohorts were thugs and bullies, too cowardly to fight in the legions, most of them getting a thrill out of abusing the civilians. They weren't restrained by the pride the Praetorians felt in their noble calling, nor, because they were recognised as real soldiers, did they have as much to prove as Vespillo's own paramilitary force. He turned the last corner onto the street that led to Carbo's tavern, dreading what he would find.

Slumped against the wall outside the tavern was Dentatus. His club was lying nearby, blood on it. Much more blood pooled on the ground around Dentatus' still body, still trickling from a rent in his abdomen. A small crowd had gathered, but they stood back, not wanting to get involved, or endanger themselves in case the trouble had not yet finished. Vespillo checked Dentatus briefly for signs of life. There were none, so he rushed into the tavern.

As his eyes adjusted to the dim light, the carnage became clear. Maybe because he had been forewarned by the attack outside, maybe just because he was the better fighter, Bucco had put up more resistance than Dentatus. Two urban cohort legionaries lay dead, heads caved in by Bucco's club. Bucco himself had multiple sword wounds, to his face, his chest, his arms. A gaping throat wound was the fatal blow, and Bucco lay on his back in a darkening pool, sightless eyes staring at the ceiling.

The tables were overturned, crockery and glassware smashed, amphorae tipped out, food thrown at the walls. Vatius, the elderly philosopher lay face down on the floor, bleeding from his head and not moving. Myia, herself limping on one hind leg, and bleeding from her mouth, trotted in anxious circles around the prone man. Vespillo checked him quickly for a pulse, and found one, weak but steady. From behind the bar, Vespillo heard a whimpering sob. He quickly moved round to see who was there.

Marsia was lying against the wall, hugging herself. Nearby, a legionary lay dead, a kitchen knife sticking out of his chest.

Vespillo touched Marsia on the shoulder. The German slave woman, lost in shock, had been unaware of his presence until that moment, and she gave a small yelp of fear and surprise. When she saw who it was, her eyes filled with tears. "Marsia," said Vespillo gently. "Where are Rufa and Fabilla?"

Marsia shook her head in misery. "I don't know," she cried, plaintively.

"Have… have the urban cohorts taken them?" asked Vespillo, any icy fist clutching his heart as he waited for the answer.

"I…don't know," said Marsia again. "Maybe. We did all we could, to give them time to get away. They had a head start. Your men, they fought bravely. When Bucco went down, Vatius stepped in their way. He held them up for only moments. Maybe it was enough. Rufa would not flee at first, but I dragged them both out of the back, told her to look to her daughter. She ran, but I don't know where, or how far."

Vespillo noticed now there was blood trickling down the side of Marsia's head.

"I came back in, to see if I could hold them up any further. I was clubbed aside, and hit my head on the counter. When I came to, that man was on top of me." She gestured at the dead legionary. "He was the only one still here. Had his cock out, getting ready to stick it in me. She spat in his direction. "Wish I could have cut his balls off before I killed him. I had to make sure first time though."

Vespillo set a chair upright. He gently helped Marisa up, and guided her to sit down. He found an unbroken cup, and a broken jug that still had some wine in it, and pressed it into her hands. He went back to the door, and looked out on to the street. He selected a young boy from the crowd, and pressed a copper coin into his hands.

"Go and fetch the *vigiles* from the fire station on the Esquiline. If you are quick enough, there is another copper coin for you when you return."

The boy raced off, and Vespillo went inside. Marsia was rocking herself back and forth, not touching the wine. Vespillo lifted the cup to her lips and made sure she drank. Then he said, "Marsia, I have to go and break this news to Carbo. He has been arrested, but he will be out soon. My men are on the way, and they will help tidy up and make everything secure."

Marsia nodded miserably, then looked up at him. "That poor child. She must be so scared. Find them, Vespillo."

"I will. Carbo and I will. By Jupiter, I promise."

Chapter XVII

Hermogenes wobbled a little as he walked home through the *Trans Tiberim* area of Rome, the crowded region on the far side of the river. The Tiber to his right was full of merchant ships and barges, queueing for mooring space to offload their cargoes from around the Empire into the huge warehouses. Brays and snorts came from lines of donkeys and oxen, harnessed to carts or bearing empty saddle bags, waited for the produce to reach them for distribution to the markets around the city. Mundane food supplies, jewellery, spices and perfumes that the wealthier Romans could afford, scented the air with an exotic mix. It all flowed through here to feed the Roman maw.

A vast population of workers lived and toiled in this region, many slaves, but also the free poor and foreigners, looking for casual labour to buy them meat or wine to last their families a day or two.

It was a perfect place for an escaped slave to hide.

Hermogenes Publii Petronii servus. Hermogenes, the slave of Publius Petronius. Hermogenes rolled his slave name distastefully around in his mind. Being a slave meant giving up everything into your master's possession. Even the name 'Hermogenes' wasn't his given name, but after his drunkard Greek father had sold him into slavery as a boy, that was the name he had received from his new master.

Having had a small amount of education, Hermogenes was eventually noticed by his master. He had risen to the position of steward of a small estate in Campania, overseeing the farm workers and providing accounts for his master. It was a privileged position, no manual labour, good living quarters, use of the best looking of the domestic slaves.

He had got too greedy though, he knew that. While it was expected that the steward would skim a little off the profits, his taste for fine wine and expensive prostitutes had caused him to take a little too much. When the auditor arrived from Rome, he knew his time was short, and taking his savings and a fast horse, he had fled.

He had easily persuaded a local warehouse owner to give him a labouring job. Realising how unfit he had become had been a shock to him. As a young man he had been able to work all day and not feel the fatigue, but good living and little exercise had let him run to fat. Two months of hard work, though, had put him well back on the path to being in shape, and soon he had received a promotion to overseer.

Now he had enough income to provide him with a basic food ration, lodgings, and some left over to get drunk from time to time. Occasionally he would sit with fellow workers in the tavern, and crow about how life was good. Those below him resented it, those above him mocked it, but he didn't care, and when he was rolling drunk, he would tell anyone that asked that being a free man was the world's greatest gift.

He paused in his wanderings. Had he heard a footstep behind him? It was very late, and even in this crowded region, there were few around, for fears of the usual muggers and cutthroats. The thought of being robbed rarely bothered him unduly - he was big enough to take care of himself, and he carried little with him in the way of coinage at any one time. Still, he felt a little unsettled as he carried on his slightly weaving journey home.

The tall warehouses cast deep shadows, which even the bright gibbous moon could not illuminate. Hermogenes found himself sticking to the light where he could. He started to wish for his bed. The wine was starting to wear off, making him realise that he was cold and tired. He turned a corner.

The punch took him full in the face and knocked him flat on his back.

For a moment, he just lay there, dazed, not quite understanding what had happened. Then a dark figure loomed over him. He looked up into emotionless eyes, and fear gripped him.

Publius Petronius looked down at the man at his feet. He presumed it was a man, although he was barely recognisable as such. The face was a mask of congealed blood. A leg and an arm bent at unnatural angles. Any part of the skin that was exposed or showed through the ripped tunic was bruised black. The stench of faeces suggested the man had soiled himself. Only the noise of bubbly breathing and the occasional groaning sob gave any indication that the man was alive. Petronius looked up at the the short, wiry figure who had brought this pathetic bundle in, and dumped it at his feet. He was surprised that the slight man had been able to carry the heavy weight with such ease.

"What is this?" asked Petronius.

"This is the fugitive, Hermogenes Publii Petronii servus."

Petronius regarded the man on the floor again.

"I asked for him alive."

The short man tilted his head on one side, his expression confused.

"You can clearly see he is breathing."

"Barely. What use to me is a slave in this condition? It will take him months to recover, if he ever does."

"The contract did not specify a condition in which the fugitive was to be returned to you."

"Did he really put up such a fight that you had to do this to him?"

The man shrugged. "Not really."

"Well, I will not pay you. You may have honoured the letter of the contract, but you certainly have not honoured the spirit. I commend you for your diligence in tracking this slave down. He has wronged me, and deserved punishment, but he was also valuable, and I had further use for him. I will pay you a quarter of the agreed fee, purely as a gesture of goodwill."

The slave hunter's eyes narrowed. "I spent a month tracking this man down. I have considerable expenses."

"That is not my concern. You have been told how much I will pay you."

"No."

Petronius looked at the man in shock.

"I beg your pardon?"

"No. You will pay me the full amount you owe."

Outrage suffused Petronius' face, his plump cheeks turning ruddy.

"I am Publius Petronius. I am a Senator of Rome," he said. "I was a consul. I will not be dictated to in my own house!"

"I am Dolabella, the *fugitivarius*. I do not fail to fulfil a contact, nor to collect what I am owed."

Petronius stared at him in shock, then cried out. "Steward. Call the porters. Have this man removed from my premises."

Several bulky slaves appeared at the run in moments. They surrounded Dolabella, waiting for instructions from Petronius. Dolabella held Petronius' haughty stare for a moment, then turned and left without a word. Petronius realised he had been holding his breath, and sighed. He looked down at the man at his feet. "Get this slave some medical attention. Let's see if we can salvage something from this debacle."

Petronius lay awake in bed, staring at the decorated ceiling, barely visible in the darkness. There were no external windows, just a slight glow under the cracks of the door from the moonlight and torches that illuminated the *peristylium*. He couldn't sleep, strangely unsettled by the slave hunter who had been in his house a little earlier. He had sent his wife away, and even spurned his favourite slave girl that night. He sighed and turned onto one side, staring at the wall.

Something cold and sharp touched his neck, and he froze.

"Do not make a sound," whispered a familiar voice, causing Petronius' heart to miss a beat.

"How did you get in here?" croaked Petronius. The knife pricked the skin, and Petronius felt a small dribble of wetness run down his throat.

"I said, not a sound. Now, let's walk to your safe. Get up slowly."

Petronius did as he was told. He had not been wearing nightclothes, but Dolabella did not allow him to dress, and his nakedness heightened his sense of vulnerability. They walked together, Dolabella at his side, knife still at his throat.

"You will be crucified for this," hissed Petronius. The knife pricked in again, drawing more blood, and Petronius gasped. They reached his office, and he stood before the safe. He paused for a moment, and looked round at Dolabella.

"Pay me what you owe me," said Dolabella. Petronius hesitated, then unlocked the safe, and withdrew a number of *aurei.* Dolabella tucked the coins into a purse on his belt. "Now double it."

"What?"

"This second visit to collect my debt has been inconvenient. This is my fee for the inconvenience."

The knife had not wavered, and Petronius sighed and counted out the same number of coins again. He rose to his feet.

"You have what you asked for. Now leave, and I will think about asking the urban cohorts to go lightly on you."

Dolabella made no movement, the knife remaining at Petronius' throat. Unblinking eyes fixed the senator's gaze. For the first time now, Petronius started to feel genuine terror. This man had done horrible things to Hermogenes, and now he was in his power while all his staff slept. He wondered where the night porter was, then realised he was probably incapacitated or dead.

"You can't kill me," whispered Petronius. "I'm a senator."

"I'm not going to kill you," said Dolabella, flatly. "But I do have a reputation to maintain. It wouldn't do for my clients to think there were no consequences for reneging on a deal."

Before Petronius could say another word, Dolabella flicked the dagger up over the senator's cheek, opening a deep flap of skin, then plunged the point into the man's eye. Petronius let out a ghastly shriek, as he fell to his knees, clutching his face. Slaves were with him in moments, but through his agony, he heard their whispered questions, asking who had done this, and he realised that Dolabella was gone.

Carbo stared at the walls of the holding cell. It was a converted cellar below the barracks of the urban cohorts, and a small amount of street level light filtered through a high, barred window. Graffiti covered the walls, scratched into the soft cement with fingernails or any sharper instrument the guards had been too lazy or incompetent to discover. "Centurion Herennius is a cocksucker," "May the gods curse Porcius, whose bad faith put me here," "Will I ever see Ambusta again?" and "Friend, watch out for the guards, they will try to bugger you while you sleep."

From the window he could hear the sounds of street life continuing, the traffic and merchants and tradesmen contributing to the cacophony. In his little cell, nothing changed. There was no bed, no chamber pot or bucket. There was a pool of stale water in one corner which he had used to slake his thirst. The opposite corner he used as a latrine. No one had come to see him yet, not a guard to bring him food, nor a friend. He had no news of what had happened since the urban cohorts had hauled him away, roughly this time the day before, and his stomach was a knot of tension and frustration. He tried not to dwell on the fates that could have befallen Rufa and Fabilla, but with no other mental stimulation, it was an impossible task. Had they been killed outright? Returned to Elissa for whatever she intended for them? Imprisoned somewhere, like him, awaiting crucifixion or some other grisly punishment for their escape?

He punched a fist into the wall. Some loose cement came away, but the wall barely yielded and his knuckles came away grazed, small spots of blood welling up. The pain felt good, felt justified. He had promised to protect them, and he had failed. Failed in his oath to them, and to their father. Dark despair threatened to overwhelm him. He looked around the cell for the hundredth time, wondering if there was something he had missed, some way out. The high window was out of his reach. Despite the unlikelihood of success, he had tried jumping and climbing. The door was solid oak, with a small cross-barred window. It didn't yield to kicks or punches, nor did anyone come to investigate the noise when he yelled. He paced the cell like a caged lion waiting for its turn in the arena, but eventually he gave up and slumped on the floor, elbows on his knees, head in his hands.

He had had time to ponder things while locked up. He thought about Elissa, and the story that Rufa had told him. Having met the woman, he now had no doubts as to the truth of the tale, and he could also see how people fell under her spell. She was intelligent, persuasive, calm. But it was her eyes, the piercing gaze, that made it so hard to ignore her, so tempting to give her what she wanted. What could a woman like that achieve, what harm could she cause, with an evil will and a band of fanatic followers?

He shuddered. Unbidden, as always, images of priestesses in white came to mind. The dark cell disappeared, and he was in Germany. Naked, bound, terrified as the priestess leaned over him, curved knife in hand. He pulled his knees up to his chest and started to tremble.

Upstairs, Vespillo took a deep breath and counted to ten slowly. He let it out and tried again.

"I must insist that you release this man."

"With the greatest respect, tribune," Lucius Mocius Poppillius said, pronouncing the title with a sneer, "you have no authority over me. I am not in your chain of command. I am a member of the urban cohorts, part of the army, not a semi-professional band of firemen and vigilantes."

"You are aware, centurion," Vespillo also laid emphasis on the title, attempting to reiterate his seniority, "That two of my men were murdered, along with several civilians, at the premises of the man you hold downstairs. We are investigating the matter, and witnesses say that members of the urban cohorts were involved. Not only do you hold no evidence against the man you have imprisoned, but he is material to our ongoing investigation. The co-operation of the urban cohorts would be noted and appreciated. It may influence our conclusions on whether criminal activities in the cohorts are due to rogue elements, or something more systemic, going up the chain of command."

Vespillo held Poppillius' stare. Poppillius' looked to one side, calculation appearing in his expression. Vespillo could tell he was wavering, but the centurion still held out.

"We believe he is involved in the illegal harbouring of fugitive slaves."

"For which you have no evidence."

"When we recapture the slaves and torture them, we will have evidence enough."

"Then at that time, you can re-arrest him."

Still Poppillius looked uncertain. Vespillo sighed.

"Very well, I will report your intransigence to Macro." Vespillo looked at Poppillius. "Quintus Naevius Cordus

Sutorius Macro, that is, Prefect of the *vigiles*. Quite the up and coming man I hear, someone who is going places in Rome. Not someone in whose bad books you want to be."

"Look," said Poppillius, and Vespillo could tell from the centurion's expression that he was beaten, and looking for a way out with pride. "We are certainly sorry for your losses, and will help with your investigation any way we can. My information is that the incident was already over when my men arrived at the tavern. They found your men and the civilians dead, and presumed it was a local gang. I understand there was some history between the man downstairs and a local gang leader. Some of my men were even killed by these gang members before they escaped. "

Vespillo considered letting Poppillius know he had eyewitness accounts of the cohorts' raid from Marsia, but now was not the time, and besides, the word of an untortured slave was worthless anyway.

"Thank you, that will be very helpful in our enquiry. But having your prisoner released to my custody will also be most useful."

"If I am releasing him to your custody, then I can see no harm," said Poppillius. "As long as we can have him back when we recapture the fugitives."

"Of course, if you recapture them, and they implicate him." Vespillo smiled. "Would you like me to fetch him, or do you have a man who can do that?"

Poppillius snapped an order to a nearby legionary, who hurried off.

"Would you like some wine?" asked Poppillius. "Just to show there are no hard feelings, just two soldiers doing their jobs."

Vespillo smiled but shook his head. "Thank you, no. I have a busy day ahead of me. Water would be acceptable though."

Poppillius frowned slightly, but commanded a slave to fetch him wine, and his guest, water. Vespillo sipped from the cup, waiting quietly now. Poppillius looked like he wanted to fill the silence, but could think of nothing to say.

The legionary returned, leading Carbo before him.

"Found him quivering in a corner," he said to Poppillius, laughing. "Dirty bastard has shat and pissed in one corner. Shall I make him clean it up?"

"Perhaps if you had provided him with access to a latrine, or even a bucket, that wouldn't have happened," said Vespillo, angrily. "You try holding it in for a whole day. Carbo, have they fed you?"

Carbo shook his head, a little numb at the sight of his friend.

"Poppillius, is this how you treat everyone before they are found guilty? It's a disgrace. I will have to consider whether to include this in my report to the Prefect. Come on Carbo, you are released to my custody. Let's go."

Vespillo led Carbo out of the barracks by the elbow.

Carbo wanted Vespillo to tell him everything that had happened straight away, but Vespillo, after saying only that Rufa and Fabilla were alive, insisted that Carbo had something to eat and drink before telling him more. He had

wanted Carbo to bathe as well, but knew that that could
wait. They sat by a fountain, and Carbo used cupped hands
to collect water to quench his thirst. Vespillo bought
sausages and bread from a nearby stall and Carbo wolfed
them down greedily.

He wiped his mouth on his tunic sleeve, and turned to
Vespillo.

"Thank you, friend, for getting me out of that place." He
had regained his composure, the terrors of captivity
disappearing once he saw the blue autumn sky. "Now I need
to know, what happened after I was arrested? Where are
Rufa and Fabilla?"

Vespillo sighed and looked down. "I'm afraid I don't
know."

Carbo reached over and grabbed his arm, looking at him
intently. "What do you mean? Are they safe?"

"That I don't know either, but I believe they are. They
had fled the tavern by the time I arrived."

"So the urban cohorts did go there. How did they know?
Cilo and Manius?"

"There's more, Carbo. There was a fight. My men
Dentatus and Bucco, they died giving Rufa and Fabilla
time to escape."

"I'm sorry. Marsia? Philon?"

"Marsia is fine. She killed a cohort legionary, but no one
will hear that from me. Philon was out on an errand when it
all happened, he returned when it was all over. Vomited his
guts up when he saw the mess."

Carbo looked at his hands, clasped together before him.
He was exhausted, not having managed to sleep in his cell,

feeling washed out in the aftermath of the panic that had gripped him. Thinking straight was difficult, but he forced himself to focus. Where would Rufa go? Her freedom was so limited as a slave, she couldn't know the city too well. Besides, she knew she wouldn't be able to survive on her own, that she still needed him. She would be too scared to return to the tavern though. She must have given him some indication of where she had run to then, a clue she could have left quickly when she realised the house was being raided.

"I want to get back to the tavern."

"Of course. Are you happy to make your way there from here? I have some reports to write, and a hundred other distractions of my job."

"I will struggle home, I'm sure."

"Well call if you need anything." Vespillo put a hand on Carbo's shoulder and looked into his eyes. "Anything."

"Thank you, Vespillo, for you all your help. I will see you soon."

Carbo made his way through the city streets, the autumnal early afternoon sun hot enough for him to sweat. He bought more food and drank from more fountains on the way back. His legs were weak from the lack of food and the general anxiety he felt. He trod the increasingly familiar route back to his tavern wearily, as the sun started to dip in the sky. As he neared the tavern, a young boy who had been lounging against a wall caught sight of him, and hared off down the street. Carbo approached the scruffy place that was his home and business, thinking that when this was all over, he should spend some time doing the place up, then cursing himself for the distraction.

He walked in through the front door, and his eyes took a moment to adjust to the dim light. The face of the figure in front of him, with Marsia seated on his lap, slowly became identifiable. It was Manius.

Carbo froze, and looked around him. Cilo lounged against a wall, stroking a terrified looking Philon's hair. Around the tavern sat six gang members. These ones looked tough, Carbo thought to himself. They were all well-built, with pitiless expressions, and gazes that didn't waver, and all were armed with clubs and coshes.

Carbo's hand dropped to his side for his sword, cursing as he realised he had not worn one since he left his house to visit Elissa the day before. He was well outnumbered and unarmed. Despair overcame him again. Surely this encounter was not survivable. He looked around again. Where were the *vigiles* that Vespillo said would replace Dentatus and Bucco?

"Welcome to my tavern," said Manius, a broad smile on his face.

Carbo didn't reply, just keeping his eyes on Manius, while his peripheral vision monitored for movement.

"Philon, go and get my guest a drink. Just some cheap *lora*, I think, nothing too special for this one."

Philon moved quickly, legs trembling, to pour a cup of wine for Carbo. Carbo ignored the proffered cup.

"You decline my hospitality, my wine, from my slave, in my tavern?" Manius gestured around him.

"What do you want, Manius?" asked Carbo in a low voice.

"Want? Nothing, Carbo. I have already taken what I wanted. Look around you. The little bucket boys your friend Vespillo left here fled as soon as they saw us. This tavern is now mine. And I must say I like it. I think I will enjoy spending time here. I like my new slaves too." Manius slid his hand inside Marsia's tunic and squeezed her breast hard. She stiffened, remaining silent, but Carbo saw the fury in her eyes.

"This will not stand, Manius. I will not allow it, nor will Vespillo."

"Vespillo is not here, Carbo, nor his lackeys. You are on your own. And when you are dead, the matter will be a moot point. Vespillo can protest all he likes then, but you will no longer be the boil on my arse that you have been. No one around here will bear witness against me either, nor will anyone try to take over this tavern. Certainly not when they have seen what we do to you."

Carbo kept his face expressionless, but Manius laughed.

"So brave, the old veteran. But I am sorry, your death will not be an easy one. You have undermined my authority around here. Before you arrived, people would clear the way before me. Now they jostle me in the street, whisper as I walk past. I have even heard laughter. Today, the laughter will end, for you, and everyone in this gods-cursed neighbourhood."

Manius nodded to Cilo, and Cilo gestured to the thugs. "Take him."

The men advanced on Carbo from all sides, and his heart sank as he found himself hopelessly outnumbered in a fight for the second time in two days. This time though, the outcome wouldn't be a short stay in a cell.

Carbo dropped into a wrestler's couch, legs spread, weight low to reduce his chance of being knocked over. Big as his assailants were, Carbo was bigger. He knew it wasn't enough, and decided he had to take the initiative.

Without warning, Carbo exploded forward, head down, charging into the nearest thug, shoulder striking into the man's midriff. The man was thrown backwards onto the hard floor, the wind knocked out of him, and as Carbo's weight followed through, he heard ribs crack. The man's club, a long stick with a nail hammered into the end, fell loose on the ground. Carbo dived for it, grabbed it, and rolled to his feet. He was backed against a wall now, and there was room for only three men to approach.

Carbo swung his club wildly at them, keeping them at bay, and they held back out of his reach.

"Get him, you cowards!" yelled Cilo. "Get him now, or you will not be paid."

The men exchanged glances, nodded to each other, then rushed Carbo all at once. Carbo stopped one swinging cosh with his club, and ducked another blow which smashed into the wall behind him with a crack. Plaster and dust flew into the air. The third man's club caught him a glancing blow across the shoulder, which staggered him and made his arm grow weak, but he gripped his own club tightly and swung it hard at head height. The wicked nail struck the third man's temple and penetrated his skull to its full length. The man stiffened, and toppled over, a pool of blood spreading from the fatal head wound. The nail snagged in the bone, however, and the club was torn from his hands.

One of the thugs had got behind him, and he shoved Carbo hard in the back, sending him sprawling forwards to the floor. Now there was room for the four thugs still standing to get round him, and they started raining kicks and club strikes. He managed to grab one foot and twist, feeling the knee pop and hearing a satisfying scream, but the others redoubled their efforts, and then he could do nothing but curl up and wait for his fate. Repeated blows to his back and legs and head were agony, and he tried to keep from crying out. A firm kick connected with the back of his head, and even though his hands cupped around it protected his skull a little, he felt darkness looming in from his peripheral vision. His head was struck again, and the darkness became complete.

Chapter XVIII

Carbo heard the sound of voices before he could open his eyes. Far off, the hubbub of Roman street life was audible, but nearby those noises were strangely muted. He opened his eyes, and found his face was flat on the ground, staring horizontally out over the detritus of the street - the broken pots and jars, the food remains, the human and animal faeces. He saw feet, hairy and gnarled, clustered in small groups nearby. He tried to sit up, but found simultaneously that his hands were bound behind him, and that his whole body screamed in agony when he tried to move any part of it. An odd, acrid smell stung his nostrils.

"He's awake," came a deep voice.

"At last, sit him up." The voice sounded like Manius. Rough hands grabbed him and jerked him to an upright sitting position. He cried out involuntarily, then clamped his mouth shut. He found himself propped against solid stone. He recognised that he was at the crossroads of the street on which his tavern intersected the Clivus Suburanus. That meant that behind him was the statue of Mercurius Sobrium, the statue that Augustus himself had gifted to the district. The crossroads were a focal point in the community, and consisted of an open, paved plaza where the two roads met, with a raised platform of marble veneered limestone. Carbo realised that he was propped against the altar to the statue on this raised platform. At a respectful distance, a small group of locals from the neighbourhood had gathered, quietly watching the scene with curiosity. Nearer were a group of Manius' men, and in front of him were Manius and Cilo. Manius had his back to Carbo, and was looking out over the crowd.

"All of you, residents of the Subura, men, women and children," said Manius in a loud voice that dripped with the lower class accent the rich and powerful mocked. "Look at this pathetic, beaten man." He turned to Carbo, and spat on him, a phlegmy gob that hit him on the side of the face. Carbo didn't flinch, but inside his heart was in despair.

"Some of you were starting to think this man was a hero weren't you?" Manius continued. "A champion of the people? Standing up to the bullies?" He turned again, and gave Carbo a kick in the side. Carbo groaned, but remained upright.

"I saw you all," he continued. "The way you started to look at me in the street. The way you muttered as me and my son walked past. Some of you even thought you could stop paying me my rightful taxes, the protection money that keeps you safe. You thought that you didn't need me, now you had your hero Carbo, and those losers playing at soldiers in between putting out fires.

"Well, I am going to show you what happens to those who defy me. I am going to show you who is in charge here. Not Carbo. Not the little bucket boys. Not the old men in the Crossroads Brotherhood or the urban cohorts or the Praetorians or even fucking Tiberius himself!" His voice crescendoed, and the crowd shrunk back a little at the anger, and the blasphemy against the divine Emperor.

"And when I have finished with this pathetic turd, we will be visiting each and every one of your taverns and cobblers and butchers and whatever else you do to scratch a living, and you will pay every *as* you owe me, and you will pay as much again for your disrespect. I will not be mocked." Each word of the last sentence came out as a roar. He gestured to his men, who had been standing around grinning. Two of them went to fetch a large jar, and between them they heaved it over to him. Unceremoniously, they upended the jar, covering him in sticky oil. He looked up uncomprehending, as the viscous liquid streamed down his hair and face. Then Cilo came into his field of view. He was holding a flaming torch.

Carbo looked down at himself, and realisation came with a sickening feeling in his guts. The acrid smell was because his clothing, which he had thought sticky with blood, was coated in pitch. The oil was lamp oil. And Cilo stood before him with a flame.

Cilo's face leered in front of his, the damaged nose just inches from his own. "Have you got any last words, hero?" sneered Cilo.

Carbo tried to speak, swallowed, tried again. "I'm not a hero," he croaked.

"What was that?" said Cilo, plainly enjoying this moment of victory, wanting to savour it as long as possible. "Speak up, hero."

Carbo had to spit some sickly tasting oil out of his mouth. He spoke in a louder voice this time.

"I'm not a hero." He looked out at the surrounding crowd. "I'm just a retired soldier, trying to make a home. I just wanted to be left alone."

"Then you shouldn't have made trouble for us," said Cilo.

"You made trouble for yourselves."

"Well we are ending it now." Cilo waved the torch near Carbo's face, and he could feel the heat. Terror started to rise within him, the unbidden memories of a clearing in Germany, white robed priestesses cackling at him.

Carbo slumped, head falling onto his chest. Utter despair overwhelmed him, and he closed his eyes. He had failed Rufa, failed Fabilla. Now he was going to die, and die horribly, bound, in the manner of his recurring nightmares.

"He is a hero," came a loud female voice with a German accent. Carbo thought it must be in his head, the Germanic priestesses mocking him. But the voice came again, and he realised the source was in the crowd.

"He is a hero to me."

Carbo raised his head, and saw Marsia. She was standing at the front of the onlookers. There was matted blood on her hair, a ruddy bruise on one side of her face. But she stood with arms on hips, staring down Cilo and Manius defiantly.

"Shut your mouth, you slave whore," said Manius. "Watch your master die."

"He fought for the Empire" came another female voice, tremorous, but loud. "Like my sons."

"He stood up to those thugs who oppress us every day, while the urban cohorts stand by and do nothing," shouted someone else from the back of the crowd.

"His mother was Atella," came a woman's voice. Carbo saw it was Gnaea, standing beside Lucius and clutching his arm. "He's one us."

A low muttering went around the onlookers, whose number was starting to swell. They no longer looked so cowed. Manius and Cilo exchanged looks, uncertain. Marsia turned to address the onlookers.

"Are we going to go back to how it was? Paying money we can't afford so these men won't hurt us? Bowing to these scum in the street, though they aren't worthy of us shitting on them?"

Sporadic shouts from the crowd broke out, "No, never." But no one moved.

"Is Carbo the only hero today?" Marsia yelled at them. "My ancestors would not allow this to one of their own. Won't you all be heroes as well?"

Vatius, head bandaged, called out in a croaky voice. "Plato said, courage is knowing what not to fear. Friends, don't think just of helping Carbo. Think of yourselves, your families, living under the tyranny of these murderers, every day scared for your lives and your livelihoods. All we have to fear, is that today we do nothing."

"Shut the old fool and that slave up," said Manius to Cilo. Cilo passed Manius the torch, stepped forward and grabbed her by the arm. A boy in the front of the crowd, no more than nine or ten, threw a stone, little more than a pebble, but it hit Cilo in the head and made him yelp. One of the thugs stepped forward and clubbed the boy in the head, and the boy crumpled to the floor, head caved in. There was a momentary pause as the crowd took in what they had just seen. His mother, a stout, dark-haired woman, let out a wail. Then there was a roar of anger, and the onlookers surged forward.

Manius' men held their ground for a short while, swinging clubs and wielding knives, but the press of an angry mob quickly overwhelmed them. Some of the thugs dropped their weapons and ran, others went down under the feet of the mob, where kicks and stamps made sure few of them would ever rise again. Cilo and Manius exchanged terrified looks, then Cilo broke and ran. Manius turned to Carbo, face twisting in anger. Then he threw the burning torch at Carbo and fled.

The torch landed in Carbo's lap. He twisted and bucked his hips, and he managed to throw the torch off his body, but the pitch and oil ignited, and started to burn. He felt the heat against his chest grow, a warmth that went quickly from uncomfortable to unbearable. He closed his eyes and screamed.

Someone grabbed his hands and cut his bonds, then thrust him onto his back. The same person then leapt onto him, smothering the flames on his body with their own, hugging him tight, starving the fire of air. The fire went out. He opened his eyes to find himself looking into the concerned eyes of Marsia, her face an inch away from his own.

"Master," she said. "Are you hurt?"

He tried to take a deep breath, and his ribs protested, and he found it hard to get enough air in. Still, he managed a small smile.

"There seems to be some sort of weight on my chest. Otherwise, I'm fine."

Marsia smiled back, and gingerly got off him, inspecting him carefully to make sure there were no sparks or hot embers on him that could reignite. Around them, the riot had stopped as quickly as it had started. Down the Clivus Suburanus, Carbo could see a group of men marching. At their head was Vespillo. The crowd, seeing the group of *vigiles* with grim expressions on their faces, melted quickly away, taking their wounded and one or two dead with them, and leaving the bodies, mostly unmoving, of the street gang behind.

Vespillo marched up to Carbo.

"I leave you alone for a couple of hours…" He shook his head. "Someone reported what was going on. I didn't think the urban cohorts would rouse themselves for a minor disturbance like this, and it sounded like you needed help." He looked around him. "Looks like I was wrong."

Carbo counted around twenty casualties.

"Manius obviously went for a real show of force," he said. "Wanted to properly subjugate the locals."

"And it turned into a rout," said Vespillo. "His power is well and truly broken now, both in manpower and morale. The locals won't let him rise again."

"Probably not. But he is a wounded animal now. He is still dangerous."

"That's not a worry for today." Vespillo held out a hand, and helped Carbo to his feet. Carbo prodded himself carefully. His injuries seemed to be superficial burns, a lost molar, bruises, contusions, and probably a cracked rib. He had got away lightly, he reflected. Vespillo took Carbo under one arm, Marsia under the other, and while the *vigiles* made sure order was restored, they helped him inside.

The *fugitivarius* slouched against a pillar, looking at Elissa with a disrespectful half-smile on his face. She returned his gaze with a cold stare.

"That's a ridiculous sum," she said.

He shrugged. "I was told by your man here," he gestured at Shafat, "that this escaped slave is valuable. That you wanted the best. That you wanted Sextus Pontius Dolabella." He swept his hands downwards to indicate himself. "Here I am."

"I will give you half that amount."

Dolabella straightened, then gave a short bow. "I think we have wasted enough of each other's time. I was obviously under a misapprehension." He turned to leave.

"Very well." Elissa hated being the supplicant, but time was running short. She looked calculatingly at the short, wiry man with the calm expression but the wary eyes. "I will pay you half now, and half on completion of your task. She, and her child, need to be in my possession by the evening of the fourteenth day before the Kalends of October, at the very latest. It is the child that is the most important to me. You may keep the mother alive to keep the child pacified if you must, otherwise kill her. If the child is dead though, you will get nothing."

Dolabella inclined his head. "Five days should be more than adequate. You will have your property back soon."

"Start your investigations with this man, Carbo. Watch him though, he is dangerous, and he seems to be in with the *vigiles*."

Dolabella laughed. "Really? The *vigiles* are supposed to catch fugitives themselves. They are hopeless amateurs, though, freedmen playing at law enforcement. They won't be any impediment. If this Carbo is involved with your property somehow, however, that will be useful. Now with your permission, I will start my work. Once, of course, your steward has sorted out the…deposit."

"Pay him, Shafat, and show him out." Elissa waved a dismissive hand.

"Yes, mistress."

When Shafat returned, she glowered at him. "Do we really need him?"

"He is the best, mistress. Everyone says so. He has never failed to return a fugitive slave when he has taken the work on."

"But I hear they don't always return alive."

"His methods are reportedly… severe, sometimes. I don't think we would want to enquire too closely what he actually does, I doubt he will stay within the law. He is also reputed to have certain urges, which mean that the property is not always returned in pristine condition. He always seems to have a plausible explanation for any damage. But you were clear that you needed the girl slave alive for him to be paid, and it seems money is the one thing that will control him."

Elissa nodded, but she remained worried.

"We need that girl. All the followers knew the importance we placed on her as a sacrifice. I never considered there would be any problem in ensuring there would be an appropriate moloch, if I selected her from my own slaves. With her distinctive appearance, that little brat was ideal. My followers will think our cause is cursed by the Lord and Lady if we do not go ahead with the ceremony as planned. We would have to delay, wait for the next major festival, maybe wait a whole year, a year in which our plans may be discovered. A year in which Carthage will remain unavenged."

"He will find her, Mistress. The Lord and Lady will ensure it."

Elissa turned to stare into the middle distance. "So much planning, so much work. To hinge on this." She faced Shafat again, and squared her shoulders. "You are right. I must have faith in the Lord and Lady. They will find her. We will go ahead." Her eyes blazed. "And then Rome will pay, in fire and blood."

Chapter XIX

Carbo lay face down, naked on a towel on the hard floor. Marsia did not have a gentle touch, and he clenched his fists as she scraped grit out of his wounds with a cold damp cloth. Pain and frustration combined in him, till he wanted to howl. He had slept soundly and only woken with the sun, starting awake as he realised how much time had gone past without looking for Rufa and Fabilla. He suspected that the drink Marsia had given him the previous night had contained poppy juice for him to have slept so well. He tried again.

"Just tell me," he said, pronouncing each word slowly. "Where are they?"

Marsia tutted. "They are safe. I will tell you where they are when you are fit to walk without support."

He opened his mouth to protest, and she pressed the cloth against an abrasion on his ribs, causing him to cry out. Nearby, Vespillo laughed.

"Give it up, Carbo. You won't win with that one. If she says they are safe, I believe her."

Carbo simmered, allowing Marsia to finish her ministrations. When she was finally done, she passed him his tunic and he sat up and threw it over his head. He made to stand, and his leg gave way, dumping him on his backside again. He looked at Marsia but no help was forthcoming there, so he tried again. This time as he started to buckle, a firm arm gripped him under the elbow, supporting him. With Vespillo's help, he made it to his feet. Placing one hand on a table to steady himself, he looked defiantly at Marsia.

"There, as good as new. Now you can tell me. They spoke to you before they fled, am I right?"

"They did, Master," said Marsia, her eyes narrowing as they watched him swaying slightly. "I'm not sure if you are truly..."

"Marsia," interrupted Carbo, his tone urgent. "There are other people looking for them. They need my help."

Marsia's expression looked stricken, and her gaze dropped to the floor.

"He's right, Marsia" said Vespillo, gently. "I know you are looking out for your Master, but Rufa and Fabilla need his help too."

Marsia nodded. "Very well. Rufa asked me where she should go. She was terrified, and I don't think she was thinking straight."

"Where did you send them?"

"Where can you go in Rome, when you are an escaped slave, with no money, and nowhere to live? You cannot stay in a tavern, you cannot stay with a friend, you cannot beg aid from a patron or master." She shrugged. "You go where all the other poor and homeless go."

"Where?" demanded Carbo.

"The tombs."

Carbo and Vespillo exchanged glances. Romans had a healthy respect for superstition, and hiding with the dead did not feel like a good omen. It did make sense though.

There would be shelter, and a crowd of other homeless amongst whom she could disappear.

"Which one?"

"I suggested she head outside the *pomerium*, to the east. There are lots of tombs that way."

"Did you tell her which one to go to?"

"No, Master. I am not familiar enough with them to have made a recommendation."

Carbo felt a surge of anger at what he took to be her irony, before he realised she was just stating fact in flat Germanic fashion.

"But she seemed to have heard of one," continued Marsia. "She said something I didn't quite understand. She laughed, a strange mirthless sound, and said, 'out of the fire, into the oven'. But the soldiers were entering the tavern. She had to flee before I could ask her what she meant."

"Then I guess we need to do some searching. Vespillo, do I have your help?"

"Of course you do," said Vespillo. He reached out an arm to Carbo, but Carbo shrugged him away.

"I can walk without aid. I've taken a lot worse and kept fighting."

"I'm sure you have," said Vespillo, and stood back, while remaining close enough to catch Carbo if he should fall. Marsia helped Carbo into his sandals, and Vespillo and Carbo left the tavern together.

Dolabella hung back in the shadows and watched the two men emerge from the tavern, and turn down the street with a purpose. He assessed them with a professional eye.

The larger one, who he presumed was Carbo, was obviously injured, and he had heard from the sausage seller from whom he had bought breakfast what had happened the previous day. It was a factor to consider. He couldn't rely on the usual apathy of the crowds to leave him to his work where this one was concerned.

The smaller, stocky one of the pair, Vespillo he guessed, walked with a back only slightly bent with age. His manner was military in bearing, and he knew from his enquiries that both men had been in the legions, and knew how to handle themselves. It was a concern, but not a major one. He had dealt with many men who fancied themselves in a fight - deserting soldiers, escaped gladiators, thugs who had stolen slaves. None of them knew how to fight the way he did. Caution was prudent, though. Besides, he needed these men to find his target. He wouldn't have to fight them, if he was sensible.

The two men continued east along the *via Labicana*, to the *Porta Esquilina* in the old Servian wall. At this bottle neck in the flow of traffic in and out of Rome, the crowds were particularly concentrated, and Dolabella lost sight of them in the crush. He remained calm, however, as he always did, and soon had pushed his way through. He reached a clearer stretch of road, and looked around, trying to identify his marks. For a moment, he didn't see them. Then he realised they had not made as much progress as he had expected - they were standing on a street corner, pointing in different directions and arguing.

He lounged against a wall, took an apple from his belt pouch and took a deep bite. No point in passing up an opportunity to rest and replenish his strength. It was impossible to predict when he might need it. So, they didn't know precisely where they were going. No matter. They would take him where he wanted to go in good time. He was in no hurry.

Rufa put her arm round Fabilla and cuddled her close. Fabilla snuggled against her, and they both savoured the warmth. Rufa looked around her. The tomb they were in was impressively large, but that meant that the air was cool, and they had with them only the clothes they had fled in. Of course, they weren't the only ones in the building. Any place that provided respite from the elements was a potential shelter for the multitude of homeless in Rome. Many slept out on the streets in the more clement weather, or took shelter under the arches of aqueducts or in porches during brief downpours. The night had been cool though, so there were a number of others in there. The atmosphere was thick with the stench of unbathed bodies, and of the excrement of those too lazy, or too infirm to go outside to relieve themselves.

It had been a good choice of hiding place. Fabilla and she were both wearing hoods to disguise their red hair, and only the destitute would brave the company, the conditions, and the presence of the spirits of unknown intentions that undoubtedly haunted the place. Rufa tried not to think too hard about the *lemures*, and she told herself that the shiver that went down her back was purely due to the cold.

She looked around her. The tomb was the final resting place of a freedman called Eurysaces. She remembered the baker from whom she had purchased the bread for the household had told her about it, and how she needed to buy a lot more bread so he could afford a tomb like that when his time came.

The building was constructed in the style of a bakery, with horizontally orientated cylindrical depressions in the front wall, exactly the right size to hold a unit of grain. Across the top of the tomb was a relief showing various stages of bread-making. The inscription on the outside read, "This is the monument of Marcus Vergilius Eurysaces, baker, contractor and public servant. Obviously." She liked that Eurysaces, dead for decades, had had a sense of humour, and she offered a silent prayer to his shade, thanking him for his hospitality and asking that he do her no harm.

Nearby, a scuffle suddenly broke out between a filthy woman, maybe in her thirties, with almost no teeth, and straggly hair, and a boy with a withered leg, over a small piece of bread. Rufa felt her stomach rumbling, and knew that Fabilla, uncomplaining as she was, must be famished as well. The irony of starving inside a tomb designed to look like a bakery was not lost on her. Soon they would have to venture out. And then what? Begging? Worse, selling herself, so they could eat?

A short, skinny man with boils on his face, wearing a tattered, dirty tunic, woke next to her. He sat up, wheezing, then coughed paroxysmally, before spitting a large gob of phlegm out. He looked over to Rufa.

"Have you got any wine?" he asked in a rough voice.

Rufa shook her head. "No, sorry, we have nothing."

He peered at her in the gloom, looking a bit puzzled.

"You're pretty," he said. "Not like the rest of the women here."

"You weren't complaining when I sucked your cock yesterday, Sentius," said the toothless woman.

"Shut your mouth, Elpis," snapped the man. "Or I will shut it for you."

Sentius turned back to Rufa and reached out a hand to stroke her face. Rufa tried not to flinch, and kept her face impassive.

"I haven't seen you round here before. You must be new. I wonder what your story is? You and your pretty little girl."

Rufa kept quiet, looking down. Sentius reached out a hand and tilted her chin up so she looked into his eyes.

"It's a bad place you know. The tombs, the streets. A woman and a child on their own, they could get hurt. There are bad men here. Bad women even. Not to mention the *lemures* that lurk in the shadows when you turn your back. A woman needs protection."

"No, thank you," said Rufa. "I can look after myself."

Sentius grabbed her arm tightly, causing Rufa to cry out.

"What sort of a citizen would I be if I left a vulnerable woman undefended. I can be your guardian, your protector. In fact, I insist."

He pulled her towards him. Fabilla looked up, eyes widening at the sight of the ugly man, and shrank back.

"No, please."

"Of course, as your protector, it's only fair that I have certain … privileges. But a pretty woman like you should have no problem obliging a handsome man like myself." He shoved her hard and she tumbled over backwards. In an instant he was on top of her, rough hands pawing at the top of her tunic. She got her hands between them and shoved, rolling her body so he tipped sideways. She tried to move away, seeing Fabilla's terror-filled face, then she was grabbed and pushed back down again. She struggled, but he slapped her hard across the face, temporarily stilling her. He drew a rusty knife from beneath his tunic, and touched it to her neck gently. Then he put it back in his belt, and as she lay, no longer resisting, he ripped the top of her tunic open and grasped her breasts painfully, letting out a throaty growl as he did so. He pulled her tunic up around her waist, exposing her to the interested onlookers within the tomb, some of whom were shouting encouragement to him. As he pulled up his own tunic to reveal his erect member, she turned her face away waiting for the inevitable. Her eyes fastened on a stone about the size of her fist. His weight bore down on her, his hands fumbling between her legs. She gripped the stone and brought it round against his head with a dull thud.

He cried aloud, rolling to the side off her, clutching his head. Rufa pushed herself up off the floor, and ran to Fabilla, grabbed her arm. Fabilla looked at her, paralysed like a rabbit caught in a hunter's lamp.

"Come on," she urged. Sentius was staggering to his feet, blood running through his fingers.

"You bitch," he hissed. "I was trying to be nice to you."

He advanced towards her, and Rufa backed up against a wall, pushing Fabilla behind her.

"Leave me alone," she whispered. "Please."

Sentius laughed and stepped up close to her, his face against hers. She desperately brought the stone around again, but he was ready for her this time, and he caught her wrist, then squeezed until her hand opened and the weapon clattered to the ground. He pushed himself against her, foul breath in her face, hardness pressing against her. He fumbled for her again. She tried to push him away but her hands were weak and trembling. Her fingers brushed against the knife in his belt.

His rod probed against her, trying to gain entry. She looked into his vacant, faraway gaze, and she gripped the knife hilt, then pulled it free from his belt. He thrust forwards, and she gasped in despair as he entered her. He let out a loud groan, then staggered back. The hilt of the knife protruded from his ribs, the blade buried deep in his chest, where it had penetrated him just at the moment he had penetrated her. He clutched it at the knife and pulled it free, and dark blood spurted from the wound.

He turned on her, amazement and rage on his face and took a step towards her. Then he sank to his knees, pitched forward on his face, and was still.

When Carbo found her, she was sitting against the wall, knees pulled up to her chest, trembling violently, Fabilla clutched to her side. He rushed to Rufa and put his arms around her. She stiffened at his touch, eyes wide, then wrapped her arms around him and gripped him tight.

Vespillo entered the tomb. He took in the scene in an instant, the terror in Rufa's eyes, her dishevelled clothing, the dead man with the knife sticking from his chest nearby. He looked around at the other inhabitants of the tomb, who were sitting quietly, like children caught in an act of disobedience.

"You all watched, didn't you?" he said. "Stood by and let this happen. Let this young mother be assaulted, without lifting a finger to help."

Sullen stares met his challenging gaze, but there was no reply. Vespillo pointed to a stocky, middle-aged man. "You. Why didn't you help?"

The man shrugged. "What's it got to do with me?"

Carbo stood slowly, unpeeling Rufa's arms from him. He stepped towards the man, who stood hastily, backing away a step. "Look, Sentius was a bad one," he babbled. "Stand up to him and he might knife you in your sleep. There was nothing we could do."

Carbo's hand shot out, grabbing the man by the throat and thrusting him against the tomb of the wall. The heavy man impacted the brick work hard enough to dislodge plaster. Carbo started to squeeze the man's neck, looking into his eyes as they started to bulge.

"That's enough."

Carbo looked round at Vespillo, ignoring the choking and kicking from the man he held.

"Let him go," said Vespillo sternly. Carbo held his gaze. "Rufa needs you."

Carbo looked over to Rufa, and the anger evaporated. He released the man, let him fall to the floor, gasping for breath, and stepped over to where Rufa sat against the wall, holding Fabilla to her. He knelt down beside her, and stroked the hair tenderly away from her face, seeing the red mark from the slap, the tear-streaks showing cleaner skin beneath the dirt. He leant forward and kissed the top of her head, then put an arm around her. He tried to pull her torn tunic back together, but it was too badly damaged. Casting around, he saw an elderly man wrapped in a scruffy blanket. He grabbed it off him, the protests quickly cut off by a warning glance from Carbo. Gently he wrapped the blanket around her shoulders like a cloak.

"How did you find me?" she asked.

"'Out of the frying pan, into the oven?' It was Vespillo, he guessed you meant the baker's tomb. He knows Rome much better than me. Why didn't you just tell Marsia where you were going?"

"I was about to, then I hesitated. I know what happens to slaves when they are interrogated. I couldn't expect Marsia to keep me secret under torture. Then the soldiers were there and it was too late."

Carbo nodded. "Come on, let's get you both out of here."

"Where to?" asked Rufa, annoyed with the self-pitying tone of her voice but unable to help it. "Where is there to run?"

"Let me worry about that." He helped her to her feet. Vespillo moved beside them, and together the four of them walked out of the tomb.

Dolabella leaned against a wall, just round the corner from the baker's tomb. A little while had passed since Vespillo and Carbo had entered the unusual building. He presumed that meant there was something of interest inside. He was a patient man. Waiting was part of his job.

Four figures emerged from the tomb. Carbo and Vespillo, with a woman and a child. The child had a cloak that covered her hair. But the woman was clothed only in a torn tunic and a blanket. Her bright red hair was on show. There could be no doubt that he had found his targets.

He considered his options for a moment, all the while watching to see what Carbo and the others did. They hesitated, Carbo and Vespillo in deep conversation, before nodding, and heading together down the street in the direction of the Esquiline. Dolabella followed at a short distance.

Carbo was walking on one side of the woman, his arm around her. The child was on the other side, holding her hand tight. Vespillo walked a little behind, looking left and right for possible threats. Dolabella moved a little faster. From the folds of his tunic he brought out one of his favourite weapons, a leather pouch filled with lead weights. He hefted it in his hand, a tight smile coming to his face.

Carbo and the two fugitive slaves rounded a corner. Vespillo was a few paces behind. Dolabella swiftly closed the gap between them. He raised his arm, and with all the force of his tough, wiry frame, he brought the weapon down on the back of Vespillo's head. Vespillo crumpled to the ground soundlessly.

Dolabella turned the corner swiftly. Only a few paces ahead of him, Carbo and the two slaves were oblivious to the fate that had just befallen their friend. Dolabella moved closer and prepared to strike.

Chapter XX

Elissa stood on a small dais before her worshippers, arms outstretched, dressed in a simple, white robe. She was flanked by Shafat and Glaukos. In the front row, she saw Scrofa and Metella. They knelt before her, heads pressed to the ground as she chanted. The words were Punic, learnt by rote from her mother, and even she only partly understood their meaning. But her followers listened to the exotic and mystical sounding words intently, awed by her presence.

This was the biggest temple she had dedicated to the Lord and Lady. It was situated in an extensive cellar beneath a fullery. The main room was large, dark and damp. Multiple side rooms, alcoves and corridors radiated away from this area.

The strong, ammoniacal odour of urine drifted down, mixing with the sweet smell of incense and the smoke from the oil lamps that cast a dim light around. The fuller was an adherent to her cause, a freedman originally from Parthia, who despite his relatively privileged place in society, still hated the Romans and all they stood for. She saw him at the back, bowed in supplication with all the rest, and she felt a momentary pride. All these disenchanted, oppressed citizens. Slaves, freedmen, foreigners, the bulk of the population of Rome. Ignored, looked down upon, abused by the elite in charge. All ready to rise up. And not in some remote part of the country, like Spartacus had, where they could be isolated, trapped, defeated by the legions. No, here, in Rome, the throbbing centre. She was going to rip the heart out of the Empire.

She knew that, numerous as they were, her people were not enough. Nor would even the others, the ones she was sure would flock to her rallying cry, have the morale, the backbone to defeat the Romans. But if the Romans were already half-defeated, if some disaster were to befall them…

She laughed to herself at the naivety of those who ran the Empire. They worried about the barbarians at their borders, and ignored the huge numbers of enemies that slept on the streets outside their luxury mansions. They thought that banning slaves from wearing a uniform so that they didn't realise how numerous they were was sufficient to prevent an uprising. Slaves lacked freedom, not intelligence. The enslaved and poor of Rome outnumbered the elite and their soldiers many times, and they knew it. All it need was a spark, a catalyst, to bring the whole shaky edifice tumbling down, like the regular collapse of one of the shoddily built *insulae* that the heartless landlords charged rent for to those who could not complain.

And then? When Rome had fallen, when anarchy reigned, what next? She could barely restrain her excitement. Then Rome would belong to the Lord Ba'al Hammon, and the Lady Tanit. She would be queen, a new Dido, beloved by her followers, feared by the Romans. The sole ruler of a new Carthage, arisen in the centre of the old Roman Empire.

Then the old ways could return. The Romans would pay for their injustices. They would become the slaves, the slaves their Masters. Their men would toil in mines, their women in domestic servitude or in brothels, their children… ah their children. The tophets would be filled with the screams of sacrifice, the cries of bereaved parents, the air rich with the stench of cooking flesh as the molochs fed the flames.

She stopped chanting and held her hands high in the air. Her heart was pounding, her breathing deep. An excitement coursed through her whole body, a feeling more intense than sex, as she felt her ambitions coming close to fruition. She let the silence stretch, savouring the moment. Then she let her hands drop.

"Rise, faithful servants," she said. The prostrate crowd straightened, kneeling or sitting up, eyes fixed on her.

"The day is at hand," she said. "The time of liberation approaches. The Lord and Lady will come. Be ready for the day. Be ready to take your freedom!"

The worshippers cried out their joy and obedience. She bathed in their adulation. Then she slowly stepped down from the dais, and walked among them, bestowing blessings as she went. At the back of her mind, a nagging doubt surfaced. Could she do it without the sacrifice? The Lord and Lady had been clear to her - she needed the girl. What if Dolabella did not recapture the fugitives? She would have to delay everything, or the Lord and Lady would ensure failure. And if she delayed, would her followers lose faith? Would all those faithful, putting her plans into place, conclude that she was words and nothing more? Would they drift away, find other causes, other cults? Isis, Serapis, Cybele, this newcomer, Mithras? Could she hold her followers to her, to the Lord and Lady, by her force of will alone?

She shook her head. It would not happen. Dolabella would succeed. She would have her sacrifice, and the gods would bless her endeavours. And Rome would fall.

Metella smiled, at peace with herself. The certainties of the faith, the calming rituals, the communion with her fellow worshippers and with the gods, made her feel almost whole again, for the first time since her husband had died.

She had donated large funds to Elissa's cult. It had pleased her to do it. What use was money to her anyway, without her beloved Decimus to share it with? Elissa and her group, who had given her comfort when she needed them, more than her money-grubbing family, more than her husband's aloof relatives, were more deserving than anyone else she knew.

As the ceremony finished and the worshippers drifted away, she approached Elissa, who was in a corner talking to her steward Shafat, and the scarred bodyguard, Glaukos.

"Mother Elissa," said Metella. She was taken aback to see Elissa turn to her with a flicker of annoyance on her face. It was only a moment before Elissa smiled benignly at her, but Metella had noticed.

"Yes, Metella dear. What is it?"

"I just wanted to thank you for the service. I wondered maybe if we could spend some time together privately, so we could talk more about the Lord and Lady, and pray together."

"Metella, I'm very busy," said Elissa, a note of exasperation in her voice. "I don't think that will be possible."

"But Mother. I thought I… was blessed. Foremost in the sight of the Lord and Lady, you said. A special one."

"We all have our parts to play, Metella," snapped Elissa. "Now, please, I have matters to discuss."

Elissa turned her back on Metella and ushered Glaukos and Shafat out of a back door. Glaukos looked back at her, a lascivious leer on his face. Metella stood staring at the door in shock. She felt completely alone. The place she thought she belonged, the woman she had come to rely on had just rejected her. She was overwhelmed with a sudden conviction that they were talking about her, laughing about her. The door was ajar, and she gently nudged it open. She could hear their voices coming from a small private chamber at the end of a long corridor, and she tiptoed down it. Standing outside, back flattened to the wall, heart racing from her clandestine actions, she could hear their words clearly.

"What will happen if Dolabella fails?" That was the voice of Shafat, she knew.

"You should have sent me to do the job, Mother," said Glaukos.

Elissa's tone was lightly, mocking. "You? What skills do you have to track down an escaped slave?"

"Who needs those sort of skills? I would just go round and kill that dumb veteran who has been sheltering her."

"What would that solve?" said Shafat. "Killing isn't always the solution."

"Sometimes it is," said Glaukos. "If I hadn't gutted that upper class twit Decimus for the mother, then we wouldn't have that silly bitch, his widow's cash to fund the Lord and Lady's plans."

Metella's heart seemed to stop. Her world began to crumble around her. All the certainties she had started to build up vanished in an instant.

"Metella has served us well, it is true," said Elissa. "She is becoming something of an annoyance now, though, with her neediness, and her cries for justice. Maybe we will need to do something about her in time."

Metella held her breath as she walked quietly away. As soon as she felt she was out of earshot, she ran, tears streaming down her face.

Scared and traumatised as she was, Fabilla could still be drawn by pretty jewellery. The woman walking towards her had long, dangly gold earrings, and the young girl's eyes followed as she walked past, head turning behind her. She saw the man behind them, saw him step forward briskly, something heavy in his hand, saw him bring the hand up. She screamed.

Carbo whirled, pushing Fabilla and Rufa aside. The cosh was already descending. Carbo threw an arm up, and took the attack on his forearm, feeling the weight of the blow jar his bones. He thrust the weapon to one side with a lateral movement of his arm and stepped forward, a roundhouse punch arcing through the air with sufficient force to put his assailant on the ground.

The punch connected only with empty air, as Dolabella ducked and stepped to one side. Carbo threw a left hook, but again Dolabella had moved, and Carbo had to pull himself back to avoid overbalancing. Dolabella stood just out of his reach, feet slightly apart, slightly raised onto his toes. Carbo recognised the stance of someone who knew how to fight, and realised he was in a real contest.

"Give me the fugitives," said Dolabella.

Carbo could sense Fabilla and Rufa a short way behind him. He half turned and said to them out of the corner of his mouth, "Run!"

Fabilla grabbed Rufa's hand and pulled her away, disappearing off into the crowds. Dolabella's eyes narrowed, watching them go, then turned his gaze back to the large man before him.

"Get out of my way," said Dolabella, his voice low and dangerous.

"You will have to come through me," said Carbo.

"Oh, aren't you the hero, soldier boy?" sneered Dolabella. "All tough from your battles against unarmoured barbarians. Let's see how you do in a fair fight."

Carbo suspected Dolabella knew all there was to know about fighting dirty, but he let the remark go. The truth was he knew a bit about street fighting himself. Very little time spent in the legions actually involved fighting an enemy. Most of the time it was training, drills, camp maintenance, and brawls with comrades and civilians in streets and taverns. A centurion had to be able to hold his own, more than hold his own in these situations or lose the respect of his legionaries completely. Carbo had never had problems before. His size had been enough when he was young, and as he got older, experience had compensated for the slowness and stiffness that ageing and scars had caused. He had never had cause to be anything other than self-confident in a fight.

The man in front of him made him doubt himself. The odds had been against him many times before, but in a one on one situation, he couldn't remember the last time he had been concerned. This man, though, the way he held himself, showed no fear, the way most people did when Carbo threatened them. Carbo watched him carefully, looking for any betrayal of intentions in his eyes.

There was no warning when Dolabella moved. In an instant, he went from still and relaxed to swinging a punch towards Carbo's throat. Carbo blocked it, and gasped when he felt a sharp pain in his forearm. He stepped back to find blood running down to his elbow, and realised that Dolabella had managed to produce a knife with such dexterity Carbo had not even noticed. Carbo cast around him for a weapon to even things up. He noticed an old piece of lead piping hanging down from a wall, bent and buckled from some old collision. He grabbed it, pulled and twisted and it came away in his hand, to give him a foot long club.

Dolabella waved his knife in small circles, a half smile on his face. Carbo took a step forward and swung the pipe towards Dolabella's midriff. Dolabella skipped back, and Carbo reversed the swing, lower again, so Dolabella had to jump over its trajectory to avoid having his shins broken.

He didn't pause though, making a straight arm thrust towards Carbo's chest even before he landed. Carbo twisted sideways awkwardly, unbalanced by his swing, and the knife grazed his ribs, drawing more blood. Carbo was a big man, and though he was losing blood, the amount was not enough to affect him yet. He knew what could happen though, given sufficient small injuries to drain him of his strength. He stepped back, holding the pipe in one hand, his left hand free.

"They are gone," said Carbo. "I don't know where. There is no point us still fighting."

Dolabella laughed. "I think my job would be easier with you out of the way."

"What is your job, exactly?" asked Carbo.

"I am Dolabella, the *fugitivarius*. I'm sure you have heard of me."

"No," said Carbo.

Dolabella frowned, opened his mouth to say something, then lunged again. This time the knife nicked Carbo's midriff, but even as the knife was moving past him, Carbo clamped down with his free hand, trapping the knife hand against his body. He dropped the pipe and wrapped his other arm around Dolabella's neck. The smaller man wriggled like a feral cat, and Carbo struggled to keep his grip, but one hand locked around Dolabella's knife hand, squeezing hard and forcing him to drop it. Dolabella twisted sharply, breaking Carbo's hold, and stepped back. Both men eyed each other with increased respect.

Carbo kicked the knife out of reach, and slowly bent to pick up the lead pipe again. Dolabella watched, and as

Carbo straightened, he threw himself forward, shoulder punching into his abdomen, arms wrapping round him. Carbo flew backwards, the breath rushing out of him as Dolabella landed on top of him. Dolabella started raining blows to Carbo's head and face, and Carbo brought his hands up to try to protect himself. He was winded, and he was struggling to get his breath, with Dolabella's weight crushing his chest. His ears started to ring, and the world began to spin, as incessant punches rattled him. He pulled his arms underneath Dolabella, and with a huge, explosive effort, he used all his strength to thrust the small man off him.

Dolabella flew three feet backwards, but rolled deftly and regained his feet. A little slower, Carbo also stood. Both men were panting hard now. Carbo was bleeding from three wounds. Dolabella was unmarked, but clearly rattled, and not moving as freely as when they started. Carbo took a slow step forward, and Dolabella circled around him. Carbo noted how he kept his weight on the balls of his feet, moving lightly, ready to spring at any moment.

Carbo slowly followed Dolabella, dragging his leg somewhat, looking slow and weak. Dolabella kept his distance, eyeing Carbo's wounds, obviously realising that time might eventually win the fight for him. He saw how the larger, older man was moving, and a sneering smile spread across him.

"Give it up, old soldier," said Dolabella. "You are getting weaker. I will make it quick for you."

Carbo bowed his head, shoulders slumping. Dolabella circled to where the knife lay and picked it up. Carbo made no move to stop him, instead clutching at his side, then sinking to one knee. Dolabella moved behind him cautiously. Carbo didn't respond. Dolabella stepped up close, grabbed Carbo's hair and pulled his head back. He reached round with his knife hand, ready to pull it across Carbo's exposed throat.

Carbo grabbed the knife hand at the wrist, dropped his shoulder and pulled hard. Dolabella flew over Carbo's shoulder, but Carbo kept grip of his wrist, stopping Dolabella from rolling away, and causing him to hit the ground with a loud thud.

Carbo had only been half-pretending. He really was feeling weakened, from the fight and the blood loss, and he got slowly to his feet. Dolabella was groaning, only moving a little. Carbo gave him a hard kick in the ribs, drawing an even louder moan. He grabbed Dolabella by the chin, gripping his jaw tightly.

"Who hired you?" he hissed, spit flying into the *fugitivarius'* face.

Dolabella shook his head. "I have a reputation," he said through his clenched teeth.

"You have your life, too," said Carbo. "You can choose to keep one of them."

Carbo squeezed harder.

"Can't…speak. Release…grip."

Carbo let his grip slacken. Dolabella opened his mouth… then twisted to bite Carbo's fingers hard. Carbo howled in pain, pulling his hand back sharply. Quickly, he made to grab Dolabella again, but the slave hunter had rolled to one side and regained his feet. Carbo lunged for him , but this time Dolabella danced backwards out of the way.

"Maybe you are right," said Dolabella. "This fight is getting both of us nowhere."

Carbo put his hands on his knees. "I'm warning you," he said. "Stay away from them. Next time, I will kill you."

Dolabella shook his head. "I told you, I have a reputation. One of the things I am known for is never failing. Besides, I get the feeling my current employer is one person it would be foolish to cross."

"What do you mean?" said Carbo, suspiciously.

Dolabella smiled. "I suspect you will find out."

He turned, and disappeared into the crowds that had made a clear circle for the fight. Carbo touched his sides, winced, then retraced his steps.

Vespillo was propped against a wall, where a kindly shop owner was giving him a cup of water. He looked up as Carbo approached, taking in his wounds.

"What...happened?" asked Vespillo, rubbing the back of his head and sounding dazed.

"We got jumped," said Carbo.

"Are the slaves... I mean the... are they ok?"

"They ran. I've no idea where they are now."

"We're here," said a soft voice behind Carbo. He spun round. Rufa was standing there, her arm around Fabilla, looking shaken, but resolute.

"I told you to run," said Carbo.

Rufa shook her head. "Where to? Where is safe for us in this city? The only place I feel we stand a chance is by your side."

Carbo looked at her for a moment, then stepped forward, taking her in his powerful arms. He held her close, feeling a slight tremor in her body.

Vespillo coughed politely. "This probably isn't the best place to be, hanging around in the streets in broad daylight."

Carbo reluctantly released his grip on Rufa.

"So where do we go?" asked Vespillo. "The tavern isn't safe. We can't leave her with strangers who might betray her. I can't have her at the fire station, even I couldn't get away with harbouring a fugitive in the offices of the *vigiles.*"

Carbo looked at Vespillo steadily, head cocked slightly to one side.

Vespillo held his gaze momentarily, then sighed. "My place it is then."

Elissa lay on her back, looking at the fresco on the ceiling of her bedroom. She had commissioned it herself, overseen the painting. It showed scenes from the second Punic war. To the left were illustrations of Hannibal descending from the Alps to surprise the horrified Roman state. Then there were depictions from the battles of Trebia and Lake Trasimene, and finally the battle of Cannae, Carthage's greatest triumph and Rome's greatest ever humiliation. She looked at the paintings of Roman soldiers, dying, pleading, bearing terrible mutilations, and the final death of the consul Lucius Aemilius Paullus, the artist being liberal with historical accuracy and depicting him being run through by Hannibal himself. She felt excitement rise in her belly, a sexual thrill, and she summoned Stathis.

Since she had taken the slave to her bed that first time, she had used him frequently, never letting him finish inside her - that would not be appropriate for a priestess - but otherwise enjoying him fully. He arrived now, eager as always, and at her command was soon standing naked and erect before her. She lifted her *stola* up around her waist and spread her legs. Stathis knelt between them, and obeyed her unspoken order, using his mouth on her with a skill that increased with each performance. She enjoyed the submission that this represented, the man being used, but the satisfaction was tempered by the knowledge that this was a slave who had no choice. What would it be like to have a man like Carbo perform this act on her? A tough, dominant Roman, for whom the act of performing cunnilingus would be the ultimate humiliation.

She closed her eyes and started to imagine Carbo was between her legs, that it was his tongue pleasuring her. The passion rose inside her. She felt her climax near, just as the climax of her plans approached. Everything was right in the world. Nearly everything.

As she arched her back, curled her toes, moaned aloud, the image of the red-headed slave girl, still at large came to mind. She slumped back onto the bed, the physical sensations of orgasm still coursing through her, but the emotional high popped like a bubble. She pushed Stathis away from her angrily. He looked confused, but stood by her bed obediently, his erection bobbing comically while he waited for further instructions.

There was a knock at her door. Shafat had learned not to burst into her chambers now. She called for him to enter, and her steward came in, taking in the scene and averting his gaze.

"Mistress, I'm sorry to disturb you, but you have a visitor."

Elissa sighed. She reached out to take Stathis' hard cock in her hand and stroked it thoughtfully. The slave remained standing, still, narrowing eyes and deepening breathing the only sign of the effect it was having on him. "Who is it?"

"It is Metella, Mistress."

"That silly woman? What does she want?"

"She won't say, but insisted she talk to you. She seemed very agitated."

"That woman is no longer of use to us. We will have to deal with her I think. Show her in."

Shafat looked hesitantly at the slave, whose eyes were closed now. "In...here?"

"Yes, I will receive her here."

Shafat nodded and retreated out of the door. Elissa lay back, one hand gently teasing her slave, looking up into his eyes. She caressed her own body idly, trying to recover her sense of relaxation. The door opened and Metella burst in, accompanied by two burly bodyguard slaves.

"I trusted you!" she cried. "How could you?" Metella took in the scene in front of her, and for a moment, shock made her pause. Her jaw dropped as the naked Elissa didn't even sit up, and just continued stroking the young slave.

"My dear Metella," said Elissa languidly, sparing her a brief glance before looking back at her slave. "Whatever is the problem?"

"You. You had him killed. My husband, my beloved."

Elissa continued to stroke Stathis. "Metella, Metella, why would say such a thing?"

"I heard. I heard you and your thug, Glaukos, talking to your steward. I heard everything! Glaukos killed my husband!"

"Maybe we should hear from Glaukos, then," said Elissa calmly. "Fetch him Shafat."

Shafat, looking unwell, bowed his head and retreated out of the room.

"Was it just for my money?" said Metella, stepping up to the foot of the bed, her voice high. "Was that all you wanted me for?"

"We all have our roles to play in the Lord and Lady's plans."

"And my husband? He was in their plans too?"

"The Lord and Lady demand sacrifice sometimes, Metella. You know that. Maybe you didn't appreciate the scale of the sacrifice. You have given up something dear to you. Soon, Rome will know sacrifice on a scale they could never have imagined."

"You don't deny it then? Will you stop stroking that boy and look at me?"

Elissa ignored the instruction. "Why deny anything? The Lord and Lady know the truth in our hearts. Soon they will descend to us, bringing fire and blood."

Metella looked at her aghast. "What are you going to do?"

Glaukos and Shafat returned into the room. Metella's two bodyguards moved closer to her, looking tense.

"The time comes. Soon the *Ludi Romani* will reach their climax. All Rome will gather, the cohorts will be fully occupied with crowd control. Then the power of the Lord and Lady will be revealed. Then Carthage will be avenged."

"You're mad," said Metella. "I'll tell the Urban prefect. The Praetorians. You will be crucified."

"Hold her," Elissa said to Glaukos. Strong hands grabbed her arms, pulled them behind her.

"Bodyguards," she cried. "Help me."

Both of the bodyguards drew the concealed knives they held and turned on Glaukos. One moved forward, then stiffened, let out a groan, and collapsed to the floor. The other, holding his dagger bloodied from where it had entered his colleague's back, turned to Elissa and bowed.

"At your service, Mother."

Elissa inclined her head towards him. "The blessings of the Lord and Lady on you."

Fear now replaced anger in Metella's heart. "Let me go," she said in a tremorous voice. "I am of senatorial rank."

Elissa finally deigned to look at the woman, who trembled before her now, pale, a sheen of sweat on her face.

"You have served the Lord and Lady well. You will be a worthy moloch for them."

"No, Mother, please…"

Elissa nodded to Glaukos. He took a knife from his belt and with one smooth motion he cut Metella's throat. He kept her hands pinned behind her and her head pulled back as the noblewoman sunk to her knees, blood gouting. Her eyes stayed wide, fixed on Elissa's in disbelief. Elissa speeded up her stroking of the slave boy, and she heard him groan. Her back arched, her eyes half closed and she luxuriated in the sensations as the slave ejaculated over her, while the blood from the dying woman sprayed her body.

"Lord Ba'al Hammon, Lady Tanit," she intoned. "Accept this moloch, and bless our endeavour."

Metella collapsed to the ground, limp, and the slave boy sighed, hanging his head. Elissa smiled. Everything would be well.

Chapter XXI

Carbo, Rufa and Fabilla stood outside Vespillo's house. They couldn't help smiling to each other at the voices raised within.

"But Severa…"

"Don't you but me! This house is made for two, not five!"

"But it's only for a short time. Until they can sort something else out."

"Why can't they make their own arrangements? Stay in a hostel?"

"Because…it's not…they just can't," blustered Vespillo.

"I don't see why not. Send them on their way."

"Now look here, Severa. I am *paterfamilias*. What I say in this house is law!"

"Maybe so, but if you want someone to cook you dinner and try to get that thing between your legs to stand up, you will show me some respect."

Carbo winced, and gently pushed open the door, stepping tentatively inside. Vespillo turned to Carbo with a look of gratitude and embarrassment. Severa also spun to fix him with a deadly gaze. She was a large, middle-aged woman, Carbo estimated her around forty years, with a handsome face that was currently lined in anger.

"And who are you? Oh, you must be Carbo, Vespillo's new best friend. I have heard *so* much about you." The sneering tone suggested to Carbo that she had frankly heard enough.

"It's a pleasure to meet you at last, Severa," said Carbo. Severa's response could best be described as a harumph. "May I introduce two ladies who are currently under my protection? This is Rufa, and her daughter Fabilla."

Rufa respectfully bowed her head. Fabilla stood behind Rufa, and slowly peered around, eyes wide as she stared at the angry woman.

Severa's face softened. She smiled shyly at Severa, and Severa smiled back.

"Rufa, Fabilla, please come in." She gestured to her slave. "Afer, show our new guests inside, and give them food and drink."

With a grateful look, Rufa ushered Fabilla into the house. Vespillo made to follow them, but Severa gripped his arm and pulled him into the street.

"Are you mad?" she hissed at him.

Vespillo looked at her in surprise.

"You want us to harbour fugitives? Escaped slaves sought by their mistress and the authorities?"

"Severa, these people..."

"These *slaves*," she corrected him firmly. "These slaves are nothing to us. Why risk our lives for them?"

"Severa," began Carbo.

"Be quiet," snapped Severa. Carbo did as he was told. "Well, Lucius Vedius Vespillo?"

Vespillo was quiet for a moment. Then he said, "I had a child of my own once."

Severa looked about to retort, then changed her mind. She turned on her heel and retreated inside. Vespillo looked somehow smaller, and Carbo clapped him on the shoulder.

"Thank you, friend. We've faced the wrath of Elissa and the justice of the cohorts, but this..." He shook his head.

"They should be safe here. Whatever her misgivings, Severa has taken them in. She will look out for them now. And she isn't stupid, she knows we need her to be discreet. Afer is a handy man to have around as well."

Vespillo poked his head round the door. "Severa, Carbo and I have some business to attend to. Please make sure our guests are well looked after."

Severa shot Vespillo a filthy look. "Of course I will. Now go and continue with whatever sordid deeds you two get up to."

Severa turned to Fabilla, who was looking up at Severa.

"How did you get your hair to look like that?" Severa hesitated, then put an arm around her. "Well, I have this lady who comes every week..."

Carbo gave Rufa a small kiss on the head. "Stay here, Severa will look after you. We will be back soon. Vespillo and I are going to sort your problems out. Permanently."

Rufa gazed uncertainly into Carbo's eyes. "Please be careful."

Carbo hoped his returning look was confident. "Of course."

The crowds parted easily for Carbo and Vespillo as they walked through the city. They were helped by the four watchmen they had brought with them, all armed with short, stout clubs. Vespillo had hand-picked them for their size and intimidatingly brutal appearances, and no one wanted to tangle with them.

"Run it past me one more time," said Carbo. "What exactly is this going to achieve?"

Vespillo sighed. "Look, Elissa is your problem. She knows you are sheltering the sla... the girls. She isn't going to let things drop, for whatever warped reason she has. So Rufa and Fabilla can never rest safe unless we can force the issue. Even spiriting them out of the city isn't really an option now, not with Dolabella on the case."

"The *fugitivarius*?" said Carbo. "He can fight, sure, but is he really that much of a threat?"

"I asked around. The simple answer is, yes, I'm afraid he is. He has a fearsome reputation as a slave catcher. He has never failed. He is also well known for his brutality. Slaves caught by him tend to have a hard time of it before they are returned to there owners."

Carbo felt a chill, suspecting that Vespillo was understating the matter.

"So, we go to Elissa's house, and force her to confess to wrong doing, and then we can institute legal proceedings to have her tried and exiled for whatever we can pin on her."

"Confession seems unlikely," said Vespillo. "We know she is up to something, we just need to find out what, and if we can get evidence of criminal activity, we could put her slaves to the torture to get them to reveal everything they know."

Carbo grimaced at that. It wasn't long ago that Rufa and Fabilla had been Elissa's slaves, and the thought of them being tortured for their Mistress's crimes made him feel sick. He said nothing though. His oath was to the two he had sworn to protect, not to the unknown slaves who had the misfortune to belong to Elissa.

"So we search her house for anything incriminating?"

"It's our best chance," said Vespillo.

"And if we don't find anything?"

Vespillo patted a small bag he carried. "I've prepared for that."

Carbo's eyes narrowed. "Are you planning to…"

"It's just a contingency plan. To make sure we don't come away empty-handed."

"What's in the bag?"

"Letters. From un-named conspirators. Elissa is planning to assassinate the Emperor Tiberius."

"Is she?"

"I have no idea," laughed Vespillo. "But when we take this evidence to the Praetorian Guard, Elissa will no longer be a problem."

"I don't like it," said Carbo. "It feels wrong."

"We may find something else," said Vespillo. "But we are running out of options."

Carbo set his jaw and continued walking.

"How do we get in, anyway. We aren't the Praetorians or the urban cohorts. The *vigiles* don't have any powers to investigate crimes."

Vespillo smiled. "Leave that to me."

Vespillo hammered on Elissa's front door, and after a few moments they heard the sound of the bar being removed, and the door swung open. A sombre looking doorkeeper appraised them.

"Fetch your Mistress, Elissa," announced Vespillo.

"The Mistress is not in," said the slave.

"Then fetch the steward, what's his name, Shafat."

"Shafat is not in, either, I'm afraid."

"Then fetch whoever is most senior in this household at this moment," said Vespillo, exasperated.

The doorkeeper nodded, and disappeared into the house. Moments later Glaukos appeared, suspicion on his face.

"Vespillo of the *vigiles,* and his friend Carbo. As the doorkeeper told you, Mistress Elissa is not in residence at this time."

"We aren't here to see her," said Vespillo, brusquely.

"Oh? Then may I enquire as to the nature of your visit?"

"Fire inspection," said Vespillo.

"What?" gasped Glaukos. "What are you talking about?"

"The *vigiles* have a duty to make sure that every household has adequate firefighting equipment. We need to make sure Rome can defend itself from the constant threat of conflagration."

"But, you have no grounds to suspect..."

Glaukos looked angry, but also shaken, and Carbo wondered at the source if his anxiety.

"We need no grounds," said Vespillo. "All households are subject to inspection at the discretion of a tribune of the *vigiles*. That's me. Now stand aside."

"I will not," protested Glaukos. "The Mistress would not permit this insult!"

Vespillo gestured to the accompanying watchmen. Two of them stepped forward and unceremoniously pushed Glaukos aside. For a moment it looked like he would resist, weighing up the numbers that faced him. Carbo felt momentarily uncertain that if it came to a fight, they would prevail against this huge man. Then he stepped back, and Vespillo and Carbo entered.

"Right," said Vespillo, addressing Carbo and the watchmen. "You, I want to see stored water, especially on the upper floor. You, go and check the kitchens, make sure the ovens are safe and well-maintained. You two, keep an eye on this big lump here. Carbo and I will look for evidence of other fire-fighting equipment, fire-blankets and such like."

Carbo and Vespillo looked around, then moved through into the *peristylium*.

"What now?" said Carbo.

"We just start looking," said Vespillo. "One room at a time. You start that side, I'll start this."

Vespillo went to the far side of the *peristylium* and entered one of the small rooms that lined it. Carbo selected the nearest one to him and went in. It was a small store room, half full of *amphorae*, the large earthenware pots standing as tall as his chest. He looked into one, sniffed, dipped a finger in. It contained a thick, dark liquid. He recognised it as naphtha, the oily, flammable substance that bubbled out of the ground in certain parts of the world.

He moved on to the next room. It was a slave chamber, with bedding for five or six. One small boy sat in a shady corner, playing forlornly with a ball. Carbo ignored him, looked around, moved some of the bug ridden blankets. He found a few simple slave possessions, charms, a few copper coins, but nothing of interest.

The next room was larger, and going from the bright light of the *peristylium* into the dark room meant that it took him a few moments to realise that there were several people within. As his eyes adjusted, he saw that there were four people, three men and a woman, dressed in simple clothes. They had been keeping quiet as Carbo and the watchmen performed their search, and they sat now, looking at him in silence. Carbo couldn't understand what he was seeing. This wasn't living quarters, there was nowhere to sleep, just a few stools, arranged in a circle. There were markings on the walls, symbols in dark red that could have been painted in blood, a circle on top of a trapezium that he had seen before. At one end of the room was a small altar, which had dried blood on its flat surface and in small rivulets down its side.

His gaze moved to the four occupants of the room, and his eyes widened as he recognised one.

"Philon?" he gasped. "What…"

Philon bowed his head and said nothing.

"I want an explanation, boy," said Carbo, firmly.

Philon opened his mouth, but he couldn't seem to find any words. He trembled and bowed his head. Carbo grabbed him by the arm and yanked him to his feet, then spun him round and up against the wall, one strong hand grasping Philon by the neck.

"Tell me," said Carbo, through gritted teeth, "what you are doing here."

A shout from across the courtyard reached them before Philon had a chance to answer.

"Carbo! *Vigiles!* Get your backsides here now!"

Carbo paused for a moment, but Vespillo's tone sounded urgent. He grabbed Philon by the hair on the back of his head and dragged him out of the room, over to the chamber that Vespillo had called from. The four watchmen also came at a run, and they entered the bedroom together.

Carbo stared, taking in the grisly scene that confronted them. As a veteran of so many years, blood and death were nothing new to him. But the naked female body, lying on her back, spreadeagled, sightless eyes staring at the ceiling, shocked him as much as a club blow to his chest armour. There was so much blood, a vast, drying pool that had spread from the rent in her throat.

Vespillo looked at Carbo grimly.

"It's murder," he said. "We have her now." He looked at the young man that Carbo still had hold of and frowned. "Isn't that your slave?"

Carbo and Vespillo stood before Philon and Glaukos in one of the cells below the fire station. The slave and the stewards were manacled to the wall, arms stretched above their heads. Both of the prisoners were naked, and Carbo's eyes were drawn to the ugly scar through which Philon had lost his stones. A stout, quiet watchman called Hercules, held a whip loosely in one hand.

Vespillo looked from one to the other, the addressed Glaukos.

"You are a free man?"

"Yes," said Glaukos. "I am a free citizen of Rome. I demand to be released. I have no knowledge of any wrong doing in that house."

"But you are a resident of the house?"

"Yes, but what the mistress does in her private chambers is her own business."

"Where is Elissa?"

"I don't know."

Vespillo nodded to Hercules, who brought the whip down hard across Glaukos' chest. Glaukos grunted, but did not cry out. The whip fell away to reveal red stripes across his body.

"Where is Elissa?"

"You cannot torture me. I am a free man."

Vespillo nodded again, the whip fell again, and Glaukos shook his chains in fury.

"Where is Elissa" said Vespillo again, patiently.

"I don't know," said Glaukos, his voice shaking but still defiant. Hercules raised his whip, but Vespillo held up his hand.

"Who was the dead woman in Elissa's chamber?"

Glaukos hesitated, but seemed to realise it was implausible that he could not at least know her identity.

"Her name was Metella, wife of the late Decimus."

Vespillo looked at Carbo. "Jupiter! She was of senatorial rank. This just gets better. I will have to inform the office of the urban prefect."

Carbo shook his head. "Not yet. We need to retain control of this. The urban prefect will only care about the murder. We know there is much more to this than the death of one woman."

Vespillo held his gaze for a moment, then nodded. "You're right, there is more at stake here. We just need to find out what."

He turned back to Glaukos. "What is Elissa planning?"

"I just live there," said Glaukos. "I know nothing of any of Elissa's plans, if she even has any."

"She is the leader of a cult, isn't she?"

"She worships the ancient gods of her ancestors."

"So her ancestors were Punic? She worships Ba'al Hammon and Tanit?"

Glaukos nodded. "It is not forbidden."

"Gods that demand human sacrifice. Is that what Metella was, a sacrifice?"

"I don't know anything about the death of Metella."

Vespillo gestured to Hercules, who laid into Glaukos with the whip, six strong blows that left him gasping for air.

"How many followers does she have?"

"I don't know anything about Elissa's religious practices."

The whip again, and Glaukos groaned aloud this time. Carbo looked over to Philon, who was trembling uncontrollably.

Vespillo stepped up to Glaukos, his face inches away from the giant. He spat his words out. "What is Elissa planning?"

"Go suck your own cock," spat Glaukos. "I know nothing of Elissa's plans."

Vespillo stepped back, and spoke to Hercules. "Continue, until I say you can stop. Make sure you pace yourself, I don't want you getting tired."

Hercules grunted his agreement, and started to whip Glaukos again, the blows falling steadily and at an even pace. Glaukos took the whipping bravely, but the pain was too severe for him not to cry out, his noises mingling with the crack of the whip and the sound of Hercules' heavy breathing as he exerted himself, administering the torture.

"Maybe your slave will be more forthcoming," said Vespillo to Carbo.

Carbo walked up to Philon. A trickle of urine leaked from the eunuch's shrivelled cock and ran down his leg.

"Why, Philon?" said Carbo, gently. "Why betray me? Have I not been kind to you?"

"Yes master. I mean no master, I haven't betrayed you. I don't know anything," babbled Philon. "I attended a meeting of a cult, I was curious to know about their gods, that is all. I'm innocent, Master. I would never betray you."

Carbo was silent for a moment, letting Philon speak.

"Please believe me, Master. I am a loyal slave. You are a good Master, I have no desire to betray you."

"It was you, wasn't it," said Carbo, quietly.

"Me, Master? No, it wasn't me. What do you mean? What was me?"

"It was you who told Elissa where to find Rufa and Fabilla. So that when we were here, she could summon the cohorts to detain us, while she sent men to capture them."

"And because of you, Dentatus and Bucco are dead," growled Vespillo.

"No Master, I had nothing…"

Carbo slapped him across the face. It wasn't a hard blow, but it was enough to shock Philon into silence.

"Philon, have you ever seen a man crucified? I have. Before that, I had always wondered how a man could die, just from being hung from a cross. Very slowly, is the answer. You are scourged, then nailed to the wood. Your full body weight is taken on the nails that stick through your wrists and your feet. If you try to shift your weight, you transfer the agony from one part to another. You are left out in the heat, with no drink. Your ability to breathe slowly decreases. You lose blood. Your wounds become infected. The pain becomes worse and worse. If you are lucky, they break your legs so you die more quickly. If you are unlucky, it can take days, and the crows may be pecking at your eyes while you still live."

Philon looked like he was about to pass out.

"You are a slave, Philon. You were in the house where a high born woman was murdered. You have betrayed your Master. You are going to be tortured, and you are going to die horribly. Tell me everything you know."

Philon licked his lips, and glanced over at Glaukos. Glaukos looked at him, and gasped out, "Say nothing, slave, or the Lord and Lady will torture you for all eternity."

Vespillo gestured Hercules over to Philon. He grinned, and walked towards the terrified slave, patting the whip into the palm of his hand.

"No, Master, please. I will tell you everything I know."

"You worthless shit," shouted Glaukos. "I will make you suffer for this."

"Take him to another cell," said Vespillo. Hercules unhooked the manacles from the wall and took Glaukos away. Vespillo unlocked Philon's bindings, and gestured him to a stool. Carbo and Vespillo remained standing.

"Tell us what you know about Elissa and her plans," said Carbo.

Philon looked an epitome of misery.

"She offered freedom. She offered a purpose in life. You free Romans, you can never know what it is like to exist only to serve. To have a life that is only cleaning, cooking, sucking cocks."

"You get your food, and your shelter," said Carbo. "That's more than many in Rome get."

"But I don't get the chance to walk away. To earn my own place in the world."

"You're a slave," said Vespillo. "That is your place. Why would you question it?"

Carbo thought about Rufa and Fabilla, how he felt about the thought of them as slaves and shook his head.

"This is irrelevant to us now. We want to know where Elissa is, and what she is planning to do."

Philon looked up, no defiance in his expression. "She intends to destroy Rome."

Chapter XXII

Night had fallen by the time Carbo and Vespillo stood quietly outside the fullery. This was the place that Philon had informed them was Elissa's main temple, waiting for the *vigiles* to assemble. It was hardly a military operation, a dozen thuggish looking men in scruffy uniforms, carrying clubs and coshes. Only Carbo and Vespillo carried edged weapons, both having *gladii* in their hands, the short stabbing swords they were used to from their time in the legions. Carbo winced as one of the watchmen bumped into another, causing him to drop his club with a loud thump. They argued in a loud whisper until Vespillo shushed them. Fortunately, the sounds of chanting from within covered the noise.

Carbo wondered if they shouldn't have called the urban cohorts. This sort of action, against a group of people threatening to disturb the peace of the city, was really their job to deal with. He didn't trust them though, not after the way they had done Elissa's bidding by storming his tavern, trying to catch Rufa and Fabilla, killing the *vigiles* protecting them. He knew that the *vigiles* were furious as well. There had been some name calling, even some scuffles between the two groups, and one member of the urban cohorts had been badly beaten, which the *vigiles* innocently claimed to know nothing about.

Philon's story still seemed unbelievable. Elissa's plan seemed insane, but then the woman was clearly not rational, with her belief in ancient Carthaginian gods, the omens that had marked Fabilla out for sacrifice, and her hatred of Rome based on a war fought over two centuries before. Even so, Carbo had not believed her plan could possibly work, until he had seen the look on Vespillo's face as Philon spoke.

Vespillo had seen enough fire in Rome to know how devastating it could be. The city had grown, even since Carbo was a boy, and its winding congested streets were lined with shoddily erected structures made of flammable materials. The *vigiles* had been formed by Augustus to combat the frequent fires, and for the most part they did a good job at quenching the outbreaks caused by accident and negligence.

Deliberate arson was another matter though. Starting a conflagration would be easy, with the right planning. Select a house in the middle of a packed area, fill it with incendiary materials such as kindling, tinder, straw and oil, and one torch could start a fire that would devastate a region, or even the whole of Rome.

Vespillo's face had whitened as Philon had spoke, revealing everything he knew in his terror of torture. They knew the date now, the climax of the *Ludi Romani* on the thirteenth day before the Kalends of October. The population of the city would be out of their homes, thronging the *Circus Maximus* and the hundreds of satellite events that would be happening at the same time. The urban cohorts would be out in force, keeping the crowds under control. People's homes would be empty, few around to extinguish a fire before it had taken hold. Elissa's plan, insane as it was in purpose, was sound in planning. It would work.

Or, it would have worked, if they hadn't found Philon, reflected Carbo. If he hadn't told them everything. Even if Elissa hadn't been so obsessive about having Fabilla as a sacrifice. If she had let the slaves go, Carbo and Vespillo would never have got involved, and Rome would never have known about the act of destruction she was planning.

Now though, they could stop the plot dead. Carbo looked around him. The *vigiles* appeared to have finally got themselves in some sort of order. Vespillo looked to Carbo who nodded, and then he gestured to two watchmen. The two men brought up an improvised ram, a delicately carved wooden beam, charred by fire, which had been a souvenir from some previous house fire, kept at the station. They would not be waiting to be invited in this time.

Vespillo pointed at the door, and the two men drove the ram into it with force, knocking it off its hinges at the first blow. Carbo drew his sword, and was through first, Vespillo and the *vigiles* close behind.

The entrance first led into a short corridor. One of Elissa's followers stood there, mouth agape at the sight of the charging men. Carbo clubbed him in the side of his head with the hilt of his sword, not pausing to watch the unconscious man slide to the floor. He burst into an open area, crowded with vats of stinking urine in which togas and tunics were dunked for the fulling process. Two of the cultists stood at the top of stairs leading down. Carbo and

Vespillo were on them before they could react, hurling them aside for the following *vigiles* to deal with. They hurtled down the stairs, taking them three at a time, and emerged into a cavernous cellar, lit by smoking torches.

Carbo took in the scene. Around twenty cultists were here, men and women, and they jumped to their feet from their prayer stances as the *vigiles* entered. The cellar had many side rooms, and Carbo caught glimpses of piles of wood, and amphorae similar in design to the ones he had seen in Elissa's house.

Shafat stepped forward.

"How dare you interrupt this sacred ceremony?" he said, in Syrian-accented Latin.

Vespillo spoke up. "You are all under arrest, for conspiracy to commit treason."

"Treason?" laughed the man. "This is a simple religious meeting. There is no conspiracy here."

Carbo regarded the tall man before him. "Shafat. We know exactly what you are planning. We know what that wood and oil in those rooms is for. We know what you intend to do to Rome. You are all coming with us, to face trial and punishment. Where is your mistress?"

Shafat half-turned, gesturing to the cultists with one arm. "This is a peaceful gathering," he said. "Tell them, Dahia."

A Numidian woman stepped forward from the crowd. "Please, sir, leave us to worship in peace."

Carbo turned back to Shafat, and saw that suddenly there was a dagger in his hand. With a quick step, faster than Carbo would have credited the steward for, Shafat lunged for him. Carbo dodged to one side, so the knife thrust just passed him, and then stepped forward to trap the knife arm against his body. Close up to Shafat, he couldn't use the blade of his *gladius* so he aimed the hilt at the back of Shafat's neck. Shafat with a desperate twist, freed himself from Carbo's grip and avoided the blow.

Dahia threw herself at him, landing on his back. Her fingers sought his eyes, and Carbo cried out, dropping his sword as he groped for her. He reached back to grip her arm, and then dropping his shoulder, he threw her forwards. She landed heavily, remaining still, her breathing showing she was out cold but alive.

Carbo looked around. The cultists had all drawn knives, and the *vigiles* charged into them with a yell. The dark room was soon a chaotic brawl, the dim lighting adding to the confusion, screams and the crashes of clubs and knives ringing out, finding targets, or missing and hitting walls and furniture. Shafat closed with Carbo, and they wrestled, faces close together. Shafat's strength surprised Carbo, religious zealotry adding power to the slender frame. The steward sought to bring his knife to work, and Carbo gripped his wrist to keep it at bay. They stared into each others' eyes for a moment, then Carbo jerked his head forward, forehead smashing into Shafat's nose, causing the steward to stagger back. Carbo kept a grip on his knife arm, though, and with a twist, made him drop the blade.

Carbo turned to see his sword on the floor, within near reach, but as he bent to retrieve it, Shafat's knee caught him full in the face. Tiny sparks of light appeared, dancing at the edge of his vision. He shook his head, then ducked just in time to avoid a two-handed blow that Shafat had aimed at the side of his head. Putting his head down, he charged into Shafat, thrusting him back into one of the small side rooms. *Amphorae* toppled over as they crashed through, spilling their oil onto the floor, which was soon slick. The fight took on a comical aspect, as all the combatants slipped and staggered, waving arms to keep their balance, many tumbling to the floor.

Shafat grabbed Carbo by one arm and swung him around. He crashed into a pile of dry kindling that splintered beneath him with a crunch. Carbo tried to regain his feet, pushing himself upright with his hands, but the brittle wood split under his weight and he fell back. Shafat jumped on top of him, face distorted with fury. The steward had found his knife again, and was pressing it down towards Carbo's throat.

Carbo was the stronger man, but he found it difficult to get leverage, and the weight of the man above pressing downwards put him at a disadvantage. His hands were slippery now with the oil that had spread everywhere, and he couldn't gain a firm grip on the knife hand. The dagger pricked his throat. He couldn't even attempt a head butt, for fear of skewering himself.

Desperately, he let go of Shafat's arm with one hand, feeling the pressure increase as his other hand tried to keep the steward at bay, panicking that the blade would sever a vital vessel. He scrabbled blindly for anything nearby, and his hand closed around a thick wooden branch. With desperate strength, he brought the branch round in a wild swing that connected with the side of Shafat's head.

The pressure instantly eased on his throat. He gasped deep ragged breaths, still feeling that his airway was not fully open, but feeling the blood start to rush back to his head, his lungs inflating. The darkness that had nearly overwhelmed him receded. Sounds that had been fading started to come back, the cries and shouts of fighting still continuing in the main room.

He managed to struggle up to his knees, still panting for breath. Nearby, illuminated by the flickering light from the one torch in this side room, he saw Shafat groaning, bleeding from a gash in the side of his head, also just starting to regain his feet.

With an immense effort of will, Carbo stood. Shafat had his back to the wall, Carbo his back to the door. They stared at each other for a moment. Behind them the sounds of battle were starting to die down. He heard Vespillo shout.

"We've got them, *vigiles*. Bind those that surrender. Kill those that don't."

Shafat looked past Carbo, dismay written on his face as he realised the fight was ending, the cultists defeated by the brutal savagery of the thugs that were Rome's watchmen.

"Give up, Shafat," said Carbo. "Elissa's followers are defeated. As soon as she is found, she will be executed. It's over."

Shafat looked down for a moment, shoulders drooping. Then he looked up, and a feral grin crossed his face. Before Carbo could react, he ripped the torch off the wall and thrust it into his chest.

The oil that had soaked into his clothes ignited instantly, the flames shooting up the steward's body, turning him into a human torch. He spread his arms wide, looking upwards.

"Accept me as your moloch, O Lord and Lady," he cried. "May your vengeance be born in me."

Carbo watched aghast as the flames enveloped Shafat. For a moment, the cultist maintained his pose. Then he started to scream as the pain took over. He beat at himself, staggering from side to side, knocking over more oil-containing amphorae. Then he slipped on the oil and fell into a pile of dry kindling. The oil-soaked wood ignited with a roar, and flames spread across the floor, lighting the oil that permeated the whole cellar.

Carbo yelled as loud as he could over the din of battle. "Fire!"

He turned and rushed back into the main room, repeating his cry. He saw Vespillo turn, shocked face illuminated in the firelight, and then Vespillo screamed orders to the *vigiles.*

"Out now, all of you! Run for your lives."

The stairs were only narrow enough for two at a time, and Vespillo hung back as the flames advanced, making sure the *vigiles* were following his orders. Carbo saw a watchman wrestling with a cultist, unable to break free. Carbo grabbed the cultist and threw him bodily into the flames, hearing his cry as the oil on his body caught fire. The watchman shot him a grateful look and ran for the stairs. Another watchman was lying against a wall, a knife in his leg, moaning in terror as he watched the flames approach. Carbo picked him up, throwing him over his shoulder. He looked around seeing that behind him only cultists remained. Lying on the floor, just starting to stir, was Dahia. The approaching flames reached her, caught her oil soaked clothes, rapidly ignited her. Shocked back to consciousness she started to scream.

Carbo hesitated, then heard Vespillo yelling his name. The tribune was at the foot of the stairs, beckoning Carbo, and Carbo ran for the exit. He gave one last glance back. Several cultists were lying wounded, others were clearly dead. The rest made no attempt to flee. Instead they held hands, and started to chant.

"Lady Tanit, Lord Ba'al Hammon. Accept us as your molochs. Your vengeance come. Let Rome burn."

The flames followed Carbo and Vespillo up the steps. Two *vigiles* relieved Carbo of their wounded colleague. From the cellar, the chanting turned into high-pitched screaming. Vespillo and Carbo looked at each other and shook their heads.

Vespillo gave quick orders to summon firefighting equipment. Within minutes, buckets were being commandeered from nearby houses, chains formed to dowse the fire. Reinforcements from the local *excubitorium*, the fire station outpost, soon arrived bringing heavier equipment. Carbo and Vespillo stood back, letting the little bucket boys do the job they were formed to do. The flames licked higher, consuming the fullery, but the urine filled vats had been made use of to reduce the spread to nearby houses. The fullery itself was not as close to other dwellings as most other buildings in Rome were, probably because of the smell, and so, with the continued efforts of the *vigiles*, the fire was prevented from spreading.

It took most of the night to bring the fire completely under control. The wood and oil had burned to create an intense heat that made it impossible to enter the building, but official firefighters and volunteers from the surrounding community worked sleeplessly, beating out sparks where they landed, soaking all the nearby buildings in water, tossing bucket after bucket of water into the burning fullery.

When Vespillo was happy that the fire was not going to spread, he put a hand on Carbo's shoulder.

"We've done it."

Carbo nodded grimly.

"It looks that way."

"It is that way. Elissa is a fugitive now. I'll inform the Urban Praetor's office. The cohorts will arrest her, and she will be tried and executed. When her properties are confiscated and audited, no one will know there are two slaves missing. We could even claim they died in this fire. They can start new lives as free Romans."

Carbo looked doubtful, not sure whether to believe it. He looked at the flames, feeling the heat on his face, watching the failure of Elissa's plan. Then he nodded wearily. "I hope you are right."

Vespillo clapped him on the back.

"I am. Now let's go home and get Severa to cook us a good meal. I think we have earned it."

The two friends walked stiffly away as the roof of the temple to Ba'al Hammon and Tanit collapsed.

Carbo and Vespillo stood in Elissa's atrium, awaiting the arrival of the Urban Cohorts. Two watchmen restrained the priestess with tight grips on her arms. Her face was white with fury. Vespillo had stationed three of his troops near her house, waiting for her return home, before news could reach her of the raid on her *domus*, or the fire at the temple. Two had arrested her, while the third summoned Vespillo. He in turn had summoned the Cohorts, explaining to Carbo that criminality of this magnitude was out of his league. As they waited, Carbo and Vespillo had had the pleasure of informing Elissa of the destruction of her temple, the death of Shafat, the arrest of Glaukos and the ruination of her plans. Carbo couldn't help a gloating sense of satisfaction at the shock and anger on her face.

When the Cohorts finally arrived, they were led by Tribune Pavo himself. His red face betrayed irritation at the disturbance, and the hue deepened when he saw Elissa restrained.

"Tribune Vespillo. You have gone too far this time. I don't know what your problem is with this lady, but if she wishes to prosecute you for your harassment, I will fully support her. Mistress Elissa, I am so sorry for the inconvenience. Vespillo, have your men release her at once."

"Shut up, Pavo, you old fool, and listen."

Pavo opened his mouth, but said nothing, and merely stood with an expression like a surprised fish.

"We have just foiled a plot by this lady to burn down Rome," said Vespillo.

Pavo looked aghast. "Don't be ridiculous. What possible evidence could you have for such a far-fetched notion."

"We found fire-starting equipment in her house here, we arrested cult members who confessed to the plan, we went to a temple which was packed with incendiary material, and during a fight with our men, this lady's steward burned the temple down, immolating a large number of her followers. "

Pavo stared at Vespillo, looking like he was expecting a punchline. He turned to Elissa, who returned his gaze with contemptuous silence.

"But…it…she couldn't…" Pavo seemed to remember his position, and composed himself. "Well, there will obviously be a trial. But if you speak the truth…"

Vespillo raised an eyebrow at this, and Pavo hurriedly continued. "I mean, when all the evidence is gathered and sifted, then suitable punishment will be administered." He motioned to two of his legionaries to take Elissa, and Vespillo nodded to his men to release her into their care. As they led her out, she kept her gaze fixed on Carbo, until she was out of sight.

"Well," said Pavo. "If all this is tr…, um, that is to say, this seems on the face of it, hmm, well, a commendation may be in order for you, Vespillo."

Vespillo inclined his head with a wry smile.

"Anyway, you can leave it with the Cohorts and the Urban Praetor's office now. We will be in touch to collect your testimonies."

Pavo swept out with the rest of his legionaries. Vespillo turned to Carbo and grinned.

"A commendation?" said Carbo. "Won't that be nice?"

Vespillo made a face. "Pavo will undoubtedly turn this around so it reflects best on him. The most I will get is some of his reflected glory."

"But you don't care, do you? It's your own honour that is most important to you, not how others view you?"

"Maybe," admitted Vespillo. "Now let's go back to your tavern to spread the good news, and celebrate with some fine wine."

Carbo clapped him on the back, and with a feeling of profound relief, he left Elissa's home.

Carbo and Rufa sat together, high in the wooden seating of the temporary arena that had been constructed for the *Ludi Romani*, the biggest and best of the annual games, which ran for much of September. The sun was nearing its zenith, and although autumn was approaching, it was still uncomfortably hot. Carbo summoned a drink-seller and bought a drink for Rufa and himself. Rufa sipped at her cup, then put an arm round Carbo and despite the heat, moved closer to him. Carbo downed his drink, gave his cup back to the drink seller, and held her close.

It felt strange to be out in public now, without having to hide. Vespillo had assured him that all they needed to do was wait a few weeks, claim Rufa and Fabilla as his own slaves as they had no owner, then manumit them. She would be free again, albeit with the status of freedwoman, not quite the same as a free Roman citizen. All Romans were beholden to someone though. Even Sejanus, the Praetorian prefect who ran Rome, answered to the Emperor Tiberius, although little was seen of the Emperor in Rome these days, and Sejanus had a free hand.

Carbo stroked Rufa's arm gently. They had made love last night, every night in fact for the last few nights, since Carbo and Vespillo had limped home from the fire at the temple, to tell Rufa that she was going to be free. Although sometimes the familiar feeling of dread started to rise in his gut, Rufa's calming presence always soothed it away, and he could enjoy her body, and his own pleasure now, like he did in his youth. Even more so, maybe, now that he realised what a gift it was.

He leaned over, kissing Rufa gently on the cheek, and she turned to flash him a smile, before she turned her attention back to the arena. The morning's entertainment was drawing to a close. It had been a mix of mock gladiatorial contests, a warm up for the later fights to the death, and some animal displays. The crowd had clapped at the display of a crocodile from Egypt, and a fight between a boar and a bear which had ended with the boar dead, but the bear so badly gored it had to be killed.

Currently an ostrich was being chased around the arena by a lion. The crowd laughed and hooted but time dragged by, and the lion's initial enthusiastic attempts to bring the bird down waned. Eventually it gave up, lying down on the arena floor with its head on its paws, while the ostrich stood at the far side of the sand, eyeing it reprovingly. The crowd started to boo, and after a while, a guard was sent on with a trident to try to prod the lion back to work. The lion roared and swept at the trident, causing the guard to jump back in fright, but would not return to the chase. After a few attempts, the guard gave up, and someone in authority must have become concerned about the growing derision from the crowd, as soon after a hail of arrows into both animals cut that part of the show short.

Carbo watched the two animals being dragged away, and sand brushed over the bloody trails they left. He wondered what his future held now. Maybe he could actually begin his retirement. He could manage the tavern, go to the baths, drink and eat and enjoy the company of Rufa. For a moment he almost felt overwhelmed at the thought. A lifetime of service, boredom and threat constant twin stresses, the horror of the Teutoberg massacre, the anxieties of the last few days, and the sudden freedom from it all, came crashing in on him. He leaned forward and put his head in his hands, muscles tensing round his back and chest as tears sprung in the corners of his eyes. He felt a hand on his shoulder.

With an effort he composed himself, then sat up. Rufa was looking at him with concern. He wiped the moisture from his eyes.

"Dust from the arena," he said. "Gets in the eyes."

Rufa gave a half smile, happy to accept his unconvincing explanation at face value, but she kept her hand on him. It was lunch time now, but few attempted to leave the arena. A date seller awkwardly weaved between the seats, and Carbo beckoned him over. He bought a handful of the fruits, and shared them with Rufa.

"Do we go and get lunch somewhere else?"

Carbo shook his head. "Only if you want to lose your seat. You have to make do with anything the vendors sell you at their inflated prices, or anything you bring with you from home. Only the Emperor gets to go home for lunch."

The dead animals cleared away, an announcer came on and proclaimed that the climax would be the *damnatio ad bestias* of a slave who had conspired to kill her mistress, followed by a gladiatorial display. Next, though was the execution of three deserters from the army.

Although the distance was too great to see the condemned men's expressions in any detail, their slumped postures showed resignation and defeat. The prisoners were forced to their knees and bent forward, one soldier grasping the hair of the first victim and pulling so his neck stretched out. The nominated executioner stepped forward. He drew a long sword and held it up for the crowd to see. The crowd cheered and he brought it down in one rapid, smooth motion. The head separated cleanly, a huge gout of blood spurting forth, then more arterial pulses, the body slumping forward to lie in a pool of crimson while the soldier held the lifeless head high. The crowd roared its approval.

Carbo glanced at Rufa. She had paled a little, and was watching with mouth tight.

"Deserters," said Carbo. "They deserve it. Leaving their comrades to fight and die in their place. They are lucky - they are Roman citizens and so get a quick and honourable death."

Rufa said nothing, and they continued to watch. The second victim was dispatched with similar aplomb. Whether the third prisoner moved at the last minute, or the executioner's arm was tiring, Carbo wasn't sure, but this time the sword did not slice through cleanly, instead wedging in the bones at the back of the skull and the top of the neck. They could hear the executioner's curses as he tried to pull his sword free, one foot on the feebly struggling prisoner's back. Finally it came loose and the prisoner slumped face forward on the arena sand. The executioner swung his sword again, but with the prisoner lying down the sword was stopped by the sandy ground before it had cut fully through.

To boos from the crowd, the executioner made his assistant hold the head off the ground, and he used his sword to slowly saw through the neck. The crowd grew restless, and started to throw food and rubbish at the executioner, who gestured back at them angrily. Eventually the head came loose, and the cheer from the crowd this time was dripping with irony.

Clowns and jugglers emerged, vainly attempting to raise the spirits of the crowd while slaves came out to drag the bodies away and sprinkle more sand over the blood.

Carbo and Rufa munched their dates. The man next to Carbo nudged him in the ribs. "What do you think?"

"It's my first games for a while. Does it get better?"

"Tomorrow is the last day of the games, and it should be spectacular. The whole of Rome will be out for that. Everything until then is just makeweight. I mean, look at those executions. Pretty poor showing, wasn't it?"

Carbo nodded. "Can't be easy though, getting it right every time. A man's neck can be pretty tough to slice through. I should know."

The man looked askance at Carbo, digesting his words, then decided to change the topic. He stamped on the temporary structure firmly.

"They seem to have built this one sturdily, at least. Not like the arena at Fidenae earlier this year."

Carbo nodded. The disaster had claimed twenty thousand lives. An old man on the other side of them who had heard the conversation though, leaned over and said, "They may have brought new laws in to prevent it happening again, but it's an unlucky year. The Emperor has quit Rome, leaving us under Sejanus. The gods aren't pleased. There are more disasters to come this year, you mark my words."

The next prisoners brought out were two men and two women, slaves escaped from the mines. Dirty and emaciated, barely able to walk, they made a pathetic spectacle. Carbo reflected that if they hadn't escaped, they probably wouldn't have survived long anyway, the mines being notorious for their mortality rate.

As non-citizens, these prisoners were not granted the kindness of a quick death by beheading. They were stripped, laid out on crosses to which they were bound wrist and ankle, and then nails driven through hands and feet. The four crosses were hauled upright, and were stood in deep holes in the ground. All four prisoners were then scourged, hooks on the whip flaying the skin so blood streamed freely down their bodies. The crowd screamed and yelled, their disapproval of the clumsy beheading forgotten. The soldiers then withdrew, and a lion and lioness were released into the arena. Their gaunt appearance suggested they had been deliberately starved, and they instantly spied the crucified prisoners who were crying out in agony. The lioness approached the female prisoner who was screaming loudest, a little cautious from the noise, then with a speed astonishing for her size, slashed her claws across the woman's throat, silencing her instantly. The other prisoners were soon killed, though the lion seemed more inclined to play with his prey before finishing it than the methodical lioness.

The lions were only given a short time to eat. Handlers with tridents, poles and whips arrived to herd them away from their meals. They resisted for a short time, growling and slashing at the handlers, but they eventually bowed to the inevitable and slunk away.

Carbo, whose eyes had been fixed to the spectacle, turned to Rufa and noticed she was trembling.

"Are you well?"

"They were escaped slaves," said Rufa, simply.

Carbo thought about it, possibly for the first time, he realised. He knew that not everyone approved of what went on in the arena, but they were in a minority, and were generally thought of as effeminate or cowardly. Why the torture and humiliation though, rather than a quick death? Was it as a deterrent? He looked around at the cheering, smiling faces in the crowd. They didn't seem to be dwelling on the warning. It was obviously just entertainment to them.

The jugglers and tumblers reappeared as the carnage was cleared away, putting up with good-natured cat calls and jeers from the crowd. The announcer then returned, and the message came back up the crowds that the climax of the lunchtime entertainment had arrived. A female slave who had been convicted of conspiring to kill her mistress was to be executed in the manner of Dirce.

"Who's Dirce?" asked Carbo of the man next to him.

The man looked at Carbo with annoyance, but obviously thought better of antagonising him. He shrugged, but asked the woman next to him the same question. She leaned across to Carbo.

"Dirce was the aunt of Antiope, who gave birth to Amphion and Zethus after Jupiter fucked her," said the woman. "Zethus and Amphion were brung up by a shepherd, and Dirce was an evil bitch to Antiope. One day she tried to get the sons to kill Antiope by tying her to a bull, but the sons recognised their mother, and tied Dirce to the bull instead. Ain't you read your Euripides?"

Carbo shook his head, bemused. In the arena below, two young men, dressed in Greek-style clothing, led a huge, muscular bull by a head collar and a pole through a nose ring. A small sheep dog herded a half dozen sheep around them. The bull snorted, and pawed the ground, but consented reluctantly to be led into the middle of the arena.

Then two guards brought out the prisoner. She was dressed in a full length loose fitting robe, and was struggling desperately in the powerful grip of the soldiers. Grimly they dragged forwards, and presented her to the two men holding the bull. The men nodded, and said some words, which didn't carry to the back of the arena. Carbo presumed it was some lines from Euripides, although the men looked more like they had been picked for their animal handling skills than their acting abilities.

The soldiers ripped the robe from the woman, leaving her naked, and then tied a rope tight around her waist. With the bull still restrained, they tied the other end of the rope around its horns. The bull started to rear, and was brought down by the strength of all four men, yanking on the ring and the collar. Working quickly, and ignoring the woman's outstretched supplicant hands, the rope was fastened tight, leaving only a couple of feet of length between the woman and the bull's horns. The bull bellowed its anger and reared again, and this time the pole attached to the ring was yanked out of its handler's hands. With a toss of its head, the rope on the head collar was pulled free as well. The two handlers and the two guards stepped back, then as the bull turned to face them, they ran.

The bull charged them, and the woman was jerked along with it. The crowd cheered loudly, laughing at the woman's attempts to try to gain her feet so she could run alongside it, laughing too at the fleeing soldiers and animal handlers. One of the handlers' sandals came loose, and he stumbled. He didn't fall, but his flight was slowed enough that he fell behind the others.

The bull caught him. It didn't slow, simply putting its head down, and tilting it slightly. Its long horn punched through his back, and protruded from the front of his chest. The bull raised its head, lifting the man who struggled like a fly on a pin. He shook his head wildly, then tossed the man so he landed several feet away in an unmoving heap.

The other three men had reached safety now and closed the iron gates in the arena wall behind them. The bull looked at them in rage, then seemed to notice the woman attached to him, who was lying with arms gripping the rope, breathing heavily. It wheeled towards her, and she rolled away from it as best she could. The rope was too short to give her any distance, however, and the bull's charge had pulled the knots too tight to be undone, though she plucked at them desperately.

The bull spun again, getting frustrated as she clambered away from it again. It tossed its head, irritated by the rope around its horns, then made a maddened charge into the centre of the arena. The woman was dragged along behind it, screaming piteously. This time, when the bull stopped and rounded on her, she was too slow. The bull stamped on her, and the crunch of the bones in her leg, swiftly followed by an agonised cry which carried round the arena. The bull stamped again, breaking ribs. Then he bent his head down and lifted the woman onto his horns, impaling her with both. He snorted and tossed his head as the woman was flung around like a doll, then he charged the arena wall.

The impact as he hit the temporary erection shuddered through every seat, and the nearest of the crowd screamed as they thought they would be thrown into the arena. The structure held, though. The bull backed away, the crushed woman unmoving on his horns. He tossed her to the ground and bellowed his anger once more.

At a hidden signal, arrows flashed out from around the arena. Struck in a dozen places, the bull roared and reared, the dead woman flung from his horns. Another dozen arrows hit home, and the bull staggered to its knees, then fell to its side. It breathed heavily for a while, until the surviving animal handler, looking visibly shaken, re-emerged into the arena and cut its throat.

The crowd went wild at the spectacle, as the slaves came out to clear away the bodies, and the acrobats, jugglers and musicians resumed their entertainment.

Carbo looked over to Rufa, whose face was set.

"She was an attempted murderess," he said. "She deserved to die."

"Not like that," said Rufa, quietly.

Carbo had wanted to see the gladiators. There was more of an honesty about them, especially to a soldier. A proper sporting contest, fought between equals, apart from those cases where criminals were sent out to fight armed men without a weapon or with their hands tied together. He saw the expression on Rufa's face though, and considered her feelings.

"Would you like to leave?"

She turned to him, showing a look of gratitude. "But you had been looking forward to the gladiators hadn't you?"

Carbo shrugged. "I've seen plenty before. Let's go home."

He offered her his hand, and they stood, their seats instantly being taken by people who had been standing at the back. It took a while to work their way out through the packed crowd, and through the urban cohort legionaries who lounged around, annoyed that their crowd control duties kept them from watching the spectacles. Soon, though, they stood outside the arena, in the forum.

"Is it always like that?" she asked.

"Yes," said Carbo, simply.

"Oh," said Rufa, looking down at the ground.

"You needn't come again," said Carbo.

"Good," she said. "Can we go home now?"

They walked home in silence, Carbo feeling guilty for reasons he couldn't explain. He had taken girlfriends to games before, they had all enjoyed it. They had all been free women, though, used to being allowed to see the games, raised as children on the blood and gore that the crowds loved. Maybe he should have realised that someone not used to such sights would have felt troubled by them.

"I'm sorry," he said to her. "I should have realised..."

She took his hand, and moved closer to him. He looked at her, and she smiled, and he felt a relief that she wasn't angry with him, followed by a realisation that this woman's feelings really mattered to him now. Not just because of some ancient oath. Because of her.

They turned a corner, two streets away from the tavern, and came face to face with Marsia. Her face was drawn with worry.

"Marsia, what are you doing here?"

"Master. Oh, thank Donner and Woden that you have returned. It's Cilo and Manius. They have taken over the street outside the tavern. And they have an army!"

Chapter XXIII

Carbo stood with Vespillo at his side and looked steadily at Manius. Marsia had told him how Cilo and Manius had turned up a couple of hours before, calling for Carbo, shouting threats and insults. They had brought with them a group of armed men, Marsia wasn't sure of their number, but she thought there could be as many as fifty. Carbo had felt a chill when he heard that. Marsia told him Manius' men had taken over the tavern, helping themselves to the stocks of wine and food, and had spilled out onto the surrounding street, smashing *amphorae*, turning over stalls, intimidating the locals.

Carbo had run straight to Vespillo's house at the news, leaving Rufa there with Fabilla and Severa, and Vespillo had gathered up as many watchmen as were readily available at the nearby headquarters. The century should have numbered eighty men, but given the recruiting shortages, illness and injury, and the men who had been on patrol on the night shift who were at their homes, fast asleep, Vespillo could only call on around thirty. He had considered sending for the urban cohorts, but they were occupied with crowd control at the games, and were unlikely to be interested in a minor scuffle in a back street of the Subura. He had instead sent for reinforcements to the nearest barracks, but it would take time to organise the off duty watchmen. The men that Vespillo had rounded up were the usual mix, hardly more than thugs themselves, and yet they still carried themselves with pride in their position. They fastened on their belts, and came with their commander, bringing clubs, hooks and axes. Taura joined them, grumbling that this was the urban cohorts' job, but Carbo thought he saw a gleam in his eye.

As they walked through the streets, word started to get around, and a crowd formed behind them. Most were along for curiosity and excitement, but a significant number emerged with weapons of their own, whatever they could improvise, or kept for defence of their homes. Carbo saw sticks with nails through them, kitchen knives, even a few illicit swords and daggers, probably once used in the military. Carbo himself carried a *gladius* that had been thrust into his hand by an elderly veteran, too arthritic to fight. It was immaculately maintained, the old man obviously still proud of his time in the army.

More than one of the followers marched along with the discipline and bearing of veterans of the legions. By the time they arrived at the territory that Manius controlled, at the eastern end of the Subura, the number of followers had doubled, not counting the thrill seekers.

They were at a crossroads, and when Carbo saw what confronted them, he muttered a silent prayer to the *lares* who guarded these spiritual places. Marsia had told him that the men with Manius were not from the neighbourhood. The gang leader's power and authority had been seriously damaged, and getting men to follow him had been difficult. He had obviously accumulated some wealth from his activities over the years though, and Carbo assumed that the thugs that lounged around insolently in front of his tavern were hired mercenaries. Assessing their bearing, their physique, the way they held their weapons, Carbo guessed that they were a mix of legionary veterans and bored gladiators.

Carbo cursed his own complacency. He should have known that a man like Manius, used to total respect in his own small kingdom, used to using whatever means were necessary to get what he wanted done, wouldn't slink away like a beaten dog. He should have known that he would want to restore his pride and position, and to get his revenge. He walked towards Manius, stopping about twenty yards away. Cilo, Balbus and the rest of the troops grinned at Carbo and Vespillo. Some of the mercenaries drew their swords and waved them menacingly.

"Get your men out of my tavern," said Carbo steadily. "You have taken enough beatings lately. Don't make me give you another."

Manius laughed. "No, Carbo. This neighbourhood belongs to me. Did you really think I would let you keep it?"

"It isn't my property, Manius, any more than it is yours. I own one tavern, the neighbourhood belongs to the citizens who live and work here."

A few cries of approval came from the locals who had followed Carbo, or were standing around to watch. Most though remained grimly silent.

"These people are sheep, Carbo. Not lions, like you and I."

"You aren't a lion. Maybe a jackal, preying on the weak."

Manius' eyes narrowed. "Give me the deeds to your tavern. Leave Rome and never come back. Or we will end this now. You will die." He raised his voice. "You will all die, all you people who are putting your trust in this man, all you little bucket boys playing at being soldiers. I will kill him, then I will let my men have their vengeance on all of you."

Carbo could sense the mood in the crowd, angry but scared. He weighed up the odds against him, the way he had so many times before in the legions. The mercenaries were better armed, all carrying swords, and many wearing breast plates or other armour. They were trained fighters. They outnumbered the *vigiles*. On Carbo's side, he also had the citizens fighting for their homes and livelihoods, but how many, and how well, he had no idea. And what about the *vigiles*? What were they fighting for? These men, drawn from the lower ranks of society, held in contempt by the upper classes by the Praetorians, the legions, even the urban cohorts. Laughed at, resented by those whose houses they had pulled down to stop a fire spreading, or who they had punished for infringements of the fire rules or minor crimes.

"Citizens of Rome," said Carbo "Do you want the freedom of your streets?"

A few nervous cheers came from the men behind him.

"Is the freedom to do your business without extortion or threat worth fighting for?"

A few more cries of agreement came this time.

"Will you join me, and these noble *vigiles,* men who work day and night in a dangerous job, trying to keep you all safe? Will you join their commander, Vespillo, an honourable man, and myself, to make these streets yours again, once and for all?"

This time, Carbo heard Marsia's voice ring out, her German accent strong.

"Carbo, we trust you. Let's kill these bastards!"

This time the crowd roared their agreement. Manius' leer faltered slightly. Then he raised his arm in the air, and brought it down.

Suddenly one of the *vigiles* cried out and fell, then another. Two of the citizens who had followed them fell too, and there was the crash of broken earthenware all around. Carbo looked around wildly, and spotted men on the roof of the tavern, and some of the other roofs, tossing tiles and pottery down on their men.

"It's an ambush!" he yelled at Vespillo.

Vespillo grasped the problem straight away. He grabbed the nearest three watchmen and ran for the stairs between two *insulae* that led to the rooftops. Carbo drew his sword.

"*Vigiles.* Honest citizens of Rome. For all of us, attack."

There was a roar as both groups of men charged forward.

Carbo led the charge, hefting the sword in his hand. Standard issue *gladii* hadn't changed much over the years, and the weight and grip was as familiar to him as his own weapon. He felt a thrill surge through him, fear, anxiety, anger, battle lust, that heightening of every sense that accompanies times of acute stress. He could hear the individual cries of anger and threat around him, the pounding of shoes on the cobbles, see the expression in the eyes of his foes.

The two groups met with a dull thud that was accompanied by grunts of effort and howls of pain. The first man to confront Carbo was a sturdy looking gladiator, a *thraex*, lightly armoured with a small shield, full helmet and a curved sword. As Carbo thrust with his *gladius*, he realised they were playing out a typical arena fight, with Carbo in the role of *murmillo*. The *thraex* caught the thrust on his shield, and swung his own sword. Hemmed in by friends and enemies, Carbo couldn't dodge, so instead stepped forward inside the arc of the swing. He grabbed the arm and hammered the hilt of his sword into the *thraex's* face. Although it only impacted the face plate of the *thraex's* helmet, it caused the gladiator to stagger back.

This wasn't the arena. Two men fighting with the roar of the crowd in their ears, glory awaiting, rarely a fight to the death, space to duck and feint and manoeuvre. This was fighting legionary style, face to face with a row of enemies, side by side with your comrades, physical and brutal. Carbo thrust his *gladius* into the stunned *thraex's* abdomen, twisted and withdrew. The gladiator clutched at his middle with a scream, and collapsed to the floor where he lay writhing.

To Carbo's left, Taura, armed with a club, was fighting an unequal battle with Balbus. Taura had already been injured, and was desperately trying to avoid the big thug's sword while attempting to land a blow himself. Balbus made a thrust for the *vigiles* centurion's chest, but Carbo blocked it with his sword. Taura took advantage of the opening and swung his club hard into the thug's knee. Balbus went down, leg shattered. Taura nodded his thanks to Carbo, then a whizzing noise filled the air, and he too went down, felled by a piece of spinning tile slamming into his leg, thrown from the rooftops.

Before any of the mercenaries could take advantage of Taura's fall, a slight figure leaped over him, grabbing the veteran's sword, setting himself in a wide stance to protect Taura and screaming out a blood thirsty challenge. The way Plancus swung his new weapon about, as much a danger to himself as to his enemies, together with the look of madness on his face, caused the mercenaries to cower back from him and look for an easier fight.

Carbo smiled at the sight, then ducked just in time, as a missile nearly took his head off. Hades, cursed Carbo. Where was Vespillo? Then another mercenary was in front of him, another veteran, and Carbo had to bring his mind back to the immediate fight. This confrontation was more even, two men used to fighting in this style. But Carbo hadn't become *pilus prior* of his cohort just by shouting and bullying. The man before him was a foot soldier, had probably seen some fighting, and knew how to handle a sword. He wasn't Carbo, didn't have Carbo's skills, tactical awareness, nor Carbo's immense strength.

They thrust at each other, then Carbo closed with the man, taking the weapons out of the equation, allowing his greater bulk to decide the issue. He gripped him tight around the chest, lifted him, then slammed him into the ground. The shock reverberated up the man's spine and he cried aloud, but Carbo kept his hug tight. Then, with a twist of his body, he hurled the man to the ground, and stabbed downwards, skewering his chest.

A gap in the fighting appeared in front of him, allowing him to take stock. Although the *vigiles* and citizens were fighting bravely, the aerial bombardment was taking its toll, in direct casualties, and in forcing them to guard themselves from the front and from on high. They had not yet been forced back, but the bodies littering the ground, moving and unmoving, showed that they could not hold against the experienced mercenaries for long.

Another missile from the roof hurtled towards him, but he saw it and ducked, seeing the tile shatter on the cobbles beside him. He looked up towards the source of the attack, and saw a man on the roof preparing to throw again. Then suddenly, he pitched forward, and tumbled down with a cry. Behind him, Vespillo appeared, raising his sword.

"Carbo, we have the roofs," he cried. "Take them."

The other mercenaries on the roofs were hurled off, some already dead, some flailing wildly till their bodies broke on the flagstones below. Carbo raised his sword in salute, then roared, "For your homes and families!"

He charged forward, and the *vigiles* and citizens renewed their attack with fresh impetus and new strength. The mercenaries rocked back at the assault. Carbo fought doggedly, trading blows, stabbing and thrusting with his sword. Slowly he tired, but his opponents tired faster. He knew from the look in their eyes now that they were going to lose, and that they knew it too. They had reached the point in a battle where the balance had tipped, and would not come back. The mercenaries had nothing to gain by throwing their lives away. They were fighting only for money. The citizens were fighting for their homes.

Carbo confronted a scared-looking *hoplomachus* who carried a spear that was useless in this type of close-quarter fighting. Carbo dispatched him with a thrust through his neck, and suddenly realised he was through the last line of defence. Although the battle still raged around him, he stepped forward, and stood before Manius and Cilo. Both men stared at him, in disbelief and fury.

"End this," said Carbo, breathing hard. "Call off your men. It's finished."

Cilo looked at his father, his bruised face twisting in anger. Then he threw himself at Carbo with an incoherent cry.

Cilo was a large man, almost as large as Carbo, and he fought with a rage that was berserker-like in intensity. Carbo for a moment was transported back to Germany, confronted by crazed barbarians who fought and killed without fear. For a moment, panic paralysed him, and Cilo, forgetting his weapons in his fury, threw a punch into Carbo's face that stunned him briefly. Cilo pressed his advantage, raining blows into Carbo's face and chest, making Carbo rock back. Cilo drew his dagger and pulled it back to deliver a killing thrust.

Carbo saw the blade in slow motion. The image of Rufa came to mind. How would she cope without him? Who would protect her? The blade came forward, straight for his throat.

With a desperate effort, Carbo's dulled mind forced his body into motion. He twisted, and the blade thrust sliced the skin on his cheek. He carried on the twisting motion, and brought his forearm round to land a blow on the side of Cilo's head. Cilo lost his footing and fell to the ground. Carbo, head clearing, remembered his *gladius* and brought it up to deliver the final strike.

A body hurtled into him from the side, and Carbo was knocked to the ground, his *gladius* flying loose from his hand. Winded, he found himself staring up into Manius' wild eyes. The gang leader closed his arms around Carbo's neck and started to squeeze. Carbo gripped the hands, surprised at the older man's strength. He felt darkness at the periphery of his vision as the blood was choked off, felt his lungs burning as they tried to expand.

He let go of Manius' hands, feeling the pressure on his neck intensify, and then jabbed both thumbs into Manius' eyes. The gang leader cried out and the pressure lifted as he gripped his face. Clear fluid leaked down both of the man's cheeks, and Carbo knew he would never see again. He reached for his *gladius* with outstretched hand, felt his fingers close around the grip, then thrust it through Manius' chest, skewering it from side to side. Blood spurted over him, and Manius stiffened, then slumped on top of him.

Carbo gasped air into his chest, the exertions of the fight and the strangulation making him feel like he couldn't even lift his arms.

A muscular, scarred, bloody-faced figure reared over him, dagger in hand. Carbo clutched at his *gladius*, but it was stuck firmly in Manius' ribcage. He tried to thrust the body off him, but his strength was gone.

"Die," said Cilo, raising the dagger. Carbo just watched, helpless.

A strange expression came over Cilo's face, puzzlement. His eyes rolled up into his head, and then he toppled over side ways. Behind him, Carbo saw Vespillo affectionately patting the club he had used to knock Cilo out.

"Always saving your cursed backside, aren't I?"

Vespillo heaved Manius' corpse off Carbo, then offered him his hand. Carbo took it, and allowed himself to be pulled unsteadily to his feet. The world spun a little as he stood, but the feeling passed. He looked around him. The mercenaries were in the process of throwing down their swords, or running. The *vigiles* were rounding up those who surrendered, binding their hands behind them with rope, but leaving those who fled. Plancus, the battle lust still on him, was being calmed down by his comrades, who were trying to persuade him to relinquish the sword. Taura had found a stick, and regained his feet. His leg looked swollen and bruised, but not obviously broken. A *medicus* was fussing around him. Taura shooed the healer away, and looked over to Carbo. He raised his club in salute, and Carbo saluted back with his bloody *gladius*.

The *vigiles* were battered and exhausted, and there were many casualties, but Carbo could tell they were carrying themselves taller and prouder now. Here at least, in this district, from now on Rome's watchmen would be treated with respect.

The citizens, too, seemed proud of their victory. Many celebrated, dancing and hugging each other. Some abused the injured and surrendered mercenaries, spitting at them, name calling, even punching and kicking. A middle-aged woman walked slowly over to where Cilo lay, breathing shallowly, stunned. Carbo recognised her as the mother of the boy who had been struck down by Cilo's thug. She picked up the dagger that Cilo had been about to use on on Carbo, and a far away expression came over her face. Cilo raised one weak hand in entreaty. The woman plunged it down into his chest. Heart blood spurted around it, and Cilo gasped, then blood welled from his mouth. Convulsions briefly shook his body, then he was still. The woman looked at Carbo.

"For my son," she said, and walked away.

Carbo left Marsia to organise immediate repairs to the tavern, and to distribute free drink and food to everyone from what remained of the stores. The citizens started a spontaneous party, and many of the stall holders contributed food and wine as well. Someone started to play a pipe, and soon everyone was dancing, singing and getting thoroughly drunk. A reeling Vatius gave Carbo a hug.

"You are a true champion of the people, my friend. A new Gracchus, come to protect the masses from evil."

Carbo laughed and clapped him on the back, causing the drunken philosopher to stagger.

Carbo felt a touch on his arm and he looked round to find himself staring into the drawn face of Brocchia. Behind her, faces carefully held emotionless, were her two bodyguards. Carbo opened his mouth, but no words came. Brocchia just looked at him sadly.

"I've come for my husband and son."

"Brocchia, he did warn them," said Vespillo.

"As did I," agreed Brocchia. "I told them, and I told you, Carbo, that this would end with death. The Parcae decided that deaths would be in my family. At least Balbus survived, though he will never walk straight again. Now may I take their bodies for burial? Will you grant a widow that?"

Carbo nodded, and showed her to the place at the side of the road where Cilo and Manius' bodies had been dumped. Even now, revellers were pointing and laughing at the corpses, spitting on them, or throwing old vegetables and fruit. When they saw Brocchia, the crowd parted and quietened. She walked to her husband and son, back straight, dignity intact. She bowed her head, and for a moment Carbo thought she might break down. Then she straightened, and indicated to her bodyguards to pick the bodies up. They did so, and she departed with the remains of her family.

Moments later, the party had started again. Vespillo came and put an arm around Carbo.

"You didn't ask for this, you know that."

Carbo nodded his head, sadly, and Vespillo pushed a drink into his hand.

"Come on, be the hero to these people, even if it's just for a short while."

Vespillo took a few drinks himself, and both men enjoyed many a handshake or hug from the local men, and not a few kisses from the local ladies. Carbo though, sore and bone-tired, wanted to get back to Rufa, and after a while he managed to persuade Vespillo that they should return to his home. Vespillo looked disappointed, but he gave vague instructions to the soberest *vigiles* to keep order.

When they reached Vespillo's home, Severa gave Vespillo a sound scolding for drinking, fighting and smelling of cheap perfume. Vespillo took it all good-naturedly, and soon Severa was holding him tight, and telling him he needed to be more careful in the future.

Rufa came to Carbo's arms, and Fabilla ran over to give him a big hug as well. Afer lit a brazier, and Rufa and Severa cooked some food for their men. After sending a protesting Fabilla to bed, the two couples spent the evening chatting companionably. Weariness threatened to overwhelm Carbo though, and he felt his eyes closing. Vespillo offered to put them up for the night in their spare room, rather than have him walk home, and Carbo gratefully accepted.

Rufa slid under the blanket with him, and held him close, kissing him softly. He was in no shape for love making, and she didn't try to arouse him, but he loved the feel of her warm body against his. Somnus, the god of sleep, soon claimed him, though his son, Morpheus, the god of dreams, did not visit.

Carbo woke early, and stretched stiffly. Every muscle ached, every part of his body felt bruised. His throat was painful, and his cuts stung. Rufa was snoring lightly beside him. He rose and wandered down the stairs. A small breakfast of nuts, dates and bread had been laid out by Afer, but Vespillo and Severa had not arisen yet.

Carbo heard a cry from outside, and he opened the front door quickly. He smiled and relaxed as he saw Fabilla playing with Afer. The tall, dark-skinned slave was chasing her in circles while Fabilla screamed and giggled. Carbo went to the table and picked up some dates. Another scream came from outside, this one more high-pitched, louder, longer. He frowned and walked back to the front door.

Afer was lying face down in the street, an arrow sticking out from his back. Fabilla had her hands over her face and was screaming hysterically. Carbo ran towards her, then felt a thud on the back of his head. His knees buckled and the world dimmed. A kick to his side rolled him over onto his back. He looked up into the face of Dolabella, who held the struggling, kicking form of Fabilla beneath one arm.

"I never fail," said Dolabella, and was gone.

Chapter XXIV

Carbo found himself being violently shaken, as he slowly regained consciousness. Sounds came back to him first, high-pitched wailing. Then he felt a hard slap across his cheek, and he opened his eyes to see two images of Vespillo's distressed face looking down into him.

"Carbo, for Mars' sake, wake up."

Carbo focussed his eyes with an effort, then sat up, holding himself still for a moment while the world swam around him.

"What happened?" said Vespillo. "Who killed Afer? Where is Fabilla?"

The memory crashed down on him like a collapsing *insula*.

"Dolabella," he said, his voice a croak. "The slave catcher took her."

Vespillo went very still, his face paling.

"Are you sure?"

Carbo nodded, head spinning again at the motion.

"Afer and Fabilla were playing in the street. I was inside. I heard a scream, found Afer dying. Then Dolabella must have clubbed me from behind. The last thing I saw was him taking Fabilla. He said to me…" Carbo paused, the memory of the words chilling him to his bones, "He said, 'I never fail.'"

Carbo and Vespillo looked at each other for a moment, acute anxiety reflected on each other's faces.

"Is he awake?" came Rufa's voice. "Carbo, Carbo, where's Fabilla?"

Carbo struggled to his feet, holding on to Vespillo for support. He looked at Rufa, heart breaking at the panic he saw in her.

"Speak to me," said Rufa, her voice rising. "Don't stand there like a mute idiot. Where is my daughter?"

Carbo glanced at Vespillo, who hesitated, then nodded.

"Dolabella took her."

Shock followed understanding in Rufa's expression. Her eyes went wide, mouth open. Then she slapped Carbo hard across the face.

"You said it was over. You said we were safe. You let us down. Oh, my poor little girl." She sank to her knees, pulling at her hair and rocking back and forth.

Carbo stood, not even raising a hand to rub his face where the stinging slap had fallen. She was right. He had failed. Failed her and Fabilla. The little girl was lost, maybe dead already. If not, soon to be slaughtered as part of Elissa's insane fantasy. His oath to protect them was worthless after all. He bowed his head, and tears appeared in the corners of his eyes.

"Carbo. Carbo!" Vespillo's tone was commanding.

Carbo looked up at him, feeling a helpless numbness threatening to overwhelm him.

"Soldier! We do not give up. We are veterans of the Roman legions. If we lose a battle, we pick ourselves up again, and fight twice as hard. Rome lost Cannae, but defeated Hannibal. You were at the disaster at the Teutoberg forest, but you were also there when Germanicus returned and regained the lost eagles."

"Only two of them," said Carbo, miserably. "One remains lost."

"Nevertheless," said Vespillo, frustration in his voice. "Arminius is dead, and Rome fights on. Can we do less, you and I?"

Carbo held his gaze, feeling the beginnings of a new resolution creep into him. But what could they do?

"Dolabella could be anywhere. Fabilla may already be dead."

Rufa screamed louder at these words, and Carbo cursed his insensitivity.

"We need to think," said Vespillo. "Dolabella would only be continuing with his task to catch Fabilla if he thought Elissa was still free. He would consider the contract void if he couldn't be paid."

"Maybe. What if he had already been paid? He says he never fails."

"If he didn't think Elissa was still free, he would have just killed Fabilla, or maybe Rufa – that would have satisfied his professional pride and kept his reputation intact."

Carbo nodded hesitantly. "He can't have taken Fabilla to Elissa's *domus*, that is still being guarded by the Cohorts. So he must know somewhere else that Elissa would go, maybe somewhere secret. Maybe he has taken Fabilla there."

"Yes, and he must think Elissa still wants her. That her plans are going ahead"

"It's the last day of the *Ludi Romani* today," said Carbo. "The whole city partying. The urban cohorts fully stretched keeping order."

"It was meant for today, wasn't it?" said Vespillo. "Probably at the climax this afternoon, the great gladiator battle."

"Yes. And he knows she needed Fabilla alive until that moment, for her…plans. Rufa, you hear that? We think Fabilla must be alive."

Rufa looked up at them, misery etched across her features.

"Carbo, please. Find my little girl."

Carbo felt his back straighten, of its own accord. He placed a hand lightly on her head. "We will, I promise."

Severa had been hovering nearby, wringing her hands, desperate to help but unsure how. Now she came forward, and gently raised Rufa to her feet.

"Come on, darling. Let's get you inside and cleaned up. You will be no good to Fabilla when the men bring her back if you are in this state."

Carbo and Vespillo dragged Afer inside, laid him against a wall. Vespillo knelt beside the body for a moment, eyes closed, and whispered a prayer to Mercury to conduct his soul safely to the Styx. He slipped a coin into the dead slave's mouth to pay the boatman, then stood. Funeral arrangements would have to wait.

"We need to talk to Elissa. Come on."

"We need to see Elissa, urgently," said Vespillo to Pavo. They stood in Pavo's office in the headquarters of the Urban Cohorts.

"That's not possible at the moment, I'm afraid," said Pavo.

"This is urgent," said Vespillo. "We think a follower of hers is involved in the disappearance of a young girl. Given the cult's passion for child sacrifice…"

Pavo blanched. "I would help you if I could, but Elissa is no longer here."

Carbo felt the knot of anxiety in his gut tighten.

"What do you mean?" said Vespillo. "You let her go?"

"No, no, of course not. She was released into the care of one of the Urban Praetor's men. It didn't seem right, imprisoning a lady of high standing in our cells, and when he came to request he be responsible for her house arrest…"

"Who?" said Vespillo. "Who requested her?"

"A rather influential freedman named Scrofa. He is not someone you refuse."

"Tell us where he lives."

Elissa was not at Scrofa's *domus*. Nor indeed was Scrofa, and his doorman had not seen him for some time. They returned to Vespillo's house in silent despondency. The look on Rufa's face, hope, then despair when she saw the looks on their faces, gave Carbo a feeling of almost physical pain in his chest.

Vespillo explained briefly what had happened.

"So how do we find Elissa?" said Rufa. "My girl, she must be with her."

"Should we try her house?" said Carbo.

Vespillo shook his head firmly. "A waste of time. Elissa is a fugitive herself now. She knows there are men watching it. There is no way she would be stupid enough to go back there."

"So who might know where she is? Glaukos and Philon are the only people we have access to that might be privy to her secrets."

"Glaukos will tell us nothing. Certainly not without coercion, and maybe not even if we tortured him. He is a fanatic. Maybe we would break him eventually, but we don't have that sort of time."

"Philon then, let's talk to him."

Vespillo agreed, and they made to leave.

"I'm coming too."

Vespillo and Carbo exchanged glances. "Rufa, I don't think…" began Carbo.

"She is the most precious thing in the world to me. She is my life. I'm coming."

Carbo raised his eyebrows to Vespillo, who shrugged.

She strode out of the door, leaving the men to follow in her wake.

Philon sat across the kitchen table from them. Marsia stood in a corner, arms folded, expression furious. Rufa stood beside her, looking dangerous. The tavern had been put back into some sort of order, though some of the chairs and tables showed signs of damage, and stocks were very low. Since Philon had been released, Marsia had been working him relentlessly.

Carbo looked into Philon's eyes, who trembled slightly. "Where might she be?"

"I don't know," said Philon, piteously. "I knew about the temple, I knew she had fire starting equipment there. But with the temple gone, Shafat dead, Glaukos arrested, I thought that was the end of it. I had put it all behind me." He looked up at Rufa.

"Rufa, I am so sorry for my part in this."

Rufa's expression hardened further. "You betrayed your Master, you betrayed me, and now my daughter is missing and in mortal danger. I don't know what punishment Carbo has in store for you. Maybe he hasn't decided himself. But maybe you will be able to lessen it, if you help us now."

"You don't know of any followers she had that she might be staying with?"

Philon shook his head. "There were some who weren't at the temple when you destroyed it. Some even quite rich. But all I have heard since is that they are all broken, believing that Elissa must have been a false prophetess if her gods could not protect them. I think Elissa is on her own, except for Glaukos, and you still have him in custody."

"You never heard of any other places of worship? Any other property she owned?"

Philon shook his head hesitantly, then paused. "There was...somewhere."

Carbo looked at him, sharply.

"Somewhere? What? Where?"

"I... I'm not certain. Just something that was said. Some of Elissa's followers had been moving supplies to a place on the Caelian hill. I thought it was maybe a store, because I thought the temple was the centre of Elissa's plans. But, maybe…"

"Maybe this place is where Elissa really meant to start her fire," said Carbo. "Maybe the temple was the store."

Philon nodded agreement. "Yes, it's possible."

"Where on the Caelian?" asked Vespillo. "It's a big region."

"That's as much as I know. I never heard any more than that."

Carbo felt frustration rise in him. So close, and yet it would take weeks to search the whole of the Caelian. They had hours at the most.

"Who else would know about this house?" asked Vespillo.

"The followers who talked to me about it are dead. Shafat would have known. And Glaukos."

Carbo sat back. They were back to Glaukos.

"Maybe you should give me half an hour with Glaukos. I would get him talking," said Carbo.

Vespillo shook his head. "Maybe so. Or maybe the fanatic would put up with anything you threw at him, and all we would have done would be to let him know we had some knowledge of Elissa's rough whereabouts."

"What would Glaukos do if we let him go?" asked Carbo.

Vespillo pondered for a moment. "He doesn't know that Elissa has been arrested, does he? So we could let him know she is at large. But if we released him without a good reason, he would be highly suspicious. He would probably go back to Elissa's house and keep his head down."

"What if he escaped?" asked Rufa, suddenly.

There was a pause while everyone considered this.

"If he escaped, he would have no reason to be suspicious. He would just count his blessings," said Carbo.

"Then we could follow him, and he could lead us to Elissa," said Vespillo.

"How do we know for sure he will go straight to her though? Time is so short."

"He needs an incentive," said Vespillo.

"He can have me," said Rufa.

They all looked at her, in shocked silence.

"What do you mean?" asked Carbo.

"Let him overhear where I am. He can take me to Elissa. She wanted us both don't forget, Fabilla and I. Glaukos may have some making up to do to Elissa, for being caught. He may fear for his life, given how much damage has been done to her plans already. If he took me, Elissa may be more favourably inclined towards him. It would prove that he hadn't been turned by his time in captivity as well."

Vespillo looked thoughtful. "It could work."

"No," said Carbo. "I'm not having Rufa in danger."

"It isn't your decision to make, Carbo," said Rufa, steadily. "It is my life. If you truly meant it, when you said I was free, then you will allow me to decide my own course in this."

Carbo tried to think of something to say. He couldn't risk losing Rufa. Yet if he didn't rescue Fabilla, he would lose her anyway, he was sure. How could they remain happy and whole, with a grief like that in their hearts? It seemed like a good plan, besides. The best they had, anyway.

Carbo took a breath and let out a deep sigh. "Very well. Let's go and see Glaukos."

Glaukos looked at them insolently. His shackles had been undone, and he had been allowed to sit on a small stool. Carbo and Vespillo stood.

"Do you have anything more to confess?" asked Vespillo.

"More?" sneered Glaukos. "I have confessed nothing to you. Confession implies a wrong doing. My actions have been for the glory of the Lord and Lady, and so cannot be wrong."

"Then do you have any more to tell us about the glorious actions you have performed on behalf of the Lord and Lady?"

"All things will be revealed in time," said Glaukos.

Carbo regarded him steadily. "Keep telling yourself that, Glaukos," he said. "Your wonderful plans will come to fruition, the Lord and Lady will descend and put Rome to fire and sword, and you will be elevated to power and glory. Just like all the other street prophets claim, for their own favourite deities. I could hear the same thing five times before I had walked from one end of the forum to the other."

Glaukos looked smug. "False prophets do not concern me."

Vespillo scratched idly at a flea bite on his arm.

"You know what, Glaukos," he said. "I don't think you concern me either. Shafat is dead. The temple is burned to the ground, but only the temple. We stopped any fire spreading elsewhere. Elissa's followers are dead, or have recanted their belief. Elissa herself has managed to avoid capture, but not for long. It really doesn't matter to us what you think any more."

"Then why are you here?" asked Glaukos.

"We have to follow the rules. You are to be executed soon, and I am supposed to make sure I have all the information I can get out of you before then. I should really have you tortured. But I can't be bothered. Your pathetic little revolution is ended, and I don't need any more from you."

Vespillo turned to Carbo. "Do you want to go and grab a drink?"

Carbo looked hesitant. "I'm supposed to be meeting Rufa. She has gone to worship at the statue of *Libertas* in the forum to give thanks for her upcoming emancipation."

"Don't you start letting that slave henpeck you, just because you are freeing her and taking her to bed. Be your own man, come and grab a drink."

Carbo smiled. "You're on. Let's leave this pathetic madman to ponder his fate."

They left the cell. The key jiggled in the lock. Glaukos heard the footsteps of the two men fading into the distance. The door swung open an inch.

Carbo stood at a distance from where Rufa knelt at the statue of *Libertas*. The goddess, the deity of liberty and personal freedom, looked benignly out over the bustling forum. She was clothed in a loose fitting robe that revealed one breast, and her head bore a *pileum*, a brimless felt hat that was worn by slaves on the day of their manumission.

Carbo ached to stand beside Rufa, protect her. Allowing her to do this felt so alien, so wrong. When he thought he couldn't restrain himself any longer, he started towards her. Vespillo, though, as if reading his mind, but probably reading his body language instead, put a restraining hand on him. Carbo shrugged him off angrily, but remained where he was, watchful, painfully alert.

Suddenly, Glaukos was beside Rufa. They hadn't seen him approach in the crowd, but they hadn't been looking. They knew his destination and had waited for him there. Carbo tensed, but held his instincts to rush forward in check. Glaukos knelt and whispered something to her. Carbo saw Rufa stiffen. He didn't know if she was acting. Probably what he had said had genuinely shocked her. Rufa stood, and without a glance in Carbo's direction, she accompanied Glaukos, south-east, in the direction of the Caelian hill.

Elissa sat on a throne. It was a plain wooden chair, with simple arms, but in her mind it was marble with gold inlay. She looked off into the distance. Instead of a cavernous room, packed with tinder, naphtha, wax and wood, she imagined herself to be in a great palace. The Lord and Lady, Ba'al Hammon and Tanit stood behind her, and she was bathed in their light. Before her, prostrate, were a million Romans, cowed and terrified before the Gods of ancient

Carthage and this Dido reborn who had destroyed their city. They waited for their divine punishment, retribution for the evils committed in the name of this one city for so many centuries. Corinth, Alesia, Capua, great Carthage herself. The *lemures* of great men who had sought freedom from Rome hovered around, delighting in the evil city's humiliation - Vercingetorix, Spartacus, Jugurtha, Pyrrhus, Mithridates, Hamilcar and Hannibal. Their mocking laughter as Rome burned was like sweet song to her ears.

A whimper reached her, and her focus was brought back to reality. Her attention was drawn to the bundle, bound at her feet. Dolabella had been true to his word. She had been tempted to pay him half the money. After all the girl's mother was neither returned to her, nor dead. In the end, though, what did it matter? When the new kingdom was created, gold and silver would mean nothing. Rufa was to be part of the sacrifice, part of the fun, as she watched her daughter die. She wasn't necessary though, the gods had only specified the girl. She had paid him his full due, and he had departed with thanks and promises to fulfil the rest of his contract. Elissa had waved that away, the mother had only ever been important to pacify the daughter. He had left her with the young red-headed girl trussed like a chicken ready for cooking.

She smiled at the image. Ready for cooking, indeed. On the far wall was the symbol of Tanit, the cross with the round head, and resting against the wall was an altar. In front of that was a statue, the twin of the one she had in her *peristylium* in shape, but enormous in size. Where the hole at the bottom of the outstretched arms leading to the fire had been only big enough for a piglet in the statue in her *domus*, this one could accommodate a child, if they were bound correctly. Like this one was. The heat coming from the flames was intense, and she revelled in it, even though it made the skin of her face uncomfortable.

Her eyes were drawn to the corpulent figure slumped in the corner. Scrofa has been invaluable to her, especially in securing her release. He had known that taking her into his custody and then letting her escape would be the end of his career in the Urban Praetor's office. He would probably be severely punished for it. His usefulness to her was ended. He hadn't seemed to care. He had started to spout fantasies about how he would be the Lord to her Lady, how they would rule Rome together. He had even tried to kiss her. She had shied back, feeling an uncharacteristic panic, a remembrance of a time as a young girl when a fat man had taken her against her will.

She had offered him wine, toasting the Lady Tanit and the Lord Ba'al Hammon. The poison had taken hold quickly. She had smiled as he died, gasping and clutching his throat.

Rats scurried around. There were still small amounts of corn from when the building had been a *horrea*, a warehouse, in this case for the storage of grain. It had been donated to Elissa by a smitten follower, though he had puzzled at what she wanted it for. He was dead now, in the fire at the temple, and would never know.

The walls were thick, brick built. There was only one entrance, a small door, too narrow to fit a cart through, with multiple locks and bars on. The original owners had been paranoid about fire and theft. No building was immune to either though. The wooden pillars and beams that supported the roof were dry as tinder.

She glanced at the tiny window leading on to the street. It was too small for even a child to crawl through, and was shuttered. The only other light came from windows high up on the two storey high walls, larger but also shuttered. Was it time yet? The light filtering through the windows was still bright. Soon, when the games were at their climax. It wouldn't be long now. She fingered the amulet that hung around her neck, the sign of Tanit that her father had given her, all those years ago. I've never forgotten Carthage, father, she thought, nor you. She hoped he was proud of her.

She stood, and reached for her ceremonial knife, hilt etched with astrological symbols. She tested the blade against her thumb, watching in satisfaction as beads of red welled up where she had drawn the edge. She would liked to have tossed the moloch into the flames alive and conscious. The lord and lady would have enjoyed the child's screams. But she was one woman, alone. She knew she didn't have the strength to lift a struggling, resisting body into the fire. She would have to cut the girl's throat first.

Maybe she could do that now? A thrill of pleasure rushed through her at the thought. No, she was capable of delaying her gratification, in order to get the timing right. She reached down and stroked the girl's thick red hair. The girl trembled at her touch. The colour of fire and flame. The image that had come to her in her dream, the Lord and Lady telling her to make this sacrifice for her to avenge Carthage, to destroy Rome. She had been working for so long. That cursed tavern keeper had nearly ruined everything when he destroyed her followers and half her stores in the temple that day. She could not be stopped though. The full stores might have been necessary if the weather had been less favourable, if it had been raining for example. Instead, the Lord and Lady had sent heat and strong winds. The conflagration would be unstoppable.

A hammering came at the door, hard, rapid blows. She tensed. Was she discovered? How was that possible? She reached for a torch, ready to thrust it into the naphtha and wood that she had made to start the fire. What about the moloch? Did she have time for the sacrifice first? Surely she must, or the Lord and Lady would be displeased.

"Mother," came a cry from the door. "It's Glaukos. I beg entrance."

Glaukos? How? She placed the torch back in its holder, and peered through the slats of the shuttered window. She couldn't see the front door properly, but she couldn't see any sign of the urban cohorts. She walked to the door.

"Glaukos? Have you betrayed me?"

"No, mistress. I swear it."

"Swear it by the Lord and Lady!"

"I swear it by the Lord Ba'al Hammon and the Lady Tanit, and may they inflict on me eternal torment if I lie."

Elissa lifted the bar on the door and opened it a crack.

Glaukos stood there, unshaven, panting. By the shoulder, he held a red-headed woman. He had brought her Rufa. She smiled broadly and opened the door wide.

Chapter XXV

Carbo and Vespillo watched as Glaukos took Rufa inside the warehouse. It was a large wooden building, nestled up close to residential dwellings and businesses, in the haphazard, unplanned manner of much of Rome. The Caelian hill was the most south-easterly of Rome's seven hills, and was densely populated. The *insulae* were so tall that one had once been ordered to be demolished, as it blocked the view of the augurs as they tried to make their observations. Carbo looked around at the combustible structures that surrounded them, tinder dry from the recent warm weather, and the uneasy feeling that had felt like a tight ball in his guts grew into stark dread.

They had followed Glaukos at a safe distance as he had taken Rufa through the streets from the forum, ascending the Caelian, and finally reaching this warehouse. After a brief conversation through the doorway, he had been admitted, and disappeared inside, Rufa in tow. They hadn't been able to see the person that had opened the door for him, but it surely could only be Elissa. As the door slammed shut, and he heard a heavy bar thud into place, Carbo felt a moment of despair. What had they done? Had they sacrificed Rufa to this mad woman and her cruel servant? Were they as bad as her? But they had had no choice. How else could they get Fabilla? And what was Elissa still planning?

Carbo studied the building. It was reasonably sturdy, built with an eye at keeping thieves out, their hands off whatever it stored. The shuttered window and closed front door gave no obvious means of entrance. Carbo wished he had a dozen *vigiles* at his back, but it would clearly have been impossible to stealthily follow someone with a group of disorderly watchmen in their wake. They could call for reinforcements now, but he didn't want to leave Rufa with the deluded priestess for a moment longer than he had to.

"Could there be another way in?" Carbo asked.

Vespillo considered for a moment. The *vigiles* often had to gain entrance to a locked building, to control a fire, to enforce fire prevention, or to make an arrest. Their usual method, though, was just to break down the front door with an axe or battering ram. Neither Vespillo nor Carbo had any particular experience as stealthy house-breakers.

"We could search around the back," Vespillo suggested.

"What if this isn't the right place, though? If this is just a stop on the way to Elissa. Or if Elissa is planning to move Rufa and Fabilla elsewhere. We could lose them both."

Vespillo nodded. "You're right. I'll stay here and watch the front to make sure no one leaves."

Carbo looked up and down the street. The warehouse was snug against the neighbouring houses on either side, so there was no direct way through to the back. He picked a direction, and walked south, weaving through people, dogs, children and livestock. A hundred yards along, a small alley led between the houses. It was barely the width of a human body, and Carbo had to squeeze past several people coming in the opposite direction, with much cursing on both sides.

He emerged into a narrow street that ran parallel to the main road. Most of the buildings here were different dwellings from the ones that faced the main road, built back to back. The warehouse though, was a bigger structure, and so reached from the main street to this back one.

Carbo's heart sank as he looked at a blank wall. There were no doors or windows facing the street on this side of the building. The *insula* next door however, had some external stairs, leading to upper stories. Carbo climbed them, until two floors up he was roughly level with the roof of the warehouse. There was no rail on the stairs, but the gap between the edge and the warehouse roof was about eight feet.

Carbo looked down. The drop was about twenty feet. It was enough to incapacitate or kill. Either way, if he fell, Rufa and Fabilla were dead too, and what would happen to Rome? He closed his eyes for a moment, then opened them again. Took a breath.

Jumped.

Pain shot through his leg, the old injury complaining about the overexertion. The weakness in that leg made the leap less powerful than he had intended. His heart seemed to pause as he thought the leap would be too short.

He landed on the edge of the warehouse roof, and fell forwards. There was nothing to grab, and he felt himself sliding backwards down the gentle pitch. Tiles came away beneath his scrabbling feet, pried loose under his fingers. Then one held, and he managed to get some purchase with one hand. He came to a halt, and took a deep breath, attempting to slow his racing heart.

He peeled a tile away. It made a dull, clunking noise as it lifted. He tried some more, but many were wedged in tight, and with little leverage, he realised it would take forever to make a hole big enough to climb through. Besides, beneath the tiles he could see heavy beams, and he wasn't sure if there was space for him to fit through if they ran close together.

Slowly, he turned himself, so he was peering over the edge of the roof. The tiles overhung the wall by about a foot. Just beneath him was a shuttered window, large enough for him to fit through with room to spare. He reached down, testing the wood of the shutters. It was in poor repair, flimsy and rotten. He could peel away some of the boards to get in, but his entrance would certainly not be a surprise. Who knew what awaited him inside? An army of cultist bowmen, arrows trained on the window to pepper him as soon as he showed himself. His entrance would have to be swift.

He wondered what was on the other side of the wall. The building was two storeys high, but he couldn't recall ever having been inside a *horrea*. Did that mean there was one room, two storeys in height, or an upper floor?

Time was running out. Rufa was in there, at the mercy of Elissa. As Caesar had said, sometimes you have to let the dice fly.

Gritting his teeth, he lowered himself over the edge of roof, hanging onto a beam that jutted out to support the overhanging roof tiles. It held his weight, although it creaked in protest. He rested his feet against the wall just above the window, and muttered a prayer to Jupiter,

Mercury, Mars and the divine Augustus. Then he pushed against the wall with his feet, the explosive power in the muscles of his leg propelling him backwards, swinging by his arms. He let his legs drop as he reached the furthest point back of the arc of his motion, then braced himself as he swung forwards.

He crashed feet first into the shuttered window, which burst apart around him, and he was through into the warehouse.

And falling.

It took less than the length of a heartbeat to fall the twenty feet, but it was plenty of time to feel terror, as the sensation of his insides being left above him hit, and the ceiling rushed away from him.

He landed on his back in a large vat of tallow. The rendered animal fat, used for candle making, was solid, but soft. He lay still for a moment, the breath knocked out of him, vision blurred. He had time to offer a brief prayer of thanks to the gods, when he heard the sound of running feet. His vision came back to him just in time to see Glaukos charging towards him, dagger in hand. The giant man dived at him, and Carbo rolled to one side, the dagger stabbing into the tallow where Carbo had been just a moment before.

Carbo continued his roll through the greasy tallow and out of the vat, bringing himself to his feet. He shook his head to clear it, reached for his *gladius*, then saw the sword a few feet away, jarred from his grip by the fall. Glaukos regained his feet, the animal fat sticking to his torso and arms. He started to circle, while Carbo watched his eyes carefully, looking for signs of an attack.

The thrust came without warning, and with surprising swiftness for a man of Glaukos' size. Carbo side-stepped in time for the dagger thrust to pass him, and circled to bring himself nearer to the *gladius*. Glaukos followed him, feinted, backing Carbo away from the sword he needed to even the fight. Glaukos appeared to feint again, but turned the thrust into an attack. Carbo, misreading, was too slow. He threw himself sideways, but the dagger sliced the outside of his arm.

The movement, though, had brought Carbo within reach of the sword, and he and Glaukos realised it at the same moment. Carbo grabbed for the *gladius*, which was behind and to one side, while Glaukos made a vicious lunge, low, expecting Carbo to be reaching down. Carbo threw himself backwards, the dagger this time slicing deep into calf muscle.

He came to his feet with *gladius* in hand. The odds had evened up.

Carbo could feel blood flowing from the deep wounds in his arm and leg, and knew that he couldn't last through a fight of endurance. Besides, he still hadn't seen Elissa, Rufa or Fabilla, in among the piles of combustible material that packed the warehouse.

Glaukos knew time was on his side as well, and kept his distance, a sneering grin fixed to his face. Carbo, though, had reach now. The giant was taller and heavier than Carbo, but not by much and the *gladius,* though a short sword, was a lot longer than a dagger. Carbo closed with Glaukos, watching the giant's smile falter as he saw the danger.

"Give up, Carbo," said Glaukos. "Your slave whore and her brat will be dead soon, gone to appease the great Lord and Lady. They are worth nothing, why are you bothering with them?"

Carbo said nothing, manoeuvring himself closer to the giant.

"You can buy another slave, if having one is so important to you. The mistress Elissa would pay you enough to buy a hundred slaves like her her, if you leave now."

Carbo made a thrust and Glaukos fended it off in a desperate sweep of his dagger, so the point of the *gladius* drifted marginally wide.

"Is she really that good a fuck?" sneered Glaukos, then, still finishing the taunt, lunged hard at Carbo.

Carbo took one step to the side and swung his sword down hard on Glaukos' outstretched hand. The sword he had kept faithfully sharpened cleaved straight through bone, tendon and muscle, severing Glaukos' arm at the wrist. The hand, still clutching the dagger, fell to the ground, and Glaukos staggered back with a scream, clutching at the stump from which arterial pulses of blood spurted. He dropped to his knees, looking up at Carbo in disbelief.

Carbo pulled his sword back to deliver the killing blow.

"Carbo, no!"

The voice was Rufa's and he froze. Slowly, still keeping Glaukos in reach, he turned.

Rufa stood, ten feet away, face pale. Behind her, Elissa held a knife to Fabilla's throat.

Vespillo heard the crash that marked Carbo's entrance to the warehouse, heard the sounds of fighting from within, and hurled himself at the front door. It barely moved. Some dust fell from around its hinges, but the door, thick wood, locked and barred, stood stubbornly firm. He tried again, but the only effect was to increase the bruising on his shoulder. He looked around desperately. Nearby, a small boy watched him curiously. He pulled out a coin.

"Boy. Run to the nearest *vigiles* station. You know where it is?"

The boy nodded, bemused.

"Tell them tribune Vespillo of the IInd cohort requires every man they have, with all their firefighting and demolition equipment. Repeat it to me."

The boy did so.

"There's another coin here if you return quickly enough. Now run like your life depends on it."

He watched the boy sprint off, then turned to glare at the unyielding door in frustration.

Carbo let all his senses absorb the situation, trying to think like a soldier, trying to ignore the fact that it was Fabilla with a knife at her throat, that it was Rufa who looked at him with hopeful, desperate, piteous pleading in her eyes. Glaukos was still on his knees, all his attention focused on staunching the flow of blood from his stump. He couldn't be completely discounted, but to all intents and purposes he was out of the fight. Before him, Rufa stood, pale and motionless. Behind her, Elissa held Fabilla by the hair, the knife across her throat, a wild, triumphant look in her eyes.

They were in a clear space in the warehouse, surrounded by the materials Elissa had gathered here. Carbo saw now how the combustible material had been carefully arranged. Near Elissa were piles of tinder wood, soaked in naphtha. Arranged around that were pieces of lumber, untouched logs of varying sizes, some carpented pieces like chairs and tables, positioned so that flames would reach them, while air fed them. There was charcoal, wax, tallow, olive oil, in various containers interspersed between the wood. Elissa had left nothing to chance. The naphtha soaked tinder would ignite at the touch of a flame, and once it did, nothing would stop the building turning into a raging inferno.

In the middle of all the material, in front of an altar that sat against the wall, a strange structure glowed brightly, giving out light and heat. Carbo recognised the design as a larger version of the statue that Rufa had seen used to burn the sacrifice at Elissa's *domus*.

Carbo stood motionless, trying to force himself to think. Vespillo would not be coming in to help him any time soon. He couldn't move on Elissa without her cutting Fabilla's throat and starting the fire. Helplessness suffused him, and that familiar, sickening feeling of panic started to rise within, threatening to paralyse him. No, gods, please. Not here, not now.

Carbo looked into Rufa's eyes. He remembered how she had been able to calm the panic in him when it overwhelmed him. He thrust the feeling down with an effort of will.

"Take me," he said, his voice steady. "If you need a sacrifice, take me."

Elissa shook her head. "The stars, my dreams, the lord and lady, they have chosen this one." She shook Fabilla roughly, who yelped. Tears were rolling down the little girl's face. Carbo knew she was old enough to be fully aware of what was happening, and knew she was facing it as bravely as she could. Carbo tried not to look at her, for fear his breaking heart would sap his will.

"But surely your lord and lady would rather they have me. A little girl is no fitting tribute to their power."

Elissa looked a little uncertain. "It has always been so. Since time began, the Lord Ba'al Hammon and the Lady Tanit took the lives of children, our most precious gifts, in honour of their greatness."

"But this snotty brat, this slave girl, she isn't a precious gift. You can purchase another for a handful of coin."

"She seems precious to you, otherwise why would you be offering yourself."

"Maybe so, but I am not the one making the sacrifice. Who would the gods prefer, this cheap slave girl, or a veteran of the Roman legions, a war hero, a *pilus prior* centurion."

Elissa narrowed her eyes. "You would do this? Give your life as sacrifice in exchange for the life of these two."

Carbo swallowed, looked at Rufa who looked back, agony in her expression.

"I would."

Elissa nodded. "Very well. The time is nearly upon us. Lay down your sword."

Rufa looked at him helplessly, shaking her head. Carbo smiled to her in what he hoped was a reassuring way, and placed his sword gently on the ground.

"Glaukos," snapped Elissa. "Stop your whimpering, and bring him to me."

Glaukos had managed to fashion a tourniquet from a strip of cloth from his tunic, and although he had not been able to tie it tight enough with one hand to completely stop the bleeding, it had slowed to a trickle. He got to his feet unsteadily, swaying a little.

"Compose yourself, Glaukos," said Elissa. "I will need your help feeding the fire with a sacrifice this big." Glaukos grunted, glaring at Carbo with grim satisfaction. Then he picked up his dagger and held it to the back of Carbo's ribs. He pushed Carbo in the back, propelling him forwards towards Elissa, but kept close enough that the knife stayed in contact, ready to give a killing thrust in an instant.

"We have a deal, Elissa. Let them go."

Carbo was face to face with Elissa, Fabilla between them, Rufa to one side.

"Oh, don't fret, Carbo. I'm not going to kill them. I honour my promises." She sighed. "Glaukos will do it instead. The Lord and Lady will be delighted with the quality of my gifts to them tonight."

Carbo stiffened. "Elissa, please."

Elissa's face twisted. "You Romans!" she spat. "So arrogant. You rule the world, and you believe that is your right. You think you can dictate terms to me, Elissa, Priestess of the Lord Ba'al Hammon and the Lady Tanit?

You will die this night, along with these slaves, and along with Rome. Tonight, a new world begins!"

She pushed Fabilla to one side, and stepped up to Carbo, pressing her knife to his throat. The knife from Glaukos on his back prodded painfully, keeping him still.

"Lord and Lady, descend to us tonight. Bring your power and destruction, fire and flame, blood and death, to the evil Roman Empire. Free your people, the men and women of Carthage, and the rest of the world who struggles beneath the Roman yoke."

She drew her hand back to strike. Rufa threw herself at Elissa, and knocked her sideways. The dagger spun away, and Elissa turned to Rufa, off balance, grasping at her. Rufa glared at Elissa, and Carbo saw a hardness in Rufa's face he had never seen before.

"Burn, you bitch," she said and thrust Elissa backwards.

Elissa stumbled into the statue, and hot charcoal sprayed out around her. She flailed her arms comically for a moment, trying to stay upright, clutching at the red hot statue, ignoring the hiss as the skin on her arms and hands burnt. For a moment, she seemed to right herself. Then she fell. The statue crashed down with her, into the nearest pile of tinder and naphtha.

The red hot charcoal that spilled out ignited the sticky naphtha instantly. Elissa screamed a piercing wail, rolling to try to right herself, but succeeding only in coating herself in the flaming naphtha. She staggered to her feet, and smokey flames shot upwards from her clothes.

For a moment, she was still, staring at Carbo. Her face had a ghostly glow, peering out from the flames at him, and he marvelled at the effort of will that kept her still despite the agony her body must be experiencing.

Her words came out in short gasps, but were clear. "Rome…will…burn."

Then she sank to the floor, body writhing until it disappeared from view in the rapidly spreading fire.

Carbo realised the pressure had eased in his back, as Glaukos had watched the scene unfold in dismay. Carbo spun his body swiftly, one arm knocking Glaukos' dagger hand aside.

"Run," he yelled at Rufa, then grabbed the giant's remaining hand at the wrist. Glaukos recovered quickly, and clubbed Carbo around the head with his stump. The force of the blow momentarily dazed Carbo, causing him to lessen his grip on Glaukos' wrist. Glaukos ripped his arm free and brought it round to slash the dagger at Carbo's face. Carbo raised an arm to block the blow, and two muscular forearms clashed. The force of the impact deadened Carbo's arm, but he managed to slide his grip down to Glaukos' wrist, and twist hard.

The dagger fell from Glaukos' hand, but instead of trying to retrieve it, he wrapped both his arms around Carbo's chest and squeezed.

Carbo had never felt such strength before. He felt himself lifted from the ground, a completely unfamiliar experience to him, and felt the breath crushed from him. Although both men were weakened from blood loss, Glaukos had lost much more than Carbo. Even so, Carbo could not break free from the bearhug, trying to pry the giant's arms away from him as he struggled to take in a breath.

He drew back his head and thrust it forward as hard as he could, forehead impacting the middle of Glaukos' face. Still the grip did not lessen, and Carbo felt darkness swimming in from the edge of his vision.

His scrabbling fingers found the giant's stump, and he dug into it, causing Glaukos to roar in pain, but grip even harder. He found the tourniquet and ripped it off, feeling a fresh spurt of blood over his fingers. Glaukos dropped Carbo in panic, clutching at the pumping wound. Carbo slumped onto his backside, gasping in air. He put his arms out backwards to stop himself falling flat on his back. His fingers gripped cold steel.

Glaukos roared and threw himself onto Carbo, his huge weight set to tip the fight fully in his favour. Carbo brought the sword round, hilt braced on the floor. It ran the giant through his chest.

Glaukos' face was suspended an inch from Carbo's. He felt the hot breath, saw the lips twist in a snarl. Then blood drooled from his mouth, over Carbo's face, and the giant went limp.

"Carbo!" Rufa's voice was a panicky scream.

Carbo thrust Glaukos' corpse from him and staggered to his feet. Fire had taken hold around the walls and was spreading rapidly through all the combustible material. Tinder was crackling, vats of tallow and wax were hissing and spitting, black smoke was curling up from the naphtha and filling the air. Carbo, still struggling for breath, started to cough.

"Carbo!" screamed Rufa again. "We can't get out!"

Carbo fought his way past the flames and through the thickening smoke to the front door, which Rufa was struggling to open.

"Out of my way," he said, hoarsely, no time for gentility. Rufa and Fabilla stepped back, the little girl pale-faced and trembling.

Rufa had already removed the interior bars, but the door had three locks on it. He shook the door, then charged it with his shoulder. It rattled, but moved little.

"Where are the keys?" he spluttered.

"Elissa had them," said Rufa, despairingly.

Carbo looked back at the roaring inferno, centred on where Elissa had fallen. There was no way back there. He rattled the door again, kicked it, thumped it with his shoulder. He looked around for something to batter it with, found a short log and hammered on the door with all his strength. Some of the wood splintered, but far too little to make an impression. He roared frustration, and hammered on the door with his fists.

Rufa put a hand on his arm.

"Carbo." He stopped and looked at her. Her eyes were full of despair, and love. She pulled Fabilla to her, hiding the little girl's face in her *stola*. Her eyes were streaming, from the smoke or emotion, Carbo couldn't tell.

"Carbo, you did everything you could. So much more than I had dared to hope for." Rufa coughed. "You were good to your word, to my father. He could have expected no more."

Carbo stared at her speechless. The air grew thicker, so breathing became hard, let alone talking. He squeezed her hand, opened his mouth, trying to find the right words to say.

The door shook with a tremendous crash. They turned, startled, and another crash came, this time accompanied by splintering wood. More blows to the door came in quick succession, and within moments, the head of an axe came through, daylight and air flooding in with it.

The axe disappeared, then a hook was pushed through the hole. It gripped the edges of the wood. There was a pause, then the door was ripped off its hinges with immense force. Vespillo appeared in the gap, face drawn with worry, sword in hand. He saw the three huddled together, and relief flooded his face.

"Thank all the gods," he cried, and pulled them out of the building. They staggered clear, eyes streaming, gasping the fresh air into stinging lungs. As Carbo's vision cleared, he saw the team of oxen that had been used to pull the door down, saw the *vigiles* in action as they attempted to fight the fire, started to work on neighbouring buildings to make fire breaks. A *medicus* approached and started to fuss around them.

Carbo and Rufa stared at each other, disbelieving. Then Carbo stepped forward, crushing Rufa into his embrace, and kissed her like it was the first time, and like it was the last time.

Chapter XXVI

The warehouse was too stocked with combustible material for any realistic attempt to douse the fire there. At full strength, the *vigiles* in Rome numbered seven cohorts, each of seven centuries, each of around seventy men, about 3500 in total. However, when recruiting difficulties, sickness and working shifts were taken into account, only a third to a half of that number were available at any one time. The first to arrive at the fire, the closest who had responded to Vespillo's plea for help, were the cohort who manned the fire station on the Caelian, with their colleagues from the nearby *excubitoria*. They numbered a couple of hundred men, soon reinforced by another two hundred from Vespillo's own IInd cohort from the Esquiline.

It wasn't nearly enough.

Aided by a strong wind, and the intense heat of the inferno that Elissa had so carefully prepared, the fire jumped from building to building with a staggering speed. Few citizens were at home, most being out watching the games, so the *vigiles* had little of the local aid that they usually relied on as the self-interested tried to save their property. On the other hand, there were fewer panicky crowds, and fewer people trying to prevent the destruction of their houses for firebreaks.

Carbo escorted Rufa and Fabilla through the narrow streets, heading back to Vespillo's house. In several places they had to turn back, to navigate around routes blocked by houses which were strangely collapsed, despite not yet being touched by fire. Carbo thought of the fire that he and Vespillo had attended, the oddly collapsed buildings then, and saw Elissa's hand at work. Fortunately, the blockages were not frequent, and Carbo guessed that they had thinned out Elissa's followers in the raid on the temple enough to reduce their impact.

Dusk was descending, and the glow of the fire was visible over the rooftops. Most of the people he met in the streets had stopped to point, muttering in alarm at the apparent size of the conflagration. He bustled past them, delivering the shaken mother and daughter into Severa's care.

Severa had endless questions, not least concern for Vespillo. Carbo assured her Vespillo was well and safe, and begged her to look after Rufa and Fabilla again. He warned all three to watch the skyline closely, and if they felt the fire was approaching the Esquiline, they should leave the city by the nearest route, taking nothing with them.

"Do you understand?" asked Carbo sternly, fixing Rufa and Severa with a stare. Both strong women looked cowed and anxious, and nodded agreement. With a crushing embrace of Rufa, Carbo left them.

The Esquiline was only half a mile north of the Caelian hill, and in that direction, the dusk sky was flickering and glowing like an angry volcano. Carbo hesitated, then thought of his tavern and his slaves. The Subura was a short distance to the west, and he headed in that direction. The streets were filling with people coming out to gaze in fear at the obviously expanding blaze. As he reached the familiar territory of the Subura, people who recognised him stopped him to ask what was happening. He ignored most, pushing through, but one young man blocked his path.

"Hey, Carbo. Where is your friend Vespillo and his little bucket boys when we need them?"

Carbo stopped, then without a word pointed to the horizon. The man followed the direction of his finger to the blaze. A low, angry sound was coming from that direction now, and even from this distance, they could hear screams carried by the strong winds. The man nodded respectfully and stepped back.

When Carbo reached the tavern, Philon and Marsia were waiting for him anxiously.

"Master, what is happening?" asked Marsia.

Carbo looked at Philon in disgust. "His mistress' plans," he replied.

Philon looked down, shamefaced.

"Are we safe?" asked Marsia.

"I don't know," said Carbo. He looked around the tavern. Vatius sat in a corner, bandage around his head, calmly sipping from a cup of wine and fussing Myia. Otherwise the tavern was empty.

Marsia noticed his gaze and answered his unspoken question. "We were quiet anyway because of the games, and everyone who was here went home once it became obvious this fire was a bad one. Well," she said, looking at Vatius, "Almost everyone."

"Good," said Carbo. "I'm going to find Vespillo and do what I can to help." He looked at Philon pointedly. "And you are coming with me."

Philon paled. "Master, no, please. I'm just a humble eunuch. What help could I be?"

Carbo stepped forward and gripped him under the chin, looking angrily into the slave's eyes.

"This is your fault, Philon, you and your mistress and your cult. I still haven't decided whether or not to have you crucified your betrayal. Maybe if you help your master and the people of this city today, I will be inclined to leniency."

Philon trembled and bowed his head. "Yes, master."

"Marsia, you are to stay here, bar the doors and do keep watch for the fire. Flee if it comes too near."

"No, master."

Carbo looked at her in amazement.

"What did you say?"

"I'm coming with you, master. My place is at your side." She reached behind the bar, and picked up a small bucket which she had clearly stored earlier in preparation for the coming fire.

Carbo shook his head. "Fine, I don't have time to argue. Vatius, would you mind keeping an eye on things here?"

Vatius raised a hand in acknowledgement, and Carbo led his slaves out into the night.

The crowds had grown, the streets more clogged now, all streaming away from the Caelian, away from the growing fire. Carbo, Philon and Marsia fought their way past panicking, fleeing people. Some had left everything, bringing only their families and any slaves they possessed with them. Others struggled with carts laden with possessions, jewellery, crockery, clothing, lamps. It was foolhardy. They made little progress, and the jostling crowds caused the contents to spill or the carts to overturn.

Only Carbo's bulk allowed them to make any progress at all. He thrust cursing men and wailing women out of the way as he continued through the crush. As they approached the Caelian hill, he encountered some people trying to make their way towards the flames. He presumed they were games-goers, trying to get to their houses, to save family and possessions. As they neared the spreading flames, the crowds thinned, and making quicker time, they soon encountered a group of watchmen. Their centurion held a hand out, forbidding him to pass through.

He sighed, frustrated at the delay in getting back to help Vespillo, but was able to see the little bucket boys proving their worth. The fire was still a distance away, but he could see that it now encompassed a large area of the Caelian hill. Under the direction of their centurion, the *vigiles* were demolishing houses. Although brick was being increasingly used in the construction of houses and *insulae* since the reign of Augustus, most dwellings still remained of shoddy wood construction, crammed together, interspersed with more warehouses of the type that Elissa had started the fire in. Although they weren't as deliberately incendiary as Elissa's firepit, they still contained flammable materials such as grain, wool and lumber, and when the fire reached one, it redoubled in intensity.

A few people protested the destruction of their homes and businesses, but the protests were half-hearted. Romans lived in constant fear of fire, had all experienced it, and knew that this was a bad one.

Carbo watched as the *vigiles* wheeled up a *ballista* towards a tall *insula* that was next in the path for demolition. With swift efficiency, they lined the bolt thrower up, aiming it at the top of the building, and at the order of the centurion, fired. A bolt shot out, its attached rope snaking out behind it, and lodged in the wood of the uppermost floor. Repeated four more times, there were soon five ropes dangling from the top floor, firmly anchored by the bolts that had struck deeply into the walls.

The centurion organised the men to attach the ropes to the yokes of two mules. He gave the order for everyone to stand well back, then had the mule drivers whip their mules forward. The mules kicked and whinnied, but reluctantly did as they were bid, straining against the ropes. One pulled through, the bolt whizzing dangerously back through the air, causing two watchmen to jump to one side.

The other four ropes held, and with a series of cracks, and then a long groan, the top two floors of the building toppled down into the street. As soon as the dust and debris had settled, the *vigiles* were moving forward with ropes on hooks and axes to bring down the remaining two stories. With the centurion distracted, Carbo beckoned his slaves, and they sneaked on down the street.

It was easy to find the general direction of the fire, by the brightness in the darkening sky and the thick smoke, but the conflagration had spread to such an extent that knowing where Vespillo and his men would be situated would be guesswork at best.

The people they saw now were a desperate collection. Many were injured, badly burned, coughing. Some reached their blistered hands out piteously towards him for help. He ignored them and walked on. Many of the taller buildings that were on fire had crumpled bodies at their feet, lying still, many with hair and clothes still smoking and smouldering. At one corner sat a man with tear tracks starkly pale against his soot-blackened face. In his arms he cradled a small body, so badly burned Carbo couldn't tell if it was a boy or a girl. Philon stared at the tableau in horror as they passed.

They came across another group of *vigiles*. These were operating a *sipho*, a big water pump, soaking a temple that was obviously deemed sufficiently important to be worth attempting to save, rather than demolish. Carbo located the centurion.

"I'm looking for Vespillo. Tribune of the second cohort. The Esquiline branch."

The centurion studied him for a moment, then nodded in the direction of the blaze.

"He was in the centre of that, last I heard. Him and his men. Idiots. The Caelian hill can't be saved."

Carbo thanked the man, and moved on. He had to ask two more groups of firefighters before he finally located Vespillo.

Face blackened, hair full of ash, the set of his shoulders showing how weariness suffused him, Vespillo nevertheless looked resolute. They were at the outermost edge of the fire. A large part of the Caelian had already been devastated, but Vespillo and the second cohort fought on.

"Get that soaked blanket on the lower walls. *Aquarii,* direct the water from the *sipho* to the upper floors. You, reinforce the bucket chain, the buckets are coming too slowly."

"Vespillo, how can I help?"

Vespillo turned and saw his friend, and look of gratitude passed over his face. He clapped him on the shoulder.

"I don't know if anyone can help, but we are going to do our best. I'm not going to let that witch win." Vespillo's gaze fell on Philon, and his expression hardened. He nodded to where a man was sitting against a wall, nursing an obviously broken and scorched arm, attended by a *medicus.*

"Pinarius there had a burning timber fall on him. Carbo, grab his axe and help the men pulling down the building next door. You two," he said indicating the slaves, "Help with collecting the water."

They did as they were told, Carbo taking the short axe and joining the watchmen who were attempting to make a firebreak. The one storey house they were working on already had a smouldering roof, but they were making progress, hooks pulling at beams, axes hacking at pillars. Carbo swung his axe, gaining grateful comments from the men he was assisting. The wooden pillar he was working on gave way, but several thick pillars remained. He looked up. The wooden roof was starting to burst into flame, and the flames had raced along so they endangered the next house, nestled up close along side.

Looking around him, Carbo spied a ladder, and a broom made of thick twigs attached to a wooden handle, both standard firefighting equipment. He threw the ladder up against the building and quickly scaled it.

The roof creaked under his weight, weakened by the flames that were starting to eat into it. Carbo wheeled the broom like a hammer, smacking the flames as they sprouted up. The flames were shooting out sparks, threatening to jump across the narrow gap to the next roof. If they did so, the firebreak they were creating by destroying this property would already have been bypassed.

Carbo extinguished a small flame, then another. He recalled the legend of the hydra, two fires seeming to spring up for each he defeated. He fought furiously, regardless. Another pillar went, and part of the roof collapsed.

"Carbo! What in the name of Vulcan are you doing up there?"

Vespillo's voice was angry and concerned.

"Buying time," Carbo yelled back, breathing heavily with effort.

A row of flames sprang up, racing towards the next house. Carbo leapt on them, flailing around him with the broom maniacally. The twigs on the broom themselves were starting to smoulder now, and the heat from the fire that was consuming the last building it had reached was intense. Sweat poured down his face, smoke stung his eyes, and he worked on. Another pillar gave way to the watchmen's axes, and now a large swathe of roof collapsed in on itself.

Carbo judged the time was right to abandon the roof. He turned round to get on the ladder, but found his way was blocked by new flames. He looked around, seeing flame closing in on him, feeling the heat. He looked over the edge, and his heart fell at the thought of another jump.

A ladder smacked against the edge of the roof on the last remaining part that wasn't burning.

"Get down here, you idiot!"

Carbo gratefully slid down the ladder. Strong hands pulled him away from the building, and the instant he was clear, men heaved on ropes attached to the remaining beams. The rest of the building came crashing down, the last flames extinguishing in the debris.

The *vigiles* cheered loudly, their success having temporarily arrested the spread of the fire in this direction. Vespillo gave them a brief moment to celebrate and regain their breaths, as he looked around him, surveying the situation. Fire was starting to work its way down the opposite side of the street, and Carbo sighed, getting ready for Vespillo to send them back into combat. He looked around and saw Philon and Marsia approaching from down the street, both carrying buckets of water. The effort seemed pitiful, hopeless in the face of the raging anger of the fire, but he felt proud of them both for their effort. Philon looked resolute, seeming to have finally found some inner strength from his desire to make amends.

As Carbo watched them, he saw the building they were passing start to list. A burning beam split and the wall of the upper storey bowed outwards into the street above his two slaves. He cried out a warning and pointed frantically. Marsia was partially obscured from his view by some of the *vigiles* and could not see him waving, but Philon noticed and followed the direction of his gestures. He looked up just as the upper wall gave way and a pile of bricks tumbled downwards.

Time froze. Carbo's heart seemed to stop. Philon barely hesitated. He thrust Marsia hard with both hands, propelling her across the street and out of harms way. A fraction of a heart beat later, the falling rubble buried Philon.

Marsia sat on her backside, buckets upended, looking in horrified amazement at the pile of cement, wood and bricks that lay on top of her fellow slave. Carbo and some *vigiles* arrived a moment later and started pulling away debris frantically. Marsia joined in, and soon they had Philon uncovered. Marsia held him, looking down into his unnaturally white face. His breathing was laboured, his chest caved in. He coughed and a fine spray of blood covered Marsia's face.

Philon opened his eyes and looked up at Marsia.

"I'm sorry for…everything."

The effort of speaking caused him to cough more. Carbo noticed a section of his chest where the ribs were broken, moving in and out like the sail on a boat flapping in the wind.

"Don't speak," said Marsisa.

Philon was struggling for breath now, his lips and tongue turning blue.

"Think…kindly…of me…"

"I will," whispered Marsia.

Philon nodded gratefully. Marsia held him as consciousness rapidly left him, and the laboured breathing stopped. She buried her face in his hair and wept.

Vespillo and Carbo exchanged glances. Vespillo shook his head, sadly, then turned back to direct his men.

A breathless young man appeared around the street corner, and came running up to Carbo.

"I'm looking for tribune Vespillo," he gasped.

Carbo gestured to Vespillo. The man took a couple of breaths, then spoke.

"I bring a message from Prefect Quintus Naevius Cordus Sutorius Macro."

Vespillo stiffened at the name of his commander, the equestrian-ranked Prefect in charge of the entire *vigiles*.

"Go on."

"The Prefect commands you to withdraw."

"What?" Vespillo protested. "We are winning this fight." He gestured at the firebreak they had just made. "We need to create another break across the street, that will arrest all spread in this direction for long enough to enlarge the break and allow us to start bringing water and *acetum* grenades to bear on the burning buildings. We can save all these houses, and who knows how many lives of those too slow and infirm to flee."

"The Prefect was firm, Tribune," said the man. "He fears that all Rome is threatened. He wants every available man creating a break around the Caelian hill, to isolate the conflagration here."

Vespillo looked aghast. "He is abandoning the whole of the Caelian?"

The messenger looked uncomfortable, but nodded. Carbo put a hand on Vespillo's shoulder.

"Come on, soldier, you have your orders. Both of us have obeyed countless commands we didn't agree with over the years. And who is to say the Prefect is wrong? Elissa intended to destroy Rome. If the fire is confined to the Caelian, Rome will cope. If it consumes the whole of Rome, who knows what the consequences may be?"

Vespillo looked defiant, then his shoulders slumped. He looked around at his men.

"*Vigiles*," he called. "You have fought bravely. You have made me proud, and brought honour on the cohort. But we have orders to withdraw. Grab your equipment, follow me."

Carbo put an arm around Marsia as the watchmen formed up. Then Vespillo turned his back on the fire, and led his men away.

Epilogue

Carbo and Rufa stood on the Pons Fabricius, the arched stone bridge over the Tiber, and watched the water rush by underneath. Fabilla was with Severa, who had taken to the child like a long lost aunt.

A pall of smoke still drifted up over the Caelian hill. The fire had burned for two days, but Macro's tactic of isolating the hill had worked. The rest of Rome was safe. The Caelian, however, was devastated. Carbo had walked the ruins with Vespillo yesterday, the day after the fire had officially ended. The ashes of the buildings still gave up phenomenal amounts of heat. They had found the centre of the fire, Elissa's warehouse. Almost nothing recognisable remained.

Carbo had kicked at the ashes, and his foot had connected with something solid and metallic. Brushing away the debris, he had uncovered the sacrificial statue. The intense heat had partially melted it, deforming its shape. Not even bones remained of Glaukos and Elissa.

Vespillo had pulled up his tunic and urinated over the statue. Steam rose up where the yellow liquid splashed. He shook and rearranged his clothing, then spat.

"She deserved worse," Vespillo had said. "She should have been hurled from the Tarpeian Rock, or ripped apart by beasts in the arena."

"She's dead," said Carbo. "That's all that matters now."

Now, Carbo reached out to Rufa. He felt cold metal beneath her dress. He insisted now that she carried a knife for protection. It made him feel better. He squeezed her hand and smiled at him, and raised his hand to her mouth for a soft kiss. Last night they had made love, but it had been less about pleasure and more about comfort, recovery, relief. They had held each other close until sleep had claimed their weary bodies.

What now? Carbo wondered. It really was over. Elissa was gone, and had no heir. Carbo would claim Rufa and Fabilla as his own, and then manumit them. Then he would marry her. Well, if she wanted to marry him. She would be his freedwoman, not his slave. The choice would be hers. He looked into her eyes, and saw his love for her reflected back at him. He took a breath, let it out contentedly.

A small urchin tugged at Carbo's sleeve.

"Sir, my Master sent me to ask you to attend him."

Carbo looked at him, bemused.

"Who is your Master?"

"Quintus Naevius Cordus Sutorius Macro. He has heard of the help you gave the *vigiles,* and wanted to thank you."

"Now?"

"If it pleases you, sir. He is about to attend a play at the Theatre of Marcellus, just across the way. He promises not to detain you long."

Carbo looked across at Rufa, who smiled.

"Go," she said. "Accept the thanks. I will wait here for you."

Carbo kissed her lightly, then followed the urchin. He wandered slowly over to the theatre, taking in the late

September air. For the first time since he had walked back into Rome, after his discharge from the legions, he felt content.

As he approached the theatre, he looked around. A puzzled frown crossed his face. There was a sprinkling of theatre goers and passing citizens, old ladies, mothers, freedmen. There was no noble here. No equestrian with his entourage of slaves, no suggestion of anyone of rank.

A cold, nagging feeling crept up his spine. He reached for the knife, turned and ran to where had left Rufa at the bridge. From a distance he saw Rufa, back turned, looking out over the river, and a slender figure approaching her. He called out but the noise of the city drowned his warning. The figure glanced around and he saw the unmistakable features of Dolabella. Thrusting people out of the way, leg protesting in agony, he closed on the slave hunter. Dolabella whirled round at the commotion, and his eyes fixed on Carbo. For a moment, Dolabella's features creased in concern.

Then Carbo stumbled over a passer-by's foot, and his injured leg gave out on him. He fell forward heavily, just feet away from Rufa and the *fugitvarius.* Carbo stretched his hand out in supplication.

"Dolabella, please, no."

Dolabella shook his head sadly. "Carbo, I did make it clear. I never fail." He pulled a sharp dagger from his waist belt and grinned. Then his features became fixed, eyes widening. He turned, revealing Rufa's knife deep in his back, then pitched forward into the swirling waters of the Tiber.

Carbo stood painfully, and staggered to Rufa, who was standing with her hands to her face. He grabbed her to him, crushed her close, and wept his relief into her hair.

THE END

Historical notes

The fire that destroyed the Caelian Hill in AD27 is attested to in Tacitus' Annals, though he is strangely silent on Elissa and her cult's role in the conflagration. Later in the same century of course, another cult, that of the Christians, would be blamed for the even greater fire that devastated Rome.

The *vigiles*, also known as the *vigiles urbani* or *cohortes vigilum*, were the first official fire-fighting organisation in Rome. They were nicknamed the *spartoli* or little bucket boys after the rope buckets sealed with pitch that they carred to do their duties. Founded by August in AD 6 to combat the frequent fires that broke out in the poorly built city. Prior to their formation, fire-fighting organisations were privately owned. Most famously, Crassus made a lot of his riches by sending his private firemen to the site of a fire, and putting the blaze out only after the owner had agreed to sell him the property at a knock down price.

The *vigiles* recruits were originally made up largely of freedmen, but take up of the job was low, so a law was introduced to give a cash bonus and full citizenship to watchmen after they had served in the *vigiles* for six years. Nevertheless, the *vigiles,* being full of the low born, and being only quasi-military, must have been viewed with contempt by the legionaries of the Urban Cohorts and the Praetorian Guard.

The *vigiles* main raison d'être was firefighting, and they had a variety of tools at their disposal for this, including the eponymous little buckets, hooks and levers for tearing down burning buildings and cushions and mattresses for people to jump out of upper floors. They also used blankets soaked in vinegar or a vinegar based substance called *acetum* which they believed helped extinguish the flames. They may also have had a sort of mechanical water pumping device called a *sipho*.

The *vigiles* also had a role in fire prevention, and were able to enter people's homes to inspect their fire fighting equipment, and even recommend that the prefect sentence those in breach of the fire prevention laws to corporal punishment.

The *vigiles* patrolled during the day, but the bulk of their duties were at night, and inevitably they became a type of police force. This mainly involved prevention and punishment of minor acts of crime, such as burglary and minor disturbances of the peace. Major problems such as riots were dealt with by the Urban Cohorts.

Sources for the lives of the *vigiles* are few and far between, and the only complete work that I am aware of is the *Vigiles of Ancient Rome,* by P. K. Baillie Reynolds, which was first published in 1926.

I am not aware of any evidence that the gods of Ba'al Hammon and Tanit were worshipped in the first century AD. However, it is possible that the religion survived in the regions around Carthage after its destruction, the tradition handed down through generations. First century AD Rome was certainly very open to new cults, with cults devoted to

Isis, Mithras and Christ all becoming established around that time.

It is controversial whether the Carthaginians did in fact practice human sacrifice, or whether this was Roman propaganda, and the Tophet in Carthage discovered by archaeologists may have been a cemetery for deceased neonates, rather than a site of child sacrifice. It seems likely at least though, that their contemporaries believed the Carthaginians indulged in the practice, and in the hundred and seventy plus years between the fall of Carthage and our story, those of Carthaginian descent may have believed this as well.

Rome was a society dominated by a tiny, super-rich elite, and the majority of books about Rome, fiction and non-fiction, concentrate on this elite, or the military they commanded. Much less is known about the lowest classes of Rome, the slaves, the freedmen, the poor free, the people who predominantly populate Carbo's world, partly because they left no written legacy of their own. However, we do know that the number of individuals in these strata of Roman society were extremely numerous, with slaves alone being estimated to make up to 40% of the population of Italy by Carbo's time. Some excellent studies of Rome's underprivileged do exist, notably *Invisible Romans* by Robert Knapp.

Although Watchmen of Rome was some four years in its creation, my research in the subject of Ancient Rome began two decades ago, when my interest was piqued by Colleen McCullough's wonderful Masters of Rome series. A complete source list would be too extensive to reproduce

here, but is available on my website
www.romanfiction.com, as is a glossary of Latin words
used in the book.

Acknowledgements

Thank you to the numerous people who commented on parts or all of this work. In no particular order, these include S. J. A. Turney, Gordon Doherty, Jerome Wilson, John Campbell, Kirsty Hooper, Dr H. Dawson, Caroline Lawrence and David Hillier. Thanks to Ben Evans and Cornerstones Literary Consultancy for the professional and thorough editing work. Thanks also to the friends who gave me encouragement to press on and finish this work, and believing in it. Thanks of course to Abigail and Naomi for putting up with the many hours shutting myself away to work on this.

Alex Gough, Somerset, 2014
www.romanfiction.com
@romanfiction
romanfiction@hotmail.com

16759829R00235

Printed in Great Britain
by Amazon